The Alters

Angie my love
and my inspiration

Ian Lenathen

To the most beautiful
woman I know.
Forever grateful to
the multi-verse for
including you in my world
Forever loved
in this life and
All others.
you are the best!!! ♡
Nothing but love Ian
xoxo

Canadian Intellectual Property Office
Registration number – 1160330 - June 18, 2019

ISBN 978-1-9991913-0-6

Contents

Chapter 1

"I've seen a butterfly possess the wind,

As it flutters here then flutters there,
And sometimes, in exchange,
The wind possesses the butterfly,
As it blows it here, then blows it there"

Barry and Debbie Thomson were married for 9 years and never used any type of birth control.
Both were prodded and probed by multiple doctors and the result was always the same.
Barry was sterile due to a bout of mumps while he was a toddler.
Debbie never wanted to give up trying and she sometimes even blamed herself.

"Ayyeee!!! God Damn it haaalp meeeeee!!!"
The stretcher was pushed down the white sterile hallway of Woman's Hospital in Baton Rouge Louisiana.
Two ER doctors held her down - Trina turned in torment.
She was a user and had become pregnant from one of her many sexual liaisons with "who knows who".
This was the answer Trina always gave when some nosy person asked her who the father was... "Who knows who?" she would always say – proud of her flippant response.
She knew who *her* father was, and *he* was a good man.
To Trina each man on top of her or behind was just like all the others.
She was young and men paid for young women. They paid more if no condom was used.
Trina always went for more.
She thought she was invincible and as usual she was wrong.
Trina was a runaway from a home, which caused her grief.
Trina was a child looking for a parent.

Trina Katalina D'Costa – what a funny name she had.
Her mother wanted to call her Katarina and her aunt wanted to call her Katelina – they decided that these names together, were too long and so they settled for Trina Katalina.
D'Costa was the same surname of her mother's father and so that stayed as it was.
Life was always a battle for Trina. She was a sensitive girl, and everyone took advantage of her generosity. When she was a baby she never cried and always shared her toys with her brothers and sisters. Her mother told her she knew who her father was because of her nature.
Her father was a man who had to travel and "meet the earth on a personal basis". He never stayed in one place for more than three years. To him it was a natural trek. To everyone else he was surely running from something. He had stopped in Jackson, Mississippi on his way to New Orleans and was offered a job in Monroe, a small town in Louisiana, just down the highway from Jackson.
They needed all the help they could get when the cotton was ready for picking.
Trina's mother always said her father was a very gentle and giving man. She didn't remember his last name. His first name had come right from the Bible. He stayed the summer and told Trina's mother she was the best woman he had ever met... "You're an angel on the planet, put here solely for the good of others," he would always say. Trina's mother loved to hear James talk. He had a way of making her feel very special.
James didn't know he had a child on the way when it was time for him to move on again.
Trina had warm thoughts about her father, and she imagined him to be exploring some interesting place in the world "meeting the earth in person".
Trina wanted to be a traveler too.
The first time Trina remembers being abused by one of her mother's boyfriends was too early for her to put an age to it. She remembered sleeping in the little room at the back with her sister when the man opened the door and came in. He was big and he had rough hands. He started with Trina, – touching her in a rough way and probing her private places. Trina began to cry, and he told her to be quiet as he

patted her on the head. He leaned in and started with Trina's older sister. He was talking and groaning she could hear her sister say "yes' and "no" as Trina fell asleep.
After that her life was a constant line of men and boys. Her mother didn't seem to bother even when her older sister cried to her about being hurt by Jakes.
"Jakes would never do that. You must have had a bad dream."
Trina's mother didn't want to lose Jakes or Carl or any of the other men who came and went through their family home.
Trina always wondered if she was dreaming while the men were touching her. She could make her mind travel away from the rough hands and she would fly over water and into "skies that had no ending, for reasons having no fears".
Trina was a sensitive child, just looking for a parent.
"We're losing her". A flurry of activity around Trina as the baby was caught somewhere in the birth canal... Trina was hemorrhaging deep inside her womb.
The surgeon worked as quickly as she could, but the trauma was too great... Trina's blood pressure was dangerously low... Trina slipped away, flying over water into skies that were unending.
As she moved, a light brighter than the sun, which didn't hurt when looked at, surrounded her and bathed her in a glow of unconditional love, touched the essence of her being as she was passing to the wave side of knowing; one dimension higher – no being - all seeing.
Trina felt the presence of the spirit manifesting, the baby girl she had carried for the past eight months.
This little girl was special.
Trina tried to linger, just a little longer in this loving event, to hold this little one, she knew so well and loved so much.
Trina felt the presence of another, manifesting, full of empathy and love, moving within the light first together, then separating from her little girl.
Sarah became sequential as Trina surrendered to the light.
The doctors cleared Sarah's air passage as she gasped her first breath... the pediatrician and nurses worked with professional intensity to clean her off, giving this new bundle a quick physical inspection before wrapping her in the blanket.

The other doctor tried in vain to bring Trina back. She was pronounced dead 10 minutes after Sarah was announced alive and well.
Sarah was sequential again.

Debbie and Barry were elated when the adoption agency called to tell them about the beautiful baby girl who had become available. They were told the story of Trina – a young girl who worked the streets and who was a known drug addict.
"The baby is healthy, though?" Barry asked.
"The doctors have checked her over and she is healthy. There was a slight problem with her lungs when she was first born but time and treatment have made them as good as new", replied the state worker on the other end of the line. "When would you like to come and see her?"
"Now" Debbie said unable to contain the excitement of this long-awaited event, "Can we come now?!"
"You can!" exclaimed Mrs. Allard, who loved this part of her work at the Agency. "I was hoping you would say that!"
Mrs. Allard smiled into the mouthpiece as she felt the need of this young couple and the happiness and excitement of the moment. She had read the file on Debbie and Barry and knew they would be good parents to this precious child, who was in desperate need of two loving parents.
Mrs. Allard had been in the baby business for almost twenty years now and she still was always touched deeply, when happiness was served.
"Come over now," She said, "and I will present little Sarah to you both. We will go over the procedure one more time and you can sign the necessary papers which are the final steps in making this little girl your daughter. I know you're in New Orleans... can I expect to see you within a couple of hours?"
"Yes!" Debbie exclaimed. "We're leaving now!"
Debbie and Barry lived in New Orleans and Baton Rouge was about an hour away straight up highway 10.
As they drove, they talked about the plans for their daughter's future. They would give her their best and they would love her no matter what.

There was some apprehension due to the mother's past, but they would deal with any problems as they came along.

Both were religious with a rich Pentecostal support network. Little Sarah surely was the gift from God they had all prayed for, for so long.

"Alleluia, Alleluia, God is great!" Debbie exclaimed as they pulled in front of the state adoption agency.

Mrs. Allard greeted them as they walked through the door. "Welcome Mr. and Mrs. Thomson" she beamed as she shook Barrie's hand before giving Debbie a lady to lady hug. "Please come into my office and we can finish the legality details, then we can go and meet your new daughter Sarah!"

The paperwork was tedious, but all had been cleared by their lawyer in New Orleans. They signed where they were asked to sign and listened politely as Mrs. Allard explained the more sensitive parts of the agreement. The child was the first concern of the state and there would be visits during the first few months to ensure the baby was being provided everything required.

Finally, all signatures were done. Mrs. Allard walked Debbie and Barry to the childcare center which was part of the government complex.

When Debbie picked up Sarah and held her for the first time, tears filled her eyes; it was love at first sight. Barry's eyes also filled with moisture as he touched Sarah's hair and stroked her cheek.

Barry kissed Debbie on the forehead as Debbie kissed Sarah....

"She is beautiful", Debbie cried as Barry put his arms around his wife and his daughter.

"She is" Barry said softly... "She is".

Barry and Debbie were ready at home with the new nursery, new baby clothes and of course all the helpers from their church.

Mrs. Allard had never seen a baby with such big blue eyes before... this little girl was beautiful, and Mrs. Allard felt connected to her in a way no other child had made her feel.

"This is your new daughter dear Debbie and Barry - I will pray for your happiness."

"Thank you, Mrs. Allard - I will pray for yours too. You have answered our prayers by bringing Sarah into our lives. I will always remember you for that."

Barry prepared the baby seat in the back of the car and waited for Debbie. Debbie sat in the backseat and Barry understood fully, as she placed Sarah into the car seat.
They waved goodbye to Mrs. Allard as they headed the car towards highway 10.
"Drive very carefully Barry!" Debbie said in a warning and protective tone.
"I will my dear." Responded Barry. "We have special cargo aboard today." Sarah had found the parents early in her life, the parents her mother Trina, never had.
"It is all good, and I love you" Debbie whispered to her child, as Sarah closed her eyes and slept.

Sarah was the center of attention at the church service as 'Reverend Paul' welcomed a new soul to the promised kingdom of Jesus Christ and to the ministry of the 'Saints of Perpetual Mercy' church, based on the teachings of the holy bible and in the living spirit of the Holy Ghost; A church whose members sometimes talked in tongues as they were overcome with the Spirit of the Holy Ghost. The baptism was a blessed event with many witnesses in the wooden pews of the little church. Sarah was dipped three times into the holy water "as John the Baptist had done with our Lord himself!" reverend Paul gleefully exclaimed.
Reverend Paul was in good form for the message that day.
The musicians - Carrie (flute and clarinet), Richard (percussion, harmonica and trumpet, when needed), old Bart (who had 'played the lead electric guitar since the first ones were invented. His guitar looked like it was the first one invented'), Sally Jones (bass guitar and violin) and Sandy (lead singer, keyboard and tambourine), rehearsed twice per week and played as if they were the Lords chosen musicians.
The music was loud, and the beat was revival!
All members of the church were in the choir, and each of them took that duty seriously. Music is a great part of worshipping the Lord, and surely the Holy Ghost was the first musician in the Garden.
"We're all children of God... children of the baptism bringing us into the family of Jesus Christ... this child named Sarah is reborn as our daughter today and she is a special child... A very special child...Like

all the special children in our church... Someone say - Thank You Jesus!!"
The assembly screamed out "Thank You Jesus!!!! Thank You Jesus!!!!" as old Bart strummed a few heavenly chords and Sandy bounced the tambourine against her hand as each word was screamed - "Thank You Jesus".
Reverend Paul was strutting now... proud to be in this place talking about his Friend and Savior... proud to be the leader of this flock; Proud to bring electricity to his people, as a witness to the sacred power of the Holy Ghost.
"The Holy Ghost is with us today and I can feel his anointing upon us! I can feel the Holy Ghost in our midst today!!" Reverend Paul was excited.
"Ou yute viglli wehd rad rol ethoe vig" he screamed in tongues... as the congregation started waving their hands in the air praising Jesus and the Holy Ghost.
"I can feel the Holy Ghost's anointing on this special child named Sarah!" reverend Paul exclaimed as he put the palm of his right hand on the face of little Sarah.
Debbie fell to her knees "Thank you Jesus, thank you Jesus!".
The congregation were jubilant, energetic, possessed in the moment - speaking in tongues and some even rolling in the isles, as Debbie fell to the floor overcome with emotion and filled with so much love for her special little girl. Barry looked to the heavens with his hands stretched above him as tears ran down his cheeks "Thank You Jesus, Thank You Jesus," he quietly sobbed... "thank You, thank You Jesus...".
The musicians were playing for the angels.
Reverend Paul, held Sarah, dressed in her white baptismal gown ... lace with silk thread... big and bright blue eyes with a wisp of blonde hair escaping from under the white silk cap which covered her head. Sarah was surely like an angel Reverend Paul thought as he spoke the words loud and clear... "Sarah Jessica Thomson, I now baptize you in the Name of the Father, dip, and of the Son, dip, and of the Holy Ghost, dip, for the forgiveness of your sins, and the gift of the Holy Spirit."

He smiled as he lifted baby Sarah up as a presentation to the congregation... "Behold Sarah... cherished child of our lord... cherished sister in our church!"

"Saints, yell out, thank you Jesus!" Reverend Paul boomed as he cradled Sarah to his chest and then handed her back to Barry and Debbie.

"Thank you, Jesus!!" every member of the congregation boomed back.

Barry and Debbie were now a family in the eyes of the church and no matter that the rumor in the congregation persisted 'one of them is surely barren'... they now were complete.

Debbie and Barry vowed to love little Sarah and to bring her up in the ways of the Lord.

Time was filled with happiness as baby Sarah brought a new kind of life into Debbie and Barrie's home. They were very proud of their little girl.

As Sarah moved from the baby to toddler age, everyone in the congregation knew she was a special child... so intelligent and advanced beyond her age. She also had deep-feeling tendencies, well known to take on the pain and sadness of other children, when they fell and scraped their knee, were in a troubled mood, and even crying with a baby as the baby cried.

In all cases she was able to soothe and comfort, seemingly without words, the troubled or hurting child.

Some of the elder ladies in the church talked in secret about the possessed and witch-like interloper (she was adopted, after all) in their midst.

Sarah learned early, jealousy is a pious observer and cruel commentator, as she felt the disturbed emotions of these elder ladies, not fully understanding what she had done to them to make them feel this way. She knew intuitively she had done nothing against them, and such pain is always self-inflicted by the pious and cruel ones amongst us.

It couldn't be denied, the other children loved her and wanted to spend their free time with her. Sarah was also known as a touching child, a tactile child... forever touching shoulders or holding hands, with every child in her circle.

Sarah was a happy child... a giving child, an intelligent child... a beautiful child and a gifted child.
She was Barry's pride and joy as well as Debbie's completeness.
Life was good in the Tomson household.

When Sarah was three, the nightmares began.
"Mommmmmy, Dadddddy" she wailed as she watched the black shadow come through the wall of her bedroom.
"Mommmy, Daddddy ahhhhhh,"
Debbie and Barry rushed upstairs and into Sarah's bedroom.
"It's ok, baby, mommy is her., It's ok, mommy and daddy are here". Debbie soothed.
Sarah was scared as she sobbed in her mother's arms...
Barry looked around the room as he stroked his daughter's cheek. "It's ok baby girl, daddy will not let anything hurt you ever! You had a bad dream, baby girl, you had a bad dream".
These nightmares persisted to the point where Barry and Debbie sought out the help of a child psychologist. It had been a bit humiliating for Debbie to ask Reverend Paul for prayers, since she knew some of the ladies in the church felt it was probably due to some form of punishment put on Sarah by our Lord Himself... for reasons unknown to them, but surely known to God. Sisters in the church were sometimes cruel in their judgments and condemnations.
At the psychologist's office, little Sarah talked about the bad man coming into her room at night. "He comes through my wall, and he wants to take me away."
She always had the same dream.
As Sarah slept, a black silhouette appeared like a stain on the wall across from her bed. It moved like the shadow of a cloud passing under the full moon. It was a man in a black robe. The shadow transformed slowly from a two-dimensional to a three-dimensional form and floated towards the bed. Sarah's eyes were closed looking like a cherub as she slept. The shadow came across her and settled around her as she stirred slightly in her sleep.
Sarah's eyes opened wide again and she screamed for her mother to come. As Debbie once again opened the door, the shadow was absorbed by the light coming from the hallway.

Once again Debbie and Barry held their daughter closely as she once again told of a bad man coming to her, through the wall.

The psychologist explained, Sarah had an innate fear of darkness and shadows. She had a vivid imagination and was very intelligent. It will pass, but till it does, be there for her and hold her when she is afraid. Debbie and Barry were always there for her when she was afraid.

Chapter 2

"In my younger days I possessed my ways - my will?

As I studied here and found out there
But somewhere in my past I was exchanged,
My life arranged, by a wind of sequence,
Carrying my body and my psyche
Through the years,
With fixed responsibility, which I had come to own
And carry out as my place in life.
To express my Love through my children...
Born of my Spirit somehow...
Thinking back to everyone I've met,
I find the Karma of it all
Forces some regret,
And I realize we all must solve our consequences,
Yet..."

Adam was born in Toronto at the same moment as Sarah in Baton Rouge.

Walter and Alison, a very successful couple, planned everything and usually their plans came to beautiful fruition.

Adam was no exception, since his birth had been planned, by Alison and Walter two years prior to their marriage, just after they announced their engagement.

This was their first child - Walter and Alison, as well as the loving grandparents on both sides of the family were ecstatic about the arrival of their new son and grandson.

Alison had always lived on the right side of the tracks, never wanting for anything. Her father, McKeon Mathews (just "Mac" to his friends) excelled as an engineer and inventor, graduating top of his class at the University of Toronto School of Engineering.

He had early successes in many patents involving computer and telecommunications technologies and was an innovator. A student of the Einstein method of thought experiments. He would think for days sometimes, about a given problem which needed a solution. He would then use his engineering expertise to mentally build a circuit or a device which would alleviate the problem, then he would do the necessary steps to start the patent process. Mac loved to invent things, building structures in thought, then manifesting them as objects used to solve problems.

Alison's childhood was loving and practical. Everything geared to furthering her father's values. Mac was a 'thinking' man who tired easily around disorganized people and 'non-grounded' people. 'My time is too important to waste on intellectual fluff.' He would often say.

'Every purpose must have a plan; every plan a purpose. In other words, it's folly to do anything if you don't know why you're doing it.

He believed life is born from chaos; engineers had a duty to provide order and scale to everything - a duty to tame the chaos.

Walter disliked the portrayal of doctors, lawyers and police people shows on tv, as if they were the heroes of society. In truth, he knew engineers are the unsung heroes - Just look around you ... from cars to tunnels to computers - everything started with an engineering plan! He thought to himself, though he was not a believer in God, intelligent design was the greatest thought coming out of various religions. God is obviously an engineer!

Walter's parents had immigrated to Canada when he was 6 years old from Scotland. He was also a graduate engineer from the University of Toronto. Walter and Mac got along famously from the first time they had met. Marrying Walter was like marrying a younger Mac, Alison always thought. She was very happy with her life and loved her husband and her parents dearly.

The birth of Adam was organized and completed without a hitch. Everything went as it should. Alison, in labor for about 4 hours, remembering each step of the classes she had taken with Walter at the hospital.

"Breathe", Walter said as he counted off the time while Alison was pushing. They were a good team and she trusted Walter's instructions.
"Bear Down" the doctor said... I can see your baby's head."
Alison pushed as hard as she could as Walter held her hand encouraging her with all the words of endearment, he knew...
"You're doing great darling... I am so proud of you...push, darling, push."
Adam was clear and the nurses immediately cleared his breathing passage and wrapped him in that special blanket which was a crude replacement from the comfort of the womb. Walter watched as they crimped and clipped the umbilical cord.
Adam cried for the first time.

"A boy darling, a beautiful little boy! He is beautiful darling; he is so beautiful!"
Alison held Adam and she was crying openly.
She knew she loved this little boy more than her own life and she made a silent promise to always stand by him in life no matter what.
Walter put his arms around his wife and his new son. He was a very happy man.
Alison and Walter looked into the bluest eyes they had ever seen.
Adam looked directly at Alison and Walter – he made eye contact with Alison first and held his focus for about 5 seconds then his eyes moved into direct contact with Walter's eyes, holding his stare again for about five seconds.
"Do you see that Walter?" Alison exclaimed, "He looked directly at us!"
"Yes" said Walter, "He looked directly at me."
The nurse attending to Alison had also seen this and it was the most intense and focused look she'd ever seen a baby experience so soon after birth.
Without any complications baby Adam was home within three days of his birth.
"Dad, I am telling you little Adam focused his eyes directly on Walter and me right after he was born – honest, I am not making this up!"
"It could be," Mac said, "but you know most babies don't focus their eyes until they are a bit older than 10 minutes."

Alison would not relinquish the point.

"Mom and Dad believe me. It's as if he looked at us and knew everything about us. I know he focused his eyes on us! It sounds strange, but he looked directly at us."

Mac and Barbara were very proud of their daughter, their son-in-law and their new grandson. They smiled in agreement... Adam had focused his bright blue eyes on them and why not? He was an exceptional child.

"You make good babies..." McKeon beamed as he watched Alison breast-feed little Adam.

Alison was totally satisfied and very happy with herself. She had made her parents very proud and Walter was like a strutting peacock. They had the most beautiful baby ever born and as far as they were concerned nobody could argue differently.

That night as Alison cuddled closely in Walter's arms at 3 in the morning, when the entire world seemed to be sleeping, she started to sob against his shoulder... Walter turned slightly and looked at her in the dim soft light.

"What is it darling? Why are you crying?"

"Oh Walter", Alison sobbed, "I can't stand the thought of ever losing our son. What if something happens to him? How can we ever protect him from the world?"

Alison was sobbing loudly as she spoke "Having a baby means you can also lose a baby... I don't want to lose our baby Walter.... I don't ever want to lose our baby... You know it happens - some people lose their children!"

Alison was sobbing loudly as the loss of her child was a possibility too hard to bear.

Walter held Alison and tried to console her "Nothing is going to happen to little Adam... He will outlive us for sure, and he is going to have a great life."

"Oh, Walter... I am so afraid of losing the most important thing in my life... the thought of losing him is unbearable".

Walter held Alison close to him as he kissed her the same way her father would, on the top of her forehead. Sometimes, the role of a husband is to protect his wife from her fears by reassuring her that everything would be well.

"The only ones who really understand the loss of a child are the ones who have children." Alison continued to sob as images of life without Adam moved through her consciousness.
Walter squeezed his wife in a comforting way... "Let's consider Adam a present to us and we will cherish him for as long as we have him" Walter appealed to Alison's more optimistic side.
"We have him now... so let's forget any thoughts of losing him and enjoy him while we can." Walter felt a tear roll down his right cheek... as he also understood the gravity of Alison's fear. He had never thought of mortality before.
Alison kissed Walter and thanked him for his comforting thoughts. She silently realized life is always close to death, and something so beautifully gained could also be tragically lost.
Alison and Walter had a changed life – where just one year ago there was no thought of needing anything but each other, there was now this magnificent new addition who totally belonged to them and who totally consumed their love and compassion.
Adam prospered as a loving child, always ready with a smile and a reaching open hand. His curiosity was his most compelling trait. Adam always had a question and at three years old, he preferred the company of adults. His vocabulary was superior, and he could put complex sentences together with a quick wit to match.
Walter and Alison started going to church every Sunday since they felt this was an important part of life for a young child.
"It does not matter what he ultimately decides about religion" Alison argued, "but we have to at least educate him at an early age that God is an idea most people in the world do take seriously."
Walter was an agnostic and he made no bones about it... "Yes darling, I agree his education should involve all knowledge... Some day he will be a great engineer or scientist and like Darwin, may rewrite the association of science and godkind."
Walter thought engineers were the least appreciated yet most important profession on the planet. He was amazed when Mac told him he felt the same way.
"Oh Walter, you and dad drive me crazy- you're both elitist engineers and you both think you own the corner of how things work!"
Walter smiled. "Well darling we do, and that is true."

Little Adam was growing up and he loved the people and the world around him. He was toilet trained at one year old and was talking in full sentences by the age of two. He was obviously a bright child - Alison and Walter always were very proud of themselves in creating such a smart little boy. They secretively gloated when comparing Adam's development to the children of their friends. Adam was in a class by himself and they knew he would need special education to ensure his genius was not wasted.
Walter and Alison started planning Adam's future as if it were a building project, with measurable goals and objectives at every turn. They researched the best schools and even considered which university he should attend.
Alison and Walter argued on occasion, since Walter always put the University of Toronto as the first step to wherever he went with his higher education. Alison always said the decision of what school to attend and what subject to study should belong solely to Adam.

"Mother, why do we look like we do?' Adam asked, his mind always curious, after the bedtime story. Alison had to answer a bunch of questions before Adam would finally give up and fall asleep.
"Well Adam, we look like we do because nature has made us this way. We walk with our legs, and digest food with our tummies, and we need our arms and hands to reach for things... our necks allow us to look around, we need our mouths to eat and our noses to smell and our eyes to see." Alison always tried to cover as much territory as possible with every answer she gave.
"Who made us like this and why is eating so important... most things that I look at have to do with eating." Adam yawned, and Alison smiled.
"You are tired baby, and you have a whole lifetime ahead of you to get your questions answered."
"Thanks mom" Adam said as he rolled over onto his side.
"Sleep well and have sweet dreams my love and I will see you tomorrow" Alison leaned over and kissed Adam on the side of his head as she tucked the blanket around him.
"Good night mommy. I love you and I will see you tomorrow, but isn't it strange that life can only exist by eating other things that have

also lived? Have I ever eaten anything which once didn't live? I am talking about all life - sea life, air life and land life."
Allison smiled once more as she tried to think if she ever eats anything that was not once alive. Salt, she thought... salt has never been alive, and I eat it every day.
"And I am not talking about things like salt, mom. You would die if you only ate salt."
Adam closed his eyes and started lifting away from his room.
He always felt like he was in a bubble floating over fields and houses.
He loved his flying dreams.
Alison closed the door quietly as Adam drifted higher into a familiar place...

I had a dream within a dream,
Where I was standing on a hill... and many people passed me by,
Stuck to the earth as they walked with their children in step.
And food was consumed from large picnic baskets,
Which kept filling up to be consumed once again.
They were enjoying their day in the sun,
Laughing and running and I got caught up in it all.
Looking at them from more than one direction,
In different planes of reference,
I realized without thinking, I am flying!
Soaring like the wind... flying, flying, flying... further and higher.
I wanted to share with the ones, who were walking,
This magnificent soaring.
But the ones who were walking wouldn't look up,
For they couldn't believe I was soaring above them,
Soaring and flying by my will alone (thank you, Father)
They didn't try to understand, and they told their children - Not to look up,
Enforced it with threats of bodily harm.
They said a trick was involved... Some slight, of hand
as they stuck to the earth.
I flew on alone until I landed on top of a hill
At the other side of the park.
I decided to walk home, since it was getting dark.

Adam drifted deeper into sleep past the flying dream in the park towards a distant light.

Chapter 3

Sometimes my mind drifts upwards,

Until I am part of the moon,
Yet at the same time under the sea...
I know what's going on,
And it feels so good "to be".
I met my mother and father early in life, shortly after I was born,
and started talking, started eating solid food and walking...
I kissed my first girl when I was six years old...
And from that time, I knew it was important,
Yet I hoped not too important.
There is so much to do.

"That child's smile could bring a pillar of salt back to life; there is so much goodness in it!" Reverend Paul said as he attended The Young Mother's Revival meeting.

Debbie beamed pride every time the minister talked in such a way, but the other Young Mothers were a bit resentful towards Debbie, since they knew Sarah was the favorite of Reverend Paul.

The meetings were meant to keep the scriptures close to the raising of the children.

"God the Father is the perfect parent and we need to bring His word to our daily work in raising our children" Reverend Paul started saying, "We've been entrusted with the lives of these young Souls and we must always put the teaching of the church ahead of all other training".

Debbie loved to hear Reverend Paul speak. He was the perfect man as far as Debbie was concerned, so selfless and warm in his giving and forgiving. He was dedicated to his church and to his 'flock' in the congregation. He was the shepherd, and this brought a great deal of comfort to Debbie.

She always felt safe in her trust for Reverend Paul.

Debbie wore the blue dress to this meeting because Reverend Paul had made such a sweet comment about how good she looked at the Prayer Revival last Sunday.
She never realized Reverend Paul even looked at how she was dressed, but since he was, she decided to look as good as she possibly could, for him.
It was a flowing dress with a full skirt becoming a little tighter on the top naturally highlighting the fullness of her breasts. Debbie felt good about her attractive looks and she appreciated it when she caught a man looking – especially Reverend Paul.
Debbie found herself doing more volunteer work for the church and was spending more time with the Reverend.
Barry thought nothing of it and was happy to look after Sarah while Debbie did her good work for the benefit of others and to help the church in its many outreach programs.
Debbie loved her efforts, helping Reverend Paul with such important work. She was doing much more than the other ladies, and it almost seemed Reverend Paul did prefer her being there, more than the others. He would always tell the other ladies they could leave early, while asking Debbie to stay a little longer, since he knew Barry was always at home taking care of Sarah. The other ladies had husbands who were not as dedicated to the happiness of their wives – limiting and controlling the extra time helping at the church - or so Sarah surmised. Most of the husbands didn't trust the swarthy, passionate Reverend Paul, with their wives. He was a good man, but he was a man, and they were men too. Men can be dogs.
The affair between Debbie and the Reverend started innocently enough. Paul had been married for seventeen years to Maraid having five children - Paul junior was seventeen, Rachel was fifteen, Ruth was thirteen, James was eleven and Caroline was four. Caroline and Sarah were best friends, and both had sleepovers at each other's home almost every weekend. Caroline and Sarah were inseparable and talked on the phone at least five times per day.
During the Sunday sermons Debbie always closed her eyes and listened intently to Reverend Paul's words... she imagined he was delivering the words directly to her.
Debbie knew she was too attached and attracted to Reverend Paul and it scared her. Barry never showed an interest in her and seemed

to have no sexual drive whatsoever, but he was a good husband in every other way. Barry was like the perfect brother she never had. Love me but never touch me (well almost never anyway).
Reverend Paul was a robust man standing almost six feet tall with broad shoulders and a slim waist. He was one of those who never had to worry about weight. He was naturally well proportioned. When seen in his Sunday white suite with his wavy hair always in a bit of a mess, fired up with the word of God, consumed by the passion of the Holy Ghost, bearing those deep blue eyes onto every member of his flock, he was downright sexy to most of the female congregation.
His animated style of preaching the good and true message, with as much body language as possible, put into every sentence... the rise and fall of his rich strong voice... he was an object of desire for Debbie. During his sermons, Debbie felt the sexual tension in her body crying out to be relieved... she was wet and ready, yet always left unsatisfied at the end. Every Sunday, after church, Debbie would go home and touch herself in needed ways until a self-induced orgasm, gushed a sweet release, and brought her back to calmness. Always with the image of Reverend Paul in her mind, imagining her fingers as his... his fingers, his cock and his tongue. She surrendered to his passion. She craved what he could give her.
Reverend Paul was a man with sexual power, demanding female attention.
Maraid was a total contrast to her husband.
Maraid was the doting minister's wife, almost always in agreement with her husband, and whenever she disagreed, Reverend Paul would quote the bible where it states in the words from God himself that a woman should obey her husband; the husband was appointed as the head of the household. How could Maraid ever argue with the word of God Himself? Reverend Paul preferred her as his dutiful companion.
She had vowed long ago to become the perfect wife to her husband and to totally dedicate herself with the following priorities; her husband first, her church second and her children third.
Maraid was a loving mother not only to her own children but to all the children in the congregation, and a loyal and faithful friend to each member of the congregation, especially to those who needed

emotional and loving support. She was truly the "salt of the earth" putting her own needs always behind the needs of others. Maraid was introduced as "my loving Saint, my loving wife" by Reverend Paul at every social and business function of the church.

It was a Wednesday night.
The church was empty except for Debbie and Reverend Paul in the office working on the accounting details regarding the previous month. Boring stuff – income versus expenses – as they worked towards the project of getting the roof repaired. A special offering was asked for every Sunday, and they were close to having the full amount needed for the contract to be signed with the Christian roofing company.
Reverend Paul had noticed the "come on" signals Debbie had been lobbing at him for the past month or so, but he played it slowly, ensuring it was not a mixed signal which could lead to an embarrassing non-encounter. He was sure, she was feeling his complimentary need and knew if she is pitching, he would be catching.
It was time to test the waters.
Reverend Paul looked into Debbie's eyes as she sat demurely across from him, wearing a tight white blouse and flared skirt. Her body was a work of art and many men in the congregation looked at her with lust – secret sinners all.
Reverend Paul stood up and walked to her on her side of the desk...
She looked at him and he could see the total surrender in her eyes.
"Oh, my dear Debbie, I find it too difficult to resist you..."
He stroked her hair and cupped the side of her face within the full palm of his right hand.
Debbie moved her head pushing her cheek deeper into his palm.
"I feel the same way Reverend... Debbie breathed in deeply, going physically limp, surrendering to the moment... "If God is Love, can love be a sin?" She asked.
Debbie stood up and stood directly in front of Paul.
Paul pulled Debbie's lips towards his, kissing her mouth for the first time... pushing his tongue gently between her parting lips... her body went limp again as she surrendered totally to the moment once again, while adding suction to the union of their mouths.

At first it was gentle but then in a wave of passion he became more persistent until her tongue met his, matching his force and passion. They were in the reverend's office and the church building was empty. Maraid was at home taking care of the children and Barry was watching the game, having given Sarah a bath and putting her to bed, at least an hour ago.
Paul moaned as his hands stroked the back of Debbie's hair then moved downwards to her back, her waist and then over her buttocks till he felt the top of her thighs under the light flared skirt. He gently pulled her legs apart as he ground his groin into her, at the top middle of her opening thighs.
Debbie pushed back until she could feel the hardness of Reverend Paul's cock. She ground with him feeling surges of desire rising higher and higher with every thrust.
"Oh my God, Paul" Debbie sobbed as she started pulling the jacket from his shoulders "I have wanted you for so long, and oh so badly!"
Paul lifted the material of Debbie's skirt until his hands were caressing her lace panties... till his fingers moved under the material finally touching the wetness of her pussy.
"My God Debbie you're so wet - my God Debbie, I have to have you now!"
With that Paul moved Debbie backwards till she was leaning against the desk. He undid his belt, undid the button holding his pants together, and pulled down his zipper. His pants fell to the floor as he reached into his boxer shorts and pulled out his throbbing erect penis.
"Put it in Debbie" he rasped as he moved his hands up and cupped and squeezed her breasts through the white blouse, fumbling with the buttons, until he had access to her bra reaching around her back undoing the clasp - her breasts were finally free for him to kiss and squeeze and see. Debbie obediently moved her hand down, circled her fingers around his penis and pulled it to the opening of her vagina. With one thrust Reverend Paul was in as he pressed Debbie's breasts into the palm of his hands moving his fingers and his pelvis in a rhythm of creation which was burned somewhere in the center of his being. He loved the first time because it was all so new again. Debbie was a mad woman as she met his thrusts with her own, pulling his lips to hers as they satisfied their hunger for each other.

"Kala mod at sans awaw de bak andel ooooooohhhhhhh!!!!" Reverend Paul moaned as the pleasure of his orgasm moved up his spine to the center of his brain then rebounded in another wave of muscular contraction towards his groin and hips.
He thrust as deep as he could as the first wave of release pushed his sperm deep into Debbie and they both thrust again, and then once again. Debbie screamed as she creamed on his cock. It was a short act, but she too had orgasmed, always on the brink of pent-up desire. It was a magnificent and sorely needed release.
They held on to each other breathing heavily till the exhilaration subsided and their heart beats retreated to the normal range again. Debbie kissed the reverend slowly on the lips. She felt satisfied and loved like she hadn't felt in a long time with her husband.
Reverend Paul squeezed her closer to him and he couldn't believe his providence once again, to have such a beautiful young woman as his lover. "Praise the Lord" he whispered.
"Thank you, Jesus!" gasped Debbie.

Reverend Paul and Debbie found many excuses to be alone especially after nine PM when the church was empty, in his office. They had time to take their time, to love each other slowly and completely. They told each other what they liked, where to lick and suck, when to hold and when to fuck.
Debbie had never felt such power and pleasure in sex. Reverend Paul couldn't believe he had such a willing and wonton woman.
She was open for anything and she only wanted to please. She loved being his private sexual playground.
Debbie loved to tease Paul with her body. She knew he loved sexy, silk and lacy panties so she bought these just for him. She loved it when in a meeting with the other women of the church she could position herself in front of Reverend Paul and slightly open her legs giving him a private view of one of his favorite playground locations. It was more exiting when she put her panties into her purse and gave him a full view of her pouty alpha and omega.
It drove him crazy, and every time he nervously cleared his throat, she knew she was getting to him.
Nobody knew what was going on between them, or so they thought. Secret lovers always give themselves away, the body language is

hard to shut down, and those who are attuned to such signals, decipher them easily and just 'know'.

Sarah knew and didn't judge it though. It was a common occurrence with many men and women, all thinking they had special secrets, when in fact in the scheme of greater things, there really were no such things as secrets. Everything we do in secret, in the dark, is exposed and bathed in the sequential consequences created in an instance, an event – which must be resolved till the truth is exposed. We waste so much time and energy in the lies we tell each other.

After these 'Women Committee' meetings, when Debbie and Paul were finally alone, Reverend Paul would ravish her like he was an animal in heat.

Debbie loved impulsive, grunting and groaning, talking in tongues, down and dirty, who's your daddy! - Reverend Paul sex.

She always, left him breathless and totally satisfied.

Debbie was hungrier than he was.

They stole moments for lust at the weekend retreats, even when Barry and Maraid were with them. Debbie loved to go down on Paul when Barry and Maraid were in the next room, causing him to moan and groan muffled, in cyclic spasms as he reached another mind-blowing orgasm.

Debbie made sure she swallowed every drop. Always looking up at him with a big smile, eyes wide open, pleased with herself for pleasing him so much.

Reverend Paul had never met a woman who loved oral sex as much as Debbie, scaring him sometimes when she did it so willingly in risky situations. He found though, the chance of being caught in a compromising position with his cock in Debbie's mouth, gave him an orgasmic rush, he had never experienced before.

Debbie was the perfect lover for Reverend Paul, and she was always looking for new ways to please him. She made sure she was properly shaved, in her nether region, and had Reverend Paul also shave his groin. She wanted skin on skin.

Maraid was a bit perplexed when she saw her king without his mane of hair, down there, but the Reverend told her he had a skin condition. Shaving improved it. Maraid believed him, of course and thought nothing more of it.

Debbie was finally a happy, satisfied, sexually aware woman, loving the feeling of being complete.

Barry had very low levels of testosterone due to his early bout of mumps. His sex drive was non-existent. He loved her but never really needed her, for physical release.

Debbie sobbed silently on many occasions after initiating a love making session with her husband only to have him roll over and say he was too tired asking if they could they do it in the morning. Of course, when morning came, Barry was always the first one up making the coffee and taking little Sarah to the front of the television to watch her morning cartoons.

Debbie was the perfect wife, providing Barry with all the support she could give him, but she was lonely, wanting to be touched, and to touch. She told him women have needs too – he had no needs.

She prayed to God to help her overcome her sexual urges. Her prayers were answered in a way she never thought would ever happen.

God had given her Reverend Paul, loving it when he called her his 'dirty girl'."

Debbie was sure Barry knew about her affair with Reverend Paul. She rationalized he approved since it took the stress of making love to his wife away from him.

Barry never initiated sex and it had been months since he had made love to Debbie.

Debbie didn't mind any more.

All things were as they should be in the Thomson home.

Reverend Paul had never had such a willing woman and all his sexual desires were met with enthusiasm. He could never imagine his 'loving Saint and loving wife' Maraid, doing what he and Debbie did together in wild abandon.

There was never a fear of pregnancy since Debbie couldn't have children and this added to the safety of the situation as far as Reverend Paul was concerned.

He was wrong.

Debbie knew she could become pregnant of course (and had a few fantasies about carrying Reverend Paul's child). She never corrected Reverend Paul about her being 'barren'.

Like most men he had automatically assumed she was the one with the problem, not her husband.
Reverend Paul painfully remembered the fear he experienced during his last affair with an unmarried and much younger member of the congregation.
He hated the abortion since he preached so much against such things, but what was he to do?
The young lady never recovered and moved out of his life back to Wilson, North Carolina, always ashamed she had killed her child, at the insistence of her Minister, who told her how much he loved her, and how they would be together 'in God's time'.
He always kept her in his prayers.
This one was different. Debbie was a woman sent from God Himself. Reverend Paul even fantasized about Debbie while he did his missionary position duties with Maraid. Maraid was happy to see the new vigor in her husband's movements and she forgave the fact that he had started talking 'dirty' as he finished the act.
Life was good and Reverend Paul's sermons were fiery and interesting.
Debbie was his inspiration and he wanted to scream about hell and damnation from the 'pulpit to the culprit!' in his church, to please her, more than the other sheep in his flock.
Deep down there was a conflict in his conscience, since he knew he was mocking God. Thank God, God is a forgiving God Reverend Paul would think during these short periods of guilt and depression. Surely all the Souls he saved would make up for his own iniquities. Amen.
As Eve had proven to Adam... no man has a chance against the charms of a woman and no woman has a chance against the charms of a snake.

Debbie held Sarah close to her bosom rocking her gently back and forth
Every day Sarah became more isolated... more alone... and Debbie was tortured by the worsening condition of her child.
"Barry, what is happening to our little girl, she is leaving us!"
Sarah was 6 years old and had been an active, bright and loving child till just after her fifth birthday.

Sarah slowly began to change becoming less active. She was retreating from the world, and no-one understood why, losing interest in playing with other children and preferring to just sit and be by herself.

"Sarah, talk to me baby... Sarah... talk to me sweetie" Debbie pleaded to a little girl who now ignored everything around her.

Her blonde hair cascaded over her shoulders as saucer like blue eyes opened wide in a vacant stare.

"Where are you baby and how can I reach you?" Debbie sobbed in desperation. "I love you baby girl, please come back to us."

Sarah now hated being touched, squirming in protest whenever Barry or Debbie tried to comfort her with a hug, hand hold or kiss. Her relationship with those who truly loved her was lost somewhere in isolation.

Sarah slipped deeper and deeper into herself – as if rejecting the world.

Sarah was the talk of the congregation and Reverend Paul solicited prayers of healing for one of his helpless lambs.

"We have a demon in our midst" he shouted from the pulpit... "a demon that is after one of our own!"

"Someone, say deliver us from evil!"

The congregation threw their hands in the air and screamed "Deliver us from evil."

Sarah was at the front of the church surrounded by the healing hands of her sisters and brothers in the Lord as the congregation talked in tongues and praised Jesus for his compassion.

"I command thee to leave this child of Jesus!" Reverend Paul screamed as he lay his hands upon the head of little Sarah, "Leave this child you vile and evil devil! I command it in the name of Jesus!"

The congregation was in a frantic state... "Halleluiah. Halleluiah" they chanted as Reverend Paul boomed out his words bombasting the evil, which had come to one of his own.

"Ouk tio eoma see eocef flaentep pareisiks" Maraid spoke softly with her eyes closed yet looking towards the heavens... her arms extended and her hands open... "I love you Jesus, please be with us and free your child Sarah and deliver her from evil."

The prayers went on, yet Sarah was away – not responding to the people who had loved her from the start of her new home days.

Debbie fell onto her knees and cried, as Sarah stared out into the midst of the crowd.
The laying of hands had no effect on Sarah's state.
Reverend Paul admitted only to Maraid, he hadn't felt the presence of the Holy Ghost as he normally did in his emotional preaching. He only felt the emptiness of his words, and he questioned his ability to lead his precious flock. Perhaps this was all a judgment of his own behavior with Debbie, he thought and kept closely to himself.
The doctors were mystified with Sarah's condition. She was given every test known. She had no physical malady's, proven by test after test, which included brain scan and brain wave analysis... all seemed normal except that Sarah was slowly withdrawing further and further into herself. They didn't rule out autism, but her positive responses to some of the brain wave tests, deepened the mystery since all seemed to be within the normal parameters of a healthy child.
Marta Armstrong, PsyD, was a professor of pediatric psychology at Louisiana State University, a position she had held, for 10 years. She was unusual since she also had obtained a degree in Pediatric medicine. Dt. Armstrong was well respected, especially for her pioneering work involving severely autistic children. She was also employed by the state government as a professional consultant, working in Family Services, with autistic children and adults.
Sarah was an interesting case since her condition involved the deterioration of her entire social skill set. She moved from being a normal, healthy child developing as she should, and had been tested earlier in fact, to be in the top 99 percentile of mental and social development for a child her age. This was verified by the State of Louisiana health records; Sarah was tested as part of a group study, by the government on the progress of adopted children.
She had a superior intellect and a vocabulary which was at least 3 years ahead of the normal development curve for a child her age.
Then without apparent cause, Sarah started dropping back to the point where she still performed sanitary needs such as washing and using the toilet and still slept and woke up within the normal bracket for a child her age.
She'd greatly diminished her interest in the world around her; almost totally stopped talking with her parents and her friends;

stopped eating properly; stopped responding to external stimulation.

This was one of the most interesting effects regarding Sarah's condition. She no longer experienced pain, and her tickling reflexes had totally shut down.

Since no underlying physical conditions had been established, Marta was called in to do an assessment of her psychological state.

During their first meeting Marta noted the fear enveloping Sarah's mother and the near detachment from the situation expressed by her father.

Both parents had agreed to sit through the first hour of the first session and if Dr. Armstrong recommended it, they would admit Sarah to the hospital for further observation and testing.

Barry secretly regretted adopting this little girl and started resenting the time and money he had to spend to treat a symptom that seemed to have no cause. She took his wife away from him rather than bringing them closer together.

"The sins of the parents are passed onto the child" he thought. "But I am not the parent, why should I be the one who suffers for her parents' sins?"

He never mentioned these thoughts to Debbie or Dr. Armstrong. He was sure his wife would never forgive him for having such thoughts. Debbie was Sarah's momma and she was committed totally to the care of her little girl.

"Well thank you for coming in today Mr. and Mrs. Thompson" Marta said, "and it's good to meet you too as well Sarah... it's so nice to meet you."

Sarah didn't change her stare which seemed to be focused at something in the far corner of the room.

"She doesn't talk anymore" Debbie said with a tear welling up in her eyes, "what is happening to her Doctor?"

"Well Mrs. Thompson, we're going to try and find this out." Marta looked at the case history of Sarah which had been sent to her from Dr. Joseph Marks, the family practitioner in New Orleans.

"Can you both tell me in your own words the sequence of events leading to Sarah's present condition... starting with you Mr. Thomson."

Barry paused a moment collecting his thoughts… "Well doctor, the first time I thought there might be something troubling Sarah was when she was about 4 and one halve years old and started having nightmares. She woke up terrified and kept talking about some man coming through the walls of her room." Barry cleared his throat as he continued, "we took her to our family doctor, Dr. Marks, and he basically told us to comfort her after these nightmares and to reassure her there is nothing in her room, and that we would never let anyone harm her."
"We sometimes spent an hour with her just rocking her in my arms until she went to sleep again." Debbie said.
"How long did these nightmares last?"
"Well Dr. Armstrong," Barry started, "they lasted about a year maybe a little less"
"Fourteen months" Debbie interrupted her husband… "they started in April and ended the following June."
Barry nodded in agreement with Debbie "Yes dear you're right."
"Did she always give the same details of the dream, Mrs. Thomson?" the doctor asked.
"Yes, it was pretty much the same each time… she would wake up in a scream and tell us a bad man was coming through her walls and he wanted to steal her. Barry always checked under the bed, in the closet and outside the window to let Sarah know that the bad man was not there anymore."
"I sometimes yelled out loud telling the bad man to stay away and never come back again." Barry said. "I was trying to show her I was not afraid of any bad man, that he better stay away or I would be after him."
"So, after these nightmares stopped did you notice any difference in Sarah's behavior?" Mr. Thompson?
"Well I didn't notice anything different until she seemed to start losing her energy and the great curiosity, she once had. I used to lose patience with Sarah sometimes because she asked so many questions."
"What type of questions did she ask?" Dr. Armstrong inquired as she started making notes on the pad in front of her.
"Well, she asked strange questions like 'Why do people die, and where do people go when they fall asleep, why do we only eat things

that were alive'... questions like that and lots more. She also had a fascination with the bible stories she learned at Sunday school."
"Can you remember some of those questions?" asked Dr. Armstrong.
"Well" Debbie started, "she always had a hundred questions when she got home from Sunday school. She was in the Juniors bible study group, so the stories told to the children were not too difficult... we showed pictures and talked to the pictures... stories about Jesus feeding the multitudes... things like that."
Debbie continued, "We explained to the children, how Adam and Eve..."
Sarah suddenly sat up straight in her chair focusing her gaze directly at Dr. Armstrong - interrupting Debbie. - "Where is Adam?" she asked with a hint of desperation in her voice.
Debbie and Barry looked at Dr. Armstrong with surprise since this was the first time, she had spoken in over three weeks.
Dr. Armstrong was startled "Adam who?" Dr. Armstrong asked.
Debbie got up from her chair and moved towards Sarah.
Sarah remained silent, returning her stare back to the corner of the room.
Debbie was waived off by Dr. Armstrong... and she moved back to her chair.
Everyone paused. waiting for Sarah to talk again...
"Sarah, would you mind talking to us and tell us more about Adam" Dr. Armstrong asked.
"We have told the story of the Garden of Eden and how Eve committed the first sin, and how she then tricked Adam into committing the second sin," said Debbie... "I think she means Adam and Eve... we don't know any person named Adam."
The three adults spent the next half hour discussing Sarah and her malady. Sarah didn't speak again for the duration of the session.
It was agreed Sarah would be admitted to the institute the following morning for further observation.
Dr. Armstrong took direct responsibility for her case and promised Debbie and Barry she should have a better understanding of Sarah and the treatment to be taken after a short time of observation, possibly no more than one week.

Chapter 4

Our breathes are measured somewhere in a count

Our heartbeats and the number of people seen,
Our children and our words,
Are measured somewhere in a count.
"They are measured by events"
It cannot be disputed. in the final analysis,
We're measured on some skein of space and time,
Measured in a count!
"How much time we waste you and I,
Putting our faces on till we die."
The murdered ones still cry out from the soil.
"As Abel did."
Who is the lesson for in this living?
Tedious toil?
"Are you one of those who feel it?"

Adam heard the inner song as he walked past the church on King Street.

He loved the music flowing from the churches and was in awe of the sessions he heard, at the Toronto Conservatory when he visited with his best friend David.

David's older sister Caroline was playing piano - she had passed all the requirements to be included in the "elite" instruction sessions provided by the "Maestros" program, run by the University of Toronto Music Department.

The search was always on for young talent and Caroline was a prized find.

Though she was only 13 years old, her technical ability was outstanding.

Her first recital held to a packed auditorium when she was ten years old brought the entire audience to a standing ovation. She was a savant.
A child prodigy.
There is always something spiritually uplifting and inspiring about a gifted child, especially one who is able to send shivers up your spine, in the delivery of a piece of music heard hundreds of times before. To some, the gifted child brought hope, proof humanity had the chance to be better, through the transcendence of the normal rules of knowledge, as prodigy gifts.
Sometimes a child is born, as a savant – born as a gift, lifting the hopes and aspirations of the rest of us.
Walter and Alison didn't know where Adam's interest in music came from since there was no real musical talent in either of their families, at least not in the known gene pool. Allison remembered her cousin Sherrie was pretty good in karaoke bars but that was the extent of music with her kin.
Adam and his best friend David Mathews were in the same grade four class and had easily become inseparable friends. They shared everything and loved each other's company. From video games to internet apps to soccer and baseball; whenever you saw Adam you knew David was not too far away.
Caroline helped Adam learn his first piano piece and after only a few hours on the keys, Adam could keep up with Caroline on the pieces she had just taught him.
Caroline wished her little brother was as cooperative as his friend Adam, but she also realized Adam was different ... he seemed to learn the music by feeling it.
Adam started spending more time at David's house after school practicing with Caroline and even David became interested in music. Caroline helped on every level from practicing the scales to reading music. The three of them worked on writing their own pieces and this is where Adam started to shine.
He had an uncanny ability to bring notes and timing together and he used his computer and the internet to meet others and test his creations with his global music loving peers. He realized the word peers had nothing to do with the word years since some of his peers were much older than himself.

Adam loved creating complex harmonies, especially where the music was written for one instrument, then phase transposed to be played by three of the same instruments, dynamically adding multiple layers of notes, timing and feeling within the same harmonic field. Adam knew early on, through his sense experience, he was a synesthete – a person with synesthesia. He had the ability to perceive one sense simultaneously, with another. In Adam's case he experienced sound vibrations, simultaneously as colors. His brain transposed sound waves picked up through his ears, as waves of color, created somewhere within the 'third eye' perception network centered in the pineal gland. He also had the unusual ability to transpose color waves created in thought, to notes and rhythms. It was quantum ability involving the light and frequencies of colors with the particle relationship of scales and notes.

Creating layers was easier to do on a synthesizer than it was with physical instruments. Writing code to make the synthesizer deliver what he felt was as easy as running the same program, with different instances executed consecutively. Each instrument mimicked a different instance of perception. The genesis layer contains the rules and physical relationships of all notes and harmonies. Seven notes – Do, Re, Mi, Fa, So La Ti – as the base of harmonics and harmonic resonances. Adam loved harmonic resonance.

Most people had trouble understanding this concept, but they all loved the final affect.

'Three-piano' pieces became the challenge taken on by the three amigos (Caroline, Adam and David), and the only place having three pianos in one room was at the Royal Conservatory.

The challenge for David, Caroline and Adam, was to write music integrated on three pianos played as one melody with multiple layers of flow. The pianos were the orchestra – the instance platforms. The rules and range of the piano was the program, the integrated and congruent notes were the data played. The limitations of one scale more than tripled in complexity and utility. The greatest hurdle seemed to be the musicians tuning out the other two pianos and concentrating on their own instance.

Sometimes there was a bit of "drifting" as Adam called it… when one piece changed its timing or harmony, with that of another.
Adam felt this immediately when it happened, stopping the practice, pointing out the problem to Caroline and David, who were surprised - thinking they were playing better than expected.
Adam was the only player, never to "drift".
The first time Adam successfully played with David and Caroline - the first three piano piece which they had jointly collaborated, was the first time he felt pride about what he could do.
Adam was able to feel and see the aura of the music as it was playing. The frequencies and created blended colors, pulsating in layers of consciousness, were a thing of beauty, only he could see.
Walter and Alison bought a piano and they hired one of the top students at the conservatory to tutor Adam. The tutor quit in frustration since Adam was not interested in following the normal teaching methods. The teacher called him an undisciplined player.
Adam was sorry, and explained this tutor was stuck in a place he had pulled away from a while ago. Adam told his dad, he tried to help the tutor, but the tutor was stuck in a rut of rote, from which he couldn't escape.
Adam preferred working with Caroline and David, who were a bit more open minded to his method.
Walter shook his head, thinking there is nothing wrong with rote learning. That is how engineers learned, and it hadn't harmed him, or so he thought.
Walter was a bit worried since most of Adams time was spent on the piano or on the computer – either talking music on the internet – or writing pieces using his computer as the synthesizer. He did realize his son was good… very good and words like child prodigy and musical genius became attached to Adam's name. He had friends and collaborators around the world – even in Turkey! Walter was totally amazed with how the internet made social connection around the globe as an instantaneous experience. He spent hours in libraries cursively writing while taking copious and tedious notes, back in his day.
Adam was accepted as a full-time student in the Royal Conservatory on his tenth birthday… and his first recital was just as Caroline's had been, with a full room and a standing ovation.

Walter received consolation in the fact Adam also had a great interest in coding and was a quick study in learning computer languages and operating systems. He didn't care that music was the driver for his programming zeal.

Adam was adept at creating new programs to add vitality to his original music – adding instruments and even voice tracks to pieces – all done electronically. Adam was becoming a young expert on synthesizers. He and his internet buddies shared and co-wrote many new subroutines without the slightest thought of commercial value. They were part of the connected generation where creativity was free and its fruits available to all without a fee.

Walter insisted Adam took some time out for sports to develop his body as well as his mind, so Adam joined the swim team at school to keep his father happy. As he did his laps, he was composing new pieces in his head.

Even though Adam was pleasing his father with his swim team activities, his music was always in his head when he was in the pool. Swimming is the perfect sport for a musician since there is a built-in metronome, provided by the frequency of the stroke.

"Music and writing are much more exciting than working on a gear, as a good engineer"

Adam sang in his head as he competed in the eight-hundred-meter swim.

He competed in the long-distance races, and always had good rhythm in his strokes.

David was also a member of the team and always beat Adam in these events. David was a great competitive swimmer while Adam considered himself to be a good competitive swimmer. He knew he would never break any records even at the local club level, while David had already established new club records in the 50-meter free style and the 100 -meter butterfly. To Adam, swimming was like the carrier for his music, while to David, swimming was his path to self-esteem. Adam's coach was angry sometimes since Adam's strokes slowed down in the middle of a good try, then sped up again without reason. Adam didn't have the time to tell the coach it was due to the ritardando and the allegro of the music he was composing as he swam.

Adam was at a tender age, yet he still understood the conversations of the adults around him, who would argue from the perception of different ideologies, about the state of the planet. He hated the violence, especially against children and he realized he was lucky to have been born in Canada. So many children had been murdered in horrible ways for what appeared to be inhumane and selfish reasons, for one cause or another.

Adam cried openly sometimes as he watched the atrocities from his safe and secure home, on the internet. Sometimes his mother Allison would cry with him.

Adam realized, flesh was the fodder of different beliefs and ideologies. He hated the lack of empathy and compassion applied to solving each 'humanitarian' rendering, usually ending in the reward of bombing and bloodshed.

He made a secret pledge to God to become a channel for the good of others. He prayed to be used as a conduit to alter people's lives for the better, a catalyst "between" rather than an agent "because of".

He wanted to give all he had for the benefit of others, with no selfish agenda.

The blue flowers on my altar,
Express my love for God,
A private alter no one needs to see,
Since God looks down,
And knows they are from me.

Adam could feel the place where love is, in the kindness you bestow, and the memories you give, to all others. To Adam it was so easy to understand.

Adam loved to learn, read and listen. He had a flair for mathematics and philosophy, the western science versus the eastern faith.

He realized early, the difference in perspective between the religious community and the scientific community. Science always moved forward by peer reviewed evidence; religion stayed fixed by deeply felt faith.

He attended the Sunday school discussions at the church but was known to ask unusual questions which sometimes left the teachers a bit dumbfounded.

Regarding Adam and Eve, Adam asked if the Adam of the Bible, had a reproductive system, penis, testicles and prostate gland, prior to Eve being created from his rib?
If the answer was yes, then Adam asked why would he need that if Eve, with her female parts, was not yet created?
If the answer was no, Adam asked when God made these new parts for Adam, and did he make them from the same rib from which he had made Eve? And, why didn't God mention the creation of Adam's new parts? He also asked why paintings of Adam and Eve showed them with a bellybutton?
The preacher teachers were taken aback by such questions. Adam was not trying to be difficult - he was serious about the questions.
"You need to have faith, Adam!" the preacher would say. Our Lord works in mysterious ways and it's not our place to ask why he did or didn't do this or that."
Adam was not impressed with this answer, but he dropped the subject out of respect. He didn't wish to make the teacher feel uncomfortable, being asked a question he had never heard before.
His father was an engineer and therefor Adam had many discussions regarding evidence and faith. His father of course was on the evidence side... "Let them build a bridge based on faith and let the builders doing the work in faith, be the first to use that bridge." Walter stated. "We don't build structures based on faith!"
Adam believed in the Christian God, but he needed to study at a higher level than the one provided by the local church. He spent hours, studying the religions of the world including historical and current day beliefs, from different sources including university lectures provided by various knowledge channels of the internet.
Adam realized our planet is a very young planet, with much knowledge and wisdom yet to be gained. He visualized the older knowledge of the older planets out there, where violence had long since been replaced by matters of the spirit and of the heart, where creation from the spirit had long ago surpassed the procreation of the flesh. There seemed to be no creative future in the religions he studied, just a reward to go to one heaven or another forever, to spend the rest of eternity inside time and space, with a judgmental god. Adam felt the universe or multi-verse would turn out to be a more interesting place than the "heavens" offered, and the future

was more interesting than receiving an eternal reward. He loved the idea of Jesus and other luminaries but hated the idea of spite, revenge and judgment.
Adam had a thirst for books. His first full novel read was all about Bilbo Baggins as the Hobbit, and then he read the Lord of the Rings. From these first books he pondered the constant quest of good over evil and the use of magic and mirrors in all battles of war or politics. There is a different mix of personalities, no matter what age of study, continuously evolving the human condition - Adam believed the differences could be classified.
Understanding comes on different levels based in the level you're living.
Could a sexual predator understand compassion? Or could a compassionate person understand the brutality of someone killing strictly for carnal control.
Events affected events. Adam wrote freely about the crimes and horrors entering his psyche from different sources, nearly every day. There did seem to be good and evil in the mix of what we are, and some of it was just too sad and too terrifying to understand.
"--- The police report the body of a young woman was found this morning in an abandoned house in downtown Toronto. She had been strangled then set on fire. The coroner reports she was sexually assaulted, suffering sodomy and rape before her death. Police are looking for two eighteen-year- old men as suspects in this slaying. ---"
And Adam, knowing poetry could be used as a bridge to deeper understanding, wrote, in keyboard strokes:
The collective thought will manifest itself and will cause a time and space occurrence that is in fact made part of the collective reality.

Thought is the builder...
Thought is the builder
Sleep gently victims of passion,
The ones who know your Soul,
Still love you and always will,
Forgive the ones, who used you so terribly,
You sacrificed yourself on the altar of life,
As flesh and only flesh,
To be destroyed,

Degraded and used
In bringing Cain back into the garden,
Your sacrifice defines the tree of Life
And all pain suffered
By the victims, in cavity and vein,
Is done over once, then over once again...
Come closer Cane
Come closer Cane
Come closer Cane
Come closer Cane
You are your brother's keeper!
Death is always close to life...
Gentle Abel still, violently dies, every day.

Adam rationalized flesh was a commodity to be used up, in the pursuit of knowledge. Nothing is learned freely. Humanity always ripped and tore old traditions apart over time and flesh was always part of the payment. Joan of Arc, and Jesus Himself died defending the perfect truth, against the selfish and non-learned infidel.

Adam made a private bet to himself- he would find the tree of life to be like a maple` shedding its leaves every season always making room for the next generation, while the tree of knowledge was an evergreen, with a constant frequency of rhythm and vibration.

"All is connected" he would tell his father... "all knowledge is one knowledge dad".

Walter was finding it more difficult to win these discussions with his son. Whenever he mentioned he could be a great engineer, Adam would counter musicians and philosophers were also engineers... the difference being they were further up on the ladder of evolution, away from the physical structures and more involved with frequencies and rhythms. Adam always smiled when he put his father's occupation on the lowest level of creation. He loved the perplexed look his father gave him since his father always thought his work was the highest form of creation.

"Dad, you work strictly in the physical layer of things... what you do is great, but it is for the sake of the physical."

"Have another spoonful of that physical cereal you're eating Adam. You may find that it's necessary to eat that physical layer stuff to survive here!" Walter always brought the argument back to what Adam was currently doing since it proved his argument that physical is what he is. He truly enjoyed the banter with his son. "And let me tell you Adam, some of the accomplishments of your so called 'physical layer creators' have made a work of art, appealing to all senses, including the sixth!"

"Yes dad, of course, even physical level engineers must eventually evolve to the higher purpose..." Adam smiled, "the creation of art as part of the physical plane is proof that we do evolve!"

Walter laughed... "You have an answer for everything don't you! Well I have to go to my physical office to do my physical creation so we can have the physical money it takes to buy your physical breakfast now." Walter said sarcastically as he walked to the door.

"Well dad, someone has to provide for the basics!" Adam laughed, "I am glad it's you instead of me."

"Goodbye son" Walter waved... "I hope you have a great day inside that head of yours today."

"I will dad" Adam smiled again as his father left for work. Adam loved Walter with all his heart and he thoroughly enjoyed the light-hearted discussions they could have on almost any subject. The arguments always ended by Adam classifying events with layers. "Life is a wave," he would say "and we all surf upon it!"

Walter told him he was stealing from Shakespeare and Elvis who said Life is a stage etc.

Adam started reading the philosophers in earnest. Kant, Nietzsche, and Kafka, the Bible, the Koran, Aristotle and Plato, Freud and Jung, Dillon and Cohen, Pascal and Smith... there was so much to do and so many scholars to learn from.

He was now 13 in grade nine at high school... he aced most of his subjects except woodwork. He always lost patience when trying build something solid from something solid.

He was required to include woodworking in his curriculum for two semesters, but the school waived his second semester and substituted another English Literature term.

Since the school, based progression on assessment tests, Adam found he was at the top-grade level in English, mathematics, music and science after his first year of high school.

He was a quick study in French and Spanish and found the language courses interesting since each language had a rhythm of its own; each a different instance of the same program. He first tried to understand the rhythm, and then found the syntax and the composition to be much easier to decipher. Adam took Latin as a personal language project since he found Latin to be one of the base frequency carriers of the other major languages. Adam also realized each language had its own pattern of colors – his synesthesia covered all sound wave variations. Every bird tweet had its own cadence and color. Adam perceived the world differently than others and this was an advantage in many regards.

"All is turning to be mathematics" he told Caroline at one of their conservatory sessions.

"If all knowledge is one knowledge, then all variances are one variance." Caroline nodded her head in agreement but in truth she thought Adam was a bit weird and hardly ever understood what he was talking about. She had her music and that was all she needed to be happy in life.

It became obvious Adam had surpassed Caroline on total musical knowledge, but Caroline was still a better technician with the keyboard. Her fingers were longer, and she enjoyed the playing more than the writing. Adam now enjoyed the writing more than the playing, and he wanted to hear his work as Caroline played it rather than how he played it. Caroline would bring "the genius to the molecules and I will bring the genius from the ether" Adam would joke. "Hmm… Okay" Caroline nodded.

Adam appreciated Caroline for what she was…and she was happy for the appreciation and the recognition.

The team of Caroline and Adam became a position of strength for the Royal Conservatory of Music and audiences were always standing room only when Caroline played a piece written by Adam.

As he moved into his teenage years, Adam was known as a bit of a nerd, but a brilliant nerd who had deep and verifiable knowledge on almost every subject. His compositions were absolutely absorbing to anyone listening, whether maestro or dilettante.

As time moved on the friendship between Adam and Caroline became stronger than the friendship between Adam and David.

David loved sports and was turning into a bit of a jock at school. He was the best swimmer in the inner-city school league and was one of those very rare athletes who excelled at swimming, football and tennis. He still loved his music, but sports and the girls attracted to sports were becoming the passion of his life.
Even though he was in high school, college scouts were already looking at David as full scholarship material.
Adam listened with both ears cocked as David told him about losing his virginity to Betty Marcos – the girl all the grade nine boys drooled over – the fantasy most of the boys in school masturbated to almost every night and morning of the week - she was fondly known as 'Betty the Body' by all of the boys and 'Betty the Bitch' by most of the girls at Monarch Park Collegiate.
Betty was the epitome of nubile womanhood. The innocence of being 16, with the body of a twenty-year-old. Betty was an early bloomer. Much older men - some even in their twenties, tried to get her to go out with them, starting when she was twelve years old. Betty was disgusted with the comments from some of these men and she didn't fully understand why they were talking to her the way they were.
"Hey girl, sit on my face and I will guess your weight" was a common insult thrown towards Betty by boys passing in cars as they honked their horns, laughed and whistled.
Betty gave them the finger but inside she was scared.
She didn't like what boys were thinking about her.
That was when she was twelve, but now she was sixteen and she had long ago realized boys of all ages treated her differently because of her looks.
She was often told she was the prettiest girl in the school with the most perfect body. It became more difficult for Betty to think of herself as more than a physical attraction. Most of the friends she had, liked her because of her popularity. Her popularity was because of her looks and she knew that.
"If you got it flaunt it" her mother told her "Just don't give it away for nothing, you're sitting on a gold mine!" Her mother laughed at that one as she poured herself another gin and tonic.
Betty was the second youngest of four sisters. They came from ancestors who were a mixture of French, German, Greek, Swedish

and Russian. All were tall and slim with full lips, blonde hair, blue eyes, - just basic good looks. Betty had developed to what everybody called, an almost perfect figure – 'thirty-four B cup breasts, twenty-four-inch waist and thirty-four-inch hips'.

The older she got the more she depended on her looks for acceptance. She was definitely the best or close to, the best-looking girl, in all of the Toronto high schools.

Summertime was Betty's favorite time in Toronto. The boardwalk by Woodbine beach teemed with boys. Betty was a roller blade babe.

When she wore her tight tank top and her short shorts, she was the main attraction. Men in their forties and fifties even stopped and smiled appreciatively at her when she rolled past, remembering the wild side of youth.

The first time she looked at David on the football field, she found him very attractive. He was almost six feet tall with light brown hair and big brown eyes. He was obviously one of the best athletes on the field and the fact he was in tryouts for the quarterback position of the Junior team didn't take away from his persona. He was muscular with bulges in the right places. She could tell he had a six-pack type of stomach and he was a runner.

"What are you looking at Betty?" Janice asked. "Mmmm, let me see – ah, could it be that long tall drink of testosterone in the blue shorts?"

"That is disgusting Janice! – my god you talk just like a messed-up man!"

"Oh, pardon moi your prissiness..." Janice mocked, "You mean to tell me you wouldn't like a little some of that?"

"I didn't say that Janice, I just don't think as dirty as you do!"

The more Betty looked the better David looked.

David noticed 'The Body' looking at him and put on his best Tom Cruise little boy smile and looked right back at her. He was totally amazed that someone like her would be interested in him, but his sister Caroline did tell him he was turning into a hunk, so maybe she just wasn't being a nice big sister.

The ball was tossed too far - David had to run it down - almost knocking Betty off her feet as he made a final lunge for the ball.

"Sorry about that" he said as he pounced back onto his feet again. "Did I hurt you?"

Betty looked right into those big brown eyes and almost melted on the spot. “No... I am fine,” she said, “Nice catch!”
David threw the ball back to his practice partner and signaled for a time out.
“My name is David” he said as he extended his hand towards Betty.
“I’m Betty” she said as she took hold of his hand for the first time and felt his strength as he squeezed just a little too hard.
“Ouch” she squealed, with a mocking smile... “I am delicate you know David, nice to meet you too!”
David apologized, looked into her eyes and said with his best look of practiced sincerity, “I will never hurt you again dear lady.”
Janice opened her mouth and inserted her middle finger on top of her extended tongue... “Pardon me while I puke, you two.”
“This is my friend Janice” Betty said.
David extended his hand to Janice with a smile, “Pleased to meet you too.”
Janice felt him gently squeeze her hand and thought, “My god he is coming on to me.”
David asked Betty if they could meet after practice at Hansen’s grill. He had seen her there after school before.
Betty accepted immediately – saying – “Well I can be there, but I don’t think Janice can make it.”
Janice stared at Betty – “No it’s ok Betty I forgot to tell you that my brain surgery was cancelled... I am free after practice.”
With that David started running towards his partner, “Great, I will see you both at Hansen’s after the practice.”
David thought to himself – “Man – they both want you!”
He was still a virgin but intended to lose that part of his history as soon as possible now that he was in high school.
Back in the locker room David’s teammates were teasing him in the shower.
“Hey Dave...” Stan Knowlton, the team captain for last year asked, “is that all you have to give her... I can give her some of this to help you out if you want” – David looked over as Stan made a stroking motion with both hands as if he was masturbating a horse.
Everyone laughed as David said... “No, it’s ok Stan, why give her horse meat when she could have prime rib?”

It was a feather in David's cap to be going out with 'Betty the Body' after only one meeting. Every guy in school had tried to make it with her but as far as anybody knew, she hadn't given it to anybody yet. Most were amazed she didn't have a steady boyfriend since she could have any boy in this school or any other school if she wanted him.

"Well tell me what happened" Adam said impatiently to David... "How did you lose your virginity to Betty?"
"Alright" David said, "we met at the football practice at the beginning of the season, before I won the first line quarter back spot." David sat back providing Adam with a pregnant pause knowing the suspense was killing him...
"AND..." Adam stammered "keep going!"
"We met at Hansen's Grill – I was there with some of the guys from the practice and they were razzing me about talking to Betty. Her friend Janice came with her, but she was a little skinny looking kid compared to Betty."
David took a sip of his coke...
"We had a plate of fries and a hamburger and we were getting to know each other better... you know... what she liked... what I liked... what she hated... what I hated..."
Adam broke in again, "Come on David, get to the good part!"
"Relax a bit Adam; I am building up to that. Give me a chance to tell the story."
David took another sip of his coke and Adam gave an audible sigh of impatience.
"We were attracting too much bad attention and some of the immature guys were sticking their tongues out trying to lick their eyebrows and stuff like that, and Caroline just came out and asked if there was someplace else for us to go."
"Where did you decide to take her" Adam asked.
"Well I had to ditch her friend Janice first, since I didn't want her to be part of my recipe... not yet anyway!" David winked at Adam and put on one of his evil smiles. "So, I told Janice we were going for a swim, and asked if she wanted to go too."
Janice looked at us like we were crazy and said no way was she going swimming... So, I took Betty's hand and walked her out of the place.

"Are we really going swimming?" Betty asked.
"No, Betty, we're not going swimming... I just wanted to get rid of Janice."
"Ah" Betty said, "so where are you taking me?"
"I am taking you to heaven, Betty... so don't say no."
Betty was disappointed once again. Another guy with only one thing on his mind. But this time she thought she may just go along with it and get it over with. If she was going to lose her virginity, why not to someone like David.
David opened the car door and Betty climbed inside.
As David got into the driver's side, he asked Betty if she had to be home at any fixed time.
"Well, my mother usually has supper ready by 6:30, but I called her before we met at Hansen's and told her I was going to catch some food with Janice and a few other friends. She knows my friends and I hang out a bit, on practice nights"
"Great" said David. That gives us a couple of hours to fill and get to know each other better - Agreed!"
"Agreed." Betty replied.
David reached over and impulsively put his right hand around the back of Betty's head and pulled her face towards his. He gave her a small kiss on the lips, removed his hand and started the engine.
Betty didn't resist but she thought 'this guy is moving a bit too fast for me'. She noticed a few of her friends looking at them through the window of Hansen's Grill with great smiles of approval, some making obscene gestures with their fists. She smiled back knowing this was her legacy... the girl who gets the boys that all the other girls want.
The car started moving and David pulled into the traffic.
"Where are you taking me?" asked Debbie.
"Well, my parents are out till ten tonight, my sister is down at the music hall and my house is empty. Would you like to go there?'
"This is our first time going out - can I trust you?"
David smiled and said "of course you can trust me... I am not a monster you know. I just want to take you to a place where we can have some privacy and get to know each other. Agreed?"

"Agreed" Betty replied once again as she sat back in the seat. She turned the music up as Rod Stewart just happened to be singing "Tonight's the night, going to do it right..."
David put on his Tom Cruise smile and thought "Yes!"
Adam was sitting listening to David's story almost mesmerized by the details David was putting into this tale.
"What?" Adam stammered "You're telling me that Rod Stewart was singing 'tonight's the night!'"
"Swear to God Adam. That song came on at a perfect time for me!"
"Wow" Adam shouted... "Sometimes the universe is such a fucking synchronistic place!"
David looked at Adam "What the hell does synchronistic mean?"
"Never mind" said Adam, "Then what happened?"
David sat back and took another sip of his coke.
"We got to my house and went into the kitchen. I asked Betty if she would like a glass of wine since I knew that was better than asking her if she wanted a beer."
David looked at Adam and put his Tom Cruise smile on...
"She told me she doesn't drink alcohol, but I said she could have a glass and sip on it if she felt like it - or leave it if she didn't. Agreed?"
"Agreed" Betty said, "I have only had wine once before and I didn't like it too much."
David looked at her and with his best professorial expression he said, "You will acquire a taste for it as your taste buds mature."
Betty hit him on the arm and said, "Oh right, I suppose your taste buds are more mature than mine - give me a glass of your damn wine!" Betty was laughing as David mocked "shocked" at her use of a swear word.
Both were actors on some stage, and they wanted to make sure their parts led to the proper finale.
The first glass of wine was sipped too fast and David being the gentleman he was, filled it again telling Betty she could sip on it if she wanted to. He refilled his glass again too, as he listened to Betty talk about her childhood and her life, living with a mother who drank too much every day.
"My mom and dad were divorced when I was six years old and then the battle began... My dad didn't pay support because he said my mom wouldn't let him see us." Betty sipped again and she was

starting to get a slight buzz from the wine. She decided she did like it after all, not realizing one red wine might taste differently from another.
She liked the taste of this one.
David looked at Betty wondering when he should make his first move. The kiss in the car had been bold but now he was unsure of how to proceed. As he listened to Betty, he realized how nice a person she was. He liked her and started to think of her as his girlfriend. He liked the image, of both of them together.
Betty was very sexy. She had the face of an angel and the body of vamp. Her eyes were blue, with long natural lashes. Flowing, thick blonde hair, full red lips, smooth skin and clear complexion.
She could be a model for toothpaste or skin cream. She had an aura of innocence and her smile and laugh were genuine and infectious.
Her body, a school-boys dream.
Perfect breasts which pushed against the fabric of her white blouse. The two top buttons were undone showing just enough cleavage to make a man think about more. She was wearing a white lacy bra and the outline of her "standing out there" nipples could be seen through her blouse.
Her waist - tiny, her hips and legs a perfect combination.
Many times. Betty had heard the boys say, 'nice legs... what time do they open?'
Betty was wearing a light blue skirt which hugged her waist and stayed tight around her bottom, flaring out a bit around her thighs and ending just above the knee. She hated hose and so her legs were bare all the way up to her pantie's underneath.
Her dress was tight enough for David to see the outline of her high cut under wear beneath the material of the skirt.
He had seen Betty on the roller blades in her short shorts and halter top and started getting an erection just thinking about her naked.
Betty noticed David move around in his chair and she had also noticed him look directly at her breasts.
'Great, another boy with a hard on', she thought.
"I am a virgin" she said quietly... David looked up from his trance like fixation on her breasts becoming embarrassed knowing he had been caught looking.

"Oh... So am I." David stammered, looking towards the window as if there was something interesting to see there.
Betty couldn't believe it "You have never had sex?" she was surprised and happy at the same time. David was a definite hunk and she was interested in exploring him a bit further.
"I have had sex with myself" he smiled... "thinking about you sometimes as a matter of fact" David was smiling that smile again and Betty found him irresistible.
Betty moved closer "Do you like me David or are you only interested in my boobs and my ass?"
David was a bit shocked at the question drawing in a gulp of air.
"Ehhmm... Of course, I like you Betty - as a matter of fact, as you were talking to me, I realized what a nice person you are, and I even imagined having someone like you as my girlfriend."
David continued, "But to be totally honest your body is a work of art and it would be an understatement for me to say it was a distraction to me... hell Betty most of the guys at school drool every time you walk by. You are an automatic hard-on generator!"
David was getting bolder since he now sensed Betty was not pulling away but was leaning closer to him... "Look"
He said as he turned to fully face her, half standing up from his chair "I have become excited just sitting here talking to you."
Betty smiled and could see the outline of David's cock straining in his pants. He sat down again, clumsily, not sure if he had done the right thing, showing Betty his hard on.
She leaned over and kissed him on the mouth, and David almost fainted as the blood rushed from his head. He was French kissing Betty the body and she was kissing him back.
They sat there and kissed for about five minutes... neither of them had experienced such an intimate experience. David thought he could stay there forever in this moment, feeling the soft full and a bit wet, kisses from Betty. He was sure he was in love.
Betty loved what she was feeling, her body was responding; She could feel her nipples becoming harder under the fabric of her blouse and bra. She squirmed a bit as she also felt a warmth spread between her thighs, and she knew she was attracted to this young man.
David was scared to move a muscle, but Betty knew what he wanted.

So many boys had tried to feel her up before – she had never let them, but now she wanted David to touch her breasts. She wanted to be his girlfriend and she knew girlfriends let boyfriends do things like that.

Betty pushed herself into David's chest and he could feel those magnificent breasts mashing into him.

Betty took David's right hand and moved it right onto her left breast and said, "You want to touch me don't you... Agreed!"

David was breathing faster as he gasped "Agreed". He cupped her breast in his hand squeezing and naturally moved his thumb and index finger towards Betty's nipple - he felt it get even harder, as he gently tweaked her nipple between his thumb and his finger. Betty was breathing faster and deeper.

David moved his other hand to Betty's other breast and squeezed and rubbed both breasts in a synchronous motion ending at each erect nipple.

It was the first time he had ever felt the breast of a woman, though he had imagined how it would feel... he did squeeze the corner of his pillow sometimes as he pleasured himself... this was much hotter and better than the corner of his pillow. He squeezed and teased each breast as he was bathed in the pleasure of the experience.

Betty moved her lips back onto his, and her tongue explored the inside of his mouth moving with the same rhythm and speed as his tongue.

Betty had taken him to heaven!

He slowly moved over to the buttons and undid each one till her blouse was open at the front fully exposing the lace bra and the swelling mounds inside.

David tried to push the bra out of the way, but it was too tight. "How do I undo this!" he implored Betty as she kissed him lightly on his lips while she reached behind her back and undid the clasp. Betty's bra was undone, and David wasted no time in moving it out of the way as he just stared at her breasts while he felt them with both hands. He brought his mouth to each nipple in turn and slowly sucked, then licked in circling motions - squeezing them together till he could almost lick and suck both nipples at the same time. He heard Betty moan softly for the first time.

"You're beautiful Betty... absolutely beautiful! I want you to be my girlfriend... do you want me to be your boyfriend?" he asked a bit nervously.
"Yes" Betty gasped. But she had been thinking as David was licking and sucking, he may think she does this with other boys... maybe he thought she was a slut or a skank!
"David, I want you to know I have never let any boy touch me before."
David kissed her tenderly this time showing a gentle recognition of the special gift she was giving to him.
"I am the same, Betty" he said softly, "Thank you for choosing me to be your boyfriend."
It was very special moment for both of them, as they slowly started to explore each other's body.
Betty touched a penis for the first time in her life as David moved his hand beneath her skirt towards her secret spot which no boy had ever touched before. Betty opened her legs slightly giving David access. She was breathing heavily as he moved his fingers up then down the crease of her vagina... David felt the wetness of her panties as he slowly moved the material a bit to the side and inserted one finger into her wetness, while his thumb found her clitoris and started to slowly rub it too. Betty started bucking her hips back and forth a little faster than David was moving his finger. He moved his middle finger deeper and was in a trance like state as he kissed Betty once again on her sweet and willing mouth, then moved down again to lick and suck each nipple in their turn. He loved this and now understood why his friends made such a big deal of it.
He pushed his finger in deeper gently pushing in then out until he felt the barrier of her hymen. As he was doing this, Betty had encircled his hard cock, still in his pants. She loved the feeling and savored each new feeling and discovery as it was happening. She felt horny for the first time in her life.
"Let's take our clothes off" David rasped.
"Not here David... Let's go to your room in case someone comes home".
David slowly removed his finger, put it to his mouth tasted it, it seemed the natural thing to do - stood up taking Betty's hand, as he moved her towards the stairs. He couldn't take his eyes off her

beautiful and perfect ass, as she was climbing up the stairs ahead of him... he was going to get laid, by Betty the Body.

Adam's eyes were like saucers ... "what happened next!"

David looked at Adam with a smile and said... "Adam, what kind of man would you take me for, if I did a tell, to you, every time I did a kiss, to some heavenly body out there!"

David got up and ran out of the house with Adam chasing him... "David come back and finish the story! I won't tell anybody."

David was laughing out loud as he jumped into his car on his way to pick up his girlfriend down at Hansen's Grill.

He had the house to himself tonight, till at least 10 o-clock!

In total frustration, Adam sat at the keyboard composing a song about two young lovers who had raging hormones. Adam needed to spend some time with girls soon or he would explode from the mystery of it all. He had a horrid thought of getting hit by a truck before he lost his virginity... what a horrible possibility he thought.

He had of course read all the books on physiology and knew where all the major organs and glands were located for each of the sexes. He knew the mechanics of everything but had never experienced a physical sexual encounter with another human being.

Adam had even helped David explaining the various techniques employed for oral sex; fellatio and cunnilingus. David got a kick out of Adam's explanations, always using "scientific" terms for things like a blow job and eating pussy, or even the more common non-gender phrase of "going down". He was such a nerd! Adam admitted he preferred terms used by the professionals in the field, and by professionals, he didn't mean pimps, sex addicts, of prostitutes. He was well read in this area of human relations.

Of course, porn movies gave the best reference to everyone – no reading required.

He knew men had to have orgasms frequently due to the nature and life span of healthy spermatozoa and he knew women had a monthly cycle bringing eggs to the womb just in case some feisty sperm cell found its way there.

He knew all about DNA or at least as much as the average doctor and much more than the average person. DNA was worth exploring. "There is the map of existence on the physical layer!" he thought.

Even though he knew all this he couldn't escape the fact, he wanted to fornicate with someone.
He knew human beings and most other living creatures had rituals for procreation and sexual relations, and he wondered if the rituals were the symptom or the cause.
"What is the primordial driver of life" he thought "Sex or the need for it - causing procreation to happen"?
This question was taking a lot of Adam's time lately as he observed as much as he could about everything, looking for associations in seemingly non-associated events.
Did Rod Stewart just happen to happen, on the radio the day David and Betty copulated (he thinks) for the first time, or was it possible, there was a matrix of synchronicity, like the field of gravity, always enabling thought patterns on the best possible path to make things manifest. He knew, both David and Betty wanted each other in a deeper and special way. The song just amplified the mutually desired choice as a positive chance. 'Follow your heart', is a common expression throughout humanity, in many languages giving anecdotal credence to this possibility. Adam believed intuition is always available to everyone, to help make heart-desired decisions... maybe.
Adam realized he sometimes fell into analyzing too much. But he also realized, under analysis was much worse than over analysis, and to him, under analysis was always the choice of lazy thinkers.
He remembered the words spoken to him from his father regarding engineering... 'You can hit analysis paralysis if you think too much of why you should or should not do something. Execution is the most important part of any idea!'.
Adam thought he may be suffering from analysis paralysis since all his waking moments were spent on thinking - not too much energy anymore, was spent on doing.
Even his music was suffering since he didn't have the desire to write like he once did. Caroline was furious with him since she wanted to continue to play his new stuff, but even the new stuff was starting to get weird and was out of reach for most music critics.
"Give me some music Adam" Caroline yelled wanting to ensure Adam knew she was very angry with him.

Adam looked at Caroline... she was older but so was he. He had spent so much time with this woman and had never really considered her as a sexual being. He loved her dearly but had never once thought of her in physical terms... there had always been music between them. Caroline was hot though, very popular with the young men at the Conservatory.
"I have to get my life going Caroline" Adam answered. "look at David, for God's sake, he is happy with his existence... he has his sports and Betty his girlfriend is to die for!" --- "My God I am 16 years old and I am still a virgin!"
Caroline looked at him and couldn't help but laugh. "Oh, so that is it, you finally have become horny? Is that why our music is suffering so much? You need to get laid?"
Adam looked at her with a scowl. She didn't have to be so cruel or so crude.
"I need to have someone to be with me - and stop making it sound like I am some animal in heat who has lost control."
"Adam" Caroline said a bit softer with a bit more sympathy, but, not liking the prospect of Adam having one girlfriend, "If you choose the route of the little wife and the picket fence and the house in the suburbs, you will forsake your gift. An artist's greatest enemy is to become average! Average people are everywhere, and they are a miserable lot. You and I are different" she continued, "we have been given the gift of music and it's our duty to the arts to let the music rule us."
For God's sake Caroline" Adam said with the same scowl as before, "I don't want a wife, I want a wench!"
"Adam have you not noticed the bevy of young women flesh always swooning when you're near them either here at the academy or when we do our recitals on the road?" Adam looked a bit puzzled here... "What are you talking about?" he asked.
"I am talking about your groupies who follow you everywhere you go... you're too dense in your music to even realize the power you already have over some women. Any number of them would gladly fuck you or give you a blow job just for the chance to talk with you or spend some time with you."
Adam was dumbfounded... he had noticed lots of females at his concerts, but he had no idea they were interested in him for

anything other than his music. He started to do a mental analysis of the previous concerts he had given - Caroline was right. On many occasions some women just hung around looking at him as if waiting for him to give the command on what was expected next.
"Do you mean to say I could have had coitus with those women after the concerts?"
Caroline looked at him with sheepish eyes and nodded "Yes". She looked him straight in the eye and said, "Your music is power Adam... it's an aphrodisiac to some of us... me included."
Caroline looked at Adam to see his reaction to her last statement.
Adam looked at her as if for the first time... "You would have sexual relations with me Caroline? Is this what you're saying to me?"
Caroline looked at the boy in front of her... "I am almost twenty Adam, you're sixteen, and even though you're so much younger than me, I have felt times when I would have done anything for you, just to be close to the source of the music you make."
"I am a slave to your gift as well as a slave to my own." Caroline said quietly bowing her head slightly towards Adam.
Adam felt for the first time his power over others.
"Will you be my wench Caroline?" Adam asked with a bit of a smile on his lips."
"Yes!" Caroline exclaimed, "but it must be between us only. I can just imagine the ruin of my reputation if it got around, I was sleeping with you. I know for one thing our parents would never forgive me and believe me I would get the full blame since I am older."
"Caroline you're always so worried about what others think." He laughed, "didn't you just tell me that it's an artist's duty not to be normal... shouldn't we be doing as many abnormal things as possible?"
"Will you promise to be discreet" Caroline asked with a humble tone to her almost trembling voice.
"Only if it does not affect my artistic abilities" Adam smiled.

Caroline moved over to where Adam was standing in the empty playing room... "If I give you my body will you give me your music?"
"Yes" Adam said as he reached over and touched Caroline for the first time. Caroline took his hand saying. "Let's find a place with a bit

more privacy than here." Caroline was in charge, of the instrument storage area. She had a key to get into this space.
There was a couch and some chairs with a table in there, and it was secure.
Adam held Caroline's hand and followed her lead, like a puppy on a walk.
Caroline unlocked the door, turned on the light, pulled Adam in and bolted the door from the inside. "Are you ready?" she smiled, realizing how much she loved and cared for this young musical genius standing in front of her. "Yes," Adam said, clearing his throat nervously. Adam's mind was running like a locomotive, going over everything he knew about pleasing a woman while also pleasing himself.
Caroline cupped his cheeks with both of her hands and moved in closer to kiss him for the first time. She wanted to make his first time special, not rushed. As she kissed him, moving her tongue into his mouth and applying a bit of suction, she moved her left hand down to his crotch, and felt the hardness of his cock. She was happy with the gasp coming from his mouth, as she squeezed him, then stroked him slowly.
"You can touch me too Adam," she said, taking his left hand, moving it slowly to her right breast... "Squeeze me, feel me... I am yours."
Adam loved what he was now doing... as Caroline moved him over to the couch, where she sat down with him standing in front of her. She reached up and with both hands, undid his belt, then the button on his pants, then slowly pulled the zipper down, over the bulge of his hard and virgin cock.
As she did this, Adam moved his hands under her blouse, inside her bra, onto her breasts... reaching the hard nipples on both sides at the same time. He was amazed, how soft and magnificent the flesh of a woman felt.
"Mm... I like that," Caroline, softly said, encouraging his exploration of her body.
She reached into his boxer shorts from the top, and pulled them down, releasing his cock.
Then she moved her head closer kissing the bulbous tip, then moving her tongue in widening circles around the head, until she moved forward and sucked his cock into her willing mouth.

"Oh my God, Caroline!" Adam gasped… "You're fellating me!"

Caroline laughed out loud and moved her mouth briefly from his cock… "I am sucking your cock! Lean back and enjoy your first blow job!"

Caroline encircled his cock with the fingers of her right hand, pumping up and down on the shaft with her mouth sucking in the same rhythm. Caroline loved giving head and she knew she was good at it.

Adam felt the energy of pleasure moving from his groin, up his spine, rebounding back down again.

"Caroline, I am going to ejaculate!!"

Caroline clamped down on his cock, gently squeezing his balls as they went tense then relaxed. Adam's hips started bucking backwards and forwards in an uncontrolled spasm… Adam, screamed four times, as he filled her mouth in four powerful spasms, with his sperm.

Caroline slurped as she swallowed the result of each spasm. Adam's knees buckled as he leaned into her, quickly removing his hands from her breasts, to use them as a brace against the couch, ensuring he would not fall onto her.

Adam was weak and satisfied, he could never imagine how great this would feel.

Caroline gently pushed him back as she licked her smiling lips. She was very happy with herself, giving pleasure to Adam.

"Now you have to give me a kiss and hold me for a bit, telling me how good that made you feel." Caroline said in a tutorial type of voice.

Adam sat down on the couch beside her, put his arms around her and kissed her. "That was wonderful," he said. "Absolutely mind blowing… you're amazing, and I love you for being my first."

Caroline hugged him back… "We're not finished yet with your lessons," she smirked… there's more to making love to me, than you, enjoying a blow job."

"I know, Caroline," Adam said, "I want to perform cunnilingus on you… I have so much to do, and I think I am going to become addicted to you and sex!"

"Well, first of all, tell me you want to eat my pussy… performing cunnilingus sounds like a medical procedure." Caroline smiled.

Okay, then," Adam said, "I want to eat your pussy!"
Caroline stood up... "Undress me." She said, "and you get naked too.... I want to see your secret tattoos."
"I have no secret tattoos." Adam stated... "Should I get one?"
Caroline laughed, "I know, I was only kidding, you're not a tattoo kind of guy. Get one if you really want one... maybe get a tattoo of a piano keyboard on your beautiful cock, and I will play if for you, haha."
They both laughed as Caroline stated again, "Undress me. You're still a virgin."
Adam was now at ease with Caroline and he wanted to give her some pleasure too. He reached over, started to undo the buttons of her blouse... as Caroline helped by pulling the bottom of her blouse out of her pants. When the buttons were undone, Adam pulled the blouse off her shoulders, until it was completely off. He reached behind her back and undid the clasp. Caroline helped and pulled her bra off her shoulders and then she took each one into the palms of her hands on the side and squeezed them together. Adam bent forward and licked and kissed each of her nipples, then cupped both with both of his hands, feeling the fullness and softness again.
Caroline noticed Adam's erection had returned. She stood up, Adam reached out, undid the waist button, pulled the zipper down, then pushed her pants off her hips, down her legs... as Caroline lifted each foot ... they were off, and she was standing in her white thong panties.
Adam couldn't remove his eyes from her body... she was beautiful with all the curves and bumps in the best places. He stood up quickly, pulled his tee shirt off, kicked his running shoes off, pulled his socks off and removed his pants and underwear, kicking them away from them.
Caroline put her arms around him and kissed passionately this time with more force than she used during the initiation to kissing. She was determined to make him a good kisser, since most women judged the passion of a man, by his kiss, in her opinion, anyway. Adam kissed back with more passion too, as he moved his hands down to cup each cheek of her ass and pull her lower body into his own.

Caroline moved her right hand down, once again encircled her fingers around his hard cock and slowly stroked back and forth.
Adam took the hint, moved his right hand into the front of Caroline's body, inserting it into the top of her panties, until he felt the lips of her vagina. She was totally shaved, and she was wet. Adam moved with meticulous precision, now learning by doing, slipping his middle finger, into her pussy, feeling the hard nub of her clitoris, with his index finger and thumb. He slid his middle finger in further, curling it upwards till he was stroking where he read her "G" spot should be. "Oh my God" Adam gasped. "This is perfect." Caroline was breathing faster moving with the movement of his finger, then kissing him hard on the lips. She was surprised to find Adam knew his way around the pleasure areas of the vagina, without ever touching one before. She was happy he had done his homework. His stroking thumb and fingers felt good. She was naturally lubricated and ready.
Caroline pushed Adam till he was sitting on the couch, she pulled her panties off, pushed him backwards, as she stepped onto the couch, putting her arms against the wall, opening her legs, till her pussy was right in front of his face. Adam looked at in awe, definitely the best-looking vagina of all primates, he thought.
Adam took this as his cue to start cunnilingus, and he did. His tongue licked right up the middle till he met the clitoris, then up and down each side of the vulva, then sticking it inside, with a wiggle and a wag. He could taste the essence of her sex. He liked it as he licked it. Then he moved up to pay attention to her clitoris as he once again slid his middle finger inside, stroking her G-spot as he held the middle of his tongue on her clitoris, wiggling the end of his tongue inside the top of her pussy. Then he moved his middle finger faster on her G-spot, while he licked and flicked her clitoris with his tongue. Caroline was twitching in spasms as she leaned into the wall and pushed her pussy into his face... she was coming, she hadn't felt this feeling before. Adam was a great pussy eater... who knew, she thought... as waves of pleasure moved up and down her spine.
She pulled away from his face, slid down and straddled him, squeezing his cock into her wet pussy... gliding it in and out with speed and precision, in an animal instinct rhythm of creation... both of them grunting and groaning as Adam yelled he was coming,

pushing as deep as he could inside her, as they both climaxed together... total bliss.
Caroline collapsed onto Adam. Adam collapsed onto Caroline. Both were totally spent as their breathing slowed down to normal.
"That was incredible, Caroline." Adam said.
"It certainly was," said Caroline. "You're not a virgin anymore, and never will be again. You're a good fuck Adam, ... who would have thought? You satisfied me. Are you sure this was your first time?" she said, smiling together, feeling comfortable and blessed.
They kissed each other as Adam was still inside her, joined at the hip and the head. They stayed in that position, holding each other in silence as they experienced the love felt between them. It was a beautiful experience for both of them.
Time to get dressed and do music.
Caroline was happy regarding her new relationship with Adam.
She hadn't realized how much she loved him... and knew she'd never be the same again. She only wanted to please him now, and Adam loved to be pleased.
Adam was amazed at the feelings unleashed by their coupling.
A rhyme and a rhythm came to him as Caroline was going down on him, once again.

"I am a sexual intellectual", she said.
"So, where do you wish to play today?
In my head, or on my bed?"
"Ah... first your bed" I heard me say.

Adam found a new relationship with the universe based on the needs of the gonads. He also discovered he had a ferocious sexual appetite.
He finally understood the meaning of 'sex is a drug'.
If sex is a drug Adam thought, women write the prescriptions!
It wasn't long before Caroline realized she could never keep him to herself. Adam now paid much more attention to the "puppies", in the audience, who looked at him with total surrender.
Caroline found it strange at first that she was not jealous. She was happy being a part of anything making Adam happy. She realized there was nothing she wouldn't do for him.
Adam tasted all that he could, and his music was an inspiration.

Every woman who slept with him thought it to be her duty, and thus, she had been the mother of the next inspired offering.

Caroline became more daring in their relationship and she had brought a few women to Adam's bed while she participated as a third partner.

Adam loved women and sex. He was addicted.

David was aware Adam was sleeping with his sister but didn't seem to mind in the least. David could understand the two of them having a relationship due to the amount of time they spent together over the last six years. Sixteen and almost twenty seems a long way apart but time would eventually bring their age difference to forty to almost forty-four, which was no difference at all.

David was pleased his buddy Adam was at least getting some.

Adam didn't dare tell David about the night he had spent with Betty. Some things are better left unsaid between friends.

Walter sat down at the kitchen table looking over at Adam who was now coming up to his seventeenth birthday in three weeks.

"Well son, we have to decide which university you will attend next year" Walter said stoically... "as you know I would prefer that you stay in Toronto and attend one of the programs offered at UofT, but your mother insists, and rightly so I might add, decision of where to go should be up to you... after all it's your life we're talking about and not mine."

Walter gave a slight chuckle realizing he wished he had the same options his son now has. Life has a way of closing doors around you as time goes on. You just get totally caught up in your career and before you know it there is almost nothing else that you're truly 'qualified' to do.

Adam looked at his father and noticed again his dad was aging just like he was supposed to do. The wrinkles around his eyes and his reading glasses were part of the trip we all take. He had become a bit mellower with less faith and loyalty towards his company than he had in previous years. His older mentors were retiring, and Walter was taking their place in the eyes of younger employees. Adam realized he didn't want to live the life his father had chosen.

"How about if I just take a year off to travel Dad - let me see the world a bit and make some new friends?"

Walter had heard this before and so was ready to respond. "Well you will have all the time in the world to travel once you graduate. You will not lose on the friendship side because I can tell you some of my dearest and closest friends, I still have today, were met during my university years."

Adam looked at his father "I want to travel a bit first dad... If you really believe I should make my own choices, let me take a year off and travel. I am younger than most university entry students so it's not like I will be wasting time. I've been told by the maestro's at the Conservatory, my music knowledge and execution are at the Doctor of Music level or above, as far as composition is concerned. I am educated.

Travel is an education in and of itself. You and mom have both told me that on many occasions, and I believe that it's true."

"Where would you go and how would you support yourself?" Walter asked.

Walter and Adam knew there was no issue in supporting himself since his grandfather had left him a sizable trust which he would be allowed to draw from once he turned seventeen.

Money wasn't a problem, but Walter hoped Adam would let his inheritance be, until he needed it to start his own enterprise. Adam never worried about money because he was always in a privileged position.

"What about your music... will you just leave all that you have done at the Royal Conservatory? Is all of that for nothing?"

What about the work you're doing with Caroline...?"

"Well my music will be with me and 'I'll be visiting many of my friends around the world who are still studying and playing. I will expand my scope and gain experience in other places, learning from other masters and adding to my versatility. Caroline is in total agreement with my traveling, and as a matter of fact she may join me from time to time. It'll be good for Caroline too."

Walter looked at his son and realized he couldn't force him or hold him to any plan to which Adam didn't agree.

"At least promise me, after one year you will start your university studies and you will consider at least starting your studies here in Toronto."

"I promise dad... I'll take one year then get serious about getting some formal degrees to hang on my future wall in some physical job somewhere."
Walter and Adam both laughed, and the conversation was done.
Adam started planning a world trip, but he wouldn't plan a location past the first one – this would be a trip based on impulse where he would follow his heart and let the universe lead him.
Alison joined Walter and Adam at the table, and they reminisced about the past.
Alison realized her son was leaving and she had pangs she'd not felt for a long time. She just wanted to go back to a time when Adam was still a little boy and where she was the center of his universe.

Chapter 5

"There is a deeper place in thought'

Where none escape before being caught,
Inside a riddle of the mind,
The search
Begins...
After the find...
Ah... let them in...
To talk of things, we cannot mention.
With no intention to cause pain,
We fall then rise then fall again,
Leaning on the strength of those,
Who do not find it frightening?
As time constricts...
Life tightening,
The definition we hold true
Of whom we are, and what we do.

Sarah sighed.

Within her mind she'd found a place, so full of self, even the thought of a word like "we" was impossible to speak.

She tried to remove herself and lift herself higher by saying the Lord's Prayer but couldn't speak the word "Our".

She vaguely remembered the dream of a man coming through the wall, drenching her with darkness, slowly sucking her out of her body, moving her psyche down in a spiral of ever denser darkness. She knew this was an occurrence manifesting from her own desires. She was moving lower and a voice spoke to her as she passed two shallow, hollow men.

"These represent the lower levels of thought on the Earth of the Son of Man.

Some only have conscience of self, others are meant to be used only for the fulfillment of the other's choice to grow anew, or wither further.

Some only see creation in terms of self. These are the spiritual children, so to speak. we're all and each, spiritual children in one instance or another. we're all and each damaged in one instance or another."

She moved lower till thought itself became a weight too hard to express. A place where self could only recognize self.

Sarah felt empty and alone.

Over and over the mantra continued ....

"ayeyahmayeyahmayeyahmayeyahmayeyahmayeyahmayeyahmay eyahmayeyahmayeyahmayeyahmayeyahmayeyahmayeyahmayeya hmayeyahm ayeyahmayeyahm"

The sound and rhythm were like an Australian pipe instrument she almost remembered from somewhere long ago.

The frequency was a constant 6 beats per second. A basic rhythm of creation or so, she thought she was sure.

"ayeyahmayeyahmayeyahmayeyahmayeyahmayeyahmayeyahmay eyahmayeyahmayeyahmayeyahmayeyahmayeyahmayeyahmayeya hmayeyahm ayeyahmayeyahm"

Lost in a mantra, Sarah changed the constant flow by inserting other sounds into the stream - at each insertion, an intersection of flows, were created. Sarah could choose on which flow to go. She didn't understand yet, why she was experiencing this layer of existence, yet she was fascinated by the thickness of it all.

She realized all life is the will of the observer. What we choose to consciously observe gives purpose to our journey. Who we choose to be in our conscious 'sight', melds our purpose with their purpose, intersects our will, our time and parts of our chosen path, with theirs – individual free will is impossible, when the will of another or the communal will of all, sets the motive and the flow.

She also realized paths could be altered by conscious desire; every sequential moment, provides an opportunity to change. We are, in the final analysis, responsible for our own happiness. "We are what we think'. We are responsible, to own and solve the consequences, we create, as a result of the decisions we make.

All is OUR all… Ah! A planet at war, is the result of communal thought, good pitted against evil, self against selfish, cruelty against kindness… hate against love. "Thought is the builder." Thinking higher or lower, changes the values we hold to be true.
Our communal thoughts add to our connected consequence.
In the final analysis, thought emanates, then animates the thicker dimensions below.
Thought will manifest.
The rape of a woman is the manifestation, of the thoughts and desires, of men who fantasize, in thought, about the rape of a woman. The thought of killing a tribe, to take 'their' land, is the manifestation of pride, greed, and entitlement within the stronger tribe.
Every tribe is the stronger or weaker tribe, in one instance or another.
Evolution over time, – only the strongest survive – by control, digestion of gentler and kinder cultures - fear, wrapped within intimidation – the Darwinian vision of genetic morphing, enabling survival consequences, within any given species, at the peril of same layer competitors.
These are the base tenets of success, within the thicker dimensions. We are mostly stuck in the resolution of our own decisions, and the consequences manifested. The bird improves the beak, mankind improves the weapon.
Sarah knew, thought dimensions could change and alter, us.
This experience she was part of, in this pit of isolation, enabled a transfer of knowledge, understanding, wisdom, kindness, empathy and non-conditional love – forgiveness and acceptance.
She realized, we're all crawling back to the idea of Bethlehem, Mecca, Haifa, Varanasi and Jerusalem – with the hope of universal love at the center.
But communal thoughts and manifested consequences based on mankind created hierarchies and greed structures, are the realities we consciously experience.
In this space, Sarah found she could step outside of her own consciousness and look at where she was and what she was doing, on a different plane of reference, in a different instance of reality -

and therefore with different perspectives, blossoming in each observation.
Sarah could travel in thought to watch the events in instances she and others, were living, experiencing short bursts of sequenced life then rebounding back to her self-centered prison in a pit of non-connected thought.
Each instance, the result of an event, each event the result of a consequence – each consequence the result of an action taken.

"Suck it, Debbie, Debbie, Debbie!" Reverend Paul screamed holding Debbie's head with both hands as she was giving him head behind the church while the congregation was inside doing the choir rehearsal.
Sarah looked on, sensing the lust of each thrust till the reverend finally started talking in tongues – "ja mandta east swoane emambeel sodomaus" as his orgasm erupted in the space, where it occurred.
This was a sexual event, agreed to, and done.
Sarah smiled with Debbie and reverend Paul as the choir started "Oh come all ye Faithful, joyful, and triumphant... Oh come ye, Oh, come ye..." just as the reverend Paul exploded once again in a flurry of bucking hips and pursing lips.
Sarah looked on as Debbie and the reverend sighed deeply with their gonads satisfied once more - no embarrassment or shyness. This was just one of the paths taken to satisfy the sexual needs, where procreation ruled the roost.
Sarah realized there is no secret activity – all secrets are known in the light.
Sarah recognized the gate, and respected the position of the event, then she rebounded immediately back to her space in the pit, once again shackled by self.

Sarah felt another rush, released again into the fabric outside.
This time to a room with a warm glow where a lady sat in the corner in front of a fire making ever changing shadows on the wooden wall, behind her.
"Sit down my dear Sarah," the woman said as her entire face glowed, as if basking in the warmth of some sure and patient truth, which

she would gladly share with anyone having a thirst for it. Sarah felt totally safe and welcome in this space and she knew it was a "wave sequential" location – not solid but flowing.
Sarah knew now, experience came in two flavors – waves and particles – which could interchange as time and space relations manifested through conscious will. Every decision was an intersection in an infinite thread. The manifestation of feelings and experience constantly reflected the will of the flow.
All experience here manifested as events, within the laws of dreams.
'My dear Sarah... what are we to talk about today?' As a new dream within her first dream started.
Sarah sat on the floor at the feet of this lady, felt the warmth of her kindness and the warmth of the fire, mix and mingle within her.
"Can we talk of truth and lies" Sarah asked as a child.
"Yes Sarah, we can, and we cannot, for every question has at least two true paths and infinite paths of lies. The road in truth is narrow, but the path of deception is wide. Lies are imaginary things."
As Sarah contemplated these words she was transformed again as she moved away from the lady and the room, pulled by another event, sensing a light, instantly reached.
She was sitting in a bar with dim lights and old smells of stale tobacco, alcohol, urine and people who had stayed away from home too long for it to matter anymore.
She was sitting close to a stranger who turned and looked at her with cold appraisal, as if her existence was a mistake in some multiversal plan.
The event transformed, she was walking in a crowd, watching seven men carry a burden, which looked like the troubles of the world, upon their backs and shoulders, as the crowd jeered them and taunted their deserved circumstance.
The crowd hated these men since they represented everything they had tried to be. Each of the burdened men, at the same time, looked up and melted into Sarah's eyes - penetrating her protection, forcing her to cry, and feel so sad about the path they had chosen to walk for the sake of others.
Then she saw in a whirlwind of motion around the men, some manifesting in sequential particles and others in sequential waves, an orgy of violence and sexual atrocities - digestion of health into

sickness – fulness into emptiness - control through fear of compassion - a mass of sacrificed martyrs - sects teaching peace and atonement - infusion of grace as a gift and the flight of a light through a tunnel.

Once again, the event transformed - Sarah was shackled in this pit by chains - by self.

She transformed again into the particle sequential - shared some space with Barry as he was sitting home alone, waiting for Debbie to return.

Barry was crying as he did many times. But only when he was alone. He had no friends close enough to share his greatest fears, for his own protection he acted out with tears.

Sarah was an intuitive empath. She could feel the emotions of others. Her time spent in this heartless place, she had been pulled into, showed her she could insert an option into the steam of the events of others. She had the ability to offer a choice which could alter the outcome. She also knew it would be a great abuse of this gift to control the thoughts of another.

Everyone had the right to make their own decisions, to meet their own consequences.

She could feel the sadness of Barry;

"I am alone in the universe.
In a world full of people
I am alone in the universe.

Sarah knew the pain Barry was feeling. She reached out to him and inserted an optional way of thinking - Barry thought about his wife and his daughter - for sure Sarah had been alone when her mother died giving birth to her. Sarah was now alone again, in this psychological medical condition she was experiencing - but he surmised, she is not alone, we're with her all the way.

Barry realized he was being very selfish thinking only of his battles and how unfair life was to him. He freely changed his perspective and opened another instance leading to a different consequence. He lifted some weight from his personal dilemma, by feeling empathy for another.

Barry stood up, gave himself a shake and vowed to be a better person for everyone around him, especially Sarah.

Dr. Armstrong came into the playroom, ready to spend another hour with Sarah. The music therapy she used with Sarah didn't seem to be working.
"Good morning Sarah" Dr. Armstrong said as she placed the new playlist onto the machine. "Today we're going to listen to some of the aboriginal sounds from Australia. played on an instrument called a didgeridoo?"
Sarah, as usual stared towards the corner of the room.
Sarah had been in the institution for almost six years now and hope was fading for her recovery.
Dr. Armstrong was intrigued with Sarah. She never talked but sometimes seemed more connected to everyone around her, than anyone else around her.
Other children wanted to play close to where Sarah was – they seemed to trust and desire her presence. Every child and some adult patients, always made a point of saying "Good morning, Sarah." Knowing they would not receive a vocal response. She had never witnessed a child not talking, having such a consistent effect of inclusion, by most of the verbally connected people.
Her mother continued to come almost every weekend for a visit, but her father hadn't been for at least the last 5 months. He hadn't given up on her, just hated to see her the way she was. He said his thought clarity regarding Sarah improved when he stayed home alone and didn't visit the facility. Debbie didn't think of it this way. She thought Barry didn't care and was a selfish human being. Barry didn't care what Debbie thought of him.
He cared deeply about Sarah and knew she would come back from wherever she was, when she was ready. He didn't believe the autism label – she was taking a break from life, and he didn't blame her for doing that. He wished - sometimes, he could also do the same.
Sarah was an unusual case, since she continued to take care of her personal hygiene and slept within the normal cycle of a normal person. She ate her meals, drank her juice, had her fruit snacks, took a daily shower, changed her clothes – everything a normal child would do... yet she had retreated from all social contact with others.
The deep base music started to reverberate through the room and Dr. Armstrong had visions of native aboriginal people running from here to there chanting in primal screams wearing as little body

covering as possible. It was a pleasant image so different from the radio wave mantras which were now the basic music carriers of the modern world.
Sarah looked up from the pit and watched as a pinpoint of light appeared high above her and then immediately formed as a glowing transparent ball in front of her. Another sequential event, she thought but to where?
"Touch the light and I will take you back, Sarah." A familiar man's voice said in a warm and friendly tone.
Sarah reached out and inserted her hand into the globe and as she did the light moved beyond speed back to sequential particle space. On the way, within the bubble of light, she experienced a surge in knowledge which overwhelmed her in its simplicity and beauty, greatly extending her compassion, empathy, intuition, kindness and expression of love.
She opened her ability to read and fully understand the motives and intentions, the needed wounds and needed healings, the truths and deceptions surrounding everyone she met.
Sarah also realized, the responsibility of this gift. She couldn't force her will under almost any circumstance, but she could enable the option of another path.
She could enable the altering of an outcome.
The universe, galaxies solar systems, and planets with embedded cultivated sequential beings - where time-based events are held in a prison of blue skies - through birthright, greed, cruelty and position, physically and mentally suppressing and manipulating, the actions and lives of others. Sequential beings stuck in a set of instances where wealth, power and entitlement distract and corrupt the manifestation of us.
In many cases, these sequential beings didn't give credence to the fact they were mortal and would die, taking nothing but their earthly experience with them when they did so. The entire lives of people could be considered as one sequential event, where the will of the 'sequential lifer' provided the consequences to be resolved, through relationships and circumstance. Sequential lifers included all life forms in the universe, observing conscious instances of sequential events, including those stuck in the pit of four dimensions and those who chose to help.

Sarah knew, to the depth of her being, the universe was an intelligent construct. She chose to help those stuck within the colored sky prisons, thinking and believing, this was all there was. They were lost in a recurring sequence of lifer events, eventually bursting out of the sequential vortex, to the dimensions of higher thought.

Dr. Armstrong was startled as Sarah's body jerked in a spasm, which almost caused her to fall off the chair she was sitting on.
"Oh my God" screamed Sarah, "I am back, I am sequential again!"
Sarah screamed as she threw her arms around Dr. Armstrong, sobbing into her shoulder. "Dr. Armstrong, I am sequential again!"
Dr. Armstrong was startled - how could Sarah know her name? She'd been non-responsive all these years.
Dr. Armstrong held Sarah tightly as she whispered. "Where were you my child?"
It is real, Dr. Armstrong, it's real!" Sarah pleaded as she talked of this spiral tunnel where darkness is too thick to let light in.
"I remember looking up and seeing this pinpoint of light so high above me, but which moved with incredible speed to the place where I had been taken"
"Who took you?" Dr. Armstrong asked.
"It is hard to explain but I will tell you all I do remember... I remember first being in my bed listening to the dull sound of the television coming from downstairs."
Sarah paused, collecting her thoughts since she was now having problems with sequence. She truly didn't know what happened first and what happened next. She had to think about it and rearrange the blocks of memory through the application of syllogism - "If this happened here and this happened there, then this must have happened there!"
Sarah said, "I am having a problem with the sequence – the place has no sequence, I had no sequence."
"You have definitely had sequence here" Dr. Armstrong stated. "I can show you daily records of the treatment you have received in the past six years."

Sarah looked perplexed and Dr. Armstrong smiled. "We have lots of time to analyze where you have been and what you have learned and also why you were taken on this very unusual journey."
Sarah sobbed with excitement and happiness as she related a place in existing things where all thought is a mantra of self.
Dr. Armstrong listened professionally as Sarah spoke of time, space, thought and grace and as she listened, she was astounded by the words, rushing from Sarah's voice.
She slowly guided Sarah out of the common area towards her private office, closing the door behind them, sitting with her on the large couch, Dr. Armstrong used during some of her therapy sessions.
The other patients in the common area were shocked and happy Sarah had finally become awake from her 'zombie' like condition.
Sarah spoke slower trying to explain where she had been.
Dr. Armstrong thought she'd become a bit delusional, creating a great story as part of her imagination, probably as a protection mechanism, brought on by her brain, to rationally explain what she had experienced. Many patients gave irrational reasons while explaining their irrational behavior and views.
But she didn't want to jump ahead to any conclusions.
Sarah was an unusual study, since she could possibly provide a window of experienced knowledge, related to autism. God knows it was needed as autism was becoming more common, every year.
Sarah was now 14 years old, and for a child who had basically been out of touch with the rest of the world for six years, she had an amazing vocabulary and an eloquence, of expression, unusual and pure, by any standard.
How could this be?
Dr. Armstrong, her staff of professionals, and volunteers had read copiously to Sarah and the other children under their care at the facility, but there was no way, this could explain the advanced level of Sarah's communication skills, whether writing or speaking – she was very impressive. It was as if she had become a child prodigy with advanced social empathy – akin to a child pianist who played the piano like a maestro, without formal musical training.

Doctor Armstrong never had an autistic case which manifested advanced social communication skills as Sarah so easily demonstrated.
Later, some would think Sarah to be a prophet, who like the Lord Himself had spent some time in Hades possibly with the devil himself, and she had survived the ordeal through the grace of God for the benefit of all.
They believed her isolation was a gift, to be shared by those who were not enlightened enough to suffer for the masses, as Jesus was alone in the dessert for 40 days.
Now Sarah was an adolescent who'd come back to the sequential world of the living from the non-sequential world of non-connection.
She'd overcome the bottomless pit and had been delivered from a place that could only be compared to hell itself.
Dr. Armstrong didn't immediately inform Debbie and Barry about Sarah's change of condition, since she thought it very important to give Sarah a chance to ease back into her previous life, as a fourteen-year old, rather than an eight-year old. Of course, Dr. Armstrong also wanted to do a proper analysis of Sarah, running some tests in the process.
Sarah was the most amazing young teenaged girl Dr. Armstrong had ever known, and she felt she'd known Sarah for most of her life. Some of her colleagues at the university, didn't believe what Professor Armstrong was relating, till they came to the facility and met Sarah for themselves.
They left stating, if everybody on the planet had this type of autism, the world would be a better and kinder place.
Her social and communication skills were off the charts, including inherent and un-learned (at least in the normal academic way) knowledge. She had a matrix like understanding of complex social subjects and interactions. Her emotional intelligence was exemplary.
After over three weeks of observation and professional interaction, Dr. Armstrong called Debbie and Barry, sharing the good news.
Debbie and Barrie were elated with the call from Dr. Armstrong though Barrie felt a pang of apprehension as he realized this adopted child would once again be part of their lives and their

responsibility, once again. Barry hated himself when he slipped into this, 'feeling so sorry for himself', way of thinking, but he couldn't help these feelings surfacing again and again. Some people think life is easier, seeking pity rather than praise. He always did his best to snap out of it as he brought Sarah into his thoughts.
They of course would drive right over to see Sarah. Sarah ran to her mother and jumped into her arms.
As Debbie hugged Sarah, she was as happy as she had ever been, "You're back with us, my dear Sarah – Thank you Jesus."
Sarah couldn't stop talking. She had a need inside of her which was full like an overfilled balloon with too much pressure on the outer skin.
She either had to talk to relief the pressure or she would surely burst.
Debbie sobbed as she held her daughter close to her. She was filled with joy and relief her little girl had come back. Barry stood back, then rushed to his wife and daughter, holding both of them in his arms.
"I missed you mommy" Sarah sobbed, "I missed you so much!"
"I missed you too, daddy!"
"We missed you too honey" Debbie cried, as she held tightly to her precious one.
"We missed you too, sweetness" Barry sighed as he realized how much his little girl and his wife meant to him.
He hadn't felt this close to anyone in such a long time and he also realized his loneliness over the past few years. Debbie was his wife, but her real interests were always elsewhere.
Barry had stopped attending church, since he couldn't stand the open hypocrisy of Reverend Paul.
Speaking in tongues while fucking his wife.
In truth Barry was jealous of Reverend Paul, wishing he could do what the reverend was doing, but in the sacred sanctimony of marriage. Still, he felt Paul was in truth, an evil and selfish man.
Barry sometimes became angry with God, wondering why he had been born this way.
Debbie and Barry had become like two polite siblings living under one roof - always caring but never sharing in the biblical sense of man and wife.

Sometimes life stops in a cycle where two sequential beings, in sympathetic polarity, settle for an answer and therefore also accept the consequence of boredom, which is sure to permeate all, and provide a sedation of dullness, never allowing risk.
This is the place where Debbie and Barry were anchored.
All is well in sex-life hell.
Debbie still loved the reverend Paul, on a regular basis, but it was now known to the general church community this affair was going on.
Some of the elders of the church pulled the reverend aside and tried to make him see the error of his ways. They talked of the devil using the weakness of the flesh and the body as an idol.
All of them in quiet times though had imagined ravishing Debbie. Some elders were downright peeved, Reverend Paul always managed to get the most desirable women in the flock, into his bed. Sarah knew lust, in thought is not an innocent act, but it's a very common act. Thought is the builder of reality and as thought exists, events manifest. It could even be argued, Paul was acting out on behalf of all the elders of every church, in a manifestation of their will. Every man, in high positions - believed they deserved to be fucked by the attractive women in their sphere of influence. They were the alpha males, after all.
We're all guilty, just to different degrees.
Like young women at a rock concert, all thinking about fucking their idol performer. It is acted out by some, for the benefit of all.
No one is guilty as a majority take part in bringing inertia to the originating thought.
Debbie and Barry were also amazed by the vocabulary and expression exhibited by Sarah so soon after her 6 years of social paralysis.
"I have so much to do" Sarah said, looking directly into her mother's eyes for the first time ever.
"I have gained so much but it must be shared!" Sarah cried, as she kissed her mother then her father for the first time in years.
Barry looked at his daughter in a new light realizing she was a young lady now. He stared at Sarah's face, her hair and the shape which her body had taken - more adult than child, as hormones took their course.

She was beautiful. Young Sarah had been totally replaced by someone new.
He had lost his daughter for 6 years and she had come back to him as a 'morphed' being. He loved her.
As Sarah held onto her father, she whispered something into his ear and Barry immediately began to sob – whatever was said, had a great effect on Barry's demeanor.
Dr. Armstrong asked Sarah to repeat her words for Debbie to hear but Sarah said, "I spoke to my dad, not to anyone else."
The emotional experience of Sarah's emergence was overpowering. Sarah pulled her hospital gown over her head and stood naked before everyone in the room.
"I want to move all of us to a higher place, where shame and shyness have no claim in diminishing who we are.
Debbie and Dr. Armstrong tried to cover Sarah, but they were not fast enough to catch her. Sarah laughed as Debbie finally threw a blanket around her to cover her nakedness.
"Sarah, cover yourself" Debbie pleaded, "It is a sin to be naked in front of your father!"
"It is a bigger sin not to be" Sarah smiled as she opened the blanket exposing her nakedness once again to everyone in the room. "We're all so ashamed of what we are" Sarah sighed, "It is what we do in private that defines our true character, not what we do in public. All of us should stand naked in front of everyone else as often as possible; to show we have nothing to hide. It is what we hide that does the damage, not what we share."
"How is Reverend Paul mother?" Sarah asked with her most innocent voice.
Debbie looked a bit embarrassed and Sarah just looked at her and smiled. "It's ok, mother! you're normal, and you would be amazed at how normal everyone is - yet they all think they are doing something special."
Dr. Armstrong waived off Debbie's efforts to close the blanket around Sarah once again. "It's ok Debbie, let Sarah act this out a bit. I don't mind her nakedness and I am sure her father is ok with it too."
Barry looked up and directly at Sarah. He was still shaken by Sarah's words to him. "I don't mind at all, as long as Sarah is comfortable."
Sarah removed the blanket and sat in on the edge of the bed.

"Thank you" Sarah said, "I am totally comfortable like this and I do not want anyone to feel embarrassed by my naturalness."
"I do feel embarrassed!" Debbie yelled, "and I do insist you cover yourself in front of your father. What is going on here? You come out of a trance which you have been in for almost six years and you act as though it never happened. What happened to you Sarah? We were worried sick about you and look at you now, sitting there naked as if nothing happened!"
Sarah slipped the hospital gown over her head and covered herself.
"Thank you." Debbie said curtly.
"You're welcome mother. I am sorry you have so much shame within you."
Dr. Armstrong wanted to regain control of her patient. "Can the three of us step outside for a minute?" She opened her arms enclosing both Barry and Debbie and moved them towards the door. "Please keep Sarah company for a moment Mrs. Hull as I talk with Mr. and Mrs. Thomson in the privacy room".
Mrs. Hull had been Dr. Armstrong's personal secretary for the past eleven years and had never seen Dr. Armstrong push anyone into the privacy room before. Mr. and Mrs. Thomson were being pushed.
"Hello Sarah," Mrs. Hull said as she walked into the room, "How are you today? it's nice to see you're back."
"Hello," said Sarah, "Do you mind if I take this stupid gown off?"
"Of course not," replied Mrs. Hull as Sarah pulled the gown over her head and off once again.
Dr. Armstrong sat across from Debbie and Barrie then started her assessment of the surprising events which had occurred regarding Sarah.
"First of all, I want you to know I am as surprised as you both are at the sudden return of Sarah. I assure you I have never experienced a case like this in all of the years I have been treating patients."
"Can you tell us what happened today?" Debbie asked, "What caused Sarah to come back to us?"
"Well," Dr. Armstrong said, "She actually - to use your words Debbie, came back about three weeks ago. I didn't tell you – I felt more assessment time was required at a professional level, and didn't think you would enjoy the pain, if she went back, after showing such progress."

Debbie was upset. "You should have told us as soon as her condition changed! I was told I could not visit due to a flu virus in the ward. Your staff lied to me!"
"In my professional opinion, I disagree with you Debbie. I also had to think about allowing Sarah to take things slowly. Everything was new to her. I didn't want to add any unnecessary stress. I hope you understand that." Dr. Armstrong explained.
Debbie was not impressed but decided to let it pass. She was not going to win this argument.
Barry looked at Dr. Armstrong as he said, "Please share with us the results of your assessment over the last few weeks.".
"Well," Dr. Armstrong started, "as you know I have been involved in experimental psychology where we use music and other sound tracks and then measure any response from patients like Sarah, who seem to have dropped out on a mental level but who remain connected at the physical level - eating, sleeping, listening, using the toilet etc. On the day she came back, I used a recording of an Australian instrument called the Didgeridoo"
"You mean that big horn looking instrument that the player blows in and the opening touches the ground?" Debbie interrupted.
"Yes, exactly Debbie" Dr. Armstrong continued. "It makes a low rhythmic sound like a group of bull frogs on a mating call."
"As I played a recording of that instrument, after about 5 minutes or so, Sarah, bolted upright on the chair and yelled 'Oh, my God, I am back!' I was totally startled."
"Do you think the music had something to do with it?" Debbie asked.
"I'm not sure but Sarah asked me to turn the music off since it reminded her of the place she had come from - I am investigating this aspect of Sarah's condition further." Dr. Armstrong explained.
"Well" Barry started, "I would like to get Sarah out of here and get her back home..."
"Not so fast Mr. Thomson," Dr. Armstrong interrupted "I want to keep Sarah here for a bit longer to find out more about her current state of mind - there is also a possibility she will relapse, and I would like her to remain here in case that happens."
"No!" Barry said forcibly, "I want my daughter home!"
"But Barry, we have more to do with Sarah here." explained Dr. Armstrong.

"No!" Barry exclaimed once again, "I want my daughter home. If you have any medical grounds to keep her here, then I will want another opinion from another doctor, and you will have to get an order from the court. I want my daughter home!"
Debbie looked at her husband with disbelief. She had never seen Barry act so aggressively before, especially to a figure of authority like Dr. Armstrong. "Barry!" Debbie said in a tone of mock shock, "We will keep Sarah here until Dr. Armstrong feels it's ok for her to come home - we have to think of Sarah's well-being here!"
Barry looked directly into Debbie's eyes with an intensity she hadn't seen before... "You, Debbie are my wife and I am the head of this household as stated by God Himself! You will do as I wish for this is a matter within our family and I am the last word of what is to be done in these circumstances. Sarah WILL be coming home, and you WILL support MY decision and that is the END of our discussion here! Do you understand that Debbie?"
Debbie sat with her mouth open totally shocked by her husband's response. He was the head of the household and he would have the support of the church since the Bible stated that unequivocally.
"Yes dear" Sarah said softly.
"Mr. Thomson, I want you to rethink this" Dr. Armstrong implored "I need to keep Sarah here for further observation."
"Then you better get another opinion and a court order, because Sarah is coming home with us today!"
Dr. Armstrong looked at Barry and tried to understand what had happened here in the last few minutes. Here was Barry Thompson whom she had always recognized as a passive individual, always the weaker of the two personalities in this marriage, putting his foot down for the first time in his life probably, while his wife immediately succumbed to her husband's irrational demand.
"What did Sarah say to you Barrie?" Dr. Armstrong inquired "when she whispered in your ear - What did she say?"
"That, Dr. Armstrong is between my daughter and me. I would like you to please get the papers ready for the release of my daughter into our care. I want to sign her out of this institution."
"Then please let me talk to her for just one hour before you take her home and please promise that we will be able to set up bi-weekly appointments for Sarah to start tomorrow. Please also confirm that

if there is any type of relapse into her previous condition, you will immediately bring her back for re-admission. You're her parents and I will not fight against your wishes, but I must insist that in my professional opinion you're making a great mistake by taking Sarah home today."

"Sarah will do better at home Dr. Armstrong" Barry said quietly. "I thank you for your concern and I do promise to bring her back at the slightest sign of a relapse, but I can also assure you this will never happen again."

Barry took Debbie's hand and squeezed it gently, "Bringing Sarah home with us is best for Sarah and best for Debbie and me too."

"Very well" said Dr. Armstrong, "Do you mind if I spend an hour with Sarah before she leaves and do you agree that I can ask Sarah if it is her desire to go home and if she would rather stay here - do you agree to respect her wishes?"

Barry stood up still holding Debbie's hand and he gently pulled Debbie up to stand beside him. "Yes, to all questions," Barry said, "But I think you will find Sarah is ready to come home now."

"We will see you in about one hour, Dr. Armstrong" Barry said as he escorted Debbie towards the door...

"Thank you, doctor." Debbie said looking over her shoulder as she was leaving.

"Goodbye Debbie, see you in an hour or so." said Dr. Armstrong.

Dr. Armstrong had a lot to do and she wanted to get started right away.

She walked back into the room to see Sarah sitting naked once again on the bed as she was talking to Mrs. Hull about "centers of inflection and infection."

Mrs. Hull looked at Dr. Armstrong with her eyebrows raised and her mouth in a bewildered frown. She hadn't understood most of what Sarah was talking about and wished she had the knowledge of Dr. Armstrong in situations like this. She had always been interested in psychology but never had the resolve to do the learning time.

"Well, Sarah" Dr. Armstrong started, "You have definitely come back with a bang, for your parents today!"

"I have your parent's permission to talk with you for the next hour or so and after our session I would like to know your thoughts on

whether you would like to stay here for further observation, or whether you would like to go home today."
"What did my father want me to do?" Sarah asked.
"He wants to take you home" said Dr. Armstrong. "But I would like you to..."
Sarah interrupted, "If my father wants me home then I want to go home!"
"Then we have one hour to talk" Dr. Armstrong stated, becoming totally professional again. "If you change your mind after we talk, just say so, since I would much rather have you here."
"I will be going home," Sarah stated sternly.
"Ok, Sarah, then let's get started." Dr. Armstrong said as she picked up her notepad and pen.
"Thank you, Mrs. Hull," Dr. Armstrong said, "we will do this privately."
"Of course, Dr. Armstrong." Mrs. Hull stated as she left the room wishing she had been invited to stay.

Chapter 6

The killer stalked his helpless prey

Until she was alone that day
And then he moved into her space
And put the knife against her face
And told her he would cut her.
She said she would do his will
If he just promised not to kill
She had so many things to be
Please use my body - but leave me.
He cut her.
And as she bled, she felt his force
Release in sexual intercourse
He pretended he was making love
With every pull and every shove
Her flesh was sacrificed!

Adam sat upright in his bed. He had had one of those flying dreams where the entire planet was just one thought away; where time and space were all connected at the same point, on some membrane of perception.

"What a dream" he thought, as he tried to remember its parts.

There were seven rooms within a mansion high upon a hill. The first three rooms were built in a sequence and each with a higher ceiling than the first. The second room had a staircase leading to a door which went into the third room, and the third room had a staircase going up and down which led into the fourth room (going up) and the first room (going down).

He remembered this place to be very simple in the dream. It was not as simple in the awakened state.

Adam sat at his computer and drew the mansion in terms of frequencies as he remembered the strata relationships.

Seven levels were contained within the structure including the surrounding white level. The red level was the base, then orange, then yellow, then green, then blue, then violet, and then white. Each color represented a separate level and all levels had steps between them. The red level and all other levels had a direct access to the white level and to every other level in the structure.
Adam thought of the stairs as access channels where one could move from one level to any other level by choosing the appropriate channel.
He closed his eyes and imagined every person on the planet moving as a field of frequencies, interacting at and between different levels, within themselves and with others.
He imagined all sequential beings, made up from quantum state particles, vibrating as colors in waves.
Adam thought of the recitals he enjoyed best, where Caroline and sometimes one or two other exemplary technical piano geniuses, played his multi-layered musical creations, especially when three pianos, morphed and blended in multi-layer retraction, expansion, retraction, expansion, filling space with the harmonics of his creations.
He had the ability to sense the visions of color flowing as waves from the center of the piano.
Created from his mind at a previous time, to Caroline's eyes on the music sheet, to the interpretation by her brain, then down her spine, into her finger, her torso and feet, her head, guided by the rhythm of her neck, nodding and swaying to the pulse of the beat. The entire room flowed in colorful fractal ascensions and contractions, somewhat like the motion of the northern lights, with more color and complexity. The ones who felt it to the core of their being as it played - with tears in their eyes, feeling the pure beauty then surrendering to a non-sequential, connection on a higher plane of reference. These were the intuitive empaths in the mix.
Adam and his doting fans felt it, as the most beautiful music ever played. He was on his way to reaching rock star status, as a composer of electric eclectic music.
Adam saw music as an ebbing, expanding - color field, felt - manifested and conducted from the "blues", harmonized in violets, sanctified in greens, till optimally purified in "white".

White as the presence of all colors relates to the higher universal, to the tribe communal, into individual sequential "am" – the 'we are' of us.
Adam met the world as a melding of color fields, where individuals projected an aura, indicating the essence of their feelings and generally, the location of their character.
Adam imagined each human body and each of the seven portals within. The sequential being side, a tactile and nerve sensing construct, run in 4 dimensions - the etheric side, a place of pure feelings, played out in higher dimensions.
Each sequential body contains gates to both sides of existence – the bridge from the spine to the pituitary – the hypothalamus.
The colors emanated from different points.
Reds and orange related to lowest glands involved with physical creation at the base – the gonads – testes in men, ovaries in women – the glands of sexual pleasure, control and procreation.
Adam studied with great interest, since he lived in this instance as a self-experienced truth - writings of various medical professors and esoteric philosophers, to understand both the sequential being, and etheric views.
In the realm of sequential being knowledge, there are seven 'ductless' glands - the endocrine system of hormone directed execution.
Two or these glands, are located in the mass area of the brain – the pineal and the pituitary, one in the neck – the thyroid, one above the heart – the thymus, three in the lower body cavity – the adrenal (two attached at the top of each kidney), the pancreas (and Islets of the Langerhans), the gonads – ovaries and testes.
The physical side of sequential beings, interface with the four-dimensional world through environmental tactile senses – muscle control, blood sugar control, self-preservation control, sexual arousal control, temperature control – any part of the interface between the body and the physical environment or sequential condition, consciously occurring. This is the realm of the nervous system, sensing - then providing sequential information, up the spine, to the brain, through synapse neuron sparking – into the hypothalamus, in a bio electrical mix, enabling the other side of the sequential being, through the endocrine system, releasing required

hormones, directly into the bloodstream or cascading downwards to other glands. – managing responses in four dimension - increasing or reducing blood pressure; heart rate; insulin production; warming or cooling the body, and so much more.

The nervous system is lightning fast - the hormones of the endocrine system are not in such a hurry, - changing conditions based on the progression or regression of the causal event, with negative and positive feedback loops and controls in play.

Both sides, the sequential physical and the etheric non-sequential side, are understood by medical schools, as silos of knowledge.

Adam knew, in fact no silos are involved – all knowledge is one knowledge.

This school of thought had no time for the ethereal philosophers – who believed the seven centers did of course, have a physical purpose, based on evolutionary hierarchies, relating to changing environments including chemical imbalances in the body – but also were portals with aethereal connections and etheric purposes.

Adam believed both to be true, since he experienced both.

He believed the hypothalamus, was the bridge between the nervous and endocrine systems in the physical realm, and the pineal gland, the bridge between the physical realm and the etheric realm. The pineal is the primordial piece. All sequential physical is emanated then animated, from thought, through the pineal.

Adam knew this to be true, and it provided an advantage.

The colors are a reference only, since in the dynamics of the sequential mix they are blended and melded depending on the mood of the communal music, and layers of the universal harmonics.

Everything is music in particles and waves.

White - Pineal
Violet - Pituitary
Blue - Thyroid
Green - Thymus
Yellow – Pancreatic
Orange – Adrenal
Red - Gonads

Adam was able to predict the behavior of people around him, by the colors and the intensity of the fields emanated.

Most people live in the lower three glands, Adam thought, but also realized every color had direct access to every other color of the spectrum.

Each wave able to be the source and destination - the carrier of each other.

Adam was always aware of color fields surrounding people.

He absorbed all available knowledge on 'aura's'.

He knew by observation and experience, the frequency of the aura showed both mood, intention and level of caring,

Anger manifested red, sympathy and empathy had a blue tinge... sex, a mixture of orange, yellow and red. Someone showing great enjoyment of a meal always had an orange tint in their surrounding space.

Adam knew we are a collective and he wrote:

'We are a collective!

I walked along King Street in changing September, with thoughts of religion, I tried to remember, the Last Supper speeches, the silver piece breaches, paying for the fall of us all.

And the fall brought a rising – that is still a surprising, event - except to the ones who fast in their Lent. Our hunger increases, our Spirit releases the poison enchantments, scientific enhancements - DNA portals of promise so true, which open old knowledge and bring us much closer to what, we once knew.

We're a collective - a selective collective.

There is spiritual surety within the pituitary – on to the Pineal - the gateway to Heaven? Where Love is our passion - so far from the hate, way we find within hell.

As I walk with the faces – look – no embraces – for strangers who share the same street. Our eyes and our smiles sometimes meet. But on rare occasions, our Spirits exchange looks of old knowledge. We Love for an instant and yet keep on walking, we Love for an instant two Spirits talking with saucer eye sighs, our Spirit soars up and away, far beyond these chains of blue skies.

We're a collective - a selective collective...

We meet when we find the courage to try, take a leap of new faith, fly through the sky... Ignoring the clouds that sometimes smother, the light of another.

Missed in the gloom of a re-opened tomb, to the sunlit embrace, of the emerging face, Pushed, into the world, from women's pain screaming, emerged from the womb,

Am I dreaming?

Or is this reality steeped in polarity belonging to one frame yet played in another, where sperm and the egg define sister and brother.

We're a collective - a selective collective.

The women have faith, thank God for their faith.

The birth channel connection with time-space dissection, forcing sequential

Karmic essential, through truth consequential, born into a lie.

Removing the stone of 'We are alone' from every thymus,

Embracing our rape and our death in each life, being the mother, the harlot and wife.

To satisfy the expletive creative, collectively drunk, in the wine of the Gonads, sometimes with violence, we digest our children, then run for protection within the collection of societies rules, enforced by its fools.

The women have faith - Thank God for their faith.

We are a collective - a selective collective.

I feel who I Love with my heart and my Spirit, in trust I move forward,

In trust I give freely, but my lower attachment creates a detachment from communal Spirit.

Will is the keel, and the sails, our capacity,

The wind, what we feel - time/space tests our rapacity

To helps us reveal, who we really are.

We are a collective - a selective collective!

Adam loved dreams which expressed themselves in waves rather than molecules.'

Adam knew these words defined his ethereal self, full of non-sequenced perception.

He knew light is the first manifestation of intuitive intelligence. We are part of some incredible progress, which can't be prevented or stopped.

The progress involves flesh and Spirit, - flesh, being the lowest denominator of all living creatures, always sacrificed for wisdom and knowledge.

Flesh is born, to be used.
Flesh is killed and abused.
Flesh is self- loved protected, to grow old - wrinkled, used - then ejected.
A new instance where we can adjust – our rebirth and re-use, of stardust.

Adam also thought about his own life now in terms of where he was spending his *energy* and realized over the past few years he was connected to a higher calling. yet was one of those living in the 'lower three glands.'

Sex, food and rock and roll are a magnificent combination. but the growth curve turns into a circle.

Adam now had a craving to bring his music higher with the urge to travel and see the event he was born on, in a personal way. He wanted to meet the ones he was meant to meet, to move above the banality of a self-centered life.

The gift of music was becoming a burden since it put Adam always at the center as if he was the one responsible for his gift.

All good art, whether in music, poetry, painting, architecture etc. involves a connection to the higher centers which are recognized by any human capable of creativity.

Adam did his morning requirements to satisfy the lower gland 'eds' which meant he masturbated, urinated, defecated, showered, dressed and went downstairs to have some breakfast.

"Good morning Dad!" Adam said cheerily...

"Good morning Adam!" Walter responded.

"Where's mom?" asked Adam.

"She had to go into work early this morning - they are doing an inventory or some such thing." Walter said without showing too much interest.

"Dad, I am leaving next week and hopefully will be back here with in the year."

Walter looked at Adam with love and understanding. "I don't blame you son for if I was in your place in life as the world is today, I hope I would do the same."

Walter continued, "You will find life goes faster than you think. One morning you wake up and find you're now part of the older generation, which you looked at with some sadness and a bit of disdain in your younger years."

"Dad!" Adam shrieked with surprise, "You're feeling sorry for yourself! I have never seen you do that before."

"Well Adam" Walter said bowing his head a little towards the floor, "I am not feeling sorry – I'm just letting you in on a reality which hits us all sooner or later, if we live past 40. I am telling you to do as your heart tells you to do. Travel where your imagination takes you and explore everything you can with honesty and passion."

Adam walked over to his father and put his arms around him. Walter of course returned the embrace, and both patted each other on the back. It was the gesture of the adult finally admitting the child was ready to be on his or her own.

"You have belonged to the world since you were seven years old Adam", Walter said thoughtfully, "Your mother and I just tried to resist the inevitable for as long as possible. You go out into the world and make us proud, for you're a fine young man with many gifts you got from who knows where. I know you will never follow my path and I am fine with that. I sometimes think and wish I could have followed the path you're on, instead of the other way around. Eventually the parent becomes pensive and then reflective on the lives their children are starting, knowing their own days for exploring and re-inventing are moving to a close."

"You have a long way to go yet dad," Adam smiled. "I don't know where I am going but you will definitely know where I am and where I have been at all parts of my travels. The internet will be our connection and meeting place, and you can visit me with mom whenever you have the urge."

"I will take you up on that son." Walter smiled, "You're so damn lucky to be the age you're at, at a time like this. Technology is shrinking the world as much as it is expanding the mind. It is damn exciting to see the fruits of the engineer being used so effortlessly by the average earth dweller."

"Engineers are the most unsung heroes of the world dad" Adam said, "I am amazed at the 'bubble gum for the brain' continuously streaming from the television sets and smart phone screens. re-chewing old segments in thirty-minute chunks., over and over, with millions of people connecting imaginary lives on sitcoms, reality shows, and game shows with laugh machines built in.

I sometimes feel superior, not wanting to waste even 30 minutes pursuing imaginary ego's while being told what type of cornflake I should be eating.

I am not a fan of the corporate advertising business model especially when enabled by a new brand of capitalism, based on subversive surveillance of off line activities, on-line, through Google, Facebook, Amazon et al. The entire planet has become a product for sale flea market. Crony capitalism is the amassing of money without morality. Very dangerous and such a waste of time and energy."

"What brought all of that on?' Walter laughed. "I didn't know you were so anti tv, market forces and internet"

"You know what I mean dad." Adam continued. "You're telling me how fast life moves and yet when most people have time, they treat it as a replenishable commodity. I am horrified to see some people watch the same episode of "Star Trek" for the fifteenth time!"

Walter started laughing, "I think I recall you watching the same music videos and also reading the same book a couple of times or more!"

Adam laughed too. "That is different dad, maybe." He laughed. "I think entertainment is aimed at the lowest denominator. Have you ever laughed every time the laugh machine laughed? It becomes a demeaning and moronic exercise. Laugh machine programmers must be the most gullible and miserable people on the planet!"

Adam continued, "Some knowledge has to be regurgitated due to the 'Oh my God!' appeal of its content, while other knowledge should just be exposed then expunged due its' banality and low reach. The masses prefer the low reach and give up too easily on the truly interesting."

Walter looked at his son with patience. "I think you will find that all knowledge is valuable, and the value is measured by the beholder. Some people enjoy your so called 'low reach' existence. Live and let live - to each his own, etc. etc. Every cliché involves a truth, in my humble opinion."

"I love you dad." Adam said warmly.

"I love you too, son." Walter smiled.

Adam realized this conversation was the turning point in the relationship with his father. From now on they would relate to each other as one adult to another. He was free to travel and meet his own path as all children finally must. With some, it happens voluntarily as it was with Adam. He was seeking his independence. While others had to be weaned on the tits of time and temerity before life experience finally forced them to get out of the nest.

Adam was a seeker - he was ready to seek.

Alison cried as she watched her son disappear through the security check point at Pearson International Airport. Walter looked on with pride.

"Come on, dear" he said as he put his arm around his wife. "It is time for us to get on with our lives too."

Adam was heading east, first to London then on to Istanbul.

Though Adam was not religious in the normal sense, he wanted to explore his relationship with the universe by connecting himself to older knowledge.

This segment of his trip would connect him to the living idea of the virgin Mary, so Ephesus was in the plan.

Adam thought if an idea survived, without causing pain or death or suffering, over centuries of time, it was probably an idea based in some universal truth.

As the Jews believed in the idea of Israel, and Muslims in the idea of Mecca, and the Christians in the idea of Bethlehem, all of which had survived from generation to generation, Adam believed in their common validity to the human psyche – worth exploring, worth experiencing and worth exposing. Though he knew it was not a perfect truth as exposed by the death and cruelty built into each idea, at different times.

He truly didn't know how his journey would turn out and was taking a leap of faith which in his own mind would prove or disprove the supposition that anyone had the ability to change their environment at any time, and a new environment would open, based on the attitude of the searcher.

It was difficult for Adam leaving the life he had in Toronto and many of his music colleagues were totally disgusted and alarmed at what he was doing with his life.

His professors were the most understanding since they each had experienced an urge to travel at around the same age as Adam was now. All had no regrets to speak of. One professor did mention that her traveling companion on her trip through Europe had been killed in a holdup making the point, changing your space does not automatically mean good things will always happen. He lost his life for the contents of his knapsack. The murdering thief took $160 and some change. As he stuck the knife into the helpless student he sneered. The one hundred and sixty-odd dollars would give this man food and some physical pleasure over the next couple of days, well worth ending the entire life of another being.

'Who cares about these foreign, spoiled losers who die like this' the killer thought as he wiped the blood from the blade.

Adam realized there are many 'ifs', but the future also changes 'if I stay here' - he knew he could be hit by a truck in Toronto - if he hadn't boarded this plane today.

He believed you had to follow your heart and take the path of most existence.

The path you felt most compelled to follow, is the path to take.

Adam didn't want to live a mundane life tied to a house and a job, forever and ever amen.

He was confident he belonged to the future he was now pursuing.

Adam knew he had the intelligence to provide a reality in different frames of reference for every combination of possible futures which could exist - every point of reference has three "consequential results" - "yes", "no" or "neither".

Adam sat back in his chair on the plane to London after everyone on board had been fed and watered, with the lights down and the white noise drone of the air conditioning system mixed with the low hum of jet engines. He closed his eyes and imagined.

The woman sitting next to him had covered herself with a blanket, with her eyes and ears closed, napping.

Adam closed his eyes as pictures and colors streamed through his mind

"All experience is experienced by all, till all finally becomes one." he thought as he drifted to a higher place and watched a young girl sleeping in her bed while a shadow moved through the wall and engulfed her.

As darkness falls into each life
Our character is tested
And those who keep the simple Trust
Will never be digested
By living on the planet Earth
Vortexing out through space
Moving to a perfect world
Through Love through Light through Grace.
And evil seeks to shake our faith
In Truth,
Through fear and separation
With lies and greed and selfish need
As nation, digests nation.

Adam dreamt he was inside a bubble of light which moved beyond speed to the young girl trapped below. "Touch the light and I will take you back, Sarah".

Adam's body jerked in the chair and he was awake.

"Your must have been dreaming." The woman sitting next to him exclaimed. "I hate it when I wake up like that. Your whole body feels like it's falling. You sort of jerk upwards".

Adam looked over at the traveling companion this instance of time and space had put him beside, and smiled.

"Yes, I was dreaming of a young girl caught in some mesh in some sort of bottomless pit – I was the knight in shining amour" – He laughed, "Who had to go to rescue the poor maiden."

"Wow" said the woman with a bit of a sarcastic scowl on her face, "I am sitting beside a kind and gentle knight!"

"All nights and all knights should be kind and gentle" Adam responded.

They both smiled at each other for the first time.

Adam reached his hand out and simply said... "I am Adam Mason."

The woman took his hand as she said "I am Jennifer Cagney, but everyone knows me as Jenny"

"Pleased to meet you Jennifer" Adam smiled.

"Pleased to meet you too Adam" Jenny smiled.

Jenny was about 25 years old with very tidy short black hair. Adam guessed she must use hairspray to keep each strand in place around her oval, pixie like face. She was not beautiful, but she was cute.

Her eyes were a shade of green, wide open with totally exposed pupils. Her face was cute in a pixie kind of way. He changed his mind – she was beautiful after all.

As Jenny moved the blanket from her space Adam could see the slim and trim outline of her feminine body, with all attributes in the right place.

He thought himself lucky to have such an attractive traveling companion.

"You had a good nap" Adam said slowly, as he adjusted his body language to indicate he was interested in knowing her better. Adam knew body language. He liked to put himself into positions with meaning when he felt it may drop some barrier and of course he always waited to see the response generated by his gestures.

As he turned towards Jenny, he opened his legs slightly and leaned the top half of his body a little bit closer to her. He looked directly into her eyes and said, "Are you going home or leaving home?"

Jenny turned slightly towards him moving just a little closer looking almost directly into his blue eyes.

"I am doing both." She smiled. "My home is in Erin, a small community outside of Toronto, which I am leaving. We can call that my old home. I have secured a new job in London which I am going to now. We can call that my new home."

Adam asked, "What did you do in Erin - and what will you do in London?"

Jenny smiled at Adam "I am an artist, but I will be teaching in London."

Adam was now more curious, "What type of artist are you and what will you be teaching?"

Jenny smiled back and Adam noticed her lowering her right leg by straightening the knee while also raising her left leg ever so slightly to expose a small opening in her defenses. Adam smiled to himself as she continued, "I am a painter and I will be teaching art. What do you do Adam and are you leaving or going home?"

Adam smiled again "Ah, my interrogation is over and yours is beginning!"

"Tit for tat" Jenny smiled back.

Adam thought 'Hmmm… Interesting choice of words' and then answered, "I am also an artist, but my brush is a computer and my

scenes are painted with notes. I am leaving home and starting what I hope will be an adventure of what you could call ‘surf and turf’ discovery. I want to know everything about everything.”
Jennifer looked closer at Adam and, in a tone of curious surprise asked, “You’re not the Adam Mason who was in the arts section of the Globe and Mail last weekend. Are you?”
Adam looked at Jenny with delight in his eyes. “It’s me.”
Now Jenny moved a bit closer on top and bottom as she shifted in her seat. She raised her left knee higher still and moved her right foot closer to Adams left leg. ‘Ah’ Adam thought, ‘Darwin to the forefront!’
Adam was happy with the dropping barriers but was a bit disappointed as well, since he would love to meet someone who hadn’t heard of him before just to see if he was as nice and as interesting as his music seemed to be.
“Wow”, Jenny reached her hand out again, “It is really a pleasure to meet you in the flesh.” Adam felt her squeeze his hand ever so slightly a little more tightly on the word “flesh”.
She is a perfect body language response machine he thought with a smile.
“Nice to meet you, again, too Jenny.”
“So, Adam do you mind talking about your music?”
“Sometimes I do Jenny” he said with a silent sigh “I would like just once, to meet someone who does not know me by my music - just to be able to talk about something different.”
Jenny smiled and looked at Adam, “So, you do mind and therefore let’s forget that I even mentioned it.”
“It’s ok, Jennifer” Adam smiled, “Sorry for my rudeness. We can talk about anything you want.”
“Then” Jenny said, “I want to talk about anything except your music!”
Adam laughed and liked Jenny just a little bit more.
“Well” said Adam “We have about four hours left in this flight, it will be light soon and the plane will be a beehive of breakfast activity again. Let’s tell each other something intriguing which we have experienced in our lives, “You start.”

Jenny looked at Adam with her pixie face scrunched up, "That's not fair, I don't even know what intriguing means in my life, I have not had an intriguing life!"
Jenny looked over at Adam and realized how much she was attracted to this young man who was younger than she was, but whom she knew had more life experience than most eighty-year old's, under his belt (she laughed to herself about the pun she had just created). She knew he had a reputation as a womanizer. Someone whom most women would gladly give themselves to sexually, on a daily and nightly basis.
Maybe he would like to do some intriguing things under the blanket on this plane she thought to herself, as she imagined being joined at the hips right here in the first-class section of a flight from Toronto to London. She'd never thought about anything like that before, ever in her life, but then again this was Adam Mason sitting right beside her with the lights down and snorers all around them, mixing with the drone coming from the engines of the plane.
Adam noted a red glow rising.
"It would be intriguing to join the "mile high" club with you Adam" Jenny whispered... "Would you like that or not" she said with a sense of embarrassment – God – she didn't believe she had just said that. He must think I am a sex starved slut puppy, she thought – "Oh God, I wish I could take that back!"
Adam looked at her and smiled. "You can take it back Jenny if you really want to. You're a desirable woman and I find you extremely attractive - but I am trying to raise my level of experience to be above the gonads! This may sound funny to you, but that newspaper article was right on the money when it talked about the so-called groupies following a music composer - this is the stuff of rock bands – not for classical piano music composers.
Over the last two years I have spent most of my time in bed with people I hardly know."
As Adam said that he pulled his blanket over to the far side of Jenny's chair and turned sideways in the seat facing her. He then pulled the blanket to the level of his shoulder. They were both covered from neck to toe.
Adam let his fingers rest on Jenny's hip, then started to slowly move his fingers in a circling motion down her left thigh till he reached the

exposed skin at the hem of her dress. Jennifer sat motionless as Adam put his hands beneath her dress and moved them upwards till he reached the side of her panties and then moved his hand under the soft material until he was holding her bare left buttock in his hand, slowly massaging and stroking while looking directly into Jenny's eyes.
Jenny started breathing heavier as she turned in her seat to give Adam more access to her body. She couldn't believe she was doing this, but he was Adam Mason!
Checking the blanket, she reached over and put her arm around Adams waist as his head moved closer and their lips touched for the first time in a soft embrace.
Adam pulled his hand away, kissed Jenny on the forehead and said "No!"
I want to know you. I want you to know me - I don't want to do a celebrity connection at the hips then watch you walk away and never see you again. Hell... I don't even know who you are!"
Jenny sat upright and arranged her skirt till she was properly covered – then looked at Adam with true surprise.
"I don't do it for you Adam – I am sorry."
"No" Adam said softly. "Sex is like a drug that keeps you from growing more than eight inches at a time – I want to know who you are, and I want to feel your heart not your genitals. Jenny. I have had so many women over the past two years. I didn't really know any of them except for one. I had no interest in knowing them – they used me for my music, I used them for their vaginas. Using will never bring happiness to anyone."
Adam folded the blanket, stood up and moved towards the washroom.
Once inside he peed and looked down at his penis. "You will not control me anymore" he said out loud. "I will control you!"
Adam washed his hand and face, brushed his teeth with the complimentary toothbrush and toothpaste provided by Air Canada.
He went back to his seat and found Jenny's spot unoccupied.
"I had to go too" Jenny's voice said from behind him.
Adam moved out of the way and let Jenny sit down. She was a beautiful woman and he looked at her with passion for the first time.
"Down boy" he said to himself as he slid into the seat beside her.

"Jenny, I want to be your friend if that is ok with you. Part of my journey is to find the levels I want to live in, rather than have the level live in me."

"Adam", Jenny said as she looked directly into his eyes, "I would love to be your friend, and by the way that is usually my line, with needy boys, you just used on me. I hope you don't think I am a needy girl, because I'm not. You have a magnetic appeal. I'm not used to guys asking me to be their friend, except of course, for my gay male friends who truly are good friends."

Jenny had a thought and asked "You're not gay are you Adam? If you are it is ok with me and you have no reason not to tell me so."

"Did you read that article last week?" Adam laughed. "I am totally heterosexual – and you're hot!"

Jenny smiled and licked her lower lip... "If you ever want to just ravish me slowly, let me know, ok?"

"Ok" Adam said as he leaned over and kissed Jenny on the cheek. "You will be the second to know."

Sex was out of the way between them and now they could talk about other things.

"Tell me about you Jenny, I want to know everything about you. Two people put together on a seven-hour flight, is an opportunity to either learn, or just ignore. I would like to take this as an opportunity to learn!"

The flight attendants and some other passengers knew Adam Mason was on the flight, and some came up and told him how much they enjoyed his work, others asked for an autograph, to which Adam quickly agreed.

The plane ride to London was interesting as Adam learned about most of Jenny's younger life and how she became an artist who now, was teaching art. Adam couldn't imagine himself as a teacher of music composition. To him teaching the craft meant you were not ballsy enough to extend the envelope and develop new thrills. Teaching meant you had stopped exploring and were at a level of self-indulgence which suited your ambition. Adam then remembered some of the passionate teachers he had during his younger years and was suddenly happy some people chose to become teachers.

Deplaning at Heathrow was a time-based experience, but Adam and Jenny didn't care, since it gave them more time to talk. Jenny felt she loved this man and could understand how young women easily fell into his bed, unable to discount his amazing charisma. He was a very special man.

Adam and Jenny stood in line together amidst the throngs of people waiting to get passed the immigration officials. Finally, they were free!

"Where are you heading Adam?" Jenny asked. "You're very welcome to share my cab if you're going downtown."

"I have to catch another flight" Adam said slowly. "I am on my way to Istanbul, and then from there I will be traveling to a village on the Mediterranean."

Jenny was truly disappointed and hadn't realized Adam was not staying in London.

"Will I ever see you again?" Jenny asked with a pout.

"Let's exchange e-mail addresses and I will write to you as soon as I am settled." Adam said as he took his pen and wrote his address on the back of the flight ticket holder.

"There" Adam tore off the piece with his address and tore a piece off for Jenny as well... Jenny wrote her address and handed it to Adam.

"ArtAche - That is an easy one to remember" Adam said with a smile. "Is art such a misery, Jenny?"

Jenny looked at Adam's address, "And AdamsNotes, is also easy to remember – is there a double meaning for the 'notes' Adam?" Jenny smiled. She was proud of herself, having an email address, defining her passion, as Adam also had. They were both committed, but he was globally accepted for his passion. Jenny had never sold a painting. "Hey – we're both artists," she said with a smile, "Cut from the same cloth!"

Adam smiled back. "That we are, sweet Jenny. That we are."

Adam walked Jenny to the baggage claim area, helped her get her suitcases onto the cart, kissed her and hugged her – then watched her move through the gate towards the customs hall. He waited till she passed the inspection, blew her a kiss, then she was gone.

Adam was happy with his new attitude and realized his internal desire structure was changing. He had proven through his meeting

with Jenny, he wanted more than sex. Maybe he was maturing or maybe another part of his essence was seeking a greater meaning. He had had so many different women over the past five years, yet only one true love relationship; Caroline. But even with Caroline, he knew, and was not proud off at all, he had used and abused, knowing she would gladly submit to his every selfish whim.
Adam felt a bit ashamed and made a mental note to treat Caroline better - to meet her at a higher level than the solar plexus and the pelvis. He wanted to respect and nurture the love he felt for her and bring her to a higher place as well.
He thought about the function and structures of the endocrine system and the chakra wheels, representing the same bio and etheric centers, knowing there were portals to each level of the body and psyche. By thought and attitude alone, we could choose and live our path.
Adam wanted to grow; to know and show non-selfish respect for each individual he met without exception. To be used as a channel for the benefit of others. This would be a tough road to follow since most people he knew were more interested in their own agendas. Most people used other people either on the conscious or subconscious level to advance their own position and sphere of influence. He hadn't been an exception to this classification.
"for the sake of love,
What a height to reach,
To kill oneself,
To teach!
To let ones alter ego, die
With a private thought
And heart felt sigh.
For the sake of love,
A height to reach!"
Adam sang this to himself as he waited in line to board the BA flight to Istanbul.
Most love at this level manifested between parent and child.
Adam had read the cases where the son had killed yet the mother continued to support her 'baby', always saying he was a 'good boy'. Standing beside him while the entire planet felt revulsion. Unselfish love is a parent's compulsion!

And surely, the idea of God himself would be better as a woman. Adam thought, since God gave birth to man and continues to do so every day through woman. If God is man, does man give birth?
To Adam - God, as Love, has no gender. Gender is a shallow classification.
Love is deeper than gender, and all ideas of gods involve love somewhere in the construct. Sometimes it is more love for one tribe over another - God loves them more, so everything they have belongs to them (since god loves them more).
"There is so much to learn!" Adam spoke out loud, causing the people standing beside him in line to look at him and smile some nodding in agreement.
Adam smiled back wondering who all these people were and what reason and tribal mores, they inherited from their families in their young years. We're born into a skein of space and time, and our birth conditions do have meaning. Our parents, our siblings, our friends, our lovers, our children, our attitudes, our kindness, our cruelty, our interface with everything, is a cause and effect construct, which goes beyond the instance we experience. Every decision is taken and not taken, in a parallel expansion of our universe, as a different instance in the multiverse, for every possible path.
As usual, Adam was overthinking. Or possibly underthinking – he didn't know which. But he knew from the center of his being, we're all part of something so wonderful and magnificent, words and feelings from sequential beings, could not express the essence of it at all.
"Where are the teachers?" he thought.
Adam suddenly felt a shaking disturbance in his stream of thought.
Two men ran through the security doors, shooting the gate keepers, in government uniforms as they ran yelling "Allah is great!"
The first explosion was loud. Adam saw people's bodies and parts of bodies, flying through, the air.
The crowd started running in all directions screaming as the two men each threw another grenade.
The explosions rocked the building and once again there were bodies and body parts bursting from the location of each explosion.
Adam rushed to the front counter and dove through the baggage weigh scale opening then scrambled to get behind the other people,

who were crouched as close as possible - cramped in the storage area under the counter.
Two more explosions pierced the air followed by more people moaning and screaming in pain, amongst the clamor of confusion and turmoil which engulfed the entire terminal space.
Adam knew one of the men was heading in his direction and he reached behind him and pulled two large suitcases behind his back for protection. He pulled another suitcase over his head protecting the woman and child in front of him, pushing his body with all his might towards the small space they were all sharing. If he did get hit, he was sure the woman and child had as much protection as he could possibly provide. His immediate concern was to keep them from harm.
He heard rapid fire gun shots at the same time as sharp thuds thundered over his head. Bullets hit the wall behind him. The man next to him let out a sharp cry of pain then became silent. Adam saw the blood seeping from the back of his shirt and realized the man had been hit by one of the bullets. Adam reached over to the man, but he didn't move or moan. He had died right there beside him.
The child, now screaming for her mother, and her mother hysterical, as she pushed the child further into the storage recess covering her totally with her own body. Adrenalin heightened Adam's senses as he tensed waiting for the next event.
A huge explosion moved the counter from its anchors and pushed everyone behind it against the conveyer belt which was still moving. Adam felt a snap in his right leg then a searing pain which hit his brain like a blade being driven into the back of his head.
Plaster, suitcases, clothing and pieces of human flesh rained down on them.
Then everything went silent.
Adam drifted in and out of sub-consciousness with a feeling like he was floating slowly higher and out of his body. Then with a thump he returned once again to feel the pain shooting from his right leg to the centre of his head.
Adam thought he was dying. But he couldn't die. There was so much to do.
In the background somewhere, could hear the sirens of emergency vehicles, arriving at the scene.

He slowly drifted higher until encircled by the Light. He felt the presence of a great Love which took away all pain, weight, and thickness. Adam was free from the sequence of time and felt an essence of pure Spirit. He recognized other spiritual instances and knew all, who had crossed over to the Light, were now at peace. Their essence folded into a kinder more loving non-sequential construct.
They were 'home', above the membrane of time and space..
They were not separate, but part of a greater plan, seeped in multiple instances, of sequential events and conditioned by cause and effect – conditioned by action and consequence.
There is no hatred, nor selfish agendas, nor judgement or cruelty - only the pure and ubiquitous essence of Love for each and all.
A sense of peace came over Adam as an intuition entered his essence. He had to go back, to the sequential heavy and thick instance he almost left.
The light left Adam. He once again was conscious of the panic and noise around him. He was sequential again and though he didn't want to be here and now, he knew he would survive this. There is so much to do.
The mother and child were still crying beside him as he moved some of the debris away from them.
"It is ok" Adam said, "We're safe, we have survived."
The woman put her arm around Adam's head and sobbed into his shoulder.
"We have survived" Adam said softly.
The emergency people moved quickly to remove the obstructions around Adam and the others with him. All fear had left him as he still felt the comfort of the light.
"This one needs transport!" he heard a man yell. Adam felt his leg being inspected and a needle being pushed into his lower back. "This will stop the pain son" a man said, "We have to get you to the hospital as quickly as possible."
He faintly remembers the woman and child shaking and crying, while standing beside him as he was put onto the stretcher. A mask was put over his mouth and he fell into a deep sleep.
Adam's leg was broken, the bone had pierced the outer skin just below his right knee. The bone was shattered by a bullet and luckily

the main artery was missed by only a few millimeters. If the artery had been hit, Adam would have bled to death. The medics had set up a triage in a church one block from the airport and the ambulances were dropping wounded and dead off then rushing back to the scene. Two other stretchers had been loaded into Adam's ambulance. One held a man in his late thirties who was bleeding heavily from his abdomen. A piece of glass still buried within his stomach area. The medics did everything possible to stop the bleeding. The other stretcher held the body of child who was barely alive when picked up but now was dead. The little boy had wounds in his neck, and in the back of his head. The medics left the child and started working on Adam's leg.

"This one was lucky" the medic said as he started sterilizing the open wound on Adam's leg. "All major blood vessels seem to be intact."

As the ambulance approached the triage, doctors and nurses were waiting to classify the severity of each victim, and to pronounce the dead ones as dead, for removal to the temporary morgue.

At least 200 people were severely wounded and probably another 50 to 60 had expired.

London was in a state of emergency as two other bombs exploded in the financial district. One bomb exploded in an elevator which had just opened on the tenth floor, killing all six people on board immediately and causing a fire to start in the elevator shaft and in the surrounding area. The elevator had been split in two by the force and the bottom part of it plunged twelve floors and came to a violent stop in the second level underground parking area.

The other bomb exploded in the lobby of a major hotel, close to a restaurant full of patrons, starting to eat lunch. The dead and dying were scattered throughout the restaurant and the lobby.

The Prime Minister declared an immediate state of emergency, ordering the home defense to take up positions at all major assets. Parliament was quickly evacuated, and the politicians were moved to a safe area under protection of the Home Office.

The queen and royal family were also moved to a safe place and Buckingham Palace secured.

"Those fucking bastards!" a man yelled within the triage as he was waiting for treatment. His clothes and face were bloodied but he

was one of lucky ones since he still had the capacity to speak and think.
"Where is my wife?" he sobbed. "Those fucking bastards!"
The man was ignored by everyone.
The call was put out for all emergency and medical personnel to report immediately to work.
T.V. news crews were dispatched to the scenes of the carnage but were held back by police and military personnel. Only emergency personnel were allowed anywhere near any of the targeted sites.
London was in a state of panic and people everywhere were on cell phones telling loved ones they were safe or trying to reach loved ones who had been lost.
Life is always close to death.
Adam needed surgery. The emergency doctor had done all she could under the circumstances. The bone in his leg was fragmented and needed to be repaired. His prognosis was good.
Adam was loaded into a waiting ambulance with two other victims then transported to the London General Hospital, where an orthopedic surgeon, who had already performed three life threatening operations, was waiting for the next patient.
Many volunteer agencies were on the scene taking the identity and destination of each patient as they left.
Victim's names, nationality and final destination were being compiled on site using an Internet connected lap top computer, into a central data base on the Red Cross disaster management web site. They were also identifying the victims in the temporary morgue.
The scene at the triage was a study in managed chaos. Professionals were doing what they were trained to do with focus and determination. Everyone was busy doing their best to repair the damage like an ant colony does when you kick away the sand on their hill.
Adam was rushed into the operating theatre and the team began their work. Dr. John Lynn did a quick scan of the wound as the anesthesiologist put the mask over Adam's mouth and nose. All the measurement wires were hooked up and his pulse was strong.
Dr. Lynn decided to do an initial operation to connect the bone fragments knowing he would have to redo some of the work when there was more time. All previous victims operated on that morning,

had bone injuries in multiple locations. At least this one was isolated to one bullet wound in the lower leg.
A bone and skin graft would have to be done at another time and a temporary rod would be put in to keep the bone together.
Within thirty minutes, Adam was wheeled into a waiting recovery room, as the operation theatre was sterilized once again ready for the next in line.
Adam slept.

Jenny was frantic.
Her first day in London turned into the worst day of her life. She'd taken a cab from the airport and it was during the cab ride that all hell broke loose. The cab driver put the radio on after noticing a stream of fire trucks and ambulances racing towards the airport with sirens blaring.
The announcer's voice was shaken while he reported the explosions at the airport followed by two more large explosions. One was in the Sherbrooke Hotel downtown and the other was in one of the main office towers of the financial district.
"Oh my God" Jenny screamed "Adam is still at the airport!"
She pleaded with the taxi driver to turn back to the airport, but he continually told her "No Miss!"
The traffic towards the airport was being detoured to clear the motorway and give the emergency vehicles faster access.
The radio announcer's voice was the only connection with information about what was going on.
"It has been verified three or more explosions have detonated at the following locations; Heathrow Airport, the middle tower in the financial district and at the Sherbrooke Hotel in central London. We can also confirm there are multiple casualties at each location. Parliament has been evacuated along with Buckingham Palace where we're told, the queen and some of the royal family residents were, at the time of the first attacks.
Initial reports from eyewitnesses at Heathrow indicate two or more terrorists were involved and have subsequently blown themselves up after facing fire from police. A triage is set up in St. Mary's church which is located approximately one city block from Heathrow and emergency medical staff and other helpers are on site tending the

wounded. We will now switch over to Marty Green who is in the airport area for a first-hand report – Marty – can you tell us more about what is happening there?"
Jenny and the cab driver sat in silence, listening to every word, as traffic slowed to a crawl. As the cab driver looked around him, he could see the same look of shock and fear on the faces of drivers and passengers in cars and busses around him.
"This is Marty Green reporting for BBC One from this horrific scene at Heathrow Airport. Smoke and flames are belching from Terminal 3 – this is one of the terminals used for International flights – and it looks like a war zone. Emergency personnel including police, firefighters and ambulance attendants are on rescue missions bringing wounded and shocked victims out of the terminal, dropping them away from the building then running back in to find more casualties."
"My God" Jenny whispered, "Adam is in terminal three! He must be in the middle of this! Oh, God please, please keep him safe!"
Jenny was sobbing now with images of Adam hurt and needing help somewhere in the terminal. "Come on now Miss, the driver said, "There is no need to think the worst, you just heard them say there are lots of people being rescued alive".
The driver wanted to comfort Jenny and wanted her to keep talking.
"Is he your husband, Miss?"
"No" Jenny sobbed, "I just met him on my flight from Toronto last night. He is a musical genius and a wonderful man. God, I hope he is alright!"
"I am sure he is Miss." The cabby said, not really sure of anything.
"I don't know the bastards who did this, but they are probably some religious fanatics... this fucking world seems to be full of religious fanatics these days!" Jenny said angrily. "Where do these miserable people come from, what have we ever done to them?!"
Jenny was angry, and she was shaking. She had finally decided to do something about her boring life in Canada and now she was in the middle of an attack which she didn't understand at all. How could any human being cause such pain and misery to innocent strangers in the name of God? It was totally incomprehensible that anyone would want to hurt anything, let alone another human being.

Her life back in Erin Ontario was so quiet – to the point she often found herself wishing something would happen just to break the tranquility. Well she thought 'I got my wish!' She had a feeling of total helplessness not knowing if her job would still be here or if the people who were supposed to meet her at the hotel, would even be there now.
These killers of the peace had taken her planned and organized trip and turned it into a total loose end.
Jenny hated loose ends!
Even her paintings were meticulously organized with every brush stroke having a purpose and a meaning. She hated disorder and chaos and here she was stuck in a taxi in the middle of London, with no control over anything!
Jenny started feeling sorry for herself and then she felt some guilt knowing other people had been killed today; people like her who were on their way to a new future; people who had planned just like she had.
Now they were gone forever, leaving behind a crowd of loved ones who would have to pick up the pieces and fill in the gaps.
She thought about her mother, father and sister in Erin and knew they would be worried sick about her. She had to find a way to reach them, but the taxi driver had tried to make some calls from his cell phone and continually got the fast-busy signal. Everyone in London was trying to make a phone call, and the network was overloaded.
Traffic had almost stopped, now moving inches at a time. The police were getting all traffic off the motorways and everyone wanted to co-operate with their efforts.
The radio announcer continued to provide new details of the attacks. Forty-five people were confirmed dead at Heathrow alone and more bodies were still being recovered.
The taxi finally pulled off the motorway and was now part of the side street traffic jam. "We will continue to head down-town Miss" he said, "But I will shut the meter off. Your hotel is about a mile from the Sherbrooke so we may be alright."
"Is your family safe?" Jenny asked, realizing she hadn't even thought about the driver's loved ones yet.
"My family lives in Maidenhead and they should be alright since London seems to be the target of today's attacks. I have tried to call

them - I am sure they're wondering where I am, but the phone network is jammed."

"We're safe" the driver said, "and we should thank God for that."

"If my plane had landed 40 minutes later, I would be in the middle of that!" Jenny thought out loud. "I wonder if Adam is safe?"

Traffic started moving a bit faster since constables had taken up positions at major intersections.

It would still be another hour though till Jenny made it to the front of her hotel.

Her suitcases were isolated for security reasons and she was told no one would be checked in or out for at least another hour.

Jenny thanked the taxi driver and wished him and his family well. She gave him a ten-pound tip which was very extravagant for her, knowing she was on a tight budget.

They hugged each other as he picked up another fare and edged his way back into the traffic.

Hotel security staff were opening and examining all suitcases and the owners had to stay close by to identify their belongings. Everyone seemed very paranoid about another bomb exploding and Jenny was happy about their caution.

She finally got her baggage checked and released and was allowed, to check into her room. It had now been six hours since she'd left the airport, she was hungry and exhausted.

Just twenty-four hours ago, she was leaving her parents in Erin taking the limousine to Pearson Airport. "What a difference a day makes." She thought to herself, as she started to cry, feeling the burden of the extra weight, so quickly added to her life.

Jenny ordered a Caesar salad from room service and left a message at the front desk in case Mrs. Cantwell asked about her. Mrs. Cantwell was supposed to have met her at the hotel but of course with all that had happened, she hadn't shown up.

After finishing her meal Jenny took a shower, closed the drapes and climbed into bed. She thought about her family back home and then Adam as she quickly drifted into a deep sleep.

Adam woke up in the recovery room. As he looked around, he realized he was hooked up to some apparatus with drip bags feeding clear liquid into his right arm.

As he looked around the room, he noticed other patients all unconscious in different beds around him. He remembered the pain in his leg and looked down, happy to see the outline of both legs under the blanket. He used his left arm to move the blanket aside until he could see his right leg elevated on some kind of traction device, complete with a cast up to the top of his right thigh.
"You're awake, Mr. Mason" The nurse in a crisp white uniform said, as she smiled and walked towards him.
She checked the tube in his arm and stroked his hair. "You have had a bit of a nasty leg injury, but you will be fine. The doctor will be in to see you soon, and he will be able to answer any questions you may have." She said reassuringly as she continued to gently stroke the top of his head.
Adam looked into her eyes for the first time and knew she was a mother of four children and a grandmother of three. He felt a great affinity towards her. She'd been a helper all her life and was a sweet and gentle spirit. Her glasses were halfway down her nose as she peered at him over the top. Her graying hair tied back and pinned beneath her cap. Her face showed some wrinkles around her mouth and her eyes, and she wore no makeup. She believed in being a natural person and was one of the few in her age group who didn't dye her hair. A gold chain around her neck, held a small and simple gold cross.
"How long have I been out?" Adam asked.
"Well let me see" she said as she looked at her watch, "It is now ten past eleven in the evening and you came in here at..." she leaned over and picked his chart up from the holder at the bottom of the bed, "hmm... one thirty this afternoon. So, you have been asleep for almost ten hours."
"I have to call my parents and let them know I am safe." Adam said slowly.
"Is there a telephone handy that I could use?"
"Well dear," the nurse responded, "I don't think you're ready to get out of bed yet but if you give me the number, I will get one of the hospital operators to phone them and give the details of where you are and tell them you're one of the survivors."

"The number to call is area code 416 555-3879. My parents are Mrs. Allison and Walter Mason, they live in the greater Toronto area known as Rosedale. Please get someone to call to say I am safe."
The nurse wrote down the number on her note pad and, added it to the proper location on the medical chart under "Closest Family Contact", also adding Allison and Walter's names as mother and father. She told Adam to lay back and relax - she would be back in a few minutes.
Nurse Williams walked down the hall to the nursing station and called the hospital operator. "Hello Gloria, this is Nurse Williams in recovery... A young man has just woken up from an operation and would like to inform his parents he is well." It wasn't the hospital's usual policy to have the hospital operators talk with next of kin, but under these circumstances, everyone was doing all they could to help and pitch in.
Nurse Williams provided the number to call and even though it was close to 12 midnight in London it would be around 5 in the morning in Toronto. She was sure his parents had probably been up half the night worrying. "Yes Gloria... his mother's name is Allison and his father's name is Walter. Just give them the message that he had a bullet wound in the leg that is not life threatening, he had undergone an operation, has a good prognosis and is recovering well.
He is not able to talk with them yet but will be able to speak with them soon. Tell them he was in luck, having Dr. Lynn as the orthopedic surgeon... on of the best in all of Europe."
Allison and Walter had been up all night trying to find information about Adam. They had called Air Canada and were told the flight had landed in London on time and they had no further information to provide.
Walter had sworn at the person on the other end of the line since he thought he was being stone-walled by the Air Canada employee. He then apologized for losing his temper. Walter was not one to lose control in any situation, yet he had yelled and swore at a young lady who had given him all the information she could possibly verify about his son's flight.
Allison was an emotional wreck blaming Walter for letting Adam go on this crazy and unnecessary venture. This didn't help Walter as he tried to rationalize every emotion he was hit with.

The phone rang as they were sitting at the kitchen table having yet another cup of tea.
"Oh my God" Allison wailed "I hope that is good news! I couldn't take the loss of my one and only child!", she wailed and started sobbing loudly again.
Walter picked up the phone "Walter Mason here" he said in the most controlled voice he could muster.
A lady with an English accent started to speak as Allison rushed to her husband's side and with her right hand covering her eyes as she sobbed "Please God let him be alive! Let him be alive!" she gasped.
Walter held Allison's hand and squeezed it hard. "Calm down sweetheart" he said soothingly "It is a call from England."
"Mr. Mason. I am calling from London General Hospital and have been asked to tell you your son is alive and well and is here." Walter couldn't hold his control anymore as he wrapped his arm around Allison and sobbed "Thank God, my dear Allison, thank God! He is alive and in the hospital in London!"
Allison threw her arms around Walter as they both wailed "Thank You God!" together.
"Mr. Mason... Mr. Mason... Are you still there?" the operator asked as she could hear the sobbing sounds coming from the other end of the line.
"I am sorry Miss" Walter said as he tried to regain his composure. "I am sorry, we're just overwhelmed and relieved that Adam is safe. I thank you so much for calling us and letting us know."
"You're very welcome Mr. Mason. I am sure this has been a horrible evening for you and your wife."
"What is she saying Walter?" Allison pleaded.
"One minute please Miss" Walter said as he turned to Allison, "Sweetheart, let me talk to the lady and I will let you know everything as soon as I find out. Please put the kettle on and make us a cup of tea, Adam is safe and well!" Allison needed something to do so she went over to the sink and filled the kettle to the very top and put it on the burner.
"Thank you, Miss," Walter said clearly now happy that he once again had control of his faculties. "Is there anything else you can tell us about our son's condition?"

"Well Mr. Mason" the operator continued "I can only tell you that he received a bullet wound in his leg..."
"Oh, my God" Walter exclaimed and interrupted.
"What is it Walter... What is wrong?"
"Adam was shot in the leg" Walter said, "But he is ok!" he added for the benefit of Allison.
"I am sorry Miss" Walter said... "Please continue."
"Well Mr. Mason, the injury is not life threatening and he was operated on by Dr. Lynn... one of the best orthopedic surgeons in the UK, this morning."
"Young Mr. Mason is doing well, and he is now in the recovery room. He talked with Nurse Williams and he asked her to call his parents and let you know that he is alive and well. Nurse Williams in turn asked me to put the call through and I am happy I was able to reach you."
"As I am too" Walter said with a tone of appreciation.
"Please let my son know we will be on the first available flight to get over there."
"I will pass that on Mr. Mason and I am sure young Mr. Mason will be happy to hear that."
"Thank you, Miss...?"
"Mrs. Knowles" the operator said. "I am Mrs. Knowles."
"Well thank you so much Mrs. Knowles for your call and your good news!"
"Goodbye Mr. Mason, and please give our best regards to Mrs. Mason as well."
"I certainly will, Mrs. Knowles, I certainly will. Goodbye for now." Walter said as he hung up the phone.
Walter had never thought that hearing his son had been shot in the leg would ever have been thanked as 'good news'.
The news reports had been going all night long and there were at least 90 confirmed dead at the airport alone, and they expected more. It was the worst terrorist attack ever to happen in London with horrible carnage at three locations.
Allison and Walter hugged each other and kissed as lovers for the first time in a long time. They realized how fragile everything was and they had taken time and each other for granted for far too long.
All things pass.

Walter patted Allison on the back. "We have to call everyone to let them know Adam is ok" Walter said as he walked over to the phone and started with Adam's grandparents, then Caroline.
Allison made a fresh pot of tea.
Nurse Williams returned to the recovery room and found Adam sound asleep. She made her rounds of each patient ensuring all intravenous connections were working properly and she changed two anti-biotic bags of two patients which were empty.
She went back to Adam and updated the personal information sheet on his chart indicating his parents had been contacted and told of his condition.
Her shift was over, but the head nurse asked her if she would mind putting in some extra time due to the number of new patients. She agreed immediately and indicated she would work a double shift if required.
The surgeons were still busy operating and some had been working solidly since eight o'clock that morning rotating for an hour of rest whenever possible.
Dr. Lynn finally finished the last operation at one a.m. He was dogged tired as he drove his car out of the hospital parking lot. His rounds would start at seven AM, so he didn't have much time to get some sleep and freshen up. He was happy about recently purchasing a new flat downtown, just a fifteen-minute drive from the hospital.
He knew a couple of his patients would probably not make it through the night, but he could do no more for them.
Multiple fractures, with a great loss of blood caused too much trauma even for his capabilities. Dr. Lynn had a large ego with great confidence in what he could do to fix broken people, and realized he lost interest quickly in the patients he knew he couldn't save.
After 15 years of surgery, he no longer felt guilt about the ones he couldn't save. Eventually we all come to a point in life, where our only option left, is to die.
He made a quick mental note of all that had to be done the next day. Adam Mason was at the top of his priority list. There was a young man he could help, and it would take about two hours of his time for the bone and skin grafts he knew would have to be done as soon as possible to lessen the chances of infection. He didn't want this young man to lose his leg.

Adam would be his first patient the next morning.
Caroline was devastated as Walter told her of Adam's condition. She wanted to fly to London with them and wouldn't take no for an answer. Walter finally relented and told Caroline he would try to get three seats to London on the first available flight.
Jenny finally woke up and it was the middle of the night in London. She quickly got out of bed and ordered some coffee from room service. It was just past two a.m. and therefore it was just past seven a.m. at home.
She phoned her mother and was happy as the call went through; a line was finally available. Her mother was relieved to hear she was ok and, she had reached the hotel safely. After a ten-minute talk about the bombing and the traffic jams, Jenny finally had to mention her meeting with Adam.
"I sat next to Adam Mason on the flight over" Jenny said, "You know the musician from Toronto?"
"Yes" her mother responded. "I think I know the one you mean."
"He was so nice mom and I think he may have been caught up in the bombing at the airport - he was continuing on to Istanbul and I am sure he was still in the terminal when the terrorist attacked."
"I'm going to try to find him today... God I hope he is safe!"
Jenny's mother provided some encouraging words and asked her to come back home.
"No." Jenny said emphatically "I will not be coming home. No terrorist is going to make me afraid to live my life and I have made a commitment to teach here for at least the next year."

Chapter 7

The world is false within our dance

Most do not want to take the chance
Embrace the place where all is true
We'd rather not; just simply 'do'
Our work and call it living!
Some have guidance from above,
To suffer, teach, to change, to Love
They force the rest of us to see,
Their pain, their loss, our sympathy
There is a price for giving!
The seventh sense, being one with Love
Exposes hate and withers fraud
The souls who preach a selfish creed
Of salvation steeped in a pious need
Accrue their just reward!
Martyrs leave a bloody stain
Innocents slaughtered once again
As bombs and bullets shatter peace
As hatred hinders Love's release
As Earth spins always onward!

Sarah knew more.

She knew life was not as it seemed, and most people wasted time worrying about things not important at all.

After her mysterious withdrawal, Debbie and Barry demanded their daughter be allowed to attend high school like any other thirteen-year old.

Dr. Armstrong intervened with the school board ensuring them, Sarah was fit to be back in school – in fact, her vocabulary, and communication skills were far beyond the grade 9 level she was entering. She would benefit from the social advantage of having friends her own age.

Sarah was very kind, always putting other people ahead of herself, to the point where some people knew she could be used for almost anything. Sarah knew when she was being used, understanding more than she said about people - their agendas, motives, fears, and insecurities.

She is and always was a highly advanced intuitive empath, in this instance.

Dr. Armstrong recognized Sarah as the most intuitive and compassionate person she had ever encountered in her professional and personal life. Dr. Armstrong was adding to her research, where autism could produce, a human being, who's brain is wired differently, not only to become a child prodigy in music, math and other intelligence indicators – but also a brain hard wired for intuition, compassion and empathy. She believed Sarah was such a person, and she felt grateful to have Sarah as a living study, and as a friend.

She would never have thought, until she met Sarah, a teenager could be such an important and insightful friend. Though adults and children loved being in Sara's circle, Dr. Armstrong felt Sarah also needed to react with others her own age. It was, in her opinion, a good thing for Sarah to be in school.

Sarah was smart in school and easily answered most questions on almost any subject. She learned it was important to hold back and not be a know-it-all smart ass. She moved her focus to the same level as her teenage friends, to ensure their acceptance of her, and also her acceptance of them. She didn't want them to feel inferior in any way. Sarah was their equal.

Her friends in school could always count on Sarah to finish their homework assignments while they pursued the "really important" and happier things like hanging out with friends down at the mall.

Sarah was a nerd who was more interested in using her time to pursue knowledge, rather than hanging at the mall or spending endless hours in gaming and social media -based internet platforms. She took her time seriously, realizing it was a linear construct, as a base carrier of memories. She realized also, if it weren't for memories, time would be a useless thing. Her goal - to create as many good memories as possible, for everyone involved.

She loved to read and explore new ideas and though she'd gone to the mall with her friends to see what the attraction was, she found it totally boring and a waste of time. She always ended up in the bookstore looking through the "true crime", "self-help", "psychology" and "world religions" sections. She was interested in anything that added to her knowledge of the human condition. Every book was an event, reported for the benefit of sequential beings – a sharing of memories, actions, consequences, atonement, entertainment and health.

After a while Sarah's friends didn't even ask her to go with them since she was such a bore on the social level.

They all agreed she was a sweet and awesome friend who could always be counted on during times of need. None of them would ever give Sarah up as a loving friend. She was one of those amazing people, who they could trust with their deepest feelings and occurrences, without judgment. Always only a helping compassion, and understanding - a tear and a touch, a hug with new hope, ensuring things would get better and it wasn't their fault.

Sarah glided through high school, learning an appreciation regarding the social expectations, for a person of her age. This was a great help in many situations, to diminish her responses, to be age appropriate rather than knowledge and feelings appropriate. There is no advantage in showing pride or arrogance for any sequential being.

Sarah was voted valedictorian by the senior classes, as she graduated with high honors, to the thrill of Debbie, Barry and Dr. Armstrong. They felt pride was okay in certain situations.

Sarah gave the shortest speech in the history or her school, at the graduation ceremony.

She stood up to the great applause of all in attendance, walked to the podium and simply stated.

"My fellow classmates and graduates, as you step out, remember four things:

First – we're all responsible for our own happiness. Making some-one else responsible is a great burden to bestow, on the ones who love you and the ones you love – Also it never works.

Second – we're all responsible for our own consequences. If you make, a decision, the consequences are yours, - if you tell a lie, every consequence resulting from that lie, to everyone involved, belongs to you. One of our greatest challenges will be to take ownership of our chosen acts and the resulting consequences. This can be sad.
Third – Before everything else, and everyone else – BE KIND. Kindness is the greatest gift, we're able, to keep on giving.
Sarah paused to add some effect as if she had forgotten her speech... ah the fourth is:
Go FORTH and multiply! –and, THANK YOU ALL, FOR THE PAST FOUR YEARS!"
Her friends and family stood up and cheered.
It had been ten-years since her start with Dr. Armstrong.
Sarah had an uncanny ability to immediately find empathy with strangers and friends alike.
She kept most of her feelings to herself since she knew most people became agitated and wary when Sarah talked to them as if she had known them for years after only one meeting.
There was a certain amount of non-comfort and denial, as Sarah went right to the heart of the matter of things people were worried about.
At first there was delight, then fear, since this girl could in a matter of meeting someone for an hour, be talking about the darkest secrets of their lives. Sarah found almost everyone had a skeleton of some sort or another in their proverbial "closets".
She could disarm people to the point where they wanted to tell all. Sarah never judged.
Sarah wanted to continue her education, studying psychology and theology; her dream was to eventually get her PhD in both subjects. She then wanted to do research and teach at the university level.
Dr. Armstrong was a positive influence in her life, and they had become friends, in the truest sense of the word.
Sarah first started working with Dr. Armstrong as a student volunteer, then was offered a part time paid position – she had become an asset to the center, showing great patience and compassion, working with both the adults and the children under care.

During their early sessions, Dr. Armstrong had become very impressed with Sarah's ability to understand the conditions of other patients in her care.

Her studies included the metaphysical aspects of living since she knew science, though very important to the ones who pursued it, could never answer all the questions life provided. Most science was time and space based and that was fine since time and space controlled all physical events. Sequence though was a delusion and she took it upon herself to delve further into non-physical occurrences. She understood the concepts of relativity, unified field, classical and quantum physics. She did feel conversations on ideas like string theory were closer to the essence of us, since those ideas brought vibration and other dimensions, into the mix.

Sarah knew, waves of different colors and intensities, were primordial constructs, in the manifestation of her ability to "read" the feelings and concerns of others. She knew through her living experience.

Intuitively to her, the speed of light in the sequential being instance, was the fastest speed possible within a classical physics term of reference.

Einstein's equations involved the mathematical relationships based in classical physics. Einstein was a classical physicist.

Quantum physics, the study of the tiny, was a bit different, but Sarah felt the physicists in this field, currently made themselves less than they could be, still wearing chains of blue skies as the frame of reference. There is an essence above this frame, where time and distance have no meaning at all.

Though Sarah didn't consider either classical or quantum physics to be as important as her relationships to sequential beings, she knew they were important in her understanding of moving to and from different instances of events making up conscious experience of life – past, present and future. The five senses of touching, seeing, hearing, smelling and tasting – are basic to the understanding of the physical dimensions we live in. But Sarah knew of neuron senses involving, balance oxygenation, temperature, and more which brought further inherent metrics to the fore. We are better physical instruments than we believe to be. Of course, Sarah did not mention

the aesthetic senses involving consciousness and feelings. Not yet anyway.
When she tried to talk with her friends about these topics, most rolled their eyes as they listened. Most had no interest in the esoteric – their greatest interest was focused on their own lives, and the "unfair" trials and tribulations they were being put through. Most didn't consider the fact they were resolving their own consequences.
How could one start a discussion about things based on intuition, at least opening up the possibility things could exist beyond time and space?
The only way she thought was to bring in the essence of thought.
Dr. Armstrong was a good friend, well educated, - a professor and a professional practitioner in her leading-edge field – A person she could vet her ideas upon. Dr. Armstrong was happy to be her sounding board.
"I have come up with two questions" Sarah told Dr. Armstrong.
"I am trying to find the primordial quality of existence and the two background constants in everything we do involve time and thought."
"Ok" Dr. Armstrong responded. "What are your questions?"
"The first one is - Could time exist without thought?
The second one is - Could thought exist without time?" Sarah smiled as Dr. Armstrong pondered.
"Hmmm" said Dr. Armstrong. "What happened to space? You always are talking about time and space and thought. Don't you consider space as a primordial possibility anymore?" Dr. Armstrong laughed.
"No" Sarah replied. "Space is simply a function of time, and therefore cannot be primordial."
"Well." Dr. Armstrong started. "I think time could exist without thought and thought could also exist without time."
"Wrong" Sarah laughed. "Think more about it. Please take my question more seriously. I need to know the reason for your responses – not just pontifical and unsupported conclusions."
"Pardon me Sarah," Dr. Armstrong said smiling, "I will get back to you on this, when I get some time to put more thought to it."
With that Sarah got up said goodbye and went out to do her duties in the ward.

As Sarah walked out of the room Dr. Armstrong watched this young lady in the long dark 'peasant' skirt with the white ruffled blouse walk away. Sarah had blossomed into a beautiful woman. Her thick and naturally blond hair complimented her light complexion and rosy cheeks with a set of beautiful blue eyes. Sarah was about five foot eight and weighed about one hundred and twenty pounds. She was slender and long legged developing in the hips and breasts just the way she should.

"You're turning into a beauty, dear Sarah", Dr. Armstrong whispered under her breath and she realized how proud she was of this young woman who was once a patient but was now a precious friend.

Adrian, under Dr. Armstrong's care, had been diagnosed as being too dangerous to be out in the general public. He was dangerous to himself and to others. His parents tried for years to get through to Adrian but had given up on him during his mid-teens since he continually threatened his younger brother and sister.

Holding a knife to his sister's throat while promising everyone in the room he was going to cut her from ear to ear was the last straw.

The police were at the scene and were ready to take Adrian out at the first sign of blood, holding back only on the pleading of Adrian's mother. She walked over and gently took the knife from him breaking down holding both of her children in her arms and sobbing. Adrian loved his mother and his little sister too.

Adrian's birth had been a joy filled event - having children was the dream of Tom and Susan from the start of their marriage.

Adrian was the centre of their universe being the only child until he was three years old. Tom and Susan decided to have more children. Melissa was born in January and Alan was born in December of the same year.

While things were normal for the most part, Adrian had a cruel streak in him and would constantly torment the cat and the dog, not in a playful way but in a hurtful way.

By the time Adrian was 11 years old both family pets knew to stay out of his way.

He had power fantasies and always, explored the darker sites on the Internet - Sites showing photographs of autopsies and war crimes, rapes and dismemberment, car accidents and airplane crashes. He

had a fixation with death, and in Adrian's mind he was not alone since web site counters were in the millions of visitors.
How could he be abnormal if this many people were interested in what he was interested in?
In his mind, his sister Melissa deserved to die since she hadn't done as she was told. He told her to clean her room and she told him he was not her boss. All hell broke loose as he proved to her that he was the strongest and therefore was her boss.
Melissa and Alan were both scared of their big brother.
On other occasions, Adrian was the sweetest person in the world. He always saved his money to buy Christmas and birthday presents for his family and was always thrilled when they hugged him and kissed him for being such a thoughtful person.
Sometimes the money to buy the presents had been stolen but Adrian didn't care about that.
Finally, Adrian couldn't relate to anyone and had been diagnosed to be suffering from paranoid schizophrenia.
"I am not a bad person" Adrian told Dr. Armstrong. "I just get frigging mad when people don't do what they are supposed to be doing."
He was 25 years old, with "big" hair looking like it had never been combed. His blue eyes were intense. Most other patients in the ward were afraid of him, since he always talked about gruesome gore and death. Adrian knew anatomy as well as some surgeons since he had intensely studied books and internet sites dealing with the human body. Dr. Armstrong thought he would've made a great pathologist if it weren't for his uncontrollable behavior, which could surface at any time for the smallest of reasons.
Sarah liked Adrian and always thought him to be a victim of life, realizing at the same moment – we all are.
He was intelligent and thought more on abstract levels than anyone she had ever met. To her his obsession with death, pain, misery, control and body parts was the result of a deep routed fear of losing control. The body and all non-played parts left after death, was something to be pondered, since it was the final state of all of us and no one could control it. Death leaves things undone and unsaid sometimes. It can be sad.
Sarah talked to Dr. Armstrong about Adrian's condition. She cautioned Sarah not to jump to conclusions.

"Most psychiatrists spend years in university learning this rule. It is not what you think personally about a patient that counts, it is about where this patient fits into the current knowledge base of what we know about psychosis and the human condition.' Dr. Armstrong explained.

"You have a few years of study yet, before you are able to give your opinion on the cause of aberrant behavior." Dr. Armstrong said in a motherly way.

Sarah thought differently, since she firmly believed there is a missing dimension in the learning prescriptions of universities and such. Knowledge is universal and universities and such do not have a corner on truth. We're all part of the same collective, and the rules of religion and tradition are more dogmatic due to the egos of those who run various institutions. Sarah included the hierarchy of professors and institutions in the mix, since some egos were the cause of the greatest damage.

Sarah thought all people should be able to participate in the search for truth, and when found, be given respect for finding it. Most institutions were more interested in maintaining the status quo, since the elders, felt comfortable in that space. Innovation suffered, since change became a challenge and a threat.

She intuitively knew knowledge and beliefs continually changed. Newton's proofs were shattered by Einstein; the Earth was not flat, no-one really believed Freud anymore, and the earth was not the centre of the universe.

She'd met people whose degrees were more impressive than they turned out to be. But they'd gone through the system getting their professional designations, usually incapable of thinking an original thought. Of course, there were some exceptions to the rule.

Universities did have great value though, since sometimes, a student would surface going against the grain of the pious and found a 'new' truth which shattered their self-important bias.

She remembered Oscar Wilde stating, 'every truth causes a scandal!' What a truth that was and what a scandal it had caused.

Sarah closed her eyes and visualized the grave site of poor Oscar at Père Lachaise in Paris. She felt Oscar's pain and his thoughts came to her as he walked the always circular path in Reading Jail. His words came to her and filled her with his sadness:

'But neither milk-white rose, nor red
May bloom in prison-air;
The shard, the pebble, and the flint,
Are what they give us there:
For flowers have been known to heal
A common man's despair.'

'Even freedom is a captured state of thought, dear Oscar.' Sarah whispered to herself. We're all prisoners in different sets of cages – most self-made.

Sarah could only be patient with Dr. Armstrong since she had the shackled anchor of a formal education attached to her intellect.

Sarah would talk with Adrian first, as she usually did.

She didn't judge in any way the things he told her - accepted every one of his beliefs as a plausible truth.

As far as she was concerned, Adrian was behaving as he should; acting out his fears in fantasies which overflowed sometimes to the sequential side of things.

He was perplexed by sequence.

People in general didn't trust unusual behavior since it was a threat to their daily routines. Most people wanted to live life without problems and would gladly turn away and ignore anything or anyone who made their lives even a little bit more complicated than they thought it should be.

People like Adrian were an intrusion to normalcy and they probably deserved whatever pain they had, due to some universal plan of 'what comes around goes around'.

Put them away and let the shrinks take care of them.

Most people were happier with a TV sitcom or an afternoon soap opera where they could watch fantasy lives without having to interact directly in any way. Most people Sarah found, would rather watch a football game or baseball game or hockey game than take the time to talk to their children or pay attention to their spouse. Most people live life as intellectual hermits, where their true self never comes out for a breath of fresh air.

All the "isms" like spiritualism, communism, capitalism, socialism, fostered and promoted mass thought based on the dogma of some prophet or guru. Every 'ism' also promoted a select few – the selective of the collective were leaders and, in most cases, proved

to be false superior beings continually impressed by their own importance, while they whittled the wood of the 'common' person into the shape which best promoted their own agendas.
"Every ism creates a schism". Sarah said.
"Exactly!" exclaimed Adrian.
"Sheep are shit!!" he went on, "And I get so tired of fighting those frigging assholes who tell me there is something wrong with me, just because I don't have the same god dammed frigging interests that they do. I couldn't give a flying frig, for the romp in the pomp these people go through - they think they are so god dammed superior just because they work their asses off to get a house that looks just like every other frigging house on the proverbial block! I don't want a god dammed house on frigging Bland Avenue!"
"That is where security seems to come from though" Sarah said.
"Secure as manure on a heap, if you ask me." Adrian hissed. "They are all going to frigging die and that is the end of that crap!"
"You're going to die too." Sarah said softly.
"Well at least I will go out fighting, not like some frigging pansy-ass who gets his name in the god dammed obituary column where everybody says he is the most boring frigger on the block and everybody loved him!"
Adrian stood up and took his clothes off. Sarah didn't mind, and she had never told him to cover himself like the orderlies continually did. If he wanted to be naked, so be it.
Dr. Armstrong was watching through the glass partition which gave her an unobstructed view of the entire 'social area' and once again she was amazed by the casual interaction shared by Adrian and Sarah. Adrian never acted out violently whenever Sarah was around, - Dr. Armstrong wondered if Sarah had some inexplicable way of disarming his fear.
She stopped worrying about Adrian's continual habit of taking his clothes off then putting them back on again at least twenty times per day. Sarah didn't seem to notice either way.
It was just another one of Adrian's compulsions by which he could prove he had control over some aspect of his life. The fact that it pissed off some of the mono-morons made it even better.
Adrian's feelings for Sarah were becoming complex. He always looked to see if Sarah was in the ward and spent most of his time

thinking about her. She was the first person he'd met who didn't continually tell him to smarten up and get his act together.

As he looked at Sarah sitting across from him, he suddenly had a compulsion to touch her. He was scared to make the first move when Sarah reached over and took his hand, kissing it then cradling his open palm against her right cheek with her hand covering his.

"We can hold hands if you want Adrian" Sarah said, as she once again drew his hand to her lips and kissed it.

"I think I friggin love you Sarah" Adrian said softly as he put his entire brain to the focus of feeling the soft warmness of her check.

"I love you too, Adrian." Sarah said softly. "I have always loved you."

Adrian pulled his hand away, stood up, put his clothes back on, then sat down again.

He reached his hand out to Sarah and she once again kissed it then cradled it back against her cheek.

Sarah looked at Adrian and said softly "Let's just close our eyes and relax together. We can try to feel each other's thoughts and help each other in a quiet, relaxing meditation."

Adrian closed his eyes and felt peace of spirit come over him as if he was cuddled up with his mother at a very young age. It was pure serenity as his mind started to drift, feeling totally relaxed, warm and secure.

His mind's eye slowly opened to images of a farmhouse burning as three children screamed from the top widows. There was no escape. He then moved into the room where the children were trapped. Two young girls and the older boy were brother and sisters, leaning out of the window screaming for help, when there was no one to help them. The heat and flames moved swiftly closer until the night clothes started to catch fire. Sometimes there is just no one around help, and only one outcome is left! Tears formed in Adrian's eyes and solely eased their way down his cheeks. Sarah was crying too.

The floor gave way as the children fell into the flames and cinders, burning in the lower part of the house. Adrian watched and knew he was the older brother who though responsible for his younger sisters, hadn't been unable to save them.

He felt the peace of the fire as it consumed the lives of these three young ones and realized some things couldn't be changed.

Sometimes we have no control as we surrender to the event. Sometimes survival isn't an option.
Next, he imagined Sarah sitting with him in a room, constructed of wood as a fireplace burned in the corner providing warmth and light, producing dancing shadows on the surrounding walls. Sarah wore a white cascading robe, her blonde hair, full and shimmering, flowing over her shoulders as she looked into his eyes. She had the bluest eyes he had ever seen. These eyes held his spirit as she spoke to him without words; they exuded forgiveness and love. Adrian never wanted to leave the sereneness of this place.
With a sudden feeling of falling he jerked awake, still holding Sarah's hand.
Adrian started to sob uncontrollably. Sarah moved closer to him and held him in her arms.
"I had a dream Sarah" he sobbed. "I had a dream and you were in it."
"I know Adrian" Sarah whispered. "I was there with you."
Dr. Armstrong walked quickly towards Sarah and Adrian concerned for Sarah's safety. She should not be holding Adrian in this way. As she got closer, she saw Adrian sobbing in Sarah's arms. She stopped, giving the two of them another minute of being alone together.
Sarah stroked Adrian's hair, as a mother would do to a small child, who had fallen and scraped his knee.
Sarah broke the embrace and turned to Dr. Armstrong, motioning her to come closer. "Adrian is ok" Sarah said, "we just had a fairly intense experience."
"Would you like to talk about it, Adrian?" Dr. Armstrong asked sympathetically.
"I want to talk with Sarah" Adrian said. "She's the only one who understands me."
Dr. Armstrong asked Sarah to join her in her office as soon as she was available. Sarah stood up and swept her hand in the direction of the office and said, "We can do it now."
"Sarah will be back soon" Dr. Armstrong said as she turned and walked towards her office as Sarah followed behind her.
"Sit down Sarah" Dr. Armstrong said as she moved behind her desk and sat in her own chair.
Sarah sat down waiting for the questions to start.

"Well" Dr. Armstrong said, "What happened out there just now?"
"I meditated with Adrian and we went back to an experience he had in another instance." Sarah said softly.
"Another instance!" Dr. Armstrong said incredulously.
"I know you don't want to believe in such things Dr. Armstrong, but I must tell you there are other places where we all experience existence. Adrian has been affected by a horrific event which happened to him while living in a different frame of space and time."
"Sarah" Dr. Armstrong said softly, "we have procedures and medicines we must follow in cases like Adrian. We practice psychiatry here based on our knowledge of psychology. We don't practice witchcraft or delve into meta-physics. I must forbid you from interfering with the treatment of my patients since you may do more damage than you may be aware."
"But Dr. Armstrong" Sarah continued, "I am not practicing anything, I just asked Adrian to close his eyes and meditate with me. He experienced certain images in his mind, and I experienced the same images."
"Sarah" Dr. Armstrong said "There has been so much study done in this field and it has not produced results like you're talking about. You probably just thought you experienced the same thing because you wanted to.
After talking with Adrian, you most likely surmised the things he had seen and filled in the gaps within your own mind."
Sarah was happy to finally share her abilities.
"But" Sarah continued patiently, "I have not talked to Adrian about the images he saw."
"Then how do you know that you've seen, the same images?" Dr. Armstrong asked.
"I was there with him." Sarah explained.
"Ok, what did Adrian 'see'?" Dr. Armstrong asked.
Sarah described in detail the burning house with two little girls and one little boy screaming from the upper window. She related how the floor had collapsed and the children had died.
"Adrian was the little boy and he was totally helpless and couldn't save his sisters." Sarah explained. "He has carried that pain into this instance and cannot shake his morbid obsession with death. This must be resolved.

He feels no matter how he lives his life he'll never have control over death, and the pain death is capable of causing."

Dr. Armstrong looked at Sarah and sighed. "You really believe what you're telling me, don't you?"

"I do" agreed Sarah, "And Adrian is going to recover."

"Ok" Dr. Armstrong said slowly "But you do realize Sarah, in some cases, like Adrian's by the way, there is a chemical imbalance involved, and sometimes it's genetic. All problems are not curable by therapy alone. In some cases, like Adrian's we must provide medication which adds balance back into the chemical structure of the brain. We have determined he has a chronic problem in his endocrine system, which causes a hormone imbalance."

Dr. Armstrong was trying to be gentle with Sarah. She remembered the troubles Sarah had as a child and didn't want to take any chances of having her relapse into the withdrawal she previously experienced. Sarah had always been a delicate child and though she was being gentle, she also didn't want to feed any delusions Sarah may have about how things work. That would be totally unprofessional and counterproductive. Though she had watched Sarah literally grow up over the past few years, she knew there was something special about the empathy she felt for people. However, she couldn't let her delude herself into thinking she was like the evangelist faith healers on tv. To Dr. Armstrong, this would be tantamount to encouraging her to live in yet another layer of fantasy.

"Do you mind if I talk to Adrian in private" Dr. Armstrong asked.

"No, of course not" Sarah said with a smile, "But I just want to let you know I am not delusional, and I don't think of myself as a faith healer in the way that you're thinking.

I am ready to start dipping into the essence of who I am. So many people need to be helped, in their transcendence from this instance."

Dr. Armstrong asked Sarah to please sit down again for another minute.

"How did you know I was thinking about delusions and faith healers? Was that just a conclusion you drew from our experience together?" Dr. Armstrong asked with a slight smile.

"Well, I just pick up things and don't question them when they come into my head." Sarah said thoughtfully. "As you were sitting quietly there, I felt your thoughts. I usually keep my feelings to myself, but I think it's time I started helping people. I know I can.
It is ok Dr. Armstrong - I love you and I realize you find this hard to believe. Just watch me and I may change your mind. Giving me some latitude, may change your attitude.", Sarah said with a smile and a twinkle in her eye.
Dr. Armstrong stood up and walked Sarah to the door. "Thank you, Sarah, I love you too and I will watch to see the healing that you do,"
"Could you please ask Adrian to come over?" Dr. Armstrong asked.
"Of course, Dr. Armstrong." Sarah said quietly as she reached out and gave the good doctor a hug.
Adrian talked with Dr. Armstrong for about an hour and Dr. Armstrong was taken back by the serenity of the discussion. Adrian talked about the dream he had and provided the same story as Sarah. He never once used the word 'frigging' during the entire hour of conversation and this was a first. He also kept his clothes on for the entire time.
He told Dr. Armstrong about the room with the fireplace in the corner where Sarah was dressed in a white gown. He told Dr. Armstrong he was in love with Sarah and wanted to get better for her.
This was a turning point for Dr. Armstrong and Adrian. He had never spoken so articulately about himself or the problem he perceived were his to solve.
"Thank you, Adrian" Dr. Armstrong said quietly, "I have enjoyed our conversation and I want you to know how much it means to me, sharing your thoughts with me."
"You're welcome, Dr. Armstrong," Adrian replied, "I want to get better!"
Dr. Armstrong was impressed and knew she had to discuss Sarah's "gift" further. It was imperative for her to find out what had happened here.
Dr. Armstrong picked up the phone, and called Debbie, to see if she would mind if Sarah had dinner with her that evening. Debbie readily agreed and Dr. Armstrong told her she would have her daughter home by 10 pm.

Sarah poked her head through the office door and with a broad smile asked Dr. Armstrong if she would like to go out for dinner tonight.
"Yes" Dr. Armstrong said, "I was just on the phone to your mother asking if she would mind."
"I know" said Sarah as she turned and walked back over to Adrian.
Dr. Armstrong picked up the phone and called 'Sarah's on Dubbin Street. She knew this was Sarah's favorite restaurant - not only because it was named 'Sarah's', but also because it had some of the best vegetarian dishes in New Orleans.
Sarah had been a vegetarian for as long as Dr. Armstrong knew her. She hated the thought of eating the flesh of an animal which was killed for human consumption. Sarah thought all life was sacred and thus only ate vegetarian meals. Dr. Armstrong made the reservation for 7 pm.
Adrian sat next to Sarah on the large couch by the window. He loved to sit here in the early afternoon since the warmth and light of the sun, bathed him in its shining glow. To the chagrin of the orderlies he always opened the Venetian blinds making the entire room brighter than it normally was. Dr. Armstrong had long ago called off the 'frigging dogs' as Adrian called them, and let him enjoy his daily dose of afternoon sunshine.
Sarah and Adrian sat in the middle of the sunbeam feeling the warmth on the back of their heads as they talked.
"I want to get better for you Sarah" Adrian said softly.
"Get better for yourself Adrian" Sarah replied. "You're the one who has to live your life, just like I am the one who has to live mine."
"I always want to be with you, Sarah" Adrian said shyly.
"That is how you feel now, but situations change as situations change." Sarah replied with a smile.
Adrian knew he would do anything for Sarah and from that day on he thought only about making himself better, so he could get out of this place. It would be a hard go and he knew it, since magical cures were not the norm of the day in a place like this.
He had been placed here due to a court order, duly signed by three psychiatrists including Dr. Armstrong. He was labeled as a dangerous person though he knew in his heart, he would never have cut his little sister. He was acting out – crying for help.

Adrian baited the cops to shoot him. Though if they did, he would have created a horrible and bloody scene, his family would never forget. He felt ashamed for the first time in his life about what he had done, and he wanted to make it up.
“Conscience is the first tenant of Love” Sarah said as Adrian sat thinking, while enjoying the company and the sunlight.
He’d never felt such peace, since his mind always raced, while thought after thought was quickly displaced, and anxiety ruled, and would finally release, into an angry scene. Adrian wanted to understand his anger. He wanted to understand his feeling of total helplessness.
“I have to tell my little brother and sister I love them Sarah. They must really hate me for the way I have treated them.” Adrian said as he bowed his head. “I don’t want to be a hateful person, but I just didn’t think anything was worth anything since it could be taken away as quickly as it had been given.”
Adrian looked directly at Sarah, “I have always been so scared to love any one because I knew I could lose them in a split second.”
“I know” Sarah said, “People think they have control of everything when they actually have control of nothing, unless they have the will to just let it be.”
“Exactly” Adrian replied. “What is the point of thinking you can control life. You may as well just have faith. Whatever will happen, will happen and there is nothing we can frigging do about it!” Adrian felt his anger start to rise again and he realized how much he hated feeling this way.
“Calm down Adrian” Sarah said as she took his hand once again. “Let’s just close our eyes and think good thoughts and visualize you getting better. You may be surprised to hear this, but many sequential instances exist where you’re not sick.”
Adrian closed his eyes feeling the wonderful heat of the sun behind him. His thoughts took him to a place in the middle of a garden where roses, growing on stems having no thorns, stretched towards the blueness of the sky. White and red roses formed a mixed and intermingled pattern in soil so warm, black and rich. He wasn’t standing on the ground but rather was hovering over this serene and silent place. He looked at the pale blue water of the pond and instantly moved towards it, feeling life teeming in every corner of his

mind. Mature white swans with signets following, leaving small waves rippling always behind where they had been. The sun's bright warmth fed all life in equal parts. He looked at the small fishes swimming just below the surface and as he looked, he found himself moving with them, easily breathing under the water, feeling as one, with each living form.
Adrian's time and space changed, and he found himself at a picnic with a red and white checkered blanket, under an oak tree, shared by two little girls who sat beside him smiling, eating the food from a large picnic basket. Then each stood up and came to him, kissing him on each cheek, which felt like a light breeze against his skin. He was forgiven only because he thought he had to be. Adrian put his arms around both children and held them closely to his chest as he whispered "I love you I love you" to each.
"Just relax and breathe deeply" he heard Sarah whisper from some place close, yet far away.
"Breathe deeply as you sleep, dear Adrian." Sarah sighed.
Sarah gently let go of Adrian's hand. He was asleep.
She had other patients to attend to, but none were like Adrian. With Adrian, Sarah knew he was curable just through his own evaluation and forgiveness of himself. Others on the ward didn't have the same options. Dr. Armstrong told her not to think of the people on the ward as her patients but rather as her friends. Some of her friends would never be able to live normal lives in this frame of reference, but of course, there were many more frame and many more references.
As Sarah went about her daily chores ensuring everyone was as comfortable as could be, she noticed Brad looking at her again. She could feel his thoughts and they were not pleasant. Brad had the capacity to be very good or very bad and these two conflicts always fought against each other in his mind. Outwardly, he knew exactly what was expected of him and everyone thought he was one of the nicest guys anyone would ever want to meet. Brad had another side as we all do, but his was a bit more grotesque than most. This didn't make him any worse or any better than anyone else. He was just more extreme in his expression of things.
Where Adrian had a fixation on death and the non-control over it, Brad had a fixation on death and his control over it. Brad knew he

had the capacity to kill, and therefore he was the one to decide who would live and who would die. He felt godlike sometimes, holding the power to kill or let live.

The first time he used this power was as a child, during the hatch of ladybugs which suddenly appeared in multitudes as the sun shone in early spring, on the back porch where he was playing. Brad was about six years old at the time - he started stomping on the ladybugs squishing them. He realized he was the one deciding which ladybugs lived and which ones died on the bottom of his boot.

By his own actions he proved himself to be correct in this assessment.

He had the power to decide which ladybug lived and which ladybug died. From this one experience, Brad imagined himself to be the king of life and death, starting with insects, then moving to small trees growing in the forest, then onto frogs in the pond, and finally graduating to a neighborhood cat he killed with a sling shot, when he was thirteen years old.

Brad's family were hunters always taking the deer hunt trip to Texas every spring.

Brad was a good shooter - any deer having the bad luck to appear anywhere near Brad and his .308 magnum scoped rifle, was toast.

Brad loved venison and catfish - he made sure there was enough venison in the freezer to last all year round. Hunting was part of the fantasy and the rifle was just another tool used in the extension of his power. He loved to shoot squirrels with his rifle and laughed as they exploded from the hit.

This power over everything fantasy took many years to fully develop and no one knew about it except for Brad and Sarah. Brad didn't know Sarah knew though.

Brad worked as an orderly in the hospital for the past four years and was considered one of the best.

Throughout the years since Sarah had recovered from the pit she experienced early in life. She had the ability to pick these types of things up about people. She knew what people were thinking, and what they were doing, was in some cases totally different and usually hidden. People loved their secret lives.

Sarah realized when she met a person who had a 'clear conscience', it was rare, and these types of people were thought to be the naïve ones.

Some even called 'meek and non-assertive' by others. Meekness was a sign of weakness.

Sarah knew these ones were the most developed sequential beings on the planet. These ones would easily sacrifice themselves and their own agendas, for the benefit of another without expectation of any reward or pat on the back.

They were not impressed by money or material wealth, but were impressed by kindness and sharing, compassion and caring.

These ones, gave in privacy, as a conscious decision to allow the other sequential being the chance to grow as a person.

Living in time, experiencing sequential events – eventually leading to a mantra of thinking higher.

The ones with the clear conscience were the ones who truly loved their fellow human being more than they loved their own life. These were the ones living in the higher self, ready to give all they had to anyone who asked for it. In some cases, the manipulators amongst us callously, untruthfully and violently just took what they felt they could.

The meek ones were like angels to children, and like children to wolves.

Brad was not an angel to children.

Some of his patients were so drugged up most of the time, who would know or care if he "copped a feel" when no-one was looking.

One of the newer patients on the ward – Cindy - who at 19 years of age, felt helpless, distressed and hopeless coping with her life. She was suicidal, but as Brad had noticed, was truly a one hundred percent young, nubile, female, with no problems in the physical department.

He helped her during the first week of her admission and really got to know her during one of the night shifts when she was in a drugged up comatose state, giving him full access to her total body. He loved the easy access gowns, worn by the patients.

It was two in the morning when he sneaked into Cindy's room, easily done when there was only one nurse on the ward for the night shift.

He made sure she was totally non-responsive to speech and touch, then moved the blankets down, till he had complete access to her body. He slowly lifted the hem of her gown upwards using his special little flashlight, for a visual examination. She was beautiful and tonight she was his. He loved his job.

After moving her legs apart, a tad, licked his fingers, then slowly rubbed the lips of her vagina and slowly inserted his middle finger. She was very dry. he made a mental note, to always bring some lubrication with him on his nightly treasure hunts. He took a picture with his phone and pushed her hospital gown all the way up, exposing her breasts. He was impressed. She was well endowed, with perky little nipples waiting for his tongue and lips. He took another picture, pulled his zipper down and released his hard cock, then took her right hand, wrapped her fingers around it, pretending she was his willing partner. He squeezed her hand around his cock and stroked it a few times. As he started to suck on Cindy's nipples, licking the fingers of his right hand again, then moving it back to her exposed vagina.

To Brad, this was heaven on earth, a non-responsive female body for him to use as he pleased.

He played with Cindy for the next hour, including trying to penetrate her vagina, but she was not wet enough to make it enjoyable for him. 'Dry bitch!' he snarled to himself. He needed some release, so he put one knee on the bed, starting to masturbate, over her angelic face. He came with three groans, as his come streamed onto her face. He took another picture – got off the bed, reached for some wet wipes, cleaning her face. He then pulled her gown down, pulled up the blanket, checked everything over to ensure he left no evidence he had been there, including putting the wet face wipes into his pocket flush it when he could.

Brad left the room with his wet wipes, his flashlight and phone in his pocket.

He sighed, she was a beauty, and he believed situations like these to be perks of the job.

Usually when he tried to penetrate his little treasures, he took precautions, against catching sexually transmitted diseases, from some 'little piece of street meat'.

Brad was experienced in getting away with things he did in private. He was full of secrets.

If he kicked the dog when no one was home, who would know and what difference did it make. If he fucked the young patients when no one was around, what difference would it make? They were there for him to enjoy, and who really cared.

Brad lived in the lower three glands. Illegal sex was the best sex as far as he was concerned since he was the one with the power. It was exciting and he preferred his 'partner' to be out of it, while he 'did' them, since there was absolutely no involvement on their part.

Nothing was complicated and it was always about him and only him. He could do whatever he wanted and make them his uncomplaining playthings.

Brad loved his job and was sure other orderlies were doing the same as he was.

He couldn't believe his luck in getting this job on the 'G' ward.

He had fucked almost every patient, who was even close to being attractive and the best part of it was, the doctors provided the drugs allowing him to do it.

Brad found it especially good when a family member visited their precious daughter or wife or sister.

Brad acted like the angel sent from heaven during the visits while going over in his mind all he had done to the precious loved ones. He always gave the "Ah... it's just my job and I am happy to be able to help" line when thanked by the visitors for taking care of their loved ones. If they only knew!

There was one person, Brad didn't like and that was Adrian.

Likewise, Adrian didn't like Brad. To Adrian, Brad was some sort of weasel who manipulated and used people to his own end. To Adrian this was totally intuitive - he never liked Brad from the minute he had met him.

Brad couldn't help but fantasize about Sarah. He would love to just get her naked and use every inch of her and he promised himself that one day she would be his for the taking.

He was scared to approach her though - to him, women were better when you didn't have to talk to them and meet them in a normal way.

"Hi Sarah" Brad said with a broad smile, as she was getting some juice from the common kitchenette.
"Hi Brad" Sarah said softly.
"Ehmmm… I hope you don't take this as a come-on… but do you think it would be possible… Ehmmm… Could I take you out to dinner sometime Sarah" Brad asked, acting shyly?
"I would love to get to know you better. No strings attached, maybe, just dinner and a movie or something."
"That is really sweet of you" Sarah said, "but I have made it a rule never to date people I am working with. It has nothing to do with you, but it's a rule that I promised Dr. Armstrong I would keep – But it is sweet of you to ask."
'Cock teasing cunt!' Adrian thought as he smiled and said… "Oh ok, I just thought I would ask, no problem. I understand."
Sarah smiled back at him as she said "Thanks for understanding. It's nothing personal."
Sarah took her juice and walked back into the main ward to finish her shift.
'Sarah's ' was almost full as Sarah and Dr. Armstrong arrived at the entrance. The seating manager checked the reservation. "Yes, Dr. Armstrong, we have your favorite table over by the window."
Sarah and Dr. Armstrong followed the manager as she led them to their table. They sat down and glanced at the menu. Sarah would order the house special salad as she always did, and Dr. Armstrong decided on the seared tuna with Caesar salad.
"Sarah, I asked you out tonight because I want to know more about your ability to read people and to discuss your relationship with Adrian."
"Ask away Dr. Armstrong" Sarah smiled…
"Well… can you tell me something about this 'gift' you say you have?" Dr. Armstrong asked.
Sarah sat back in her chair and started talking.
"Ok - but I want you to keep an open mind and give me a chance to talk freely." Sarah said.
"I promise I will let you talk freely, and I will listen." Dr. Armstrong said sincerely.

Sarah took a deep breath and started. "Ok - where is the best place to start? First, I will give you some information about yourself in order to validate some of the other things I am going to tell you. Your mother's name was Lenora and she died when you were thirteen years old. Your father's name is Joseph and he is living in Detroit. You have two sisters named Veronica and Lynne and they each have two children. They are also living in Detroit."

"Are you two, ready to order?" the waitress asked with a bright inviting smile.

Dr. Armstrong quickly ordered the food, for them both, wanting to get back to the discussion.

"Ok, correct on all counts." Dr. Armstrong stated. She knew there was nothing in these facts any person seeking information would not be able to find out. She had talked with Sarah over the years about her family. She was not too impressed so far.

Sarah smiled and said, "I know, this is easily found information about you, but I just wanted to ease you into the discussion, with some facts, you can agree with." Sarah said with a smile, "Let's get a little deeper. You had brief affair with another psychiatrist twelve years ago and it was a lesbian relationship." Sarah said slowly.

"How did you know that?" Dr. Armstrong asked with surprise. She knew she had never told Sarah or anyone else except her therapist about this relationship.

"Uh... uh... Dr. Armstrong" Sarah smiled, "You agreed to let me talk while you listened. You have nothing to worry about since I have total respect for your privacy, and you're quite boring and normal in your secret adventures. I will never judge you.". Sarah smiled again.

"Ok," Dr. Armstrong said with a little more reservation. "Please continue."

"The woman you fell in love with is married to a doctor and they are still together living in Cary, North Carolina. You still talk to her often, but the affair is over. Her husband, Dr. Arnold Missic is a professor at North Carolina State University, and has been in a wheelchair for the past fifteen years as a result of an automobile accident.

He is paralyzed from the waist down and is bitter about his condition, sometimes blaming his wife, since she was the one driving, when they were hit by the drunk driver.

Arnold and Cathy have not had a sexual relationship since the accident - this is one of the reasons why you both got involved at the lower levels.
Cathy didn't think cheating with another woman was as serious as cheating with another man, since intercourse didn't occur."
The waitress came with a basket of bread and put it in front of them.
"Oh. I love the way they bake this stuff here," Sarah said with a smile as she reached over and put a slice of the warm treat on the small plate in front of her.
Sarah took some of the vegetarian garlic butter, spreading it onto the fresh bread, watching it melt into the surface. She picked it up and took a bite. "Mmmm."
"Please continue Sarah" Dr. Armstrong said in a professional tone.
"Please let me bring the question I asked you earlier today, into our conversation, since it's relevant to what we're talking about. - Thought is the primordial quality of life.
When you answered time could exist without thought, you were incorrect. All time involves sequence and sequence must be perceived. Time is the assimilation of sequential events, and thus can be defined.
Thought has no definition since it's not time based. We could relate thought to conscious awareness, where thought could be thought of, as the bridge between the now and eternal.
Therefore, thought is the primordial quality of life. Thought could exist outside of time, but time could not exist outside of thought, since all time, no matter how measured, involves a sequence – Thought assimilates, yet doesn't require sequence – it's essence is from a higher place."
Sarah looked over at Dr. Armstrong with a smile. "Can I butter one of these for you?" she asked as she picked up another slice of the cooling bread.
"Yes please" Dr. Armstrong said, "I would love one."
Sarah buttered two slices and handed one to Dr. Armstrong. "Excuse my fingers" she said with a broad smile.
Sarah ate her slice and continued.
"I mention thought and time since they are key to understanding the way things work.

All things thought can manifest in a time space creation. All creation is the result of thought. Thought has a universal context in time and space and that is why, for example, any person coming into this restaurant who is asked 'what is this?' Sarah picked up the water glass and held it above the breadbasket, "Would answer 'it is a glass' and if another person who just came in from England was asked 'what is this?' Sarah lifted the glass once more, "that person would also answer 'it is a glass'. Universally this object is defined as a 'glass' to any observer who looks at it. The molecules making up this glass have a time space relationship which is universally perceived as a glass by anyone who looks at it, within the same time space instance."

"Here you go" the waitress said as she put the house specialty salad and in front of Sarah and the seared tuna and smaller salad in front of Dr. Armstrong. "Is there anything else I can get you two?"

"I will have a glass of the house Chardonnay" said Dr. Armstrong.

"I will have a glass of iced tea." said Sarah.

"Coming right up!" beamed the waitress.

"Ok" Dr. Armstrong said, "Thought is the primordial quality and all created things are manifested in a universal time and space relationship. Is that what you're saying?"

"Yes" Sarah stated with authority. "Thought emanates, time animates the three dimensions below."

"This idea is old," Sarah, continued, " Take the stories of Jesus in the bible, when he healed, turned water into wine, or brought Lazarus back from the dead – any miracle you want to name, by any teacher or mystic prophet – emanates from a place of timeless faith, and animates as a sequential occurrence – an event. We have the ability to alter the universal aspects of objects and lives – in effect if we have conviction and faith, we can change time space relationships and therefore the perception of what reality is."

Dr. Armstrong and Sarah each poked their forks into their salad and raised it to their mouths.

Sarah finished chewing then continued "As you know, when I was a little girl, I had this recurring dream that some evil person was coming through my bedroom wall and wanted to take me away. To me the dream was real, and the evil was real. It turned out I was taken away but the place I was taken to, provided me with knowledge which I believe is universally true."

"I remember that Sarah." Dr. Armstrong interrupted, "And even though I believe, you were in a place, I think you were actually withdrawn from the world and your mind made up for its boredom, shall we say, by creating this fictional place."

"I love you so much Dr. Armstrong," Sarah smiled. "but I say with the greatest of respect for you and what you do, you must open your mind a bit, because there is a place on the edge of reality where thought interacts with time on a non-sequential basis.

The place I was in is real and my experiences are real. We sleep because we need to dream. Dreams are reality too, but not thick, four dimensional and sequential reality."

"Ok Sarah" I am sorry for interrupting, "Please continue."

"I have learned we're totally upside down in our cultures and life.

Our value system is out of kilter, and we're living on a very young planet.

By that I mean, there are older more advanced societies and cultures out there all at different levels of development. This may sound strange to someone with your training, but I say respectfully, if we're on a young planet then the sequential knowledge base is also young with lots to be learned yet."

Sarah paused and sipped her iced tea while Dr. Armstrong took a sip of her wine and ate a fork full of fish.

"Mmm... this is so good, Sarah." Dr. Armstrong said as she savored the flavor of her tuna.

"Imagine a universe where both good and evil is a path towards wisdom, through exercise and experience. Imagine the idea of Caine and Abel as different manifestations of the same Spirit, where the physical structures are put in place solely to negate all forms of 'self'. Imagine Caine and Abel as a representation of two distinct paths. Imagine a spectrum of events with 'all giving' at one end and 'all taking' at the other and the consequences lived out in sequence for every decision made. Caine is at one side of the spectrum while Abel is at the other. One burns the mantle of total self, while the other burns the mantle of total non-self."

"You're talking about karma, Sarah." Dr. Armstrong interrupted once more.

"In a way, you could call it karma, but on a universal scale. By universal I mean all things experienced which involve sequential cause and effect. Every action has an effect not only in one life instance but in all life instances... ripples on a pond require the interaction of all molecules of water in the pond - even the ones at the far edge, only because they are part of the same cohesion – the same membrane."
Sarah continued. "We're connected in both the higher and lower dimensions, and in the lower dimensions we think we are alone. We have a hunger – a need to feel we have a higher purpose.
For many, religion fills that need. We think we are children of God, and if God is love then we are all children of Love. We are special in our tribes and are part of something higher.
We feed our need, in the emanation of a higher, benevolent place of love worship animated as a church – a synagogue – a mosque – a forest clearing – a holy place where we meet our god. But we're tribal in our remedies. Our church is a bigger self – still separated from others, by our superior sense of our tribal self. Other gods are lesser gods – other tribes are lessor tribes.
The same occurs with nations – each country with a special niche – making each better in one aspect or another, from the rest. There's a built-in fear of differences, a need for secure territory, resources and material wealth to prove the worthiness of our choices taken, and the play-out of all consequences manifested. Some consequences take us deeper in, to a thicker and stickier place – where self is our priority – above all others. We kill, we steal, we manipulate and control, raping and cuckolding as we go. Power, digestion and self-preservation as we live in the lower three glands."
Sarah leaned back in her chair trying to find the words which best expressed the thoughts she was trying to parlay.
Dr. Armstrong had finished her meal. She tried to follow all Sarah was saying but small thought blocks continually surfaced in her mind negating Sarah's argument. To her, self-preservation and self-worth were the cornerstones of a healthy personality. Compassion and empathy were important traits but if these were not balanced by a great sense of self then surely a life path leading to abuse by others would be the result.
She had seen this binary waltz in too many patients to disregard it.

An abused person usually has low self-esteem and no self-worth. On the other hand, people who were too self-centered were also her patients. Surely a balance in self and non-self-centered traits was the best combination.
Sarah continued. "The best combination for someone living here and now is a balance between both, but here and now is not the end point of the journey."
Dr. Armstrong smiled and shook her head "Did you just read my thoughts again, Sarah?"
"No Dr. Armstrong." Sarah smiled back, "I don't read thoughts. I am called an '*Alter*' in some sequences. The sequence we're in doesn't have a name for what I am, yet.
Every sequential being is given the chance to give. The ones who have come into great wealth, are given the opportunity to provide a positive action in the lives of those who are here for their purpose.
The ones who have intellect, are given the opportunity to give to the ones who are here for their purpose.
Opportunities are provided and we create our personal sequence by our choices. Everything we have is a gift, and everything given is a gift.!
Trials and tribulations are a gift. They provide the opportunity for all of us – no matter what side we're on, to choose a consequence in everything we do, that is a positive and non-selfish action. Every day we're presented with the ability to love and forgive others or only love ourselves and use others."
"If I may interrupt you Sarah" Dr. Armstrong said, "What do you mean by 'in this sequence and 'in some sequences'? Also, how do you define 'God' and what do you mean you're an 'Altar'?"
"I don't use the word god, too often but when I do, it's because biblical terms in my explanation, provide an immediate reference, to the idea of unearthly and earthly constructs.
To me, the god of the bible is too small to describe the size of the playground, so to speak, we're playing in. The idea, God is Love, is the right vibration, but the actual bible is populated with the concerns and greed of sequential beings – in a tribal hierarchy. To me the ideal idea of God, is Love. I know, when love becomes more important than god, then there will be no further need for religion. Does that make sense to you?"

Dr. Armstrong answered, “Yes, and I am glad we’re not going to get into a great discussion about religion.”
Sarah continued, “Life’s quest to emanate kindness. Open kindness is the greatest gift we can give to one another. This is not the purview of science where every truth must be reduced to an equation, like $E=mc^2$. Empathy equals Morality times Compassion squared does not cut it, since we lose the precision of mathematics, in higher, non-sequential dimensions. Feelings don’t do math.
Kindness factors into outcomes, emanating from humane responses, as a manifestation from compassion. We know kindness is a truth, but we have no mathematics to support that truth. We know it and other aesthetic essences are truths – we experience them every day. Aesthetic essence is not currently the purview of science, though many scientists animate these aesthetic behaviors every day of their lives.
In my experience, thought is the builder – thought emanates then animates the four dimensions below.”
Dr. Armstrong was amazed that Sarah could articulate these ideas so well. “Your words are beautiful,” she said.
Sarah smiled and continued, “I wish I could use a more descriptive word than ‘essences’, but this is the closest word to the condition I am conveying to you.”
“I understand.’ Dr. Armstrong replied, as Sarah continued.
“We live our lives as if we had control over where we will be five minutes from now, and yet we’re continually given signs, this is not necessarily so.
Five minutes before a fatal car crash the participants almost never know they will be dead within ten minutes.
We forget life is always close to death - we forget there are universal consequences in play, which in the blink of an eye, will change our total perspective of who and what we are. In the final analysis in each instance, we are on loan to each other.
Sometimes we resonate through synchronous events in other frames of reference not yet perceived in the current sequence.
Some people settle for an answer which gives their psyche a sense of peace, yet the same seemingly random outcomes apply.”
Sarah took a sip of her iced tea, and wistfully asked Dr. Armstrong, “Am I boring you yet.”

"Not yet." Dr. Armstrong replied, "But I am biting my tongue, not wanting to interrupt your interesting stream of thoughts." Sarah smiled as Dr. Armstrong continued questioning the logic of it all.
"If the idea of God is Love and we're all part of Love's creation, why don't we all just call God, Love, in all religious constructs?"
Sarah continued to expand the idea of love and God. "Each time we choose to give of ourselves we embrace the idea of God, because we have chosen to Love.
Each time we feel compassion and act upon it, we embrace the idea of God, since we have manifested Love.
Love is always the child inside we're so afraid of losing.
To love or not to love, is a freedom of choice, of which we're all endowed.
Each time we choose only for the betterment of ourselves, our family, or our tribe - we diminish the growth possibility of each circle.
We are the cause and effect of love.
We each are given sequences beginning at birth, with the ability to give back or to keep for ourselves. all that is given to us.
If all only gave back, we would resonate as our true selves.
If we think only of ourselves, we can manifest the idea of hell, to ourselves and the ones we use and abuse to meet our selfish needs.
In some cases, sequential beings live in the idea of hell - a psychopathic or sociopathic orgy - coercing, digesting and controlling – using and abusing, not caring or even recognizing the damage done to others. They take no responsibility for the consequences they create, always blaming another who usually was a victim of their cruelty.
In other cases, people live in the idea of heaven and give all they have.
We live in a soup of collective decisions, interacting and melding with collective consequences. it's a magnificent set of sequential events vibrating, then resonating, then vibrating again and again.
Our individua path, vibrates and resonates with the choices and consequences in the mix of our sequential contemporary events.
We're continuously a universal instance of what is, attached to instances of what was and a group of instances of what could be.
Collectively we're all part of the same one – collectively we are us.

Dr. Armstrong sat back and reflected on the depth of the words just spoken. "I thank you for your explanations Sarah," Dr. Armstrong stated with sincerity. "I wish I had the insight to turn on my phone, to record your words. Do you mind if I start recording our exchange?"

"Not at all," Sarah said. "But I think I have covered most of what I wanted to tell you." Sarah said with a smile. "Oh, you also asked me why I referred to myself as an Alter."

Sarah waited for Dr. Armstrong to test her audio recording skills. Dr. Armstrong nodded and said, "You're on!"

"I am called an 'Alter' spelled A L T E R, Dr. Armstrong, not 'A-L-T-A-R', as you assumed, because I have the ability to alter perceptions as I am doing with you now.

I am a catalyst with the ability to apply compassion without judgment – what you may classify as a highly intuitive empath.

I know you have written some interesting papers on my experiences, and you're correct in your assessment of my autistic-like condition. My brain is "wired" a bit different than most - autism is the start of a global transition involving most sequential beings - where we will be able to transcend our current antisocial and psychotic behavior, to reach a kinder and gentler set of communal sequential events.

I see the larger picture of what and who we are.

Some will love me because of this, and others will hate me as a result of this. Though we all have the ability to alter perceptions and change the path of others, we currently do it mostly for greedy and very selfish reasons.

I am a social and essence catalyst – a catalyst does not manipulate, to change - unlike being an agent – an agent forces and controls change, mainly for the benefit of the agent."

Dr. Armstrong sat back trying to assimilate the answer to her questions but still had a warm and fuzzy feeling regarding the relationship of love and god. God is the idea of love, understood on different levels by each tribe with a different need.

The waitress came back and cleared the empty plates from the table.

"Can I offer you two anything else this evening... maybe a coffee or a tea?"

"I will have a cup of Earl Grey please" Dr. Armstrong said with a smile.

"I will have some lemon tea." Sarah also said smiling.

"If we're all together why do some people go through life with disabilities while others are given perfect health? It seems totally unjust to me when I see some children suffering greatly while others do not suffer at all." Dr. Armstrong stated.

"You will find this response perplexing, but here goes. we're a collective mind and each experience holds its own wisdom and set of choices and consequences." Sarah said quietly.

"In Adrian's case, there is a feeling of - let's call it sequential being guilt, for lack of a better expression. He has experienced loss to the depth of his being.

But loss adds knowledge. The process involves different instances of sequential experience.

In one sequential instance, we do not have the wisdom to understand why certain 'bad' things happen but if we could look at the entire picture, we would be better prepared, and would show more empathy towards the ones who have chosen each experience.

Adrian can't release himself to a position of trust.

He has internal conflicts which continually put his perception of self against the world around him.

He hates the fact he can be hurt, and others can be hurt, seemingly through no fault of their own."

The waitress came back with two pots of tea and both Sarah and Dr. Armstrong stirred the pot with their spoon adding more flavor to the brew on each spoon press.

Then Sarah continued "I see the bigger picture, and I see lives as a group sequence. I do not see the future, but I see the place where we're now in the larger sense of the word.

We're both selective and collective at the same moment and individuality is real only to the point of the observer.

Individuality is a choice which teaches us compassion and allows us to feel empathy and forgiveness towards another. Or it allows us to experience self-love, proving the sequences involved with our self-perception and inner reflection.

Attila the Hun, Charles Manson, Ted Bundy and Hitler are individuals who chose the path of self - Jesus, Buddha, Confucius and others, are individuals who chose the path of love.
We all are someplace in-between working our internal conflicts against our external stress. Individuals can either choose to be an agent of self, or a catalyst of love.
In this instance, I am a catalyst altering perceptions, offering positive consequences."
Sarah continued. "Brad is on the self-focused side of the spectrum."
"Brad? - you're talking about Brad on the ward?" Dr. Armstrong asked with curiosity.
"Yes" Sarah replied. "Brad is self-obsessed. His perception involves only what is best for him and he feels others are here, for his benefit only.
It is his choice to create the consequences he will manifest by his actions. In this life, he is one of those who will hate me."
"But Sarah," Dr. Armstrong interrupted once more, "Brad has been with us for over two years now. We consider him to be an exemplar to others. In fact, as you know, we gave him the night supervisor's job he applied for, due to his work ethic and willingness to help wherever he was needed. Are you saying Brad is not performing as he should?"
"Brad is performing exactly as he should, Dr. Armstrong" Sarah replied. "I am not here to judge his motives, but I am using him as an example of the instances we choose to live."
Dr. Armstrong made a mental note to learn more about Brad's performance in the ward.
"You continue to use the word 'instance', can you elaborate further on what you mean by that term," Dr. Armstrong asked.
"Yes, I can do that." Sarah replied, "But be warned, this explanation is the most counter intuitive idea, I have talked about so far." Sarah took the final sip of her tea and continued.
"Imagine your life, from your birth to your death, as a sequential event. I think you will agree; it is. It's a sequential strip of time and space. Where you were born, the time you were born, who your parents are, your siblings, your aunts and uncles, your friends, the schools you attended, who you married, the children you spawned."
"Spawned!" Dr. Armstrong exclaimed, with smile on her face.

"Well pick the words you want - pushed out, dropped, birthed?" Sarah laughed.
"Please continue." Dr. Armstrong said, thinking it was good she remembered to record due to the complexity of Sarah's explanation. Sarah continued.
"It is complex – I know, but it's self-evident as sure as we're sitting here in this restaurant space at this time in our life, or should I correctly say this instance.
In our lives, we live in many mansions – every instance is a mansion, a closed set of sequential circumstances, relationships, cultures, dogmas and knowledge – delineated by the consequences of a root choice – the vetting of a caused event. Every consequence creates a new instance."
Sarah gave Dr. Armstrong a moment to ponder her words.
"Okay – let me try and figure this out. I was born, and I will die – my life between those two events is an instance?" Dr. Armstrong asked.
"Your birth is the root instance for this event." Sarah continued. "Within this root instance – the one we're sharing now – every time a decision is made, not just by you, but by all contemporaries who share this instance, another sequential path is opened. we're part of a magnificent flux of energies – expressed in all dimensions."
"Okay, Sarah – thank you for all of that ... I think I am getting a headache," Dr. Armstrong said. "I have a lot to think about, but if what you say is true, which I think it is, since I have total faith in you, there will a sea change in the way we look for answers."
"In this instance." Sarah added.
"Is there anything you would like to add before we go?" Dr. Armstrong asked.
"Well you did ask me to dinner to talk about what happened with Adrian this morning, and we haven't talked about that yet."
"Okay," Dr. Armstrong said – "Tell me more."
"I think the discussion we just had may help in your understanding." Sarah said.
Dr. Armstrong nodded her head in agreement.
Sarah started. "Let's go back to today when you watched me with Adrian. You were able to watch me at that time, since I decided to visit Adrian first – as I usually do – In another instance of our

experience, I went to someone different than Adrian. In that instance, we were part of another set of events.

In the Adrian first instance, we went through our day, which included you calling my mom, and asking if you could take me for dinner tonight, we're still part of the same instance.

The intelligence and love involved in these sequential being instances and events is magnificent.

Imagine a great decision tree, like the dendrites and the terminal branches of the axion in a neuron structure, where every decision creates a sequential experience for all possibilities, as unique strips of time and space.

That is the beauty of us. Birth and death, for individuals and dynasties, are simply the beginning and end of grouped events, of instances.

Birth or death in one instance, has no meaning or relevance to birth and death in another. Birth and death are root events in a specific instance. No-one really is born or dies – birth and deaths are only real in the bottom four dimensions.

We are, that we are – the collective us.

Now imagine - every decision you had the opportunity to take in your life, and the decisions of all your contemporaries, were taken as they occurred and started another instance of the strip. If your government went to war, that branch may create another instance, where a random contemporary took the choice to shoot you – and you were killed – ending your involvement of that instance – if the government decision was not to go to war, a real-time instance of the consequences of that decision - where you didn't go to war, and lived a long and happy life, with many children and grandchildren, would be your birth to death experience of that instance. Of course, if you went to war and the contemporary enemy on the other side didn't choose to shoot you – you would not have died in that instance. He may have felt compassion for you, and decided not to shoot, providing a kinder consequence for you to experience, as you decided to shoot him. That is the beauty of us."

"Can I get you two something else?" the waitress asked with her ever present smiling face and happy attitude.

"Just the ticket please dear." Dr. Armstrong replied.

Sarah continued. "In this instance, I want to go to Adrian first – since in this instance, I can alter in a more positive way, his resolution of the torment he is feeling. Thank you, for such a lovely dinner."

"You're welcome dear one, it has been an interesting evening and you have given me lots of things to think about. I am still baffled at how you knew about me and my friend. Please don't let that get around or my reputation will be in ruins. I am not a lesbian by the way. Are you sure there was no 'slight-of-hand' involved, in your knowing so much about my secret deeds?" Dr. Armstrong laughed?

"Don't worry about that Dr. Armstrong - your secret events are still a secret, but in a higher place – well known by all." Sarah laughed back.

Brad slid down in the front seat as he watched Dr. Armstrong and Sarah leave the restaurant. He had followed them and watched them through the restaurant window. He was still upset with Sarah for refusing him.

Brad hated rejection and he especially hated it from a prissy little 'cunt' like Sarah Thomson.

His plan was to find out everything about her schedule - when she left for work; when she got home; when her parents were out; when they were home. He was going to show her she couldn't just toss him to the side like some asshole she had no use for.

Brad imagined all the things he was going to do to Sarah and licked his lips in anticipation as he watched her get into Dr. Armstrong's car.

Brad would be smart though - she would never know it was him.

He had to wait for the right time and would ensure she was unconscious during the "fun time".

He found a way to open the drug cabinet on the ward, and nobody seemed to care about the fact some potent pills had gone missing.

Brad felt his penis harden as he imagined his power over her.

"In time my sweet treat, in time!" he whispered to himself.

Brad followed Dr. Armstrong's car making sure he wasn't noticed.

He loved the excitement of what he proudly called "the cunt hunt".

Brad was no stranger to rape and though little Sarah would have to wait, he had plans to find another 'pussy face' to satiate his building passion tonight.

He pulled his car onto the side street watching as Sarah opened the door and walked towards the front door of her house. She turned and waved at Dr. Armstrong as Barry opened the door to let her in. For just one moment Brad thought he had been found out as Sarah turned and purposefully looked up the street towards his car.

'No way' he thought. 'I am too far away. It's too dark for her to see anything - shit I am becoming paranoid myself!' he thought as he laughed out loud.

Once the door was closed behind her, Dr. Armstrong put her car in gear and drove down the street.

Just for a bit of fun, Brad decided to follow her.

This is how he spent many nights, driving his car and following women driving alone. It was exciting like hunting big game. Brad had become very good at stealth. No one ever knew they'd been followed right to their front door.

If a woman was particularly attractive, and seemed to be his type, Brad started a file on her, and would proceed to find out as much information as possible.

In some cases, these women had become his plaything, like a cat and a mouse.

"Rape is such a fucking power trip" he said with a smile, "No pun intended!" he laughed out loud.

Brad knew he was too smart to be caught. He never worried about such an ending.

Part of his 'thing' was impersonating other people. With wigs and clothes that changed his appearance. He could look fat or look thin, look Latino or like some white 'asshole' businessman in New Orleans for some boring convention.

In every case so far, no rape had been reported.

The women were too afraid to come forward and he would always remind his victims he could still get at them by placing one of the pictures he always took, during the 'dirty deed' on the windshield of their car, or in their purse with a note telling them once again he was watching and would kill them next time if they told anyone about their 'date'. One picture usually did the trick, and Brad loved the power to scare the shit out of these women by abusing them again through fear.

New Orleans was an easy prey city since the cops got bogged down on murder more than rape. 'Hell, sex is everywhere in this place and if a woman gets raped, she probably deserved it,' Brad thought. In Brad's mind, the women he raped wanted it and so he was just doing them a favor.
Brad lived the life of two different personalities. At work he was everyone's friend. He knew the buttons to push and was very good at his job.
He preferred the other life as a predator, always looking for the next opportunity like a hungry croc in the bayou, waiting for its next meal to innocently appear.
Brad loved the power surge he felt in making women helpless. If they didn't do as they were told, he would cut them. Just one little slice of the blade was all that was needed as an attitude adjuster.
His victim's fear was like a drug to his senses and sometimes when the victim was too willing from the start, he got angry.
He wanted them to resist and feel the force of his fist. There was nothing more exciting to Brad than to have a woman do his every wish - and do it with gusto. They were as powerless as ladybugs under his boot.
Brad watched as Dr. Armstrong put her car into the garage of her home. She lived alone and would be easy prey, but she didn't fit the profile of what he liked. The ones who turned him on were usually young and vulnerable, with blond hair and slim bodies.
He drove into the night back to the French Quarter. It was only 9:00 PM, and the night was young. The bars would be teaming once again with tourists in a party mood.
He parked his car at the curb just off Bourbon Street and started walking.
The "persuader" was sheathed in the side of his boot.
He had bought this attitude changer at the army surplus store; a ten-inch blade used by the marines, sharp tempered steel with a blood trough and a serrated edge on the thick side of the blade. Brad knew the scarier the knife, the easier the submission.
Brad went into O'Malley's first, a bar with two large pianos serving their famous 'Hurricanes' to willing patrons, who sometimes got so drunk they couldn't walk out of the place. Being drunk in New Orleans was part of the fun.

He sat at the bar and started watching.
A group of young women were singing along with the music, drinking as if it were their last day on Earth. He watched the youngest looking girl at the table. She had long blond hair and blue eyes, with a clear complexion. She looked wholesome, like some Iowa farm bitch in the big bad city for the first time.
She was obviously drunk and was standing up moving her Hurricane from side to side like a German beer drinker at Octoberfest.
She wore dark blue shorts and a white blouse with a gold bracelet around her right ankle, and one thumb ring on her right hand.
She also had a gold chain with a small cross around her neck. Brad studied every inch of her body from the long, tanned legs which met at a well-rounded ass - then upwards to a slim waist and a nice set of tits pushing against the fabric of her blouse.
He could see the outline of a white flimsy bra, her nipples visible as hard little knobs, to any man who wanted, to look.
'Little cockteaser!' he thought to himself with disgust.
He liked what he was looking at and went into his fantasy world where he could, with his mind alone, make her fall in love with only him.
He imagined stripping her slowly and licking her exposed skin as she begged him to give her more.
Brad was starting to get an erection as he imagined her, straddling his lap fucking him with everything she had.
"Nice tits, huh!" the man sitting beside him exclaimed. Brad turned to look at him and said "Yea man! She's a fox." Brad had been too obvious and focused.
Brad finished his drink and left the bar. That son of a bitch had noticed him looking and thus she was now out of bounds.
Brad never allowed himself to be connected by anyone to any of the girls he took. This asshole didn't realize it but by just talking to Brad about the sweet young thing he was looking at, he'd probably saved her from an hour or two Brad's kind of fun.
'Hell, she had too many girlfriends with her anyway,' He thought as he walked towards the 'Pink Pussy Cat' a little further down the street. As the jazz band played - some of the crowd jumped and danced with great abandon, as usual.

This bar was known as a 'swinger' hangout by locals and tourists alike – lots of men, women, and couples, looking to hook up for a bit of the strange. Brad thought these people were 'pigs', who had no respect for their spouse or boyfriend - not caring if in many cases it was the man, pushing the women to fuck with other men or women complaining to their men, they needed more cock and were pissed off, he couldn't get it up anymore. Some women would do anything to keep her guy happy, and some men were pussy whipped cuckold's controlled by their forever horny wives.

There was one chair open at the bar, so Brad sat down, ordered a Bud and once again started watching.

This time he caught a girl looking at him. Brad was a good-looking guy, with a muscular build, and short cropped hair. He looked good in his blue jeans with his favorite black silk shirt, his black leather cowboy boots, worn on the inside. Standing six feet tall, weighing about 190 pounds.

Brad never wore jewelry.

His eyes were brown, his face was chiseled, with a strong chin and a dimple in the middle.

He'd been told on many occasions he looked a bit like Michael Douglas.

The girl looked at him again and smiled. Brad smiled back. She was twenty-something with short blond hair and a cute face, with blue eyes, red full lips and a small button nose.

She was wearing a white t-shirt and a short blue skirt which showed her tanned thighs. She was also wearing white sandals with crisscrossed straps. Her breasts were small and perky, and it was obvious she wasn't wearing a bra under her shirt.

She was by herself, and he picked up his beer, then walked towards her small table.

"Howdy girl" Brad said with a bit of a Texan twang. He would be from Texas tonight and he morphed into his role easily. He'd played this Texan cowboy type on many occasions before and the women seemed to love a cowboy.

"Would you give me the pleasure of your company, and can I buy y'all another drink?"

"Sit down and join me." The girl said with a smile and what Brad thought to be a German accent.

The girl reached out her hand and said "My name is Gretchen, and I am visiting from Germany..."
"My name is Chuck" Brad smiled back as he sat down and brought her hand to his lips and kissed it. "I am in town for a couple of days on business, from Dallas Texas."
"Welcome to Nolin's, Gretchen!" Brad beamed. "I surely hope we're treatin' y'all right here!"
"Are you a cowboy?" Gretchen asked with a wide smile "I always wanted to meet a cowboy from Texas!"
"Well we Texan's always consider ourselves to be cowboys." Brad smiled back. "I do have a ranch just outside of the big city with a couple o' hundred head of first-class Texas beef. I've been riding' a horse and rounding up the doggies for as long as I can remember! – My daddy taught me well!"
Brad and Gretchen ordered another drink, as Gretchen told him how she had come here with a girlfriend who had a bit too much to drink last night, and decided to rest a bit longer and start a bit later today. Gretchen was 21 years old and this was her first visit to the United States. She loved jazz and didn't want to miss even one minute of her time on Bourbon Street.
They ordered another drink and Brad looked at his watch. It was ten o'clock and he had to be in work by midnight, so he didn't have much time left.
He danced with Gretchen and she was very responsive to him. Hell, he could have taken her back to her room and screwed her, and he knew she was looking for a man, and having her first cowboy was a bonus boner.
But that's not what he wanted.
"I know another place on the other side of town where the music is better than this. BB King is a-playin' there right now" Brad smiled, "I would love to take y'all there if y'all are ok with that."
Gretchen looked at Brad and wondered if she could trust him - he had been so nice, telling her about his ranch and his family back home. "BB King! I have heard of BB King; I will just go and tell my girlfriend I am leaving this place." Gretchen said.
"Hell, there is no need for that - we will be back here in an hour or so - let her sleep a bit more girl."

"O.K., Chuck" Gretchen agreed as they picked up their plastic cups of beer and walked out the door. Brad held Gretchen's hand as he walked her to his car, opened the door, as a Texas gentleman would, went around to the driver side, got in and started to drive.
Brad drove north onto Interstate 10 then up towards Lake Pontchartrain.
Gretchen started to worry a bit as the city was lost somewhere behind them.
"I thought you said this place was in New Orleans?" Gretchen asked.
"It is just up the road a bit more, honey - it's called the 'Halfway House". Sit back and relax and y'all can get another beer from the cooler in the back." Brad said confidently. He pulled off the highway onto a darkened road previously used by one of the refineries. The road had been closed for years.
Gretchen finally began to get scared and she realized she knew nothing about this man.
"I want to go back, Chuck. My girlfriend will wonder where I am, and we have been driving for almost half an hour already."
Brad drove on, till he found the small dirt road almost hidden by the growth of bushes and trees. He turned into the road and reached down, pulling the 'persuader' from the side of his boot. The car stopped as he swung the knife around and put it against Gretchen's neck.
"Do exactly as you're told little girl and y'all will get back alive tonight." Brad said quietly.
Gretchen pulled back as her eyes suddenly opened wide with terror.
"OK!" Gretchen said with fear in her voice. "Put the knife away, you don't need that. I will do what you want me to do."
Brad hated this type of woman who gave up before he had even started. He tightened the grip on the handle of the knife and smashed it against her lower jaw.
Gretchen's head snapped back with the impact and she started to cry loudly as she felt the point of the knife break the skin on her neck as a trickle of blood flowed onto the top of her white top. Brad reached over with his left hand and roughly squeezed her right tit.
"Lift your hands in the air, bitch!" He hissed. Gretchen, still crying from the assault on her face, quickly raised her hands above her head.

Brad twisted the persuader in front of her eyes then rested the flat edge of the blade on her right cheek as he held it tightly in his right hand.
His left hand was free, and he didn't waste any time, assaulting her tits, first on the outside of her top, "Lean forward!" he hissed, and as she did, Brad grabbed the bottom of her top and pulled it up, till it was above her raised elbows.
"Nice titties, Gretchen." he said as he moved his hands from one to the other, squeezing roughly then softly. He was enjoying Gretchen's fear and the feel of her flesh. Brad moved his hands to Gretchen's right breast and put the nipple between his thumb and index finger, then tweaked it, first softly then hard, until he knew he was hurting her. Gretchen gave a squeal every time he tweaked hard. "Oh, you like it a bit rough, don't you, baby! Tell me you like it rough!"
"I like it rough." Gretchen sobbed.
Brad could feel his hard on pressing against the inside of his jeans.
He looked down at her short skirt covering her thighs and said, "C'mon girly open those legs a bit and let me see what you have down there." Gretchen was tense as she opened her legs. Brad moved his hand down to the hem of her skirt and slowly started to lift it towards her stomach. He watched as the fabric of her white panties could be seen covering his prize.
"Mmmmm sweet thaaang! Damn you're looking good!" he smiled as he started to move his middle finger over her crotch, applying enough pressure to separate the lips of her labia. His finger moved the panties aside and he forced one finger inside feeling the wetness of her opening. There was no pubic hair. "My god girlie, you shaved it for me!"
Gretchen was sobbing - she had already decided to do whatever he wanted her to do. She didn't want to die. He could take her body and she would make him feel good. He would be her boyfriend tonight and she intended to be the best girlfriend he ever had.
"You know what I want girlie." Brad whispered in her ear as he forced her face towards his. "Kiss me like you mean it girl and if you don't do it right, I will cut your throat in the middle of it'"
Gretchen kissed him with as much passion as she had kissed any man as he roughly moved his bony finger in and out of her vagina.

Brad didn't cut her. He removed his finger and put it to her lips. Gretchen put her mouth around it and sucked on it. She had just finished her period yesterday and was happy about that now. She didn't know how he would have reacted if she was still on her period. 'This one will be good' Brad thought as he opened the car door on her side and pushed her out, making sure he had the knife to her neck during the clumsy exit. He got out of the driver side and moved around the car.

They were now standing together beside the car. "Lift your arms in the air again, girlie… that's it… stretch them as high as you can reach."

Brad took hold of both sides of her top, pulled it over her head, then tossed it to the ground. He reached down and licked her bare neck, starting where the blood had trickled, all the way down to the nipple on her right breast, then bit hard making her squeal again. Gretchen felt the chill of the night air as her nipples began getting harder due to the cold. "You like that don't you girlie." Brad said as he reached back and cupped both cheeks of her ass first outside of her skirt – then moving her skirt up and his hands to the inside, squeezing her ass through the silk material of her low-cut panties. Brad's erection caused him discomfort as it continued to push hard against the front of his jeans.

"Open my zipper and pull my dick out" he ordered with satisfaction as Gretchen brought her shaking hands down to unbuckle his belt.

"Come on girlie" Brad rasped. "Give it a little squeeze first." Gretchen moved her right hand down and squeezed the hardness moving her hand back and forth in a stroking motion. "You sure know what you're doing sweet thing" Brad said as he grabbed the zipper of his jeans and pulled it all the way down.

"Kiss me again, and you better have my dick in your hand before we stop kissin' sweet thaang." Gretchen leaned forward again and kissed him with all the passion she could muster. She wrapped her hands around his cock and pulled it out, squeezing and stroking as her tongue kept the pressure against 'Chuck's' tongue in her mouth.

She felt 'Chuck's' hand on her shoulder pushing her to her knees and she didn't have to be told what to do. Gretchen put 'Chuck's' cock in her mouth and started sucking. His hips moved hard back and forth as he abused the softness of her mouth.

"Take it deeper, cunt!" he yelled as he pushed his cock down her throat, with both hands on the back of her head. He pulled her head into his groin, till Gretchen's lips were close to the base of his cock. Gretchen started to choke, not able to breathe as he held her head in that position. Gretchen thought she would pass out.

Brad pulled back as Gretchen gasped for air - he pulled his cock out of her mouth.

"Oh, you're such a good little cocksucker!" he rasped, as he pushed his cock back into her mouth, holding her head as he pumped against her throat. She sucked hard and tried to make him come, but instead, Brad grabbed Gretchen by the hair and pulled her up, back onto her feet. He turned her around, till she was facing the car, as he stood behind her.

He pushed her face onto the hood of the car till she was bent forward with her ass up in the air. Brad pulled her short dress all the way up. He slipped the knife under the side of her panties and cut them off.

Gretchen braced herself for the worst but instead he rammed his cock into her vagina. He moved quickly battering her hard pushing his cock to the hilt with each thrust.

Brad started moaning then came deep inside her.

Brad became limp as he pulled out, picked up her panties and wiped himself off.

"Y'all better not have any diseases girlie, or I will find y'all and kill y'all!" Brad said, happy with his Texan accent.

He then pulled Gretchen off the car and threw her to the ground. Brad removed his phone from his pocket, clicked the camera app icon, and kicked Gretchen in the stomach as she lay helplessly on the ground.

"Cunt!" He yelled – "you spoiled the whole fucking night! Get on your back and open your fucking legs!" Gretchen did as she was told scared again at what was going to happen next.

She saw the bright flash as Brad took the picture of her spread-eagled on the grass. "Open your pussy and let me take a nice picture of it too!", Brad ordered, as he changed to video mode. "You're in the movies, bitch – is this your first porn film?", Brad laughed.

Gretchen reached down and pulled on both sides of her pussy, opening it as he wanted her to do.
"Squeeze those muscles, bitch – I want to see my come, seep out of that hole!"
Gretchen pushed as hard as she could, as the light from Brad's camera exposed her to the lens.
"Stick your finger in your pussy then put it up against your lips and stick your tongue out a bit – look sexy for me, or I'll cut you."
Gretchen felt totally helpless as she did as she was told – wanting this to be over. If he was going to kill her – she wanted to die quickly.
Brad continued with the video, showing her bruised face, her wet finger on the tip of her tongue as she opened her mouth.
Tears swelled up and she started sobbing, thinking about her young brother back in Germany – wanting to see him again.
Her eyes were closed, waiting for the next command, as she heard Chuck, walk briskly away from her, after slamming the passenger door shut. He got into the driver side of his car, closed the door after doing up his belt and pulling up his zipper.
He re-sheathed his knife, put the car in reverse, backed up and drove to the edge of the bush road, turned right, hitting the gas to Interstate 10 where he turned right and headed back towards the city. No little bitch was going to make him late for work, he thought. He loved this part of his life, satisfied and in control.
Gretchen lay sobbing in the middle of nowhere, but she was relieved to be alive.
Things could have been much worse she told herself. She looked up, past the treetops to the stars in the sky and wished she was back home again.
She stood up slowly, gathered her clothes and continued shaking and sobbing as the weight of what had just happened to her, sunk deeper into her psyche.
She'd never been raped before and she couldn't understand why this had happened to her. She pulled her top over her shoulders, rearranged her skirt, then started to slowly walk towards the road. Thank god he never took her shoes, she thought.
The night sky was filled with stars and everything seemed to be just as it was before this happened to her.
Gretchen knew she would never be the same again.

Her innocence and trust had been brutally abused by this monster. She hated cowboys.

Brad showed up for his shift at the ward smiling and greeting everyone he met on the way in. Inside his head he was still a bit pissed off, since the little 'girlie' had been a bit too co-operative for his liking. He had enjoyed it though.
It was just another quiet night on the ward as Brad checked the roster to see if any of the younger female patients had been given heavy doses of sleeping medication. He smiled to himself when he read the name of a new 'weirdo' in the ward. A seventeen-year old who had overdosed on sleeping pills and alcohol. He smiled in the thought that he had another night of new discovery ahead of him. "God, I love my job!" he proclaimed to no-one there.

Sarah was having a restless night, feeling a tension in this instance, with, knowing something was wrong.
She sat up, turned on the tv and saw the breaking news. Multiple groups of terrorists had attacked Heathrow airport, the financial district and a hotel in London. Many casualties were reported.
Her thoughts took her to the place where the bubble of light had rescued her. Adam was part of the mayhem.

Chapter 8

We people standing on the shore

Looked up and saw the stars above
We knew the way and wanted more
As we made sweet holy Love.
There was no jealousy or pain, no gender rules, just wanton lust
There was no guilt there to explain, as we intertwined in trust.
The energy within our sphere
Moved up the helix of each spine
One day became just like a year
All light became one shine.
We soared on as one embrace, above the stars, beyond the sky
Immersed within our vortex pace, watching sequential days stream by.
As each returned, our dream was done
We slowly moved apart
All returned to being each- one
Old wisdom in each heart.
From our place upon the shore, flesh is sacrificed by division,
Each portal is an open door, our paths are our decision!

Adam was the first one on the operating table.

Dr. Lynn's skill as a surgeon once again impressed the support team in the operating room.

He was a consummate healer and this young man was lucky to have him as his surgeon. The operating theatre clock hands moved from 8:15 to 11:45 as each fragment of bone which could be saved was saved and grafted back.

The drilling holes required to insert the small stainless-steel rod had been done with the precision of some ancient watchmaker as Dr. Lynn fixed the tibial fracture. Dr. Lynn finished with his work,

allowing the support staff to apply the bandage and cast to Adam's leg.
Jenny had breakfast in the hotel restaurant amidst the security in the lobby and at the entrance to the eatery. Her purse was searched and with apologies, a woman security guard took her into a private booth and performed a more intimate body search.
The front page of every newspaper in the UK cried, "COWARDS STRIKE LONDON!", "HUNDREDS KILLED IN DASTARDLY DEED!", "LONDON ATTACKED!" and "BABY KILLERS!" were typical screams from the front pages of the Tabloids. Each had pictures of the gore and detailed accounts of ordinary people who'd turned into heroes risking their own lives to save others.
Jenny was determined to find Adam today and to reach Mrs. Cantwell. She quickly finished breakfast then left a message at the front desk for Mrs. Cantwell just in case she made her way down to the hotel.
The concierge told her the Red Cross was working diligently, compiling a list of the injured and they could be reached via telephone manned by volunteers who had access to the data base. On-line access was restricted.
She took the number from the concierge and went back to her room, picked up the phone and dialed the number. A recording stating the Red Cross was trying to respond to everyone as quickly as possible and an operator would be available as soon as possible. "Please do not hang up since your call has been put into a queue and will be answered in sequence." Jenny waited for over 20 minutes, re-listening to the recorded message every two minutes. Finally, a human being came on the line... "Red Cross, my name is Jim, and how can I help?"
"Hello Jim" Jenny started... "My name is Jenny and I need to contact a friend who was at the airport when the bombing occurred yesterday. His name is Adam Mason. He is a Canadian who arrived from Toronto, on Air Canada and is on his way to Istanbul."
"Before we start Jenny, we have been asked to tell all callers our information is not complete and we will not provide information on known deceased persons, since the next of kin is being notified through the proper channels set up by the authorities."
"Understood." Jenny responded.

"I also must state if the person you're looking for is not in our information base, it does not mean the person is deceased nor in one of the local hospitals. Our information is not complete, but we're verifying as we go. "What is the name of your friend, again?"

"His name is Adam that is A-D-A-M, Mason. M-A-S-O-N." Jenny responded spelling each name with slow deliberation.

"One moment please." Jim said. Jim typed the name Adam Mason and waited for the information to appear on his screen.

"Jenny, we have one Mr. Adam Mason listed. He was transported to the London General Hospital by ambulance from the Heathrow triage yesterday morning."

"Can you tell me more about his condition?" Jenny asked with relief he was not dead or missing.

"No Miss, we're not authorized to provide further information and as a matter of fact we don't have other information." Jim responded. "Please take proper identification to the hospital with you since your credentials will be checked by hospital security."

"Thank you so much!" Jenny exclaimed as she quickly pushed the button and disconnected the phone.

Jenny called the front desk and ordered a cab.

Within two minutes she was in lobby of the hotel moving towards the waiting taxi.

She didn't know where the London General Hospital was, but the cab driver told her it was about a twenty-minute drive, possibly longer due to traffic.

This was the second longest cab ride Jenny had ever taken, since traffic was horrible. It took about 40 minutes to reach her destination.

She finally reached the front entrance of the hospital, paid the driver and ran inside to the reception area.

There were people mulling about in every corner of the waiting area and she had six people in front of her, all waiting to talk to the information clerk.

Finally, it was her turn - she asked for information on Mr. Adam Mason.

"What is your relationship to the patient, please?" the clerk asked.

"I am his friend and I flew into London with him on the flight from Toronto two nights ago." Jenny responded.

"May I see your passport please, miss?" the clerk asked.

Jenny quickly provided her passport and the clerk wrote information from it onto a form,

"Thank you, Jennifer." the clerk said as she handed the passport back to Jenny. "Please have a seat and one of our staff will be with you as soon as possible."

"Is Adam ok and is he in this hospital?" Jenny implored.

"Please have a seat Miss and we will be with you as soon as possible." the clerk replied once again. Jenny felt helpless as she walked over and stood against the wall with the others. All seats were occupied.

Finally, after a half hour wait, Jenny's name was called - she was led to a small side office by the attendant.

Jenny sat down on the visitor's side of the desk as the attendant opened a folder in front of her.

"Mr. Adam Mason was operated on yesterday morning and is back in his room. He has a wound in his right leg but the doctor's state his prognosis is good – his injuries are not life threatening."

"May I visit him?" Jenny asked.

"I am sure he will be happy to see a friend," the attendant responded with a smile.

"He is in room 609 - the security desk will provide you with a visitor badge which you must wear, while you're in the hospital."

Jenny thanked this kind lady, then waited for another 20 minutes in the security desk line, got her clip-on ID after being processed once again, and headed to the elevator, exited to see Adam once again.

Jenny thanked the security guards and walked towards the elevators.

She considered herself lucky since most visitors were sent back to the waiting area for one reason or another, unable to visit their friends and loved ones.

The elevator was packed with hospital staff and visitors. She pushed the button for the 6th floor and patiently waited as the lift stopped at every floor on the way up.

The door opened at the 6th floor and Jenny felt her heart start to race. She was a bit nervous and promised herself not to cry if Adam's injury was too gruesome to look at.

She finally reached room 609 and entered. Adam was on the bed with his leg raised and his eyes closed.
"Hey, you" Jenny said softly, "Are you asleep?"
Adam opened his eyes and smiled, "Hi Jenny. Good to see you! How, on earth did you find me?"
Adam opened his arms as Jenny moved towards him, "You're easy to find!" She hugged him, like she had never hugged a man, before.
"I'm so happy to see you're still alive, Adam." Jenny felt the tears well up from her eyes as she started crying. "I am sorry, Adam," Jenny sobbed. "I promised myself I would be strong for you." Jenny held Adam tightly and realized how strange life is. Here she was in a hospital holding a man she had only met two days ago - now he was one of the most important people in her life.
"We never know where life is going to take us Jenny." Adam said as if he had read her thoughts, "You came here to be a teacher and I was on my way to Istanbul; now look at what has happened."
Adam smiled and was genuinely happy to see his new friend once again.
Jenny kept hold of Adams hands as she moved back and looked at him. She noticed the cast on Adams leg and stopped sobbing. She was here to be strong for Adam.
"How serious is your injury?" Jenny asked with concern, not really knowing what else to say.
"Well I was shot or received shrapnel in my tibia, and the doctor told me no main blood vessels were damaged. I think I was very lucky. One man was killed right beside me." Adam said slowly
"My hands were not injured so I still can play the piano and my brain is still intact. I am luckier than some and unluckier than others."
Adam and Jenny spent three-hours together that day and Jenny forgot about Mrs. Cantwell and the school.
She was where she wanted to be, realizing the main reason she'd come to England was to meet Adam. She'd never felt such closeness and empathy towards any other man in her life.
The hospital staff asked Jenny to come back again tomorrow, since Adam was due for a body wash, medication and sleep.
She kissed Adam lightly on the lips and hugged him again. "Can I come back tomorrow?" she implored.

"I hope so!" Adam beamed back. There was a growing connection, not based on sex, but based on a true feeling of compassion and friendship. Could a man and woman of approximately the same age, be loving friends, without exchanging bodily fluids? 'Yes' Adam hoped.
Walter, Alison and Caroline arrived early the next day going directly to their hotel then to the hospital from the airport. Severe damage had been done to the terminal building - International flight passengers were re-routed once inside the terminal. The airport re-opened as quickly as possible, in a 'stiff upper lip' reaction UK people were famous for, but passengers were delayed due the reduced space available, and increased security.
Security measures had also been tightened and thus it took over two hours to clear customs and retrieve luggage. British soldiers could be seen with exposed weapons.
Everyone on the flight from Toronto was nervous, yet also happy since security had been tightened. The delays added safety – no-one could argue or complain about that.
They purposely booked into a hotel which was a five-minute walk from the hospital. Walter, Allison and Caroline, called the hospital from Canada leaving a message for Adam, they had booked a flight and would be seeing him "tomorrow".
Adam was elated when he received the message, knowing his parents and friend, were in the air, on their way to see him.
They got a cab at the airport, checked into the hotel, settled with their luggage in their rooms, had a shower and change of clothes, then headed out together on their walk to the hospital.
Once in the hospital, Walter, Alison and Caroline went through the same procedure as Jenny had the previous day. Jenny was not aware, the older couple and young lady in the security line, were here to see Adam, until she overheard the conversation as they reached the security desk.
They were father, mother and friend, to see Adam Mason. Jenny didn't know how to respond. Adam hadn't mentioned his parents were flying over. As they were leaving the security area, Jenny called after them. "Excuse me," Jenny said a bit louder than she had meant to, causing most people in the proximity of the line, to look at her. She then made eye contact with Allison, held her hand out, in a

shake my hand gesture, saying "My name is Jenny, and I am also here to visit your son.' Allison walked closer and shook her hand.
"Nice to meet you, Jenny," Allison said, then she introduced Walter and Caroline as well.
Caroline looked Jenny up and down in a stealth sort of way, noticing the curves of her body, all in the right places. As she shook Jenny's hand with a smile, she was thinking, "You're such a dog in heat, Adam!" She was not jealous though, thinking Jenny was just another one of Adam's sexual diversions, and a beautiful one at that. She was happy for him.
"We will wait for you," Walter said, since Jenny was the next one in line to be processed. She quickly showed her ID, picking up her visitor badge, then walked to join the group.
Jenny told them she'd met Adam on the plane, she lived in Erin Ontario, and was here on a one-year contract to teach art. Jenny realized she was chin wagging too much, but she was nervous, and was excited to meet Adam's parents in such an unusual way.
They pushed into the full elevator, stopped once again at every floor and finally got off at the sixth. Jenny was in the lead as she showed them the way to 609, then stood back to let Adam's parents and Caroline go in first.
Adam's eyes opened wide with joy, as Allison came towards him first, throwing her arms around him and kissing him on the cheek as she started to cry.
"I'm good, mom," no need to cry... it's so good to see you, thanks for coming."
Walter moved in, gave Adam a manly hug and shook his hand.
"Good to see you dad," Adam said.
"And you too, my son!" Walter exclaimed.
Caroline was next as she put her arms around Adam, kissing his neck and squeezing him tightly.
"Ah, Caroline," Thanks for coming."
"Nothing could stop me from coming to you!" she said with a lump in her throat.
Jenny walked in and Adam, smiled again. "Jenny, you're here too! – Did you meet my mom and dad and my friend Caroline?"

"We met downstairs, Adam, in the line for our visitor badges." Jennifer said as she walked over and gave Adam a polite hug. She didn't want to make a bad impression on Adam's mom and dad.
Over the next few days, Jennifer became friends with Adam's parents and Caroline. Caroline wasn't sure what to make of Adam and Jennifer's behavior, they acted like friends without benefits.
Mrs. Cantwell finally got in touch with Jenny and allowed Jenny at least another week in London to ensure her friend was ok.
Jenny Googled Caroline - she was amazed to see the accolades and awards Caroline had won - named as one of the world's greatest, on the piano. Jenny realized she had fallen into a group of accomplished, famous Canadians – she was amazed.
Jennifer also felt sad and a bit inferior, comparing her life and talents to those of Adam and Caroline. She wondered why they even bothered with her at all. Yet. Caroline was genuine and very nice – not snobby or bitchy at all.
It was now apparent, to Caroline – Adam and Jenny were not just fuck buddies. They had a good and open relationship going on, and they loved each other's company. Caroline's attitude was, 'Any friend of Adam's is a friend of mine.' Caroline knew she was a bisexual woman now, liking both men and women. She was sorry, Adam, wasn't just fucking her, since she would have liked a bit of Jenny pie too.
"Take as long as necessary, my dear." Mrs. Cantwell told her, "Your friend is your main concern at the moment."
"Thank you, Mrs. Cantwell," Jenny said, "I appreciate your generosity."
"Well it's the least I can do, since you never intended to be in the middle of this terrorist thing when you accepted the position."
Jenny didn't want to leave Adam – she was having second thoughts about her whole future as an art teacher in England.
Adam was healing quickly – it was not long before he was on crutches walking to the hospital lounge. There was a piano in the lounge, and it wasn't long before Caroline and Adam enthralled the hospital staff, patients and visitors with magnificent music.
Jenny knew Adam was a pianist, but she was not ready for the mini concerts played by Adam and Caroline. The music was mesmerizing to all who listened and even Dr. Lynn stopped by to be part of the

small audience when Adam and Caroline played. Adam's raised leg fully stiffened by the white cast fit neatly below the piano keyboard and his wheelchair was just the right height for him to easily reach the keys.
Caroline always worked the pedals.
Jenny was falling in love.
"Adam, I have something to talk to you about." Jenny said as they sat and listened to Caroline playing one of Adam's pieces, "I don't want to teach art in England any more – If you wouldn't mind, I'd like to travel with you and work on my art with you as my mentor."
Adam looked a bit surprised. "I am not a painter, Jenny - how could I ever be your mentor?"
"I envy you and Caroline; you both have made me realize art is the most important expression in life. Let me finish, please" Jenny said softly as Adam was about to interrupt her. "I want to learn more - your music has inspired me, and I want to paint from experience, and from my heart. I have enough money to travel for about one year and I want to spend that money to learn from life, instead of spending life to earn money, I want to spend money to earn life. Do you understand what I am saying?"
Adam looked into Jenny's eyes... "I understand completely what you're saying Jenny, since that is what I will be doing for the next little while."
"I know we have just met over a week ago, and I know you may feel this is impulsive of me, but I think I would die if you continued on from here and left me behind. I would surely just shrivel up and die."
Adam smiled and took Jenny's hand as Caroline was playing the soft and romantic interlude of the piece, "Jenny, life is an impulse to me – I am not one of those who can settle for a nine to five job driving to and from work each day – though God bless the ones who do it. I believe we're surrounded by intelligence and we're collectively on a slow trek of discovery slowed by too much caution, status quo expectations and fear. But in saying that, I want you to know I am not a conventional thinker. I choose ethereal over material, not impressed at all with the money, so dear to most. If I lived to be comfortable, own six or sixty houses, with no debt, a portfolio of the best investments but, never had an original thought to bring knowledge and joy to others, I would surely die a failure."

Adam briefly thought about the hypocrisy of this, since he knew he would never have to worry about not having enough money, but he planned on sharing his gift with others.

Jenny continued to listen, as Adam continued...

"You're more conventional as far as I can tell. I see you settling for an answer with a house in the country and small children being properly trained on how to act at the supper table." Adam smiled as he said this, "Please don't take offence because the world needs convention to survive – the children must be taught, the country homes must be built and lived in. Maybe someday my views will change. Could you live your life in leaps of faith Jenny? Are you brave enough to go against the norms of the world?"

Jenny looked at Adam a bit perplexed... "I know I want to be with you, and I know you know more about life and passion than I will probably ever know. You're right though because one day I do want that home in the country with the children misbehaving at the supper table, but I don't want it right now. I want to be the kind of mother, who tells her children interesting stories about the things their mother has done. I want to be able to walk my talk!"

"We all live life at different levels Jenny and the level I am seeking is simply a true union and communion with the complexity of this planet. I don't want to follow communism or Catholicism or Judaism or socialism or any other "ism" that you may mention.

I want to clean the slate and follow my heart to wherever and whomever it may lead me."

Adam paused for a moment and continued. "I don't want to fix myself to another single person implicitly defining a unison based on binary equivalence and personal compromise. I feel we're a collective and the coupling of purpose for the benefit of two, becomes a detraction and betrayal of what we really are. Spirit is not binary or unary – It encompasses all, doing it all at once. I want to find the common truth – in doing so living in the upper centers of the collective mesh – not in the lower ones where the main driving force of life, becomes the preservation and duplication of self."

Adam looked directly into Jenny's eyes as he continued, "Think about the decision you're making – be sure – I am a bit of a vagabond, though I realize a vagabond with specific passions, and a healthy dose of financial means – but, never-the-less, a vagabond."

Jenny was learning to love her time with Adam in the lounge – especially in the afternoons when the sun streamed through the large window, with heat and light from the sun, warming them as they thought and talked.

"I will think about it, Adam," Jenny said as Adam closed his eyes, surrendering to the music. Jenny closed her eyes as well. She started thinking about it.

As Caroline's playing seeped into his essence, Adam imagined himself once again flying over distances not restricted by time and space, trying to experience in his minds' eye the manifestation of the words he had just spoken.

As he flew, he reached a place where there was no fear, food or sex. He realized we're each a quantum of the universe, hindered by the lack of a bigger picture, showing who we are and where we fit in, to the greater scheme of things.

In this small, thick dimension, we only find meaning about us, by ourselves, seeking knowledge following rules and laws, discovered through our constant curiosity. Our source is the ecosystem in which we live. Our preferred tools and boundaries are first classical - then quantum mathematics.

Adam knew mathematics defined the lowest part of knowing – though a very important part. Mathematics proves the lower layers of what and who we are. The laws of mathematics are part of the root instance. Each root instance could have different lower layer laws, and thus a different set of knowledge mining, tools.

Having a set of different root instances? – Not a known topic yet, but string theory based on vibrations, was a start. It hadn't yet been realized the membrane between the sequential instance were a basis enabling the separation of consequences. As far as Adam was concerned, Jenny had the right to exercise her decisions and meet the consequences presented. In this instance of this consequence, Adam and Jenny would interact.

Jenny thought for a moment then said, "I don't want to tell you I totally understand what you're saying, but I do want you to know, I want to be with you. And by the way" Jenny smiled, "I think you're a living example of individualism. We can never totally leave the 'isms' since any new idea gaining mass appeal, eventually becomes an 'ism'.

Adam opened his eyes… content with where he was, squeezed Jenny's hand and smiled back. "You're right" he said, "Life is a prism which reflects every 'ism, including individualism – the last fortification from every other 'ism'".

Jenny laughed at this bit of wit. She was happy being with this special man.

Caroline finished and the small audience once again gave her a standing ovation. The nurses were used to the piano being used in sing-a-longs of old, world war II songs. "It's a Long Way to Tipperary", and "Pack Up Your Troubles" were a long way from the sweet melodies this same piano was giving these days.

They were amazed at the wealth of music this piano could deliver when played by a master or in this case a mistress of music.

The hospital workers all agreed - never underestimate the possibilities of an instrument, properly played.

Adam was strong enough to leave the hospital and was already making plans to continue his journey.

Walter and Allison tried to talk him into coming back home, but Adam would not listen.

Caroline gave lots of space to Adam. She respected the feelings Jenny and Adam shared.

She did try to initiate some oral sex, when she was alone with Adam in his room, but Adam had cupped his hands around her face, saying "You don't have to do that. My music is yours, always," as he pulled her towards him and kissed on the forehead.

For the first time in her life she felt the pangs of jealousy.

She didn't mind sharing Adam on the physical level, but Jenny had touched Adam somewhere higher. She couldn't believe the story Jenny told her about the incident on the plane – Adam had rejected her sexual advances! She had never had sex with him.

Jenny called Mrs. Cantwell and told her of her change of plans. She was going to Turkey. Mrs. Cantwell was disappointed and tried to talk Jenny into staying but to no avail. She did mention Jenny had signed a contract and there were commitments to be adhered to. Jenny said she was sorry she couldn't honor the contract she'd signed. Mrs. Cantwell wished her well and blamed the terror attack at the airport more than Jenny for her decision to leave. There were extenuating circumstances.

Adam treated Caroline differently – she was not happy with the change. She would rather comply with his sexual whims than be treated with the respect of a 'loved friend'. Caroline felt part of her world was slipping away from her and it was being done in such a gentlemanly manner, she had no means to protest.
She made a point of catching Adam when they were finally alone.
"I need to talk with you Adam" she said softly as she sat beside him on the sofa in the patient lounge.
Adam cupped her face in both hands and kissed her gently on the lips. Then moved his arms around her and held her closely to him...
"I just want you to know how much I love you Caroline, and how sorry I am for the way I've treated you over the past few years. You were my first lover and I used your feelings for me against us. I am so sorry for acting in such a selfish way towards you."
Caroline moved back a bit and looked Adam directly in the eye. "What are you talking about? I have never felt used by you! You have given so much to me and I want you to know how much I appreciate what you have done for me. You were not selfish at all with me, and in fact, I think I have been using you! – I love loving you. I am addicted to your touch."
Adam kissed Caroline lightly on the cheek. "Caroline, I have used you sexually... I have taken something beautiful and made it ugly. I have manipulated your feelings for my own satisfaction."
"Well Adam," Caroline responded "as I just said, I have used you too. I have manipulated you through my sexuality and believe me I have enjoyed everything we have ever done together!" Caroline once again looked directly into Adam's eyes. "I feel we're losing something between us, and I don't want to lose it."
Adam kissed Caroline once again on the cheek. "I made a promise to say I was sorry to you while flying here and I want to make sure you understand what I am sorry about.
We spent so much time together and I coerced you into having sex with me. I am sorry for doing that."
Caroline smiled as she continued to look at Adam... "I wanted sex as much as you did. Sex is like a soothing salve on a throbbing wound. I love having sex with you and I don't care if it is just you and me or if there are others with us as well.

I could easily make love to you while you make love to Jenny and it would not bother me at all. But to think that you're not having sex with Jenny and yet you still love her, makes me confused and a bit scared. I don't want to lose you Adam.
By the way, the first time with you, started as a sympathy fuck. I wanted your music back and felt sorry you were such a horny little virgin."
"That is the point Caroline" Adam said slowly, "We're more than sex and your feelings prove that I have used you. I want to break the structure of sex in my life. A woman is not just a vagina or a mouth ready for me to ejaculate into whenever the urge hits me. A woman is more than a depository for my sperm. I want to explore that side of life where sex is not part of the relationship equation. In my own experience, sex has proven to be a distraction. It's easy to build everything around it, to the point we worship at its altar, dropping to our knees in holy submission every time an erection appears. I want to move that energy higher?"
"Women also like sex Adam - Don't think you men have the only corner on sexual pleasure, and we love ejaculation!" Caroline laughed at this admission. "I love having sex with you. It completes me as a person and gives greater meaning to our music.
I have never told you this, but I play better when I am thinking of you fucking me as I play the piano. It adds to our music in a way that can't be explained. It adds to the meaning of the whole experience. Our music would be banal without our sex and if you take it away, I will surely lose the root of my passion."
"The way you're talking my sweet one" Adam said, "You're comparing sex to a drug... and I think you're correct. we're given the choice of which locus to focus our intelligence upon. I choose higher."
Adam sat back on the couch and closed his eyes. "The point I am trying to make Caroline is that I want to be celibate for at least the next year. I want to love women but without bringing sex into it. I want to experience the knowledge gained by that approach, I want to meditate and focus on the higher centers of my being and while doing so, I want to learn more about my higher self.
We both have this passion for music, which allows us to touch other people some place deep within their own souls. it's a precious and

mysterious gift which I do not want to waste on my own self-satisfaction. The universe does not exist for my own satisfaction and aging proves we have so little time to choose on which side of self, either 'ish' or 'les' we will die upon."
"You're going to be a monk" Caroline exclaimed with a guffaw. "Adam you will not be a good monk! Also, I think women will become angry with you for rejecting their advances – women love the control felt by uttering the words 'yes, ok, let's fuck!'. It's a liberation from the sublimation of us, by men. Who would have guessed we, us women, like to fuck more than men do! It scares some of them to death!"
"Well, the monks may be onto something, but they do it in isolation as a penance in purgatory." Adam replied. "I want to do it openly, in front of the world, not hidden from it. If women become angry because I am saying no, then that is part of the lesson gained."
"I'm serious when I say Adam, women love sex as much or more than men do. We love the orgasmic high from below. And it's even more explosive when shared with a man we love. I love you. I want to be with you." Caroline said forcefully. "If you're on some celestial mission, I want to be one of your 'nuns'."
Adam laughed out loud. "Caroline, you will not be a good 'nun'!"
"You don't know what type of 'nun' I will be, but - if you ever have the urge to merge at a lower level, I will also be your little holy harlot."
Adam shook his head smiling. "I don't want a harlot and I don't need a 'nun'."
"Well that's too bad because you have both! – Your choice which one you want me to be at any given time" Caroline laughed.
Caroline learned long ago, Adam had a certain genius for capturing the future and was always ahead of the curve.
Besides she felt she needed a bit of adventure in her life. Her life was too meticulously planned and a bit boring, with everything built around her and her piano.
"Adam, I have lots to do to get ready for this little adventure we're going on, so you will have to excuse me. What is the weather like in Turkey?" she asked almost as an aside... "I will have to buy some clothes."
Adam looked at Caroline with a whimsical smile on his face.

"So, just like that, you're coming with me? I can't believe how impulsive you can be on something like this. You have commitments all over North America with various symphony orchestras in various cities and you're now going to toss that aside and come to Turkey?" This was more of a statement than a question and Caroline stood up, smiled happily and said "Yes" as she quickly kissed him on the cheek and walked out of the lounge towards the elevator "Just like that!"
"When are we leaving?" she called back as she was walking "How much time do I have?"
"As soon as possible" Adam answered back. "Take as much time as you need."
He knew he had at least another month of physiotherapy to complete before he would be ready to travel. He was looking to move into a rental three-bedroom home, which had a study and a Steinman piano.
This had all happened so suddenly – Caroline called her agency in Canada to tell them the change in plans. They were pissed, since her schedule for performances had been meticulously planned.
She told them she was travelling on a sabbatical with Adam, making it more palatable for the cancellations to be accepted by their fans. She would chalk her decision up to character development.
She trusted Adams instincts totally.
Jenny and Caroline were moving in with him, they decided, and this is why Jenny included only three-bedroom homes in her short-term rental search. Adam knew he was being manipulated, but in this case he didn't mind.
Adam was alone in his room as he pondered how his personal trek to Turkey had now swollen to three people without any planning of his own. He thought about the events of the past two weeks and couldn't help but realize the thoughts and actions of terrorists killing and maiming innocent people who seemed unconnected in any way, had now changed the final course in at least three lives, and without a doubt, countless more.
No teaching for Jenny – No concerts for Caroline - No seclusion for himself.
Adam thought about the law of cause and effect which becomes self-evident in life as events unfold. In the final analysis any event

has the built-in potential to change the entire sequence of the world. Every death has a circumstance and a consequence built in, and the ones taken violently may have the same potential effect as the ones who die of natural causes in the middle of the night in the middle of a snore.

If all death involves a circumstance and consequence, then each birth must have the same effect.

It then follows, each event can be considered as the birth or the death of a consequence and therefore each consequence as the birth or death of an event.

There are spiritual laws of events and consequences, higher and outside the laws, of pure mathematics.

All events become a consequence and all consequences become an event.

"What comes around goes around" he said to himself once again out loud.

Adam wanted to explore this thought further. He started his mental process of "auto relaxation" which was the term he used for meditation.

In this state he allowed thoughts to come from any level – they didn't have to be logical or make sequential sense. All thoughts generated were unrestricted by bias.

It was a condition he referred to whimsically as "instance storming" allowing his mind to create or receive thoughts without screening by the conscious.

Adam closed his eyes and imagined a white sheet hanging from a close line on a sunny summer day at Whistler.

The line had no connection points, it just seemed to be there, attached at some distant place which was part of the supporting consequence to this piece of its existence. A gentle breeze slowly moved the sheet closer to him, and the greenery of the grass and trees provided a perfect contrast to the whiteness of the snow-capped mountains, the blueness of the cloudless sky and the whiteness of the sheet.

His mind's eye moved closer to the sheet until his entire focus was just the whiteness of the sheet. He sensed the warmth of the sun and started breathing deeper.

Adam felt the centers opening as energy moved higher in his spine, from the lowest to the highest, each vertebrate tingled and vibrated to a higher spiritual frequency and lower physical rhythm, until the entire double helix was in resonance. His mind's eye was now in the essence of existence as images ebbed and flowed, allowing him to acknowledge, all spaces, at all times.

In a dream image he viewed non-connected sequences which created events and consequences at each center of his being. He was aware of the greater presence of all centers; of all humanity living and dead, sequential and non-sequential.

He was in the state 'We are.'.

Adam felt peace as images moved across the whiteness of his mind. The tome of life was open to his awareness and he intuitively understood how simple the whole thing is.

When the big picture is seen, the smaller occurrences of self-pity, self-deception and self-centeredness become almost un-eventful and inconsequential in the scheme of greater things. But all must be experienced by self, to reveal the final truth. From the third level he thought in prose;

Jerusalem, Jerusalem, in fire you will pass,
As heat from splitting nuclei, will sanctify your mass,
As the ever-wailing guilty ones,
Get on their knees and pray,
The covenants meted in the past, at this time, melt away!

Adam watched the nuclear explosion start as an event in Libya, once again destroyed the Temple of Solomon during "Tisha B' Av", became a consequence in Israel.

He watched the reprisal, as an event, started in Israel, ended as a consequence in Tripoli, then Tehran. Adam watched as the first nuclear consequence happened as an event during the "Tisha B' Av" on July 16th in the nineteen-forties.

This was deemed a success by all - Jewish scientists were impressed, but also sad, bringing this destruction as a possible instance, including events and consequences too. All possibilities are inevitable.

Then he watched the nuclear destruction in Japan less than one month later. Two cities evaporated. All nuclear events occurred in

the same vision, each in a different frame of reference, but attached by a common membrane like the sheet at Whistler Mountain.
Adam watched as entire families vaporized on both sides of the occurrence. The vacuum caused by the explosion sucked the air out of every living thing within 600 meters of the blast center and in some cases caused living bodies to literally explode from the cellular level outwards.
Within one half of one second the heat evaporated all liquid whether water or blood within 1000 meters from the center of the initial explosion. Tens of thousands of people died within two blinks of an eye, without pain or physical anguish. They simply disappeared in cellular rapture from the face of the earth.
Every building within 1 mile of the blast disintegrated into dust ruble caused by the explosive pressure of over 9 tons per square meter, adding to the radioactive mass of the forming mushroom clouds.
Within three blinks of an eye, all wooden structures which hadn't been pulverized – ignited from the direct radiant heat caused by the explosion.
All sequential beings within this same radius ignited and burned like some gasoline filled torch. Some of these took a few seconds to die in brief agony.
Further out, sequential beings were savagely cut into pieces by flying debris which moved at hundreds of miles per hour outward from the blast.
Thousands of people were simply sucked into the center of the expanding nuclear furnace, disintegrating into flesh and bone ash, as they joined the mushroom whirlwind.
Three miles from the blast sequential beings were instantly exposed to massive doses of radiation, cooking them like some great microwave device causing them to char from the inside out.
Four miles from the explosion sequential beings died slower.
Within six miles of the blast human beings wandered in a dazed state, praying for the mercy of God to take them to another level.
Radiation sickness fell like some black rain from the sky as the mushroom cloud expanded and drifted with the wind.
The ones who survived were less blessed than the ones who were gone.
From the fourth level, Adam thought in prose:

Death and destruction - gnashing of teeth –
observed in three layers - Beneath.

He realized in a flash of intuition – we all are good – at different times, evil at other times.

There's no communal judgement or regret just knowledge gained from consequences, we beget.

In each instance and each event of each instance, we're damaged or healed to different degrees.

Adam then focused on the fifth level and watched multiple occurrences in the levels below, each in parallel within different frames of reference connected in thought by a membrane of communal experiences – both good and evil.

In a quantum moment all possibilities are lived and experienced. Choices and consequences gave birth, to give birth to all possible event sequences.

Adam realized the idea of god in each instance, is not always good – yet the choice of kindness altered perceptions, moving towards a higher vibration.

So much is hidden from the hermit consciousness of a focalized observer.

Adam opened his eyes suddenly and realized the horrors of the images seen.

He knew we are part of something wonderful, executed by the will of selfish and loveless acts, disguised as benevolent actions, proclaiming allegiance to the will of one god or another, manifested as the promised agendas of the "prophets and the saints", and also a balance of compassionate and kind acts based on empathy and love. We are the evil and the good, of us.

To some sequential beings in some instance, there is no allegiance, except to oneself.

The children are sacrificed on the altar of selfishness.

Flesh is the fodder, the fuel - of knowledge experienced and gained.

Love is the balance of the equation and the preservation of self whether as an individual, a family, a state, a country, or a tribe – is less than kindness and love. In the lower and thicker dimensions, self is the primordial worry. In the higher dimensions, self is a shallow illusion. There is no self.

In the thicker dimensions, doing unto others that which you would not do unto yourself, is a common choice, based in self-aggrandizement.
Adam knew, we would meet every consequence caused, as a personal affront, as a law of spiritual cause and effect.
"Be still, and know we are love," Adam said out loud.

The big stories on the internet celebrity sites and celebrity magazines, told tales of Adam, Caroline and a mystery woman named Jennifer, living under one roof, in a cozy little love nest, just outside of London.

Chapter 9

E=mc²

Empathy = morality (compassion)²
I wish it were that easy,
But feelings don't do math.

Dr. Armstrong, still amazed and impressed by the dinner conversation she had with Sarah, regarding her intuitive and some would say, psychic capabilities - called meetings with her professional peers at both the university, the hospital and the government.

Her objective, to explore other opinions about the ability of Sarah to sense not only feelings, but also memories and thoughts of others in real time.

Dr. Armstrong shared the recording, also relating how Sarah knew about her personal experiences – private experiences, which she would have no way of knowing, by normal means.

Dr. Armstrong also took Sarah's description of her abilities seriously. She stated she was an intuitive empath, and could alter the perceptions of others, without judgment or self-gain involved. She was a catalyst, rather than an agent.

Dr. Armstrong also documented Sarah's psychological history since she was first introduced to Sarah, when Sarah was six years old.

Sarah did display the symptoms of a late development autistic child, but her condition was different, due to the come-back she had shown.

Her language and communications skills improved tremendously as she was withdrawn and non-verbal. She'd somehow become more eloquent during the time of her withdrawal.

How could that be possible?

Dr. Armstrong's colleagues were also intrigued, but they felt further tests were required to ensure Sarah's abilities could be proven, under the scrutiny of scientific methods.

Since Sarah was willing at any time, to discuss her condition with Dr. Armstrong, she decided to just ask her.

"Hello Sarah," Dr. Armstrong said as Sarah came into her office, gave her a hug and sat down.

Sarah smiled widely – always enjoying her time with Dr. Armstrong.

"Do you mind talking with me about your abilities, which I greatly respect, and I don't mind telling you – of which I am totally in awe. If you're the evolution of us, count me in to help build the road.

I want to understand, from your point of view, the intricacy of your condition - Do you mind if I record our conversation?"

"I am happy you're asking me, Dr. Armstrong," Sarah beamed. "I am one of the first empath savants, to be born into this event instance. Please record on." She smiled wider and then continued.

"I am 'wired' for want of a better term, differently than most of our contemporaries, and if you did an MRI of my brain, you would see the frontal lobes are a bit larger and a bit denser than others, my pineal is larger and there is a greater density in the area of my thalamus and hypothalamus – my pituitary is also larger.

The physiology of my brain, my nervous system and how my endocrine glands manage the hormone reaction to other systems in my body, is slightly different than others.

The lateral orbitofrontal is denser and a bit larger than average – and as just mentioned, my pineal gland is larger and more sensitive to light than others you have seen.

The pineal not only produces melatonin, as is the current position of scientific and medical knowledge – it also is the gateway to communal and universal thought.

The pineal gland is the connection to the quantum elements – not based on electrical sensing, but rather based on photonic sensing.

It is the first level of consciousness outside the constructs and sequential limitations of four-dimensional space and time.

While current scientific knowledge is based on the physiology of the organs and systems, manifesting as our bodies, there is a great deal of knowledge yet to be learned.

Indeed, I would say most scientific treatment is focused on the bottom three layers of the glandular hierarchy.
Layer one is the physical layer – electrical – nerves and neurons. Reporting to and through the physical six senses, fed by the external conditions detected and passed on by the nervous system, through the hypothalamus and the pituitary."
Dr. Armstrong interrupted, "Six senses? I assume you're talking about an extra sensory perception?"
"Well, you call it extra sensory, which does apply if you consider the portal of the pineal gland as a gateway to the non-sequential – it's outside of the sequential being, sensory construct." Sarah responded.
"By the way, Sarah," Dr. Armstrong continued. "You talk well about the most complex parts of our human bodies – where did you learn this level of detail."
"We all have the capacity to learn about ourselves, and others too if we're inclined to do so" Sarah said, "Through the pineal and the thalamus my visions come to me, I intuitively know. The pineal is the dream portal – the gateway to sequential and non-sequential."
"Well I can tell you for sure, the current knowledge of science does not endorse what you're saying about the pineal gland - we know it secretes melatonin, which helps in the regulation of sleep cycles for people. That is a current scientific fact." Dr. Armstrong said.
"That is correct, of course, Dr. Armstrong – but there are more facts to be discovered – especially in the area of the pineal gland, and also the cerebellum," Sarah replied "The discovery and understanding of photo-neurons will help greatly in moving this knowledge base forward."
"We're adult friends now? Do you agree Sarah?" Dr. Armstrong piped in.
"Of course, we are, Marta!" Sarah beamed in.
"Oh, my goodness, Sarah – please stop doing that with me! I was just going to ask you to call me Marta from now on. We're not on a patient/doctor relationship anymore." Marta responded.
"Done," said Sarah – "But I think I should always use your doctor designation when we're in front of patients and clients. You will always be Dr. Armstrong to me!" Sarah said.

"Okay, I'm glad that's settled." Marta smiled. "Are you able to give me an explanation, I can relate to, and understand, how you know what I am thinking and what I am going to say next – there is no reason for you to have assumed I was about to ask you, to please call me Marta. It's rather disconcerting to tell you the truth. I'm not sure I like it."
"I think I can at least get you to a point where some of this makes sense – theoretically - since no experimental, scientific, peer reviewed, and evidence-based proof does not currently exist." Sarah paused then continued.
"You know all the trouble over the idea of the 'Big Bang Theory?'" – Marta nodded positively as Sarah continued –
"Saying the creation of any universe is the result of a Big Bang? - the worst misnomer in history of modern physics, in this instance. A more accurate descriptive name to use is 'Genesis Root Instance'". Sarah looked to Marta for a reaction, but no reaction was given. Sarah continued.
"A genesis root instance occurs when a new four-dimensional universe - like ours – is formed from the higher dimension of thought.
Thought emanates then animates the four dimensions below.
If we all thought higher, kinder – manifested empathy, incarnate, - our actions and consequences would resonate closer to us. There are some instances where this is the case, and it's a beautiful path to experience – creating a kinder and gentler instance of actions and consequences – which basically defines four-dimensional consciousness, possible only through a higher, resonant emanation from thought.
Thought is the builder – what we think, we become – what we think, we are, in the instance being experienced. Our individual and communal thought produces a consequence of kindness or a consequence of cruelty. Our experience drives our need. "
Marta was amazed, as she listened to this seventeen-year old, who has no formal training in anatomy, psychology or physics – she was still confused by the relationship of the big bang and the root instance.
And Sarah continued, "Okay, let's go back to the term big bang as it relates to the more accurate term – generic root instance.

Remember the philosophy thought experiment – 'If a tree fell in the forest, and there was no-one around – would it still make a sound?' Of course, it wouldn't, since there is no four-dimensional observer, and thus no tree to fall. This is the fallacy of the term 'big bang' – there is no big bang in the creation of an event instance. It's the root event required to inflate a four-dimensional construct, and it is one reality of all potential realities which will exist in our four-dimensional space. An example of one element having more than one possibility for existence is water --- this molecule, made of or two hydrogen atoms and one oxygen atom, can co-exist as ice, liquid and steam."

Marta felt herself getting bogged down in details.

Sarah smiled and continued, "I know this is a ton of detail, but if you bear with me, I will get to the bigger picture which you will understand, but which you may not like. The only relevant point of what I just said, is that the idea of a "big bang" should be purged from all references relating to how we began. Get rid of the big bang picture in your head, and think of a root instance created by thought, whether communal or personal, which enables every possibility to be manifested under the laws of mathematics and physics inherent to the root instance, created. The silly argument of 'how could something come from nothing' is a shallow position. In the four-dimensional construct of universes and environments, thought emanates then animates the four dimensions below. All physical structures are thoughts prior to being structures.

Thought is the builder and is one dimension above our four-dimensional constructs, emanated then animated. Thought is the portal, the gateway, connecting time space reality to the ethereal.

I am saying, there are many instances, animating many realities.

This of course could be thought of as a ridiculous explanation - but don't forget, it's also based on the laws of quantum mechanics - the laws of the small – manifesting as particles or/and waves.

The mathematics of quantum physics, provides the field of possibilities - possibilities, filtered and folded into a sequential four-dimensional construct, provide the field of probabilities. What is possible is always greater than what is probable. This statement is key to understanding what we are – being sequential is highly probable.

We belong to a wonderful idea."

Marta looked at Sarah for a moment, then said, "You have given me lots to think about, Sarah.

I will have to parse our conversations into smaller chunks to ensure I fully understand what you're suggesting. But thank you so much for this initial session."

"Well, the largest hurdle is understanding the big picture of what we are. Our four-dimensional experiences limit us to four dimensional proofs. Thought is a quantum quality based on pure wave emanations. The pineal gland is the gateway and protocol keeper, between the four-dimensional experience and the fifth dimensional experience of, thought. There are no particles in the physics of thought. And the possibilities of a pure wave experience, exceeds greatly the probabilities of a particle-based construct. Light, and all it touches is a photonic animation of thought. The pineal gland is a portal of light and a portal of thought – a two-way door, to less and more.

But every center of action and consequence, from the Root to the Crown, from the Gonads to the Pineal have a direct path to and between each other, each a locus – with a local and universal focus – to express, as part of the DNA encoded, experienced probabilities. Each event instance includes a path of personal and communal probabilities. We're evil and saintly, cruel and compassionate, narcissistic and empathic in different instances of events and times. We do unto others, what others have done unto us, and no negative or positive consequence will go unresolved." Sarah laughed – "There, I have included a biblical reference for those who require it and have just did your parsing work for you."

Sarah wrapped up her monologue by concluding, "Every decision we make, leads us to probable and sometimes possible consequences. Every decision taken, is a root instance. All decisions are taken.

When a probable selfish consequence surrenders to a kinder possible consequence, transcendence occurs.

We all move forward towards resonance in four-dimensions."

Sarah sat back with a huge smile "Are you sorry you asked me, Marta?"

"My immediate question is, since you know so much, why are you here?" Marta asked.

"I am a possibility outside of the normal probabilities – I exist as an anomaly in this instance, and I have the 'goods' for lack of a better term, to enable a transcendence – a new root instance – moving us toward a more resonant result. But I can only act as a catalyst – not as an agent. Every person, every communal tribe have the ability, to think higher and cause a transcendent path – or not. When all paths transcend, resonance of purpose is reached, - the four-dimensional experience is no longer needed, and collapses."
"Okay, thank you Sarah," Marta exclaimed, "I am happy you're an anomaly in the instance I am in – I am amazed at your grasp of logic and possibilities, and feel jealous I am not in the same place as you. I have spent my entire life trying to figure all of this out!"
"Ah, but you are Marta," Sarah smiled, "In a different instance of you. I have seen you there, as you have seen me here."
There was a knock on the office door, as Dr. Armstrong's assistant popped her head in. "Excuse me Dr. Armstrong. Your 10 o'clock appointment has arrived."
Sarah stood up, walked over to Marta and gave her a hug. "You're beautiful," she whispered in her ear.
"You are too, Sarah. To be continued." Marta smiled.
Sarah walked back into the general area, noticing Brad looking at her from the other side of the room, with that transparent smile he thought was his best foot forward.
Sarah smiled back as she moved towards the large window – towards Adrian.
"Snotty bitch," Brad whispered to himself, "Soon you will be my private playground, bitch." His smile growing wider as he noticed her smile back.
Adrian stood up beaming as he acknowledged Sarah approaching, "Can I give you a hug Sarah, it's so good to see you." Sarah opened her arms folding Adrian into her personal space, feeling his vibrancy returning, as they squeezed each other tightly.
His decisions were more coherent – he wanted to get better. She spent the next hour talking with Adrian about his new attitude and his wish to reconnect as a good and purposeful human being.
Adrian was in love with Sarah. He loved the way she accepted him, without judgement or pontification. He realized he was responsible for his own decisions and the consequences they brought. He

thought more about potential consequences now, and wanted to hurt no-one, including himself. His new goal was to be a helper to those in distress as Sarah had helped him.
The news swept the ward quickly since it was a very unusual situation, and people were in shock talking about it. Jordan Taylor, one of the young women on the intensive care ward, was four months pregnant. She had stopped menstruating, and when this condition persisted for three months, a physical examination by a gynecologist was ordered.
To the surprise and shock of all, Dr. Laura Watson simply stated, “She is pregnant!”, as she completed her examination.
She was seventeen years old and had been under the long-term care facility of the institution for five months, after being admitted as the result of a drug overdose.
Dr. Watson did a full peer reviewed report to the hospital board, including the legal team, since she was sure, she had been impregnated within the last three months – four months maximum. She had been impregnated while under the care of the hospital.
All males who had access to her, from orderlies to the professional staff, were asked to provide a DNA sample.
Jordan’s parents were totally distraught and angry. Their daughter had suffered a horrible consequence after someone spiked her drink with a debilitating drug at a college frat party, which she and her three girlfriends didn’t tell their parents about. Jordan became comatose as she was sitting with her friends - no-one had touched her. She just passed out. Tests of her non-alcoholic drink, her blood work, and CT scan, indicated an overdose of Phenytal was the cause of her comatose state. She was an innocent young lady out for new experiences, with the protection of her girlfriends. It was not fair at all, what happened to her.
Her parents were now mortified another monster had used her, so badly. Their lawyers were instructed to sue for as much damage as possible and the hospital insurance, was hoped to be enough to cover the damages done.
No-one wanted this, to go to court.
Brad was in shock. As far as he was concerned - he had just fucked her – without a condom, three times. How was he to know she was in heat?

"These fucking bitches always make my life more complicated than it has to be!", He hissed to himself.

He would have to figure out a way to fake his DNA or do a quick exit and get out of town.

Brad received the DNA permission form in his employee email box, asking him to sign it and return it to HR within the next three days. He also read the non-agreement statement, which informed him of his privacy rights.

He didn't have to give a DNA test if he didn't want to do so. This protection was afforded by the government of Louisiana, to block corporations from using this genetic information against employees. Genetic information can reveal many things about an employee, indeed some things the employee does not know about himself or herself, such as their chances of being susceptible to genetic diseases, ancestral history, family relationships and even mental health history and expectations.

Brad knew he had a good chance of not being forced to sign, due to his privacy rights. He indicated on the form, he didn't approve of having his DNA taken, due to privacy concerns, afforded to him by the laws of Louisiana.

He planned to talk with the other paid volunteers, male nurses and orderlies, to convince them not to sign this request. He knew the more he could convince not to sign the document, the less unusual his refusal would be.

"Can you imagine, our employer knowing about a genetic disease possibility – which we may not even know of ourselves – and use that against us by taking our jobs away, to keep their insurance premiums at a minimum?" Brad asked the other males on the ward.

Brad smiled, knowing he could convince a few of his male colleagues with this argument. He started talking to them in earnest, every chance he got and soon knew at least five of his co-workers would not sign the agreement, based on their fears of privacy invasion. Who knows, a couple of them were probably also fucking that sweet little peach on the ward.

When Brad met Jordan's parents the next day, he put on one of the greatest show of his life – crying with Jordan's mother and hugging her distraught father – Brad was one of their favorites over the last

couple of months, since they felt his compassion towards their daughter, and witnessed the care he provided her.
"What kind of monster could do this, Brad?" her mother implored.
"Don't you worry Mrs. Taylor – we will get that son of a bitch – If I get to him first, I will personally kick the crap out of him!" Brad said with tears running down his cheeks.
Brad was proud of himself. He started to think about Sarah, and how he could get her under his control.
Brad had connections in the "date rape" community of dealers. His three favorite "chemical persuaders" as he called them, were "Roophies", "Liquid X" and "Special K". All available on the street, which could be slipped into a "bitches" drink as a liquid, powder or pill.
He loved to see his quarry slipping into what seemed to be a drunken stupor, then in most cases lose control of their legs and arms.
His MO as he called it, was to slip the drug into her drink, wait for 10 or so minutes, then introduce himself as a local nice guy. Once the drug took a deeper hold, he would escort her out saying she had overdone it – and get her to his car.
From the car, he could take her anywhere he wanted. He always took pictures, like a hunter with his trophy.
Using these drugs provided him with his ideal partner – no talking, no fighting – just fucking. This was a different MO than the one followed when he raped an unwilling partner – using his Marine issued knife as the blade persuader. He hated it when these women were too docile and just gave it up without a fight, since it was almost the same as a druggie experience, except for some bruises on their face where he had hit them for some special effect.
He did enjoy dropping his "drug experiences" off in funny places – like on people's porches – naked and spread eagled, with cum filled pussies.
What a laugh he had as he looked at the pictures afterwards.
He also made sure he would never do the druggies in New Orleans – he had a bevy of beauties in Baton Rouge – attending LSU. The college girls loved a good time.
Sometimes he would drive to Lafayette or Lake Charles – sometimes even venturing into Mississippi for a taste of something different.

He never heard on the local news, anything about these women. They didn't know what happened to them – no memories of how they got there, probably too embarrassed to tell anybody.
Brad wanted to use his chemical persuader on Sarah. He would love to have that haughty, taughty, hottie under his control and fuck her while she was totally out of it.
He rubbed his crotch and got a hard on just thinking about it.
Sarah came into the staff kitchen as Brad was finishing his coffee. She sat down beside him with a smile on her lips. "Good morning Brad," she said in a happy tone.
"Good morning, Sarah" Brad smiled back – "it is almost good afternoon though."
"These days are going too fast – I am like a machine sometimes, as I do my daily rounds. But I must admit, I love it. Taking good care of my section, trying to ensure everyone is as good as they can be." Sarah said.
"I know what you mean Sarah," Brad piped in. "To me it's the best feeling in the world helping everyone who needs to be helped. We're special people Sarah – not everyone is as compassionate or are born with the empathy you and I have, Sarah. We are alike in so many ways." Brad tried to make some points with Sarah – it was unusual for the two of them to be in private place alone together. He sharpened his focus since his prey was in range.
"Is it usually quiet on night shift? Does everyone just sleep all night? Do you have some special issues?" Sarah asked.
"Sometimes as I make my rounds, I provide a sympathetic ear for those who are not ready for sleep and want to talk a bit about their families. Sometimes they cry and just need a hug." Brad answered.
"Sometimes I also spend time in the rooms of the non-responsive ones Sarah," Brad continued with as much emotion in his voice, he could muster, "I talk to them and tell them they are not alone. I think sometimes I do get through to them, since a finger moves, or I hear a soft moan. I just have this feeling inside me – I want to help everyone I can."
Sarah looked at Brad with a smile. "I think it's best when we all try to help each other Brad."
"Sarah," Brad continued, "I know you don't date people you work with, but I would like it if we could at least spend some time together

– get to know each other – not as a date, but as friends, with no benefits included."

Brad looked for a reaction from Sarah and noticed her smile – a small smile, but a smile.

He continued, "I am working nights and you're working days, so that leaves the evening when we're both free. Maybe we could go for a coffee, dinner, anything at all. I promise to be a total gentleman – I would rather have you as a friend anyway. What do you say, is there any chance at all we could be friends?"

Brad moved his head forward, with a big smile on his face – "Please say yes! I want us to be friends."

Sarah looked directly into his eyes and said, "You need a friend Brad, and I will be your friend – no funny stuff though – I am not looking for a boyfriend – just a friend, friend."

"Thank you!" Brad exclaimed. "You won't be sorry, I promise you."

Brad was so proud of himself – now he had to get some roofies and get this party started. He would have to be smart though, since he knew Sarah was very smart. He had watched her from afar and knew she had some kind of special way with people. The freak Adrian was like putty in her hands and he was a tough guy. Brad stayed away from Adrian – he was scared of him - Adrian was some kind of psychopath – wanting to knife his sister and all, taking his clothes off and putting them back on again – always glaring at Brad whenever he was anywhere close by – what a fucking weirdo.

Yet he cried in Sarah's arms – like a baby.

"Well," Brad asked. "When would you like to go out, and what would you prefer – dinner, a coffee at Starbucks – a walk down by the river?"

"Well, if you don't mind, since we're both members of the same health club, why don't we do a workout together and have some juice afterwards?"

Brad thought this was a stupid idea – how could he talk to her and use his charm on her, if they were in a fucking gym? The juice bar was not a very intimate place.

"That sounds great, Sarah," he beamed. "When would you like to do it?"

"Well I am busy for the next two nights, but we could do it on Thursday night if that is good with you. I could meet you there at seven?"

He would rather have picked her up – but the hunt was young. He knew he would eventually charm her into his 'web of influence'.

Brad had seen her at the health club, and she was hot. The local hard-ons had tried to pick her up - she was always polite but not interested. To Brad, it was unusual in New Orleans, for such a fox, to be without a boyfriend or two. This city rocked on music, food and sex, with a different set of drunk and available, good time lady meat, arriving every week.

Maybe she was gay.

Sarah truly felt the separation from morality and humanity Brad was experiencing in this instance. She couldn't interfere as an agent of change, but she could alter perceptions as a catalyst. She didn't know where the choice of meeting at the health club came from, but she knew and understood it was the correct choice for Brad.

In fact, this was a point where transcendence could occur. Sarah was a catalyst but didn't remove an option for Brad – he could have said no, but in this instance, never would say no. Brad was at a point, in this instance, where he only had one choice due to his internal separation from morality and humanity. His only desire was to control and abuse Sarah - nothing else mattered – he was driven by a psychotic delusion, where he was the top of the predatory chain – manifesting as his superior relationship with women.

His psyche emanated only from the hormonal relationship put forward as reality by the bottom three glands. His self-worth emanated and was animated by his relationship with a reality not including compassion or love for others.

Others were there only to be used.

They were there for him, and he controlled them. Like the lady bugs on a back yard porch in the spring when they were hatching – he alone controlled which ones would live or die, as he had stomped on the ones he decreed would die by his will alone – and expected thanks from the ones he allowed to live.

Brad took pleasure in abusing domestic pets – dogs and cats – sometimes killing cats – showing cruelty to dogs – kicking them –

punching them- hitting them with sticks. He was the center of power over these lesser beings.

He was superior, and to him, most women were lesser beings.

His power was transformed as he grew older towards the "weaker" sex. They were now the ladybugs, the cats and the dogs - he was the master of their fate and the creator of their fears.

But it had to be done in secret.

Brad was afraid of anyone finding out about what he was doing. He was smart enough to know there would be hell to pay, if he was found out.

He was scared about the DNA request, until he figured a way out of it – he would refuse to comply along with the others he convinced to do so as well.

The wanton killing of ladybugs and cats along with the sexual abuse of women, had to be a private matter, otherwise people would get the wrong impression of the type of person he was.

Brad thought of himself as a good guy – he didn't want to be misunderstood. He lived a psychological disconnection between who he was and what he did.

The next couple of days went quickly - Brad ensured he reached the health club at six, just in case Sarah decided to show up a bit early. He wanted to spend as much time as possible with her.

He was not in a good mood, since Dr. Armstrong had expressed her concern and disappointment regarding the three male employees who had refused to provide a voluntary DNA sample. She requested each employee to have a private meeting with her, separately on Friday morning. Brad was scheduled for 3 PM, the third and last slot on her agenda. He would not have time to speak with the other two prior to their interview, since they were both slotted in a 9 and 9:30 AM on Friday morning. All the employees who had given voluntary samples had been cleared of suspicion, putting extra pressure on the three non-tested, to get it done, or deal with a "more intense" investigation by the police. This case was being treated seriously as an aggravated rape.

Jordan's parents were religious to the core – the baby was innocent and if all went well, with Jordan's condition, they would keep the baby and love the baby as their own.

Dr. Armstrong tried to get Sarah to elaborate on the statements she made regarding Brad at dinner – but Sarah responded she had nothing left to add.

Brad liked to impress the ladies at the gym - bench pressing 100 kg was his showoff trick. He had waited by the dead lift station, waiting for Sarah to come in, and when she finally did – he lay on the bench and started pressing the bar bell, with 100 kg of weight, up and down.

"Hi Brad," Sarah said as she walked up to him.

She felt the trauma rise just as Brad turned to look at her. His right elbow gave way and the bar, fell across his neck – his eyes bulged out as he tried to scream in pain.

"We need help!" Sarah screamed, as two men ran over, removing the weight. Brad was in trouble, as he gasped for breath. His eyes were bulging still, full of fear and begging. He needed help. The emergency button was pushed as the manager called 911- a flurry of activity was going on around Brad.

A doctor who just happened to be working out, close by, used the emergency medical kit, which contained an emergency tracheostomy kit, to slice into Brad's trachea – inserting the tube, with instructions to those around him to raise Brad from the waist so his neck and head were supported at a 30-degree angle. Brad was in shock but was breathing through the tube installed by the doctor. The first responders arrived, secured the breathing apparatus, put him on the spinal board and secured him, then moved Brad to the Ambulance.

Sarah knew Brad had crushed two vertebrae in his neck and would be paralyzed for the duration of this instance. He would experience the agony of helplessness and remain institutionalized. His brain was not affected – thanks to the quick work of the doctor. He had been "lucky" since the major veins and arteries in his neck hadn't been punctured. His voice box was destroyed - he lost his ability to speak, The police obtained a DNA sample from the hospital, and it was determined, Brad was the male responsible for the rape and impregnation of Jordan. The police also presented the evidence gained through access to his phone and all pictures and videos taken of young women in distress or drugged were added to the case

against him. The videos of Jordan being raped on several occasions added to the aggravation of the crime
He was convicted of aggravated rape and sentenced to 60 years in prison, but due to his medical condition, he would serve his time in a state institution.
Jordan's mother and father were shocked and in a state of disbelief, when Brad was charged. They couldn't believe how wrong they'd been about his character – they would never trust anyone again. He was a monster.
Brad was helpless in this place and had to endure the cruelty and shame of being used by a couple of the 'guards' and a few of the other inmates, using his mouth as their personal sperm depository. They knew the sordid history of this scumbag and were happy to give him the same treatment he had given to others.
The fact Brad was forced to give them 'bad Brad blow jobs', never able to tell anyone about it, added to the poetic justice life sometimes deals back.
Payback is a bitch - tearful, fearful Brad - was their bitch.
Secrets are important, only to those who need them.
Brad reached an event, giving him a chance to transcend and escape - not in this instance but in a parallel sequence for sure.
He met himself and understood.

Sarah talked with Dr. Armstrong about her future. She provided a few sessions where Dr. Armstrong continued the recorded interviews – Dr. Armstrong opened a new field in autistic studies which included the first study of "Empath Savants".
Sarah was given peer authorship on the papers – she was published at the doctoral level – and had become a star with those who had such interests in psychology.
Non-believers in the power of thought were changing their focus on a planetary level. Both Dr. Armstrong and Sarah were deluged with offers to present their findings at top shelf conferences around the world.
Sarah realized she needed to move on from Louisiana. Marta was a gift, a great friend and a staunch supporter. They decided to respond positively to a few of the requests from the many offered around

the world. Each offer, fully expense paid with a generous stipend – the universe was unfolding as it should.
The first conference – Istanbul – hosted by the International Conference of Community Psychology and Turkey Psychology Association
Their keynote speaker topic would add knowledge in the area of Autism Savants.
With Dr. Armstrong's guidance and recommendations from leading learning institutions, Sarah was enrolled directly into the Doctorate program, bypassing the normal procedure – as she had an almost perfect score in all entrance and acceptance standards provided by the various universities.
At the end of the process, the various universities were competing for Sarah to come to them. No university had encountered a person with this level of knowledge and intellect. She could have become a professor based on her entrance performance.
She was a true genius savant.
As Sarah's fame grew, more people became interested in learning more about her abilities – not believing the amazing stories told about this young woman, whose mother was a street prostitute and father was "who knows who".
To many, Sarah became a shining light against the politics, greed and selfish empowerment of governments and corporations worldwide. The bottom line was a line established by bottom feeders. They were part of the "dung ball beetle" model of economic success - where the size of the dung ball amassed, provided the material wealth and therefor top of the heap elitism and entitlement, deserved.
The people of the world in this instance, were weary of these shallow pursuits – ready for more meaning in life than working – getting into debt – working more and dying.
The entitled elite didn't give a damn about any one's children and quality of life, except their own. Everyone seemed to be commoditized and monetized for the benefit of a greedy few. People started identifying these material elites, as "the money moron class". Sarah knew the elite were the lost.
Sarah recognized this to be a transcendence point where a future like Star Trek where the money moron elites were recognized as Ferengi.

It was a battle to limit life to the expression and portals of the lower three glands – sexual power, planet digestion and tribal fear – a hierarchy topped by old men, older families, and older tribes hanging on to the status quo of materialism.

To Sarah, material wealth is an oxymoron.

Dr. Armstrong received her PhD from Harvard and remained close to the psychology professors, keeping their friendships alive, helping in the post doctorate programs to provide clinical relevance to theoretical postulates – she presented Sarah's capabilities to the elite group of professors, responsible to ensure all PhD candidates were fully vetted, including thorough defense of their thesis.

There was a tad of political pressure from the university to show some progressiveness regarding Sarah, since every major university in the world was competing for Sarah to join their program.

If indeed she showed exemplary results passing the PhD requirements, including the vetting of her thesis defense... they would provide her with a doctoral degree and nominate her for the post doctorate distinction - having her as a research fellow to move Harvard further ahead in the blossoming area of Autistic Savants.

The professors agreed to vet Sarah under the sponsorship of Dr. Armstrong.

Harvard would be a representative sponsor at the upcoming conference in Istanbul, so they had about six months to award the PhD degree to Sarah and have her and Dr. Armstrong represent Harvard as the keynote speaker while providing further input to the various panels also presenting. This was a very unusual process and there was great disagreement on its validity from some academic centers.

Tenured, brilliant professors didn't like this invasion of their procedures and traditions. How could you have such a prestigious academic degree if you never were academic.

The pop culture magazines ate it up, as Sarah became a new symbol of the powerful, intelligent, capable, gentle and feminine woman.

Sarah had millions of followers on social media. She was a star.

Chapter 10

There is a space in subliminal secrecies,

Where we emanate then animate our timeless tome,
Within harmonic, flawless, frequencies
Transcending a coded genome.
We reach for and yearn for the "We are" above,
Through – Resonance, Empathy, Compassion and Love.

Walter and Allison were disappointed Adam would not come back to Canada with them. Allison cried and Walter had a tear in his eyes as they said their goodbye's.
Caroline assured them she would take good care of Adam and Jenny piped in, she would too.
Adam was ready for the next step in his adventure.
Jenny and Caroline were becoming great friends. They shared everything together, getting ready for the trip.
Adam did exceptionally well, learning and doing his physiotherapy. After his final meeting with Dr. Lynne, he provided Dr. Lynne with a signed copy of an original score music sheet, along with a digital copy of the piece, played by Caroline.
Dr. Lynne was elated as he played it while Adam was sitting with him. The piece was magnificent – starting off slowly, in a calming mood – then suddenly breaking into a hard and violent stream of aggressive notes – then back to slowly and sweetly.
It was a musical interpretation of Adam's experience so far in London.
Dr. Lynne hugged Adam and joked "Break a leg, on the continuation of your journey."
Adam laughed, "If I do, I will be sure to call you."
The terrorists were successful in the instigation of tighter security at the airport along with the installation of over 400 high definition cameras at all strategic locations.

For three months, Adam rented the country cottage with a Steinman piano in the main room, Adam, Caroline, and Jenny were in a happy place – good music, good wine good food and excellent companionship.

It was wonderful.

Jenny's parents finally relented in asking her to get back to Erin, as they realized their daughter would never be home to stay, again. They were happy for her and couldn't believe she was travelling with Caroline and Adam – two rock stars - of a new music creation, a deeper interpretation, which reportedly transcended all other music. Some "intuitive critics" stated the music put forward vibrations, which interpreted the beautiful and ugly world events – exposing kindness and cruelty, hopefulness and hopelessness, the love and the hatred, within everyone's life experiences.

Jenny's parents didn't understand but knew something important and different was happening in the entertainment space. They left their dear Jenny in London, wishing her the best of the best on her new journey of opportunity.

When the convalescence time was done – Adam, Caroline and Jenny were off to Heathrow, ready to board a British Airways flight to Istanbul.

Caroline and Jenny worked together on the research of this place, with the help of Adam's Turkish musician friends, found a villa with a Steinman piano – and a beautiful view of the Bosphorus.

The place was expensive, but when you have money, everything expensive is not expensive at all. Jenny was amazed at the villa where she would be staying and was asked by Caroline to contribute $600 Canadian per month,

The villa was leased for $8,000 per month - $7,000 if prepaid – Caroline had her lawyers do a quick look at the contract, change a couple of clauses regarding maintenance, security and insurance, responsibility, and once approved, transferred $42,000 to the villa owners Barclays Bank account in London. It was not necessary for Jenny to prepay her portion.

Adam and Caroline were also excited, since Caroline's agency arranged an evening to perform with the Istanbul Symphony Orchestra – and other locations were also interested in producing some highbrow shows. Adam would be brought in as the guest composer/conductor – Caroline the music savant.

This trip to Istanbul was turning out to be a very good choice for Adam and Caroline.

Caroline used her business team in Canada to keep the schedules accurate for rehearsals, household needs, money transfers, promotion updates, and everything else which had the possibility of having a loose end.

Her entertainment legal team negotiated 20% of the door revenue, with zero percent of the production costs, on behalf of Century Millennial (CM) Music Inc. CM in Caroline's mind – stood for Caroline Mathews. Her marketing guru talked her out of using her name in the official registration of the company.

They were expanding their reach, making a good living while doing so.

Caroline hired Jenny as Artistic Director International Venues.

Jenny's responsibilities included setting up meetings with the artistic community in countries visited, providing access to Adam and Caroline if warranted.

Since Jenny stayed with Adam and Caroline, they could easily talk and decide quickly, the benefits of playing here against there.

Jenny had her picture on the web page along with contact information and her responsibilities as the gate opener for international venues, requesting Caroline's and Adam's inclusion in their performance road trip. Some venues requested full orchestra involvement as well as smaller venues with a Steinman Grand piano.

Adam and Caroline asked Jenny to look into the local school venues, planning to offer a free concert to different schools in the local regions.

Jenny became very busy, very quickly. Caroline and Adam were in great demand.

Jenny was now making $110,000 US per year – all expenses paid, and she was meeting the greatest artists in the word, at after concert receptions. She couldn't believe the change in her life, just because of a random seat selection on a flight from Toronto to London, and also the fact, if the terrorist attack hadn't happened, her life would be completely different – she was selfishly happy the terrorist event happened that day.

She sometimes thought personal good could be randomly created by another person's tragedy and even death. She was a living proof. Adam never came on to her, always treating her with love and great respect – and for that she was a bit disappointed.
Jenny had a few, two in the morning - wine talking encounters with Caroline, where they both admitted being totally in love with Adam. Jenny and Caroline understood each other now, on many levels – and Jenny was learning so much about art, business management, and the humanity of harmonic music. She was very lucky to be with such beautiful and totally open friends.
Caroline told Jennifer of her first time with Adam and how she saved him from a life of virginity – they both laughed at that. Caroline also was truthful about being attracted to women and men – as far as she was concerned, it was about love, not gender.
Jenny started thinking, as Caroline knew she would, what it would be like to be loved by another woman, especially a woman you loved and a woman who loved you too. Women, like men, also have their personal needs.
Everyone was happy with the rented villa - it was a magnificent space - the people of Turkey were a special breed – always open and helpful. Istanbul was a sophisticated city with great museums, art galleries, live theatre, dancing and eating establishments.
Jenny's parents were shocked to read about their daughter in the Wellington Advertiser newspaper – as "Local Artist Hits Gold" – explaining how local artist Jennifer Cagney – was living the dream with great success in Istanbul. They bought a computer, connected to the internet, via WiFi and Bell, received training from a local high school student, got an email address and started communicating with greater ease. They couldn't believe they were making video phone calls with Jenny in Istanbul - no long-distance charges. The world was a different place than they were born into, and they finally realized they liked it, after getting over the fear.
Walter and Allison, also followed the news, connecting frequently with Adam. They were very happy to see their son and his friends, having great success and making a good living from the music they loved.
Walter was resigned to the fact, Adam would never be an engineer, never coming back to finish university as they had discussed. He was

very happy for the path Adam had chosen, realizing the path had also chosen Adam.

Walter felt his life seemed much smaller now, but he was very happy growing older with his love, Allison. Allison and Walter still walked hand in hand along the boardwalk at 'The Beaches' in the east end of Toronto, still loving each other to the very core of their beings, while sharing precious time with a circle of friends, met during their university days.

They loved what Adam was doing, and loved what they were doing too.

Adam spent the first few days at the villa, in a meditative mood as he melded into the culture, history and creative energy of this amazing city and country.

He was in the right place.

The villa was like a marble palace, every room furnished with a Turkish theme, including large comfortable couches and pillows, a separate entertainment room, the piano room, four large bedrooms, equipped with decadent drapes, carpets and king-sized beds – each with an en suite bathroom. Adam stayed in the master bedroom at the insistence of Jenny and Caroline. His en suite bathroom was equipped with a full jacuzzi and Turkish steam bath.

The dining room could seat 18 people at the large cedar custom made table with white leather cushioned chairs. The kitchen was fully equipped, with stainless steel amenities and an eight-burner gas stove.

The Turks had a flair for interior design, even making marble warm and inviting.

In the evening, the terrace was softly lit with discreet comfort corners for romance or good conversation. In front of the terrace, the amazing Bosphorus - two bridges in view, joining the European and Asian continents.

Adam finally met his good internet friend Okan and his wife Cigdem - it was a wonderful evening. Caroline and Jenny joined in the conversations and of course Caroline played a few pieces on the piano.

Jenny, Okan and Cigdem had tears in their eyes – totally involved and aware of the magical music.

Okan studied software system science at MIT, and worked with Google, and some other major software companies, as an architect. He was six feet tall, with long wavy black hair which went nearly to his waist. His eyes always in the state of "sparkle". Okan also loved the architecture of music and was amazed how Adam so effortlessly, put notes and harmonies together. There was no other composer in the world, living or dead, able to create what Adam created.
Cigdem was also an accomplished, Turkish woman, with a PhD from UCLA in clinical Psychology. She was a joy to spend time with - totally comfortable being a non-judgmental counsel and helper to many in her life, both professional and personal, as a student of the trials and tribulations of our common human condition.
She was also the founder of one of the top psychology practices in all of Turkey and the lead representative of Turkey at the Society for Personality and Social Psychology in Istanbul. Both Okan and Cigdem spoke multiple languages, including English, French, Arabic, and Spanish – Cigdem also had mastered Hebrew. They were an impressive pair, and it was obvious, totally devoted to each other. Both were very accomplished in their fields and both were 33 years old.
Cigdem had dark hair like her husband - healthy and wavy, but her hair was cut at her shoulders. She was slim, like Okan, and had a better sense of fashion than Okan. Okan always wore a black T shirt, light colored pants and leather shoes with no socks. He looked like a rock star or, a top of his world, software geek. Okan was also skilled on the piano and the acoustic guitar – but he decided not to play the piano in Caroline's presence.
Okan and Adam produced some great synthesizer music in the past – with themes capturing their interpretation of the sound of the universe, always with heart beats underneath. They both loved creating haunting alternative tunes, with Adam composing most of the notes, and Okan tuning the synthesizer software to provide the greatest contrast and harmonies. Both had released the music and the software to interested developers around the world as an open source system; no charge – no patents – shared knowledge.
Adam did write a new piece he called "Istanbul" and he practiced with Caroline for a couple of days – refining the score and the requests to Caroline as he moved the piece forward.

Jenny watched Adam close his eyes as Caroline played, sometimes rewriting the harmonics in his head as he went.

After a day of playing, Jennifer sat with Adam in one of the cozy nooks of the terrace enjoying a bottle of "KK" Pinot Noir.

"What do you do, Adam?" she asked, "when you close your eyes, you're transported to a different place,"

"I do, Jenny", Adam replied. When I close my eyes, I see the music as intermingling colors – multiple frequencies flowing together as a single experience. I have learned to ignore the sound of the instruments – whether they be piano, orchestra, or ukulele."

"Ukulele!" Jenny exclaimed in disbelief.

Adam laughed – "No, I am only kidding – I have never met a ukulele, though this is not a slight – Ukulele's are cool."

"I see, the music as a group of waves, ebbing – strong and weak – blue, violet, green, red, with white and black embedded. I seek the black and fill it with color – I marvel at the white – it is where resonance involving all frequencies resides. White is the greatest music of all – but ineffable in four-dimension speech."

It quickly became time to rehearse with the Istanbul Philharmonic Orchestra, and it was a wonderful experience for Jenny, Caroline and Adam. They were treated like music royalty – but the orchestra musicians found Adam to be a perfectionist.

Adam wrote the score with the orchestra as the ocean - the piano as the moon, with the moon in control of the flow.

He explained this to everyone – Caroline knew what to do since she had worked with Adam for such a long time – some of the musicians were confused – Adam told them to play the score in harmony, visualizing the moon pulling and letting go of the ocean, far below.

As they played Adam closed his eyes, not listening, but watching the ebbing and flowing of the waves, in colors filling the magnificent hall. When someone missed the influence of the flow, Adam had the ability to stop the orchestra, and give guidance to a specific musician – sometimes the oboe, sometimes the flute, sometimes the French horn, the percussion or the violins. Adam was an equal opportunity fixer.

It was a long day and a grueling rehearsal, but at the end of it, when Adam finally congratulated them for such a magnificent effort, after playing through the piece two times without a quantum flaw.

The musicians knew they were in the presence of greatness – humble and caring greatness. Each of them, knew they were a better musician at the end of the rehearsal, than they were at the beginning. He brought each of them into the moon and ocean vision as they played. He moved them into the visual beauty of a full moon with an invisible reach moving the hands of Caroline, as she moved the draw and push of the oceans – till a balance was reached – a harmonic balance – always with pure resonance in sight.

Caroline, as usual, was flawless. She understood and experienced every sweet spot, moving easily from wave to observed wave.

At the 'wrap up' talk, Adam stated "If I have done this work correctly today, and I think I have - since I never did receive a 'dirty look,'" Adam made the punctuation visual, with a big smile while looking at Caroline as she returned the visual of a pointed finger of her right hand, as she wagged it up and down, smiling as she did so.

Adam continued in a more serious tone, "You can now consider yourselves as part of the growing order of global synesthetes." He smiled again as he looked at some puzzled and confused faces, on most of the players in front of him – and elaborated – "Your sense of hearing has an effect, on your sense of visualizing the harmonies, colors and frequencies of the music you're creating. Believe me when I say, this hall and the minds of empathic listeners, light up with color and emotion as you play.

Our success in creating an exceptional experience for our audience, will happen when my conducting, and our playing join as one, with their perception, creating resonance within the flow of musical magic. This sounds a bit surreal – but I have always found it to be true, in all the music that I do." Adam paused, then continued.

"I know many of you wonder where my 'gift' of music was spawned... as you have experienced from your parents and friends, often wondering and asking about your abilities and gifts. You're playing with one of the best orchestras in the world, and thus you're all gifted musicians." Adam was willing to talk openly about his journey, and added, "I will explain my experience to you if you would like to spend a bit more time in the hall today?"

Adam smiled everyone yelled "YES!" and so he continued, "I was lucky enough to be born as a synesthete. A higher-level autistic like condition where one sense not only has an effect of causation on another, but where all senses have a different measured effect and causation on all, of the others.

Some of my autistic brothers and sisters, do not have the feeling sense filters, I was gifted with, and thus their brain is a confusing network of firing neurons, sourced from various senses – uncontrolled.

Some of my brothers and sisters find solace and build neuron paths by following the same sensual sequence, like tearing paper to thin strips with unbelievable straight edges, rocking back and forth – as they desperately try to understand their place in the human community. They experience the world differently."

Adam looked at his musician audience and then stated, "Now this is the hard to believe part – not yet proven or considered by the communal research of current neurology and psychology, but surprisingly stated as being possible by the quantum physics community – and we all know how weird and nerdy those guys can be," Adam laughed, as he continued. "I also have the ability, to do it backwards – backwards being a funny word since one person's backwards is another's frontwards – but I digress.

What I mean by doing it backwards, is I have the ability, using my 'third eye' for lack of a better term, some believing the third eye nomenclature defines the pineal gland, to observe and understand, a resonance of harmonies in waves, then transpose downwards, as simple notes almost automatically written, on a musical score sheet."

Caroline piped in and said as she laughed – "Adam – you're talking too fast – use more whole notes in your speech."

Adam agreed as he smiled back at Caroline "Ladies and gentlemen – I will slow the pace. I do get excited when I talk about myself, and Caroline doesn't like it." Adam said as the members of the orchestra laughed out loud.

"As we rehearsed today, I closed my eyes, using my sense of hearing to stimulate other senses – seeing, touching and feeling vibrations – I know, not by listening, but by seeing the harmony and synergy of the various sections – and within the section, an actual musician – just a little sharp or flat – I stop the flow, give advice and direction, to the contributing creator, then start again – we grow as we go."

Adam paused, adding a whole note to his speech. Then continued, "Please take no offense if I gave you direction – it was done for harmonies sake. I would ask everyone who goes over this score for personal practice during the next couple of days to embrace synesthesia. If we're successful, you will not need a conductor – let your own rhythms and intuitions guide each of you as part of the whole unfolding creation.

If I stand with my back to you and my front to the audience, play the colors in the hall. Your communal creative energy – played as one harmonic and resonant flow, will alter, not only your thought shift to a higher enchantment – but also the deep experience and feeling of the ones you're playing for – all of them will be raised with you, whether they are compassionate, empathic or instinctive. Our music will profoundly alter the depth of experience – and open higher portals."

Adam looked at the Artistic Director and Chief Conductor of the Istanbul Philharmonic Orchestra and thanked him for his efforts to make this possible.

"You're so welcome, Adam – we thank you, Caroline and Jennifer for accepting our offer to have you as our very special guest. it's our honor." The artistic director responded.

Adam looked at Caroline and asked her if she had anything to say.

Caroline looked at the orchestra, pointed to Adam with a smile, and said whimsically, "What he said."

That got a loud laugh.

The artistic director thanked Adam once again as they shook hands - the orchestra gave Adam and Caroline a standing ovation - ready for the concert slated to occur in a few days.

As they were having dinner that evening with Okan and Cigdem, Jennifer spoke of the amazing words Adam provided in his closing remarks that day.

Cigdem was very interested in the connection to autism – and she told Adam, this line of research is occurring in the science of Psychology – led by a Psychology team from Louisiana and Harvard University.

"As a matter of fact," Cigdem said, "they are the keynote speakers at our global conference next week. There is great excitement in our group about one of the speakers, who is not only a fast track PhD in

neurology and psychology at Harvard, but is also a practicing autistic like, empath savant.
This is a new category of study – extremely interesting to me, and I am their host while they are in Istanbul!
If you guys would like to meet them, come as my personal guest."
"I for sure would like to see that." Jennifer said.
"Me too," Caroline said.
"I'm in." said Adam – "Hate being home alone."
"You can come too Okan, but you need to pay for a ticket." Cigdem laughed.
They toasted their good fortune of meeting in this special place in Istanbul.
Caroline caught Jenny looking at her in a special way, as she unconsciously licked her top lip then smiled the sweetest smile.
Caroline had seen that look before and knew Jenny was becoming curiouser and curiouser about loving possibilities. They had spent a few evenings together – discussing everything under the sun without judgement or advice – they would be loving friends for life, no matter what physical experience happened between them.
Caroline loved Jennifer almost as much as she loved Adam - if Jenny was pitching – she for sure, would be catching – maybe together, they could entice Adam out of his self-imposed dry and dreary drought.
Caroline felt the moisture increasing deep between her legs – she certainly was horny, especially after playing Adam's new creation earlier, with the Istanbul Philharmonic Orchestra. Adam's music was an aphrodisiac – probably turned Jenny on too - she needed a sweet and loving release – a sexual tension release.
She was glad she wore her panties under her loose dress today.

Chapter 11

All things possible,

Are inevitable.
Imagine that?

Sarah believed, in this instance, there is a communal inertia, where instinct and 'might makes right' choices and consequences are animated over critical thinking, compassion and empathy.

She also believed, in this instance, autistic-like sequential beings, with unusual and amazing skills, regarding music, math, memory, art - manifested early in life, were part of the evolution – the creation of the next layer of the brain, above the neocortex – enabling a path where kindness is chosen over cruelty, where the pineal and pituitary outshone the adrenal and pancreatic centers of being.

Sarah was a mystery to some of the psychologists and biologist probing and prodding her physiology and psyche.

Some were envious of her talents and what she could do.

For those interested in her physiology, Sarah allowed a state-of-the-art scan of her brain, which produced images, showing a larger frontal lobe, a larger and denser pineal and pituitary, a denser cerebellum, thalamus and hypo thalamus, than normal.

Some neurologists calculated the number of neurons within her brain exceeded one hundred and thirty billion, based on the capacity, density, fold count and electrical/wave activity, compared to the about 100 billion neurons contained in the average and normal human brain.

Most of the extra neuron activities were a result of her larger frontal lobe cerebellum.

She was a beautiful woman in every way but was described as a tall forehead type of person – an intelligent and aware person – a person not to be underestimated or taken lightly.

She also was very kind, with no interest is self-aggrandizement – no narcissistic tendencies – never manipulating or judging – but a bit too altruistic for some people's taste.

Academic purists also resented the way she brought other academic disciplines in as a wholistic mix of knowledge as if there were no boundaries between disciplines. They didn't believe Sarah when she often stated, "All knowledge is one knowing."

Nobel Laureates felt the smudging of disciplines to be an error. They believed more evidential knowledge of a given subject will be gleaned by specialists in that subject, when objective focus is applied.

Sarah answered these criticisms by simply stating, "All knowledge is one knowing – there is no compartmentalized versions of evidential truth."

She knew compartmentalized knowledge, like compartmentalized religions, allowed more hierarchies and levels of power for the persons (mostly men) in charge of any given compartment. In the end Sarah thought, compartmentalized knowledge provided a safe harbor for those important people, who were insecure in their own position.

She allowed an electroencephalogram (EEG) to be done three times with different durations, including a sleep analysis.

Sarah was personally interested in the Gamma wave tests – believing, this wave enabled further wisdom regarding actions involving the pituitary and pineal glands. The generation of blood carried particles and enzymes, manifesting as hormones did have an influence in the perception and reaction of the nervous and endocrine systems. Waves manifesting as an analog field outside of the body, also outside of the four dimensions in instance.

Gamma waves interacted with photo-neurons, and this was still an unknown entanglement in this instance.

All waves were important, but the one least understood in this instance was the Gamma wave. She wanted to expand the knowledge in this area – showing the pineal was not just a producer of the melatonin hormone, but also acted as wave - particle converter. She was one of the few people on the planet who knew there were photo-neurons in the mix.

"We're spawned from the elements of our planet - our planet, spawned from the elements of the multiverse - ergo we're spawned from the elements of the multiverse.
The multiverse is an animation of our communal and individual thought and thus is the result of our conscious creation." Sarah said to Marta. Marta tried to parse this statement but was unable to do so. It was a complex construct all around – she didn't know the intuitive logic casually being espoused by Sarah.
Sarah also started a daily blog on social media and within four months had over millions of followers. She was becoming a celebrity, approaching the threshold of becoming a viral thought leader and force.
Sarah's mantra involved choosing kindness first.
Sarah and Dr. Armstrong were in a whirlwind of preparation.
Harvard University agreed to put Sarah's non- academic history to the side, as they accepted to hear the dissertation, and her oral defense, with the objective of awarding her a PhD duly vetted and signed by the Chairperson of the Psychology Department.
She was officially a Harvard PhD candidate and could use this tittle as she pleased.
Dr. Armstrong was her mentor, providing the process and logistics regarding the procedures which were to be followed prior to her dissertation defense session.
The topic of her dissertation centered on autism and various savant manifestations – she would argue the human brain in these cases is "rewired", so to speak, in the hypothalamus, thalamus, cerebellum, various areas of the cortex, the pituitary gland and the pineal gland.
The brain mass of all sequential beings could be mapped on a hierarchy of evolved development. Brain Stem (life enabling functions – blood pressure, heart beat, appetite) - Amygdala – right and left (anger, fear, sex, basic survival instinct), the Limbic system (emotional responses, compassion and cruelty) and the Neocortex (reason, creativity, social responses, language, vision, movement) and more.
The lessor evolved beings related to their instance reality with less tools.
"The average person knows nothing about these terms." Sarah sighed as she looked at her friend, sponsor and mentor - Marta.

"You're not writing for the average person", Marta said with a smile. "The Theses Evaluation Committee expect your work to be presented as a result of real research – in your case, you don't sit pondering over books and lectures which support the base of your doctorial argument. You're basing it on intuitive reasoning by-passing the research work, all other successful candidates have had to do. I don't know if that makes you lucky or cursed." Marta responded. "They will expect you to use the lexicon of the profession though."

"Hmm," Sarah sighed again – "If you really understand a topic, you should be able to explain it to a ten-year old, said an old master once before.

Maybe I could write a song, like the bone song – you know – the wiggling toe bone's connected to the spine bones, the spine bones are connected to the brain stem, the brain stem's connected to the reptilian spot, the reptilian spot's connected to the amygdala, the amygdala's connected to the limbic, the limbic is connected to the neocortex and they all have neurons in between - I could make sense of all these profession specific names and nomenclature in a poem, and present the poem as my thesis." Sarah smiled.

"Don't even think about it, Sarah." Marta said sternly.

Sarah's dissertation put the argument forward, neurophysiology – the electromagnetic actions of neurons in the brain and nervous system - is the bottom layer on which psychological acts and consequences occur.

Sarah linked not only the particle actions and consequences of the electromagnetic nervous and endocrine systems, but also the wave actions, outside of the sequential being, to universal and multiverse-al actions and consequences.

Though most cases of autism animated the sequential being, isolated from the norms of societal interactions, there were a few random cases where the neuron population was higher - the connectivity of the neurons, denser – producing a superior level of accomplishment, for that sequential being.

Creativity and intuition were the resultant psychological benefits of those endowed with a wider, denser association of neuron paths and networks.

Some of these sequential beings excelled as savants – early 'geniuses' by easily playing full concerto piano parts – easily drawing and painting excellent works of art – easily remembering events and sequences exactly as they happened on any given date in the past – easily providing correct mathematical calculations, faster than a calculator – easily remembering thousands of numbers associated with the square root of pi, easily reconstructing an area flown over, as a painted and penciled diagram, with every building, tree and road (and even the vehicles on any particular road) in the actual observed place, sometimes representing miles of reconstructed visual observation, redrawn from memory – easily counting cards in a casino, beating the 'house' at their own game to the point they are barred from playing.

Having any of these amazing 'gifts', ensure a social audience and acceptance by people impressed with such things, adding to the social skills of these special autistic sequential beings.

The autistics without such obvious special skills are set aside – without appreciation or acceptance. The average autistic child is not understood or properly studied.

They exist in an experience, with differing attributes of spatial memory – non-sequential connections through the hippocampus and temporal lobes. The experience a time/space level, a notch higher where actions and reactions are not sequentially important – events are nontemporal – as dreams are nontemporal.

Sarah argued, autism in all its forms, involved a heightened level of consciousness, individually focused on various aspects of human accomplishments in music, art, science, intellect, creativity, cruelty, selfishness, kindness, compassion and empathy.

She argued nothing classical or quantum, could exist without consciousness, and the lowest form of consciousness is thought.

Thought emanates then animates the four dimensions below.

The four dimensions below, manifest the possible paths to be taken – either moving away from or towards harmony and resonance, with a consequence to wither or bloom.

Resonance exists when all actions and consequences, exist as one action and one consequence – the action is empathy for all – the consequence is love for each.

We're here, in every instance, to resonate towards our highest calling.
We're here in every instance, to resonate, individually and communally towards love.

Our future moves always, towards us embracing a universal truth:
There must be compassion and empathy for all – before there can be love and acceptance of each.

Sarah expanded the thought about consciousness being a space/time skein – a membrane – a taut field of particles and waves, transcending and surrendering from and to, to and from, our physical and ethereal observations.
Though current theoretical quantum physics is knocking on the door of multiverse realities, the thought is too strange for most to visualize and realize.
Sarah didn't present too much on this context, since the academic worlds of neurophysiology and psychology – were not ready to embrace this construct, and rightly so.
Sarah knew the relationships between cosmology and neurology was a simple jump.
The cosmologist works with a bigger head.
Proof of concept was the rule of the dissertation - Sarah presented her self-evident truth - the scans of her brain – using her own physiology, psychology, intuitive and extra sense capabilities as proof of argument.
During her oral presentation, she shocked each of the committee members by expanding on their questions of personal experiences or professional experiences in details no one could possibly know.
Sarah pointed out it was not magical or extra spiritual – it was due to the evolutionary physical development of the human brain, providing further development and utility, supported by self-evident truths - we're expanding our creativity and knowledge naturally.
Sarah took Marta's advice not to expand too much on the capabilities of the pineal gland and its relationship to the cerebellum in connecting universal thought over a membrane connecting all instances as one instance – it was too radical for the committee and too scary for their places in the hierarchy, due to the problems

presented by disagreeing with the solutions they had pushed and persuaded – They wanted no conflict with the current status quo, especially if their name was included as an author of the paper challenged.
Sarah knew, status quo added nothing to innovation and new paradigms – status quo just added tons and tons of drag - a remedy against bruising ego's and diminishing hierarchical positions, of those taking full benefit of the status quo platforms.
The status quo malady is also present in everything concerned with business and commerce. All CEO's rigged the system to milk the status quo billing – eliminating innovation.
In psychology and philosophy, truth was sometimes self-evident.
Sarah used the self-evident postulates as the basis of her argument.
She wrote the thalamus, in lower forms and more debilitating forms of autism could misfire in its functional areas responsible for the coordination of sense information relayed from the spinal cord, and response strategies delivered to the pituitary and pineal glands as well as the various lobes within the cortex.
She would also postulate; neuroscience is the physical layer on which all sequential being psyches arise. Sarah knew if the neural activity between the peripheral and central nervous system, via the brain stem to the thalamus then onto the pituitary or pineal glands was "broken", or the signal network through the thalamus misfired, the physiology of the sequential being would be affected for the duration of that sequential instance.
In other words, if we're born with a neuron malady, manifesting as misfiring or non-filtering of neuro-network sources and proper destinations, we will live a misfunctioned life in the instance or instances, where this malady occurred.
It is akin to holding a football in your right hand, and when you start the neural process required to throw a ball from the right hand, the left leg bends at the knee as if it were an elbow, and flexes straight as if you were throwing the ball. The ball of course is still in your right hand, but your brain believes you have thrown it. Confusion and frustration arise in the sequential being experiencing an instance with this malady.
Life is easier learning a rote sequence like tearing a newspaper page into perfect strips, while verifying the result, alone, where actions

produce the proper and expected consequences – even if the work was, in the final analysis useless towards growth to greater things.

Sarah defined sequential beings as all living contemporaries, fixed in an instance of being sequential. There were multiple instances with associated and disassociated events making up the total wave experience towards synchronicity and resonance. It was a normal occurrence for sequential beings to experience many event instances in time. Time is always measured locally to the given consequential instance.

Sarah's problem was separating knowledge into given places of responsibility – adhering to the mistaken conclusion, knowledge was compartmental in nature.

To Sarah, all knowledge is one knowing, with the lowest point of knowing being driven by the physical manifestation of the four-dimensional vortex present in every multiverse.

The fact is a person with deep knowledge in quantum physics is separated on purpose through university curricula, from a person with deep knowledge in neurology or psychology. This is done on purpose for mostly historical reasons supporting the departmental hierarchies and institutional specialties.

Sarah believed PhD curricula would produce better results if the knowledge centers - bridged the knowledge of each "discipline" into one knowledge.

"You know, Marta – neurons are made of leptons and quarks at the quantum level." Sarah said.

"Oh, please Sarah, don't start talking about positive and negative ions – I am a psychologist, not a physicist or engineer. We assume all the stuff below brain and emotion science is there as it should be."

"Case closed," said Sarah with a knowing smile.

Sarah's greatest problem with her thesis was separating psychology, neurology, cosmology and quantum physics as a separate scope of science.

She wrote her thesis, presented it to the Harvard committee – did her oral dissertation - argued her case - proved her suppositions – received her PhD, with the caveat she would spend 5 years as a Harvard post doctorate research fellow – working with other post

doctorates – researching the effects of autism savants on psychology.
Sarah had proven, by her own self-evident examples, the idea of empath savants was a new topic of discussion and discovery.
Harvard now, led the study of autistic psychology and would sponsor the attendance of Dr. Marta Armstrong and Dr. Sarah Thomson at the World Psychology Conference taking place in Istanbul.
Sarah's parents, her younger brother and some of her friends from her church - attended way back then – including Reverend Paul and his good wife Maraid, proudly attended the graduation ceremony in Boston. They were very proud of the parts they had played in Sarah's success.
Her young brother, Trevor – was born as an "unexpected gift from God". There was whispered rumors within the church elders and the congregation, about how much little Trevor looked like Reverend Paul. Barry, Debbie and Reverend Paul, all knew the truth about Trevor, and they loved him without judgement or legal malice. God works in mysterious ways – Barry was happy Trevor was a Thomson, his name would carry on.
As Barrie hugged Sarah after the graduation ceremony, he whispered into Sarah's ear – "Thank you for telling me to be the male force in our family way back then. You told me I would have a son and you were correct. I always believed you somehow knew what was missing in my life."
Sarah kissed her father on his cheek, feeling the emptiness Barry had known until his son Trevor, came into his life. He made sure Trevor was never exposed to mumps in his early years.
Reverend Paul and Debbie cooled it a bit – no longer passionate spontaneous lovers. The birth of Trevor scared Reverend Paul, since he knew Debbie was surely barren. He thought God had somehow intervened as He did with the virgin Mary Herself. He started thinking of Debbie as some holy women – to be revered. He never interfered with her again. Debbie was good with that since she finally had a baby, totally belonging to her and her husband. The universe was unfolding as it should.
It was a happy celebration, at the post ceremony light dinner at Sarah's Café in West Cambridge. Marta and Sarah – had booked this

spot, on purpose – saluting the good times they had at Sarah's restaurant in New Orleans over the years.
Everyone enjoyed the meal, the happy atmosphere along with the comradery and high spirits at the table. Before the meal was served, Reverend Paul gave an opening prayer asking our Lord to take care of Sarah in her travels and experiences, and to ensure she came back home to New Orleans every now and then, for the benefit of her family and friends, who loved her dearly.
The food was delicious – the memories were golden – spirits was high – laughter was easy.
Everyone at the table now addressed Sarah as doctor Sarah – except Barry and Debbie. She would always be Sarah to them.
The waitress came over to the table with the ticket.
"Please bring the ticket to me," Marta said. She stood up toasted doctor Sarah once again, and thanked everyone for the love given on this very special occasion,
"Did you hear about the bombing in London yet?" the waitress asked. "I can't understand why such things happen in this world. It just came over the news now."
"What happened?" Dr. Armstrong asked.
"Oh, some religious crazies just blew up some buildings and the airport. There are dead and injured everywhere. it's just terrible how these fanatics can kill innocent people for some radical cause that only they believe in. I will be right back with the machine for your credit card payment."
Dr. Armstrong looked over at Sarah and noticed tears rolling down her cheeks.
"Why are you crying dear?" Dr. Armstrong asked as she moved her hand over to lightly brush a tear away, and then dropped her hand down to hold Sarah's hand.
"It has started." Sarah sighed as she squeezed Dr. Armstrong's hand returning the closeness and feeling of compassion.
"What has started?" Dr. Armstrong asked quietly as she moved her head closer to Sarah.
The waitress came back with the payment machine - Dr. Armstrong looked at the items on the ticket, put her credit card into the slot – added a 25% tip – waited for "approved" then handed the machine back to the waitress.

"Thank you very much for your generous tip!" the waitress smiled, as she gave the customer copy of the receipt to Dr. Armstrong.
Sarah said quietly. "We're now part of a communal instance, leading to ascending events." She stopped crying, telling Marta, she soon would be together with a kindred spirit she deeply loved.
"You never told me you had a boyfriend," Marta said – "I have to meet this very lucky guy!"
"You will." Sarah said with a smile, "And so will I."
"Ah," Marta responded – "This man is in your field of intuition. I believe you!" she said. "I will never doubt your intuition again. You have too much going on in that frontal lobe of yours." Marta took Sarah's hand and gave it a loving squeeze.
The goodbyes at the Boston airport the next morning were emotionally charged.
Sarah and Marta had a lot of work to do with the post doctorate research committee, exploring the grant availability for their new research. Marta loved what she was doing and loved the friend and confidant she had found in Sarah.
Trevor gave his big sister a hug and told her how proud he was to be her brother – Debbie was crying – Barry was like a peacock – strutting with pride – He loved his family.
Reverend Paul, hugged Sarah too, saying "God bless you my child. You're always in our thoughts and prayers." Maraid hugged her too "Bless you dear Sarah – you have such an exciting and purposeful life!" – then they walked through the gate and were gone.
Sarah and Marta were lucky enough to lease an apartment in Cambridge. The building was well maintained, the furniture upscale – owned by the university.
The internet and the newspapers were abuzz with blogs and stories about Sarah. She was the most popular and famous psychology PhD the university ever had - Sarah was happy when the university offered her a PR person and an executive secretary – shared – as a buffer between her and the various news outlets and talk shows interested in booking her for an interview. Sarah never sought to be a celebrity, but she had gained the adoration and admiration of many around the globe, due to her adherence to empathy and empathic acts.

Sarah smiled, seeing Adrian on one of the talk shows, telling how Sarah had helped him out of his dungeon of depression and depravity. He talked about his time with Dr. Armstrong in the mental health institution in Louisiana.

Adrian openly stated, "I can't tell you the calming influence Dr. Thomson shared with all, in difficulty at the institution. I am cured of the malady, which took me from my family, and caused great pain for them and a sense of total loneliness for me. Dr. Thomson was the most positive influence in getting me and many others, out of our guilt based, thought walled prisons. She is a catalyst and played the starring role, in altering my future. It doesn't surprise me at all, she was given this great honor by Harvard university. She is the smartest and most loving person I have ever met, and I feel blessed having her presence within my life. I believe her accomplishments, at Harvard, gives her a new platform, for the benefit of us all."

The audience agreed and applauded loudly.

Adrian completed his high school diploma with honors and was accepted by LSU, on his way to become a clinical psychologist – his goal - to work at the same institution in which he was a patient. Dr. Armstrong continually encouraged him, to be the best he could be – also telling him a position at the institute was his, after graduation. Adrian worked at the facility, in the same role Sarah held when she had helped him. His sense of purpose was restored. His nightshift work was exemplary – every patient safe under his care.

"We have our tickets, our hotel is booked, our presentation is ready, and we will be the guests of Dr. Cigdem Alpar.

Marta made a point of looking up the bio for Cigdem, learning about her family, field of study and her academic history.

She was an accomplished, intelligent woman. Both Sarah and Marta looked forward to meeting with her in the molecules. They did meet her over an internet video call, which went extremely well.

After the call, Sarah said, "Cigdem will become a life-long friend, in this instance." Marta once again believed her and was happy to hear it.

"Istanbul here we come!" Marta laughed as they went through the gait towards the plane.

Sarah leaned back in her first-class chair and remembered the light – coming down to her bottomless pit of heavy thought – she knew

Adam was the one who told her, 'Touch the light – I will take back'. Intuitively she knew Adam is in Istanbul – she could feel him stretching towards her, as she reached towards him.

Chapter 12

But when we choose to take a chance

Embrace our dreams and dare to dance
Our lives as they were "wished" to be -
Our feelings soar in harmony -
Our universe expands in rings -
Enabling amazing things,
We radiate our inner light -
And re-give the gift of our insight.

Jenny and Caroline were in a state of primal attraction. They were falling in love, not just in a friendly way – but in a highly sexual, new relationship possibility – targeting our horniness way. They longed to hold and touch – to kiss and kiss some more.

This was a new and exciting discovered feeling for Jenny. She had been curious during high school about what it would be like to have a 'girl on girl' experience but had eventually liked boys too much to give it a try. There was one occasion - a sleep over at her best friend's house – they had experimented with lightly kissing each other and touching each other's breasts – both chickened out to take it further. She did realize though, girls kiss better than boys. She liked the kissing.

Adam noticed the attraction and was not perturbed at all, knowing Caroline was bisexual, with a healthy appetite for intimate physical, panting, entanglement.

Adam was happily surprised on the numerous occasions when Caroline brought another woman to his bed – a women willing to play on both sides of the experience. Some agreed, only to get the chance to fuck Adam, and some agreed due to the music played by Caroline – music they related to from a deeper core of the moment. The ones attracted to Caroline were easily ascertained – they made love to each other as only two sensual women can. Adam was there,

and was sated and satisfied, but the woman was there for Caroline – Adam, just a necessary part of the negotiation.
It was obvious - the ones who were there for Adam - loved cock more than pussy, and Adam was happy about that too. The ones there for Caroline – loved pussy more than cock.
Occasionally – the woman liked both, as Caroline did. These sessions were the most satisfying as the woman obviously was comfortable getting and giving – pussy and cock - in different combinations of poses and creative positions.
Jenny wanted to please Adam, but since leaving for London, Adam turned into an asexual being.
No matter what sexy outfit or topless bikini she wore, Adam always mentioned how sexy and beautiful she was, but never moved it further – Caroline was the one licking her lips as she looked at Jenny.
Jenny finally decided a young woman like her, had needs. She'd lived with Caroline for about three months now - both of their menstrual cycles had synchronized - as nature does, when competing healthy women live together.
Caroline and Jenny were ovulating at the same time - both needed orgasmic release and relief heightened around the same time.
Female needs were definitely a bit hotter and more demanding during ovulation.
Adam, Caroline and Jenny finished dinner --- Black Sea oysters, on the half shell – Louisiana hot sauce – baked Portuguese sardines - Spinach salad with poppy seed dressing – fresh baked local bread – dipping garlic sauce, a cheese platter and 3 bottles of Bùzbăg Turkish wine. They were feeling good, as they moved to the comfortable and small private area on the terrace – with big cushioned couches.
They brought their wine with them.
Adam sat on the big chair as Caroline and Jenny chose the couch directly across from him. This area of the terrace was covered and therefore safe in rain, offering a magnificent view of the Bosphorus and the traffic on the bridges.
Istanbul is a beautiful city at night.
Adam laughed as he said, "You two are looking unbelievably desirable! I can feel the heat you're both generating – you both glow with that CFMN glow, only ovulating pheromones can produce. I love it!"

Jenny was wearing a silk bright colored top, tied at her waist with black pedal pusher tights, hugging her shapely shape with emphasis on her very appealing posterior. She reminded Adam of Betty the Body, an instant hard on generator – she knew it and she liked it. Raw and innocent femininity was her strength. Men were easy, but she didn't want men. She wanted to be loved and she wanted to love back. Jenny knew if she felt like having a man – she could easily get a man, and sometimes she did.

Every man it seemed except Adam.

She had masterbated a few times – coming easily at the image of Adam making love to her as she easily loved him back.

Her face was angelic – pixie like angelic – full lips always close to a smile, blue eyes, high cheek bones, clear complexion. She had a beautiful feminine demeanor, kind and compassionate – loving everything about art.

Adam watched her on occasion cry beautiful tears as she listened to the music played by Caroline and created by Adam. It didn't surprise Adam at all, how easily Jenny had fit into their lives – no hidden agenda – no manipulations - no self only, interest – just an amazing pure and true presence – given freely and openly.

She was a joy and she was hot!

Caroline, sitting beside Jenny, was a different kind of fish. She wore only two pieces of clothing – a silk type gown hugging her breasts and her ass – poetry in motion as she moved. Caroline was confident – feminine and strong willed.

She knew what she wanted and chased it till it was hers. Her hair was shorter than Jenny's, light brown – her lips full, but a little thinner than Jenny's – she laughed more than she smiled, with a gusto attitude that all things were possible.

Caroline stood at five foot seven inches, with a long lithe body – perfectly proportioned. Adam knew well, she had a healthy sexual appetite as she had proven, first in that locked back room at the conservatory in Toronto and then in many and varied risky places – like the front seat of the car, when Adam was driving – giving him a blow job – as truckers blew their horns.

She was a mischievous lover, and Adam loved the spontaneity.

Caroline was always ready to do something out of the bounds of normality.

She claimed her attitude helped her as an artist – you had to be willing to move the boundaries of normality to be creative.
The worst thing you could ever say to Caroline is she's normal. That would be like a slap to her face – make her cringe. It was her greatest fear – so she fed the dragon – did dangerous and outrageous acts – kept normality away from her door. She played the life as she played the piano – always pushing forward – never reaching back.
Caroline always looked delicious – her athletic and lithe body style, built for adventure and fun. Her body was a playground.
Caroline was done with the cat and mouse game she had played with Jenny over the past little while which felt like an eternity... she wanted to make love to Jenny and she wanted Adam to watch – and hopefully join in – since both Jenny and Caroline wanted to make love to Adam.
Adam watched as Caroline moved closer to Jenny, stroked her hair – lightly slid her left hand onto Jenny's right cheek, using her thumb to lightly stroke Jenny's skin – as her other hand – combed slowly through Jenny's hair on the left side of her beautiful head – as her eyes fixed onto Jenny's eyes – as her head and body moved closer – as she kissed Jenny's lips – as she had dreamt about on multiple occasions.
Jenny responded by gently kissing back while surrendering to Caroline's tongue as it parted her lips and moved gingerly, to and from - side to side, finding Jenny's tongue responding back. This was a green light to Caroline, as she moved both of her hands through Jenny's hair, cupping the back of her head and gently pulling her closer enabling a deeper and more passionate kiss.
To Jenny the kiss is the most intimate part of making love to another. The sensual kiss, the soulful kiss - done passionately is the surrender and the victory of mutual passion.
Jenny surrendered as Caroline pushed her tongue deeper into her willing mouth – then Jenny pushed back as Caroline surrendered to her desire.
The game was on and both were ready to play.
This was a new sensation to Jennifer – though she had lightly played with her best friend on the sleepover, she had never kissed another woman with such willing passion and hunger.

She kissed back as Caroline moved her hands slowly onto Jenny's neck, kissing as she caressed – lightly touching and teasing as her hands made their way to the fullness of Jenny's breasts. She squeezed and moved both hands in circles, with her palms putting gentle pressure on the hardened nipples, responding beneath the silk material of Jenny's top. Jenny's breathing became deeper as Caroline trailed her tongue from Jenny's lips, moving to her neck kissing and licking – Jenny squealed her approval and delight as she reclined back giving Caroline full access to her body. Caroline moved her lips back to Jenny's lips and kissed her deeply again as she pushed the material from Jenny's shoulders fully exposing Jenny's breasts as Caroline moved her hands – skin to skin – gently tweaking both nipples between her thumbs and index fingers. She kissed Jenny again, then trailed her tongue back to her neck - kissing as she moved – as her hands cupped Jenny's breasts pushing them upwards – Caroline moved her lips onto Jenny's left nipple – kissing, licking and teasing – then trailed her tongue to Jenny's right nipple as she kissed, licked and teased. Jenny gasped – as she felt the wetness between her legs increase. Jenny moved her hands to Caroline's head feeling the movement from one nipple then to the other.

She wanted more.

Caroline pushed Jenny's top down till it was draped loosely around her waist, then started kissing and licking down Jenny's body – stopping here and there to pay attention to one location then another. Jenny had felt the pressure of Caroline's thigh against her pussy and she grinded into the pressure – gasping on each thrust. Caroline moved lower hooking her hands around both sides of Jenny's tights, pulling them down along with the top, till they were past her thighs – past her knees, past her feet and off.

Caroline sat up on her knees as she looked at Jenny with her lacy white panties – covering a wet spot between her legs. She then moved her right hand to the inside of Jenny's thighs until she could move her middle finger up and down the covered wetness of Jenny's pussy. Jenny moaned deeper and for the first time, moved her hands to Caroline's breast and squeezed. Caroline slipped her finger past the fabric of Jenny's panties and slowly and gently, pushed it into the creamy folds as she brought her wet finger up to Jenny's clitoris, circling it around with expert knowledge of what made women feel good. She hooked her hands around Jenny's panties and pulled them off.

"Jenny sweet Jenny." Caroline smiled, "I am going to eat your pussy – the first time you will experience this from a woman – and I am going to make you cum. Beware my love, you may never need a man again" Caroline groaned.

Jenny gasped, "Oh my God, Caroline! I love you so much!"

With that said, Caroline moved her head between Jenny's legs, inserted her middle finger back in to the wetness of Jenny – then started licking Jenny's clitoris, curling her middle finger upwards till the tip could put pressure on Jenny's G spot, in a synchronous pressure pattern between her tongue and her finger.

Jenny started bucking up and down, making guttural animal sounds as Caroline increased the pressure and the frequency of her tongue, inserting her index finger into Jenny's pussy, adding to her pleasure. Caroline then started the pattern with her tongue. Licking up and down between the lips of Jenny's pussy, darting her tongue in and out with her fingers as she moved, down then up the lips, ending up at Jenny's clitoris, where she did the synchronous pressure again between her G spot and her clitoris.

Jenny felt the waves start in her pussy – moving up her spine – reaching some place deep within her brain, then moving back down again at the speed of lightning, then back up and down again in waves of pleasure she had never felt before. She didn't realize she was making so much noise, and she didn't care either.

Jenny's hands were clenched on Caroline's head, as she twitched up and down – uncontrolled - in the throes of her orgasms.

"On my God!" she gasped, as the ripples from her pussy and her nipples moved higher then lower then higher again.

Teeth clenched, fists tight, hips bucking – primal spasms – orgasms.

Caroline lifted her head and grinned like Lewis Carol's Cheshire cat. She was very proud of herself – bringing so much pleasure to her best friend, on her first woman on woman experience.

Jenny was calming down – breathing back to normal – totally sated and elated with her first lesbian experience.

She loved it.

Surely Caroline is best oral lover in the world.

Caroline smiled as she kissed her way back up Jenny's body sucking and licking each nipple on her journey, till she reached Jenny's mouth and kissed her deeply once again. Jenny kissed back tasting her own juices as she did. She was in heaven as she lay back holding Caroline in her arms.

"I want to do the same for you Caroline." Jenny said, "I don't want you to think I am a selfish lover."

Caroline hugged Jenny tighter – "I am good, Jenny. The first time you will be spoiled. The next time we can spoil each other. I got off just watching and tasting you get off." Caroline said with a smile.

"You're amazing – I have never felt like that before. Thank you." Jenny said. "I needed that! I promise you the next time, I will love you back the way you just loved me. You have taught me what I need to know."

Caroline looked at Jenny – realizing this woman was a gem.

"Well that sounds much better than what the boys say," Caroline said with a twinkle in her eye.

"Don't tell me." Jenny said – "I know the answer to that one!"

Both Jenny and Caroline spoke at the same time. "Thanks babe – I owe you one."

They both laughed.

Both Jenny and Caroline forgot Adam was still sitting across from them. His big chair was about 6 meters from their couch – Adam was sitting in a dimly lit shadow.

"That was beautiful," Adam said softly. "I have music in my head based on the love shared by both of you – you two are in love, in love in a beautiful way."

Both Jenny and Caroline looked at Adam, then at each other. Jenny felt embarrassed Adam had seen her in such a wanton state.

Adam stood up and walked over to them – "Do you want some more?" he smiled, as Caroline removed her silky gown and threw it onto a plant. Adam held his hand out as both Caroline and Jenny pulled him into their midst. As Adam kissed Jenny – their first real kiss – Caroline was undoing the belt around Adams shorts, pulled the zipper down, hooked her hands around the waist band of his shorts and underwear – pulled them off - then put her mouth around this special cock she loved, but hadn't seen for a long time.

The three of them made love – sweet love for the next two hours – in all combinations possible. Jennifer experienced her first triangular kiss and then her first triangular bliss. Two women and one man was a special combination, when all three loved each other as openly and deeply as these three.

Jenny squealed with joy as Caroline came for the first time against her tongue and lips.

They fell asleep – fully sated – happily exhausted. Adam was on his back, Jenny on her right side and Caroline on her left side. Adam held both Jenny and Caroline in his arms. Three lovers in love, sleeping in each other's arms – a beautiful scene – serene.

Jenny had learned well – but like Caroline – she knew she liked cock as well as pussy – she could easily live and love with both.

Adam couldn't believe, during his and Caroline's early years, Jenny lived just a few miles from Toronto up highway 10, in Erin and they met on a plane to London.

Each of them fed the lust and need required by the bottom three glands, while drenching each other with love and empathy from the four glands above.

They woke up early the next morning in a state of bliss, laughing as they untangled themselves from each other. They showered together in Adams bedroom, washing and kissing in the warm flow. Caroline and Jenny were willing and able to start another sexual session, but Adam stepped out, leaving them to play together.

Caring is sharing.

Adam threw his robe on, went to the kitchen – started the coffee machine then went to his music room - scoring the music he had seen the previous night as Caroline and Jenny physically loved each other for the first time.

Their physical hunger extended to something more beautiful, when Adam entered the mix – as they moved and moaned in all giving sensual sexuality.

Adam was composing – seeing the frequencies and colors – the harmonics - the striving for and finally reaching a three centered resonance – one Love.

Adam sensed then saw the first colors vibrating at base frequencies of reds, oranges and yellows – at the start of the sexual coupling between Caroline and Jenny.

As their kisses and caresses became deeper - the greens and blues came into the mix. As Jenny and Caroline orgasmed on more than one occasion – the indigos, violets and white came in.

Pulsing states of frequencies including some infra-reds and ultra-violets, not detectable by the normal human eye, but seen by Adam. Those not seen, he sensed.

The orchestra musicians were amazed when Adam stopped the rehearsal and pointed to one musician or a group of two or three on different instruments – the flute – the French horn and the oboe and correct each of them as required. Adam didn't do this with his ears, but rather with the colors he experienced – as the orchestra played. He could see through sense, the places in the piece – where harmonies were not pure.

He never stopped Caroline – she always waved in harmony.

All music is a wave with every wavelength included - Adam was a quantum savant.

The human ear is a poor instrument when interpreting the full dimension of music.

Adam knew the emotions – sadness and joys felt through music, due to the interaction of quantum portals – particles and sequence in the heavy layers – photons and thoughts in the lighter layers.

Harmony manifested a deeply rooted emotion of connection - resonance, a deeply rooted communal experience of oneness.

As Adam scored the notes – the instrument vibrations - he captured the intensity, sensitivity, hunger and loving positivity, aggression and surrender in waves as they had occurred.

Caroline and Jenny came into the music room, as Adam was finishing the piano part of the lust love score.

"Did you score?" Caroline laughed, looking happy and satisfied as she walked towards Adam with her arms open for a hug.

"I did", said Adam, smiling --- as he hugged Caroline and brought Jenny into the group hug, "At least three times if you include my work this morning."

Jenny had never been happier in her life and still didn't understand how her life had changed so dramatically - now in love with two of the most amazing people on the planet.

"May I?", Caroline asked Adam as she looked at the large screen, full of notes and rhythms on the two-dimensional electronic surface the new and original composition.
"Go to the piano", Adam said – "I will send it to your screen."
Adam and Jenny moved to the large couch in the music room, as Caroline looked through the entire piece. She sighed deeply and started playing from the beginning.
As Caroline played, Jenny had tears in her eyes – in her mind, she relived the beautiful connections she had experienced the night before – Adam captured the energy and the mood – and Jenny responded in joy.
Music is personal, evoking memorable events.
Adam smiled as he looked at Jenny, squeezed her hand and whispered – "I am so happy you see it – you have to feel it, before you see it. Music is a memory of opportunities gone by, and possibilities to come."
It was a beautiful moment for Jenny, as she experienced for the first time in her life, her connection to an everlasting truth – we are us – every child is our child – every pain is our pain – every tear is our tear. We start as 'me' – transcend to 'we', then move en masse through harmony – to resonance in spirit – to us.

Dr. Armstrong and Sarah were settled on the Turkish Airline jet – ready for their 9 or so hour, non-stop flight from Logan Airport in Boston to Istanbul.
Since the flight was over 4 hours in duration – they were flying first class – a condition of their contract with Harvard University – any flight over 4 hours duration warranted a first-class seat.
As they took off, Marta took Sarah's hand and squeezed. "This is going to be a great trip Sarah – are you ready for everything?"
"I have been waiting for this for most of my life", Sarah responded, squeezing back.
"Well let's wow them at this great convention.
Cigdem sent an email saying she will be waiting outside the arrival gate when we get there. I really can't wait to meet her in person, she sounds like the ideal person to hang out with it Istanbul – Imagine, born in Turkey, educated at one of the best universities in the USA – with a PhD in clinical psychology – then returning to

Turkey to open and lead a professional practice with six other PhD's on board, and a support staff of fifteen! With all of that – still had time to start a professional association in Turkey which is now recognized around the world. She is certainly a go getter and a doer!" Marta said

Sarah agreed – Cigdem would be a great asset and resource, especially since part of her practice involved the study of autism in Turkey.

The Captain wished everyone good morning over the plane's intercom, stating we were now over the coast of France and from there, would be heading a little bit south and a great bit west directly into Istanbul.

They had slept quite easily since the flight left Boston Logan at around 11 PM Boston time and landed in Istanbul at about 4 PM Istanbul time – which was about 9AM Boston time - Great time to fly without disruption of their circadian body clock.

The landing was smooth and easy as Marta and Sarah looked at the city below them. It was a large city built on two continents – Asia on one side of the Bosphorus and Europe on the other with two main bridges connecting them, and a population of about 15 million people.

Sarah and Marta were booked into a five-star hotel downtown on the Europe side, and the conference center was part of the hotel complex.

The plane landed – Marta and Sarah easily went through the passport control booth, collected their luggage – easily moved through customs. As they walked out of the security control point - they were met by the smiling face and beautiful eyes of Cigdem.

"Marta and Sarah." Cigdem yelled with a huge smile on her face.

Marta and Sarah walked quickly towards her and the three of them had a group hug – full of joyful energy - finally meeting each other in the molecules.

"It is so good to see you two – welcome to Turkey!" Cigdem said.

"And so good to see you too, Cigdem!" Marta said.

"We're happy to be here – thank you for your presence, Cigdem", Sarah said as she hugged back.

"Okay, our driver is over here. Let's get you to the hotel – it's a long flight and you must be ready to unpack and settle in --- as you know,

the conference venue is the Istanbul Hilton hotel and you have been booked into a two-bedroom suite. I hope you will be happy with the arrangements." Cigdem said as they got into their limo – their suitcases were put into the trunk – Cigdem paid the baggage handler – and they were ready to drive into one of the most interesting cities in the world.
It was a beautiful afternoon.
Sarah felt the close presence of Adam.

Adam and Jenny listened again as Caroline replayed the piece – as she was playing, Adam added the scores for other instruments on the screen of his one-and-only composition device. Adam's expertise in synthesizer and musical app designs came together in the invention of this device which utilized AI algorithms to look ahead and insert the score for an instrument or group of instruments, based on an individual or initial score.
Adam was asked, on many occasions to productize the device – he could make a 'fortune' – Adam was only interested in the music with no interest in selling a product. To Adam, this would be the greatest betrayal an artist could make to art. He didn't patent the algorithms or the apps themselves – his creations were open sourced – well used and appreciated by many music creators, planet wide.
As Caroline finished her second run of the original piano score, Adam had the scores done for every instrument in the philharmonic orchestra on his screen.
Jenny looked at Adam in amazement – "You're so far ahead of the world when it comes to music Adam," she said – "I am so in love with you and what you show me we can do."
Adam smiled and replied, "It is all part of my AI – meaning Adam's Intelligence, don't be too impressed." They both laughed.
Caroline came over and gave Adam a tight hug – "Thank you for your music my love – that piece is amazing – I could conjure up an orgasm listening to that. What does it sound like with your orchestra?"
Adam hit the play button on his device - every WiFi speaker in the house came alive with Caroline's piano, initializing the experience – then the scores of each instrument came in as part of the experience – the feelings were amazing – as Caroline sat beside Jenny, holding

her hand as they re-experienced to the bottom of their being, the beauty and pureness of their love.

Adam leaned back and watched the colors as harmonies built into a final resonance.

It was as beautiful for him now, as it was the previous night when this unique sequence of feelings and emotions were animated in four dimensions.

This was the first time Adam had written a score about the experience of sexual gratification, building to the harmony of both physical release and spiritual expansion.

Sex without love fills a need, burning in the lower three glands – an oil change.

Sex engulfed in love is a gift we freely give and receive, involving all portals from the gonads to the pineal – an overflowing cup of lust, compassion, empathy and joy.

Cigdem, Sarah and Marta arrived at the hotel after focusing on the "tour information" Cigdem freely and expertly provided as they drove through the city from the airport. It was obvious Cigdem was very proud of her Turkish heritage and this great city she had been born into. The architecture, the domes, the ancient streets, the teeming of people – the commercial diversity – the street vendors – the energy buzz and the timeless feelings, were all part of Istanbul.

Once checked into the hotel, Cigdem went to their suite to ensure all was copacetic and there were no surprises.

"Cigdem, this is delightful – what an amazing view!" Marta said.

"It is going to be a pleasure staying here, Cigdem," Sarah piped in.

The suite had two separate bedrooms, with the living room and office in between – all rooms had a magnificent view of the city and the Bosphorus.

The furniture throughout showcased pure Turkish design and style – beautiful and well appointed – the carpets were a work of art. It was easy to see the depth and pride of Turkish artistic craftmanship.

Cigdem said she would see them in the lobby in an hour or so... giving them a chance to freshen up and get settled in.

Both Marta and Sarah hugged her once again and then she was gone.

"Sarah, this room must have cost a fortune – talk about travelling first class!"
"I think the university is paying our expenses, Marta," Sarah said with a smile. "Harvard has a lot of money, I think."
"Okay," Marta said, "I am going to my room to unpack, have a good shower and be ready to meet more of Istanbul with our friend Cigdem in an hour or so. See you later."
Sarah laughed as she went to her room and did the same.
She looked out the window searching for a villa, down by the water – found it, then blew it a kiss.

Cigdem called Caroline and told her she had an hour or so to kill.
"Come on over!" Caroline said, "You can kill it here with us."
The villa was close to the hotel – It took Cigdem 11 minutes to get there.
When Cigdem entered she heard the music – stopped and listened to the most vibrant notes, running together with a piano lead and the orchestra following.
She walked into the main room as Caroline and Jenny stood up and moved towards her with an open-arms welcome. Adam turned the music off.
"What is that amazing music??" Cigdem said loudly. "It touches my soul!"
Caroline laughed as she responded, "Oh, just a little something the three of us cooked up last night," as she looked at Jenny and winked.
"Would you like a glass of wine, and why do you only have an hour or so, to spend with us?" Caroline asked.
"I just dropped two American friends off at the Hilton, have to be back there within the hour to take them out for dinner – though they are on Boston time so maybe we will have lunch," Cigdem laughed.
"You have probably heard of one of them since she has been on the news lately, not just in North America – but around the globe. Her name is Sarah Thomson."
Adam sat up – "Sarah is here!" he exclaimed.
Jenny said, "I have surely heard of her – very well known in Canada – some people think she is a real psychic – and she has a podcast with millions of followers. She doesn't agree with the psychic label –

calls herself an 'Alter' – She's an amazing person, from what I have heard of her.
Why is she in Istanbul?"
"She is the keynote speaker at our conference which starts on Monday. We have psychologists, neuroscientists, cosmologists, biologists, two philosophy professors and even a couple of theoretical physicists flying in to attend. We have never seen such a response from different scientific areas of interest." Cigdem said.
Caroline gave her a small glass of wine. "Thank you, dear Caroline – I can't stay too long so forgive me if I don't finish this." She took a sip, then continued – "As I mentioned previously, you're all welcome as my guest and you will get to meet the famous Dr. Sarah Thomson and her almost as famous colleague, Dr. Marta Armstrong - I find them intriguing and beautiful."
"That sounds wonderful," Adam said – "As long as you and your magnificent husband, Okan, and your two American guests – will be our guest at the concert next Thursday night."
"That is a deal Adam!" Cigdem said. "Okay I have to go – don't want my esteemed colleagues to think us Turkish people don't respect other people's time."
"You and Okan are welcome here anytime, Cigdem – see you soon!" Jenny said.
Kiss, kiss, hug, hug – kiss, hug, and she was gone.
Adam leaned back and said softly to Jenny and Caroline – "I know Sarah well – we're cut from the same cloth so to speak - born on the exact same date at the exact same time – me in Toronto – Sarah in Baton Rouge." Adam paused as he let these words sink in for Jenny and Caroline.
"We're spiritually entangled – and though we're ALL spiritually entangled – Sarah and I are entangled 'Alters'. Adam made a quote sign with his fingers as he said the word Alters, then continued, "I am, in this instance, a quantum fully functional autistic like savant – Sarah is an empath fully functional autistic like savant, again in this instance. Together we enable the altering of actions and consequences – we enable a chance for all of us to ascend."
Caroline and Jenny were perplexed.
"Ascend to where?" Caroline asked.

"You may think I am a bit delusional," Adam continued – "but, in my quantum intuitive view, we're stuck in four dimensions – a prison of blue skies, where we each are 'born' and move through time – event to sequential event – till we die.

Events are linear memories with a bit of time in between - memories, past events, brought forward in our minds - events are sequential and happen in a linear path. I brushed my teeth - I had a shower - I got dressed and had a cup of coffee (thank goodness)" Adam said with a smile, then continued, "I washed my uncle's car with my cousin Mary, almost 15 years ago.

Life is an observed experience of sequential events, over multiple parallel instances, within parallel concurrent times.

The future begins a petasecond (or less) from now.

The past ends when nobody thinks about it anymore.

The 'big bang' is the root instance of this universe, created by action and consequence taken and met, in another.

Every universe creates a new instance of sequential events - these events also include the creation of other universes – when linear decisions spawn resultant consequences - each consequence creates a new instance, in a concurrent yet separate time - each instance is the root instance of a new set of consequences.

Everything possible is inevitable – in the multiverse model all that can happen will happen.

The idea of a multiverse rather than one universe is supported by the mathematics of quantum mechanics – 'String Theory' - it's still a theory - supported by current mathematics".

Jenny and Caroline looked at Adam a bit perplexed. Where had all this come from?

"I have never exposed this level of myself to either of you before – though the music I create, could only be created from a deeper dimension of comprehension." Adam thought everyone already knew that.

"Are you serious, Adam?" Caroline asked. "You know the famous Sarah – the genius from Baton Rouge, everyone on social media is talking about? You actually know her, or do you know her from the exposure she gets on the internet? I don't think you ever mentioned her?"

Adam realized Caroline and Jenny were more impressed that he knew Sarah, rather than the deeper sourced information he had parlayed.
Adam responded – "I know her, Caroline – as I know myself – we were born into this instance, as one event into this shared concurrent time."
Adam looked at Jenny and Caroline and started to laugh. "Okay, you're both impressed I know Sarah. Can I give you more background in how we know each other and who we are?"
"Of course," Jenny said. "Sorry."
"Okay" Adam said, and then continued.
"The three of us here share time with each other as separate entities – we're sharing this sequential instance.
Caroline, you and I started sharing time together through my friendship with your brother David – we're still within this sequential experience. Jenny, we're sharing time together in this instance, due to the random event of you and I having seats together on a flight from Toronto to London.
From the time of our first meeting, we have shared our observations and experience. After the attack and my injury at the airport, Caroline joined us and the three of us are now together.
Currently we three – are sharing what would be correct to call, a contemporary instance with shared events.
We all share on this beautiful planet – time and events with all contemporary sequential beings.
Contemporaries is one of my favorite words," Adam smiled, then continued. "It is a one-word definition of all living - NOW - sequential beings - from an ant to an orca, from an uncle to bird – a sequential being, just born, to a sequential being about to die. Before birth and after death, they are non-contemporaries.
So, our contemporary mix is always in a state of great flux, defined by the concurrent time, birth and death events of every living sequential being in shared time."
Jenny pursed her lips with an incredulous kind of look – "Adam, are you saying there is more than one universe and other parts of us live in all of them? That is a real weird thought for me to agree with. What the hell are we trying to do with our split parts all over the place or should I say places?

Plus, I think it will be interesting when we meet Sarah – to see if she agrees, you know each other so well without ever meeting."

Caroline squeezed Jenny's hand, looked at Adam and added, "What she said!"

Adam smiled lovingly at his two bewildered friends and lovers, "Yes, you two! Instances in parallel places, are observed by us and are therefore, real. Did you ever watch a movie made to have more than one ending?

Other realities, other starts and endings, where we never met as we did in this instance, also exist.

You and I met on the plane Jenny due to the randomness of the seats we were given. You will not believe me when I say there are instances, where we sat beside every other person on that plane, and where every person sat with every other person on that plane. There are instances where we never met since we didn't make it to the plane for one reason or another. Every person on that plane missed that flight for one reason or another – including the pilot and the co-pilot. The plane is a constant in a connected process of instances.

We exist in a flux of possible futures generated through the funnel of consequential pasts.

Every physical construct – like a planet or a plane has multiple instances attached to its reality. Every physical construct involves multiple particles and waves at a quantum level.

Randomness is an underlying part of the mix. Everything possible, is inevitable."

Adam paused to let this idea sink in – it was totally non-intuitive since our lower intuition is only concerned with the reality observed within a given life, and the observation within one life, is focused on the actions and resulting consequential events within that life.

Every instance is a wormhole at the quantum level.

Every reality - a quantum reality.

Adam knew his brain is different, in both architecture and topology – his intuition going beyond the focus of one instance, into the multi-dimensional focus of multiple instances.

He is a highly functional autistic like quantum savant.

He realized without trying, he could bore people to tears, as he seemed to be doing with Jenny and Caroline.

His most difficult task was expanding the imagination and openness of those who never thought about such things - making explanations simple enough to alter perceptions. His ability to create such amazing music added to the credibility of his thoughts – he is a genius, as we all are in one instance or another.
Adam looked at Jenny and Caroline. "Please indulge me in this – I am trying to tell you why Sarah and I are entangled – and there will be a test for you two after I have explained it." Adam laughed and continued, as Jenny and Caroline cocked their heads forward pretending to be totally enthralled by what Adam was saying.
"The thought of a multiverse will take some time before moving from theoretical physics to experimental physics - and an expansion of imaginative brainpower as well.
The universe is one instrument - the multiverse - an aesthetic orchestra."
Caroline and Jenny were silent as they thought about what was said. Both were a bit sadder, since they realized the physical relationship between the three of them was over. They knew this intuitively and experienced the sadness together. Adam was now part of a larger purpose.
"Well," Caroline said, "I know both Jenny and I love you more than life – I also know you have always been a truthful beautiful friend – I stand with you and will participate and hopefully contribute to your aspirations as best as I am able. I don't understand all you have said, but I want to learn – I want to understand."
Jenny looking a bit solemn added, "What she said."

Cigdem was waiting in the lobby when Sarah and Marta walked out of the elevator.
Kiss, kiss, hug – kiss, kiss – hug.
"You two look great," Cigdem said as she smiled. "I know to you both, your body clock time is closer to lunch than to dinner. So, I don't mind eating a lunch meal if you're so inclined to do so."
"No way," Sarah said, "I am hungry, ready for a dinner size salad."
"Me too" said Marta – "But I will have more than salad. I think Sarah was a giraffe in her last life – she eats too many leaf's, in my opinion."

"Okay – I know the best place and we can walk to it from here. I have booked a table at Old Ottoman Café – serving great salads and vegan food - delicious carnivore dishes as well."
Everyone was in a happy mood as they walked into the street – Istanbul was a special place. Sarah felt the vibrations, the fervor and the kindness – she also realized the darker side too, but the darker side was common to every place on the planet, in her experience.
The meal and the ambiance – the service and the company were all magnificent. Over a glass of wine at the end of the meal, Cigdem mentioned they had all been invited to a special concert, as the guests of the composer and starring musician, occurring with the Istanbul symphony orchestra. She said they were special friends introduced to her by her husband, who met the composer in various internet music groups.
"Perhaps you have heard of them," Cigdem stated, "They are Canadian, but I think their music is a gift to the world. Caroline Mathews is the pianist – Adam Mason is the composer – they also have a friend – Jennifer Cagney, who is travelling with them, and is also Canadian – they are delightful. I have invited them to our conference, and you will meet them there."
Sarah smiled and said, "I know Adam like I know myself – we were born into this instance, as one event – into this shared time – on the same date, at the same second – Adam in Toronto, me in Baton Rouge. We will finally meet in the molecules, here in Istanbul."
Marta was not surprised since she believed Sarah earlier when she talked about Adam. Nothing about Sarah surprised Marta anymore – she knew when Sarah said something about anything – she was speaking the truth.
"You know Adam?" Cigdem said with surprise. "This is going to be a great conference."

Somewhere in the Middle East , a group of fighters were waiting for the decision to carry out the suicide bombing plan in Istanbul.
They received the affirmative and put the plan in place to kill as many as possible, at an upcoming conference, where foreigners were in attendance. Their objective – to kill as many as possible – including the American speaker who had become so popular around the world telling lies about how the universe itself functioned. Lies

about the domain of God and the truth written in the holy book, written by God Himself.

There were six sleeper cells in Turkey ready and able to kill indiscriminately for their religious cause – the foreign sinners would die and go to hell - the martyrs would go to heaven with a special seat beside a thankful god.

The entire middle east was a tinder box – ready to explode on many fronts to protect the various god given rights – of multiple tribal factions, each believing God was on their side to help win their cause for land, and punish non-believers, for their indiscretions against the word of the true god.

The true god gives favor to each tribe – each tribe is the chosen one. Even tribes worshipping the same god, broke into factions, where only their interpretations of the holy book – were real. There are many types of Christian - Evangelicals, Protestants, Catholics, and more, all believe in Jesus – though not necessarily in the Trinity, and in the Christian god. Yet each faction within one religion – becomes more attuned to the real god and becomes the favorites of the real God.

Each religion and the factions within each religion think down on the other's feeling sorry they will never see god – since they don't believe the true words.

The Muslims, the Jewish, the Christian and Hindu – all special in their own beliefs, each with their own internal factions, worshipping the true god or gods.

The most aggressive religious tribes were monotheistic – usually beginning in dessert environments, where nature was unkind. These religious men of god formed raiding parties to kill and enslave those of different beliefs – power over other lands and food supplies, as gifts from god himself, were part of the rewards.

They sacrificed children and animals to god, for special needs like rain and good crops.

Land is important and most fights are about the rights to land – god promised and given land in some cases.

Followers of a false god didn't deserve to live – and in many cases the ones who worshipped false gods (all of them at one time or another) were nothing in the eyes of their true god – and could be

enslaved, raped, subjugated and killed with their god's approval and encouragement.
The god you served was mostly a tribal hereditary choice – or as the result of missionaries sent to conquered lands to expand the number of believers.
Martyrs - a special breed of the creed, received next world rewards promised for killing non-believers – who had no value in the eyes of their god.
The disciples of Jesus were eventually killed as martyrs – the offering up of Jewish martyrs during the crusade for the sanctification of god's name – who would rather die than forgo their religion's beliefs in favor of their generation to generation – hand me down, tribal truth.
If religion is based on love - as most propose to be, it's a love meant to protect and promote their own.
Each god has no patience for the 'truth' of another. The worship of 'false' gods – punishable by an eternity in hell, or some other applicable eternity of horror.
Every religion creates atrocities against every other, at different times, under different power balances and unbalances.

Sarah and Marta spent an excellent Sunday with Okan and Cigdem visiting the amazing historical sites of Istanbul. Cigdem was a proud and loving host, adding color to the ancient themes and histories sewn into the cultures of Istanbul.
She knew her city and the history of Turkey and was happy to share her knowledge. Okan also added color protesting when Cigdem blamed many of the discords and various wars, on the egos of older men – angry at the age they had become.
Cigdem gave expert descriptions of the contents and history of Topkapi Palace – Sarah and Marta touched the glass case said to hold the hand of John the Baptist – it was a bony hand, they thought. She also talked about the importance of Turkey in the Christian faith – which she didn't believe but found interesting. How while dying on the cross, Jesus said to his favorite disciple John, who was standing with his mother, Mary – "Woman, behold your son." And to John "Behold your mother."

Cigdem was enthusiastic as she continued to comment. "Many people don't know, John the apostle – not the Baptist - brought Mary back to Ephesus and built her a small dwelling, which to this day is called 'The house of Mary'. John's basilica is also there. John was exiled to the Island of Patmos, by Rome, after refusing to deny Jesus as the Son of God. From this location. John wrote the last chapter in the New Testament – Revelations while he was on Patmos and I don't know what happened to Mary, after John was sent to Patmos. Perhaps she is buried there – or just went to heaven body and soul." Cigdem laughed.

"Turkey is a mostly Muslim country full of Christian history", Cigdem said proudly – "Even though we have been fighting with the Greeks for centuries", she laughed.

During a pleasant and interesting lunch where Cigdem, Okan, Marta and Sarah discussed the relationships of gods, faith, philosophy in the context of common psychology, only Sarah was aware of the couple sitting a few tables from them. This couple pretended to take pictures of the café and themselves, but Sarah knew she, Cigdem and Marta were the target of the cameras.

These photos were downloaded to the active cells verifying the identity of the 'must die', targeted sinners.

Sarah understood the gravity of the events to follow when she ended the discussion with, "When love becomes more important than god – then there will be no further need for religions."

Everyone agreed to this.

Sarah and Marta were dropped off at the hotel after a wonderful and informative day, so they would have a bit of time to finish off the details of the keynote speech, to be given at the conference the next morning.

As Sarah and Marta walked through the hotel lobby, they were greeted by many conference attendees. Everyone looking forward to the next couple of days, meeting and greeting other professionals in their field – many considering this to be the most important conference ever. A breakthrough was about to be demonstrated which could change the course of humanity.

"Well we're as ready as we ever will be." Sarah said to Marta. They shared a half bottle of wine, kissed and hugged each other – "Sleep well", "You too", retiring to their bedrooms.

Sarah looked once again at the villa with its lights still on – "Tomorrow, dear Adam -tomorrow – always another tomorrow, tomorrow"

Six AM seemed early – and it felt that way since it was much earlier in Boston. Both Marta and Sarah were slowly adjusting to the new time zone and were ready to go.

When Sarah entered the living room, Marta had coffee ready with Turkish pastries already delivered fresh from the hotel kitchen.

"I pre ordered this last night", she smiled, "come and get some – we're going to hit the ball out of the park today! Imagine the discussions we will have tonight at the reception? I am excited and talking too much." Marta laughed.

"Marta, you think of everything." Sarah said smiling, as she sat down at the table with Marta. "Just to run through this morning's agenda - After the opening ceremony with a video feed from the President welcoming all participants to Turkey, then the traditional dancers, we will be introduced by Cigdem, as the dual presenters of the keynote address."

You will go to the podium first and introduce me as your prodigy."

Marta broke in – "I will not introduce you as my prodigy, Sarah. You found me. I will introduce you as my distinguished associate and colleague, which you are!"

Marta paused, then asked, "I haven't brought this up, hoping you would, but, you haven't – what is the meeting with you and the great composer Adam going to be like?" Do you know each other physically or is it totally in both of your minds - no disrespect intended - If you would rather not talk about it of course, I will not ask again? You know I will be thinking about it. Well you normally know what I am thinking about."

"It's not a big deal." Sarah said. "Let's get this done, you will see it as it unfolds."

"Okay, I can except that answer. I guess I will just have to be patient and meet this mysterious man." Marta said.

One hour to get ready – and it was tight. Marta and Sarah went into scurry mode as they morphed from their pastries and coffee look into their confident professional business attire – Sarah didn't like to be so bound up with such conservative attire but Marta had insisted they visit her favorite clothing emporium in Boston, to be fitted in a

conservative style, from accessories to shoes. They were here to get their message delivered - a force to be reckoned with.
The conference centre was on the second floor of the hotel and this was a great convenience, from room to conference floor in about 8 minutes.
As they entered the crowded space, Cigdem moved towards them – kiss, kiss – hug, kiss, kiss – hug. “You two look wonderful.” Cigdem said.
They were both greeted by many colleagues, known and unknown, as they moved through the hall towards their VIP seats at the front of the room.
Okan stood up to greet them – kiss, kiss – hug, kiss, kiss – hug.
“Good morning, dear friends”, Okan beamed. “I am so looking forward to your presentation.”
There was a commotion at the back of the room as Jenny, Caroline and Adam entered the hall. They were well known to this audience through the music they created. Cigdem excused herself to Sarah and Marta – “I will be right back with my special guests.”
Cigdem greeted them with two kisses and a hug for each - she invited them to follow her to the front of the room. As they walked forward the room broke into a spirited applause – Adam and Caroline smiled and nodded their appreciation for this kind response. Jenny felt a sense of great pride as she walked with them. Adam looked forward and locked eyes with Sarah – they both smiled as Marta stared in awe, not believing the intensity of this moment. She felt a shiver run up her spine, knowing she was witnessing a special moment in time.
The hall was almost full – over 800 delegates from around the globe – happy to be witnessing this great event.
Okan walked towards Adam with his hand extended as the first bomb went off, blowing Okan’s arm from his body, as he flew through the air – being ripped apart by ball bearings which had been strapped around the suicide bombers body. Cigdem was also shredded and died instantly as her husband had. Sarah and Adam went into a slow-motion response able to see and keep their locked eye connection, until they too were blown to pieces by the nails and ball bearings. Jenny and Caroline were torn apart – Marta’s torso

exploded away from her head and limbs --- the carnage was horrible and cruel.
The first bomber made sure the high priority targets were eliminated – the second priority – to kill and maim as many people as possible.
All prime targets were eliminated... 'thanks be to God'.
A second and third suicide bomb exploded in other parts of the hall.
Blood and body parts scattered in all directions.
It was a sad day in Istanbul.
More than four hundred delegates killed and many more injured – the hospitals in Istanbul were full.
When the world heard of the attack - Adam Mason, Caroline Mathews, Jenny Cagney, Sarah Thompson and Marta Armstrong and many other leaders in their field, were killed so cruelly, the entire planet mourned the loss.
No one could understand the futility of it all.
Alison and Walter Mason – were devasted beyond words.
Barry and Debbie Thompson – were devastated beyond words.
Jenny's parents heartbroken forever.
The world sobbed and cried for the loss in Istanbul.

Chapter 13

Choose Kindness First.

Somewhere in the Middle East, a group of fighters were waiting for the decision to carry out the suicide bombing plan in Istanbul.
The commander had many opportunities on the table and decided to cancel the Istanbul opportunity in favor of an attack in New York City.
The sleeper cells in Turkey went back to sleep. The sleeper cells in the USA were waking up.
A dirty bomb shipped, on its way to Philadelphia – It would be loaded in three pieces onto three different trucks and shipped to New York.
The supreme commander had given orders to all regions, to focus all field assets to this project.
Six Turkish sleeper cell members made plans to go to either Philadelphia or New York City. The dirty bomb and all logistics were funded by a very rich nations – the people of the USA needed to be taught another lesson, they were not invincible.
The dirty bomb could kill over four million people and leave the ground area contaminated for hundreds of years.
Most people in the world were sick and tired of the violence and cruelty.
They were ready for another path, but no one knew how to do it.
Many tried through meditation, and higher thinking, with great results for individuals or small groups. In most cases, these sects would eventually fall back into the hierarchical structures. The more aggressive or the more manipulative ones – would rise to the top, subjugating those now defined as lower.
Hierarchy usually involved a tiered structure, where all male participants were greater than the female. The females were helpers – not fully participating in the thicker part of the work.
God is male therefore women are not endowed with His image.

They are lesser beings.
How could anyone argue with that – it was a self-evident truth – to men.
The religious zealots believe they are doing the will and work of god – being ready to kill or die for the good of god, was the locus of their lives.
Above all, the idea of their god as the true god must survive. Children learned by rote and rod, to live their lives, obedient to old men who say they know the mind of god.
Sarah looked at the bigger picture of multiple instances sequentially experienced in concurrent event portals.
Every event horizon is the result of a decision consequence.
Her opening remarks would lead to the proof on no free will. Everything was the result of a consequence – when every consequence is experienced – the need for any idea of 'will' is no longer relevant.
"What a treat having you as our guide, Cigdem. Thank you so much for your hospitality. I never realized Istanbul was such an important city in the history of mankind." Marta said.
Cigdem replied – "My pleasure. I love bragging about my city and my country."
Sarah was enjoying her time in the sun, after savoring the taste of a chopped Turkish salad – with pomegranate dressing – tasty.
"I must add my thankyou as well. Cigdem." Sarah piped in. What a great day! I am sorry Okan had to leave before this wonderful terrace lunch."
"Well," said Cigdem – "I have a surprise for you both. Okan is with Caroline and Adam and we're invited to their villa, close to the Bosphorus – They're waiting for us now. They want to meet you both before attending the keynote address tomorrow morning. Are you up for that?"
"Of course," said Sarah.
"Let's go!" said Marta. "We're always ready to meet new friends, especially new friends who have gained the love and respect from the entire planet."
Caroline and Adam were a famous couple indeed.
Their concerts were sold out as soon as they were announced.
Okan and Adam met over the internet when in their early teens.

Adam was endowed with a great sense of music which, in some cases seemed outside of normal human abilities.

Okan was anything networked or computed – a gifted coder, and system architect - able to put tight functions and procedures together – for a specific objective – reams and reams of function and procedure, beans.

They named their machine "Charlie" – as a joke – no special meanings to any of the letters – Charlie was just another member of the creative circle.

They were a compatible pair, in the design of music machines – synthesizers above and beyond the normal design metrics.

Adam was one of the first to add artificial intelligence into the generation of electronic music.

Charlie - created by Adam and Okan – imbedded machine learning techniques to add anticipative and deterministic algorithms – enabling the fleshing out of all orchestra instruments, from a single piano input.

Adam wrote a piano score, Caroline played it, Okan tweaked Charlie, added instrument by instrument till the harmonic sound of an entire orchestra filled the room – with music magnificence.

Adam then used his magic, providing finer tuning to the crowded mix.

When everyone was satisfied with the result, the piece would be sent to the transposition processor – and printed as a full or partial score depending on the objective of the transposition.

The moving of notes optimized harmonies, fine-tuned by Charlie's machine learning algorithms.

Caroline was amazed how her one score piece could be transformed into a full orchestra soundtrack – with her solo spots created by some secret sauce software, she knew nothing about.

Adam and Okan didn't want to commercialize their achievements, and due to the continual creation and improving machine learning procedures – Charlie improved exponentially.

Adam was the final arbiter though – he was dimensions ahead of Charlie. Charlie was a master of predictive and definitive rote.

Adam added emotion to the note structure – feelings to the created field, where every instrument was an individual contributor to the emotional mesmeric masterpiece.

His brain was built differently – the top layer of his cerebellum had 8 times more neurons than the average brain, and his frontal lobe was larger and denser as well.

Adam knew this – no one else did, except Sarah.

Sarah shared Adam's brain physiology, though she had applied her difference in a different way.

In this instance Adam and Sarah were "Alters" - able to transcend the thick realities of the three lower glands – active within the four lower dimensions - sequential instances – observed in multiple waves – where everything possible is inevitable.

From the lowest and cruelest bottomless pit to the highest, kindness enlightened, harmonic, all.

Manifesting an observed balance of knowledge – where every sequential being experienced transcendence of the thick.

In this instance – Adam and Sarah transcended.

Transcendence is possible for every sequential being. Transcendence is thus inevitable.

In the final analysis, Adam and Sarah were not special at all, in other times and multi-verse spaces, which formed the membrane of their observations, they were clawing tooth and nail – to move forward – lift higher, driven by the communal universal appetency to transcend.

Cigdem, Sarah and Marta were on their way to the villa.

It was a very happy occasion.

Sarah and Adam - finally meeting in the molecules.

Okan, Caroline and Adam were on the front terrace as Cigdem pulled into the driveway. They stood up and walked towards the car.

Sarah and Adam locked eyes as they moved towards each other, both streaming tears of joy, they reached out and held each other, tightly.

Cigdem, Marta and Okan – stood back in awe – a soft white light surrounded Adam and Sarah as they moved back in their minds eye, to the event where this sequential root instance began - to the Woman's Hospital in Baton Rouge - to the General Hospital in Toronto.

Both Adam and Sarah exchanged all observations of their individual sequential being experience. When the sequence reached the point where Sarah was stuck, in a bottomless pit, able to jump from one instance to another, Adam moved beyond speed to that lonely cruel place and told her to touch the light. As she did, she jerked on the chair as a young girl – becoming conscious again surprising Dr. Armstrong as she did.

Sarah and Adam then moved through the sequential experiences and observations lived in this instance by each, until they reached the present time – standing in the villa driveway, holding on to one another in the thickness and heaviness of the molecules.

They were sequential again, and aware of all each had done, with whom, to reach this place and time within this root event instance.

As they slowly decreased the pressure of their embrace – they kissed each other and felt the deepness of their love and purpose. Their eyelids were closed – blocking physical vision. Their pineal portals, fully aware, as they visualized beyond thought to the resonance of the light, dimensions higher.

Both Adam and Sarah didn't want to be sequential again – but they were.

Adam then gave Marta a hug – he knew everything about her.

Sarah gave Cigdem and Okan a hug – she knew everything about them.

"Wow" Marta said, "You two are enigmas, I don't know what to say."

"Just say nice to meet you Adam and Caroline," Sarah said.

"Nice to meet you Adam and Caroline!" Marta laughed.

They moved into the villa – Adam and Sarah holding hands, acting as if they had been together forever, without a hint of lust in their love. Caroline could think no harsh or jealous thoughts about this new woman in Adam's life who apparently was not new at all.

They moved to the comfort of the back terrace, with the comfortable cushions, chairs, loveseats and couches. This was a soothing place.

Adam and Sarah moved to the loveseat, – Okan, Cigdem and Marta to the big couch opposite Adam and Sarah.

Caroline went to the kitchen and came back rolling a small serving table, with chilled wine, cheese and tapas. Okan got up and did the honors of pouring the wine and putting the "snacks" on the large table in the middle of the sitting circle.

Caroline chose the big chair between the couch and the loveseat. She felt like a fifth wheel on a double date but would not have chosen any place else to be in the world at this time.

When everyone was settled with their drinks and their snacks, Adam spoke – "I have an idea which you may or may not be interested." He paused, then continued, "I would like to provide a musical backdrop tomorrow morning – with the help of Caroline and Okan of course, preceding and during Sarah's keynote speech."

"Everything is planned," Cigdem said. "I want to make sure the opening flows – the sound system is set up and ready to go – we have no piano on the stage – the event planner would not be chuffed to find out her work was done for naught."

Okan held her hand – "We have thought about that my dear Cigdem – we would never do anything to put your conference in a dimmer light. The music will enhance Sarah's presentation – Charlie will know when she is speaking and will provide a perfect changing volume, impressing on the audience, the message, also as music."

"Sarah and Marta – what do you two want to do?", Cigdem asked.

"Well", said Marta – "I defer to Sarah – she is the main attraction – oops, can't say that anymore since Adam and Caroline are also a huge attraction. If your music is part of the conference Adam and Caroline – we will make headlines around the world. I am sure the handlers from Harvard would be over the moon."

Sarah squeezed Adam's hand and simply said – "I want to do it."

"Okay" said Cigdem, "What do we have to change – who do we have to call?"

"I am taking care of all of that Cigdem, but I would like you help and approval and help with some of the logistics – We have wireless speakers I need installed this afternoon and a booth where I can sit with Charlie and a piano for Caroline. After this part of the presentation is done, we go back to your event planning – this is the only change over the three days." Okan said.

"Oh, my goodness" Cigdem said – "I can't believe the presentations of the conference speakers will be exciting in anyway – how can you follow an act of Adam, Caroline and Sarah?"

"Let's order some food." Caroline quipped – we have a bit of work to do, but not much.

The ladies sat together trading stories and enjoying each other's company – waiting for the food to arrive – Okan and Adam went to the music room and started doing magic with the new composition."
Cigdem asked Sarah, how she and Adam could be so calm now, after such a spectacular first meeting.
"There is no stress in love." Sarah said. "Everything physical is the lowest part of knowing.
A birth event of any sequential being is a lonely experience. We're trapped in a sequence of actions and consequences – we miss who and why we are – we cheat and steal and lie and manipulate others, not realizing everything we do – every decision and consequence we manifest, is done in the light when we think it's done in the dark. There is no such thing as a secret – but the concept of secrets, have consequences. Adam and I overtly resonate with awareness of higher thought – where the pineal is our lowest portal of our physical experience. Each sequential being is locked in a cage where the bars are blue skies."
The doorbell rang and the food is here – Caroline had a favorite restaurant Turkish and US cuisine.
The ladies set up the dining room table – various dishes – multiple flavors – excellent food.
"Come and get it" Caroline yelled as David and Okan were coming out of the music room.
"We're ready, Caroline – after dinner we need you to play a composition. I think we will enjoy it." Adam said.
The meal was full of joy and lively conversations.
"Okay, I am ready." Caroline said. "To the piano I go – once again!"
Charlie displayed the new creation to the screen on Caroline's piano. This was the start of the score to be played the next morning, but all was not exposed.
When Caroline sat down and started scrolling through the score on the screen to take a first look at the complexity and simplicity of the piece, Charlie lit up the speaker system with a low comforting vibration - like waves caressing the shore on a remote Caribbean Island - using carrier wave frequencies between 6 cycle per second and 14 cycles per second, the Theta and Alpha frequencies created in the brain.

Adam explained – "Charlie will play this as the hall is filling up – unobtrusive – relaxing – putting everyone at ease. It will not be audible to most but will be soothing to all.

As we get closer to the hall being filled, Charlie will start mixing higher carrier frequencies, between fifteen and one hundred cycles per second – subtly raising the alertness of the brains in the hall, while also having the effect of putting most of the audience into a synchronized feeling of anticipation and wellness."

"Well it is working on me," Cigdem said.

"And me too," Marta added. "This could help some overactive patients in calmness sessions."

"I am relaxed," said Cigdem as she leant into Okan with a satisfied smile on her face.

"Our human ear can't hear the sound of this wave range." Adam continued – "Though some sequential mammalian beings like elephants communicate by stamping their feet on the ground – creating a frequency of about 14 cycles per second – which can be 'heard' by other elephants at great distance, but I digress - Our objective in using these infra-low frequency waves is to promote relaxation, calmness and well-being to those sitting in the hall.

At the appropriate time, the lights in the hall will dim a bit, and Caroline wearing her best white angelic gown, will walk to the piano – wait till the applause is done, sit down and start playing."

Caroline felt comfortable with the score and started playing.

The background sound diminished but was still present adding subtle harmonies to Caroline's keystrokes.

Adam continued to narrate – "There will be applause and Charlie will subdue the sound, then signal Caroline on her screen to start playing again. There will be a four-minute musical interlude with Charlie adding harmonics and Caroline playing the lead." Adam said as Caroline started her four-minute stripe of notes with emotion.

The mood – haunting, conveying a lost and empty place – yet there is a ray of hope – harmonies - plotting their escape – expanding their space – pushing all things possible – gathering the separated – as one.

Then the music changed – Caroline playing a solo interlude – climbing from a bottomless pit of isolation – moving towards the

higher light – stretching forward rather than reaching back. Joined by others with the same intent.
The theme - moving to a new position – transcending the current mindset.
The opening would be magnificent – all were sure.
Everyone was ready.
Okan set up a live podcast over the internet covering the keynote speech – millions of viewers were already signed up for the event.
Both Sarah and Adam were cherished by their fanbase. The ones who wanted to reach higher – the ones tired of the constant hierarchical wars and money manipulations by the sequential beings of the lower three glands – fight or flight – digesting the planet for money, - sexual power plays, subjugating females to a lower place on the pecker order. The sequential beings of three-dimensional mastery – the Darwinian proof of might is right and survival of the fittest – the ones with the weapons – ready to kill without remorse – the killing of "them" for the sake of the non-inclusive, 'us'.
Millions of sequential beings in this instance were ready to ascend – to transcend these chains of blue skies – thinking higher.
As the new introduction was played through, Cigdem was happy with the results.
It was time to get some rest.
Okan and Cigdem bade their good nights – as Caroline finished her magic.
Marta and Sarah – would ride back with them to the hotel ready for the hope of tomorrow.
Adam held Sarah, as they continued to connect in thought, through the pineal portal.
They were now together as all others would be. There is no hierarchy of "us and them" in the higher dimensions, experienced solely as - "We are".
They kissed and departed connected. Marta hugged Adam – not sure at all, what was happening – but taking it all is as an extension of truth. She loved Adam and Caroline – without knowing why - she trusted her feelings.
Adam and Caroline were happy they had come to Istanbul - Caroline was also happy her "hubby" Adrian would be arriving on the weekend, to attend the Istanbul symphonic orchestra presentation

– featuring Adam's compositions – Okan's technical mastery and Caroline's keystroking.
They were also happy Cigdem, Okan, Marta and Sarah would also be attending as their special guests.
Adam knew he and Sarah would be together working to bring higher thought – towards love, away from self – towards kindness, away from cruelty – towards empathy, away from narcissism – towards compassion.
This instance of planet Earth is ready for a change – ready for a transcendence from the influences of the lower three glands to the influence of the upper four, then ascending beyond.
Thought is the builder, which emanates then animates the four dimensions below.
The multiverse of congruent instances, experiencing every action and consequence possible in the mix. We're truly part of a magnificent mix.
Adam wore a silk black shirt with white slacks and black shoes – his hair tousled – as the hair of a genius should look – exuding charisma - stunning in his approachability and his simplicity. He was sexier in the molecules than his pictures could portray – and women noticed – understanding why he had so many groupies in his late teens. He changed though – losing interest in the sexual offerings of women – becoming more interested in expanded humanity development.
Some women were disappointed when this change occurred, especially those blessed with a body no man could refuse – except Adam.
Adam spoke with all who extended themselves to meet him, giving autographs for those who asked and allowing pictures to be taken for those who wished for a photo proof too.
Caroline was backstage having her own dressing room – slipping into her white silken gown – with hair cascading over her shoulders – she was beautiful – graceful – artistic -vulnerable, confident and poised.
Okan was in the control room with Charlie.
Cigdem was with Sarah and Marta in their dressing room – The hall started to fill.
Charlie started the low frequency carrier wave – no sound but a sense of relaxation filled the room.

Okan, with the podcast screen in front of him - over two million people joined-in so far. The count was increasing quickly. "An online world event", Okan said out loud to himself.

Charlie was doing well – Okan was happy – Marta, Sarah, and Cigdem had been joined by Caroline – who looked spectacular in her silk and shimmering gown.

"Caroline – three minutes – Cigdem, 9 minutes – Marta and Sarah, 11 minutes" Charlie announced over the dressing room speaker.

Caroline gave everyone a hug with huge smiles and a "Let's do this!" attitude, all around.

The hall was full – Charlie presented a soothing set of notes – then Charlie announced, "Ladies and gentlemen, – we present to you, Caroline Mathews Tranter."

Caroline walked onto the stage – the audience, totally surprised at this change on the program, enthusiastically stood and gave her a standing ovation.

Okan checked the podcast which now had over 40 million people around the world viewing live on screens of multiples sizes. This was by far the largest on-line audience ever experienced.

Charlie then increased the volume as the phrase "please be seated" from a deep base chorus – the volume cascading higher as everyone, happy to be part of this – sat down in unison.

Caroline turned to the audience and bowed in appreciation – walked to the piano, sat down stretched her arms above her head – brought them down, put her fingers on the keys and started playing.

The sound was haunting - the space silent, as she played – Charlie put one spotlight on Caroline - the house lights were off, except for the dim glow of the emergency exits by the closed doors.

The audience moved into a meditative state as the brainwaves of each reinforced the feelings of all. Synchronization – common experience – empathic membranes – teary eyes.

The feedback from the podcast participants was also moving towards the meditative and empathetic state.

All participants were thinking higher – love being higher than hate – kindness more natural than cruelty – sharing more pleasing than hoarding.

Adam closed his eyes and felt Sarah's isolation, as she experienced the bottomless pit, where even the word "our" was too heavy to be spoken.
Adam watched the harmonics – thick and difficult – moving only within the portals of the lower three glands – with a perception akin to the quicksand of material things – holding and sinking the sequential beings, caught within these instances of continuous actions and consequences. These ones didn't seek a higher reality – material comforts were a sticky choice - where material wealth proved to be an oxymoron – a deception – a trap – where those who died 'rich' were poorer in obtaining kinder and empathetic consequences – sinking deeper into the quicksand of the lower three glands.
Adam knew, the material dimensions are the lowest part of knowing.
But, the enlightened contemporaries within each instance stretched higher, using the consequences taken within each era, knowing the stretch for greater knowledge, based on truth was a tedious and arduous journey. But the only journey worth following - escaping the stickiness of material masters which in the final analysis worshipped and became material slaves.
Caroline closed in on the four-minute mark - Charlie was ready to add music in support of Cigdem coming out to introduce the keynote, speakers. Okan was overlooking the entire process – watching multiple thousands of heart shaped symbols rising within the various screens, the on-line audiences expressing approval and thanks for the experience.
This live pod cast was a viral event.
As Caroline raised both hands away from the keys, the audience gave her a sitting ovation, thankful for the piano interlude, respecting the flow of what is yet to come.
Charlie started the transposed melodies from Caroline's solo piano piece, as music once again filled the room, the sound of wood flutes, supported by oboes, violins and French horns – a country stream with water falling over a set of small falls - ebbing and flowing waves – escaping, transcending – with no expectations or goals.
As Charlie was putting this forward, he announced – "Please welcome Dr. Cigdem Olpar, one of Turkey's most prominent

professor's and practitioners, for everything psychology and neurology. She is the host of your conference and is responsible for everything happening here.

If you feel inclined, please give her a heartfelt welcome."

The audience once again broke into a loud and lively applause – some exuberant attendees putting a whistle into the mix.

As Cigdem walked to the microphone – Charlie brought the sound down and put a warm glow spotlight of her as she walked to the podium.

"Thank you all," she said. "Such a wonderful welcome – I hope you're all enjoying my city – and you consider it your city over the next few days. Welcome!!"

Cigdem looked over to Caroline with a great smile, "Isn't Caroline wonderful?" The audience broke into another applause and Charlie added a drum roll and cymbals to the hand percussion din.

"We're so happy to have her here – along with Adam Mason – Adam – please stand up and take a bow."

Charlie put a spotlight onto Adam as he stood up and took a bow. Once again, the audience erupted in applause with the occasional yell of appreciation. Adam sat down not enjoying the cameo appearance Okan had included without letting Adam know – as Okan laughed out loud in his control booth – Adam smiled, knowing it's all good.

Some people in the audience - in multiple locations – whispered this was the best conference opening they had every attended, wondering how much an appearance of Caroline Mathews and David Mason cost – never mind the cost of Sarah Thomson and Marta Armstrong.

Charlie dimmed the hall lights then put the single glowing spot back onto Cigdem.

Caroline lifted her arms above the keyboard with a small spotlight only on the keyboard – Caroline started a one piano piece – quietly – emoting a sense of anticipation as Cigdem continued her introduction.

"I have the pleasure and honor to introduce our keynote speakers this morning – two stellar personalities in our professions – who are bringing a new sense of wonder and appreciation, not just in our professional circles, but in the circles of humanities around our beautiful planet. I can announce a virus has occurred this morning – a worldwide virus. My husband Okan, who some of you know, and hopefully others will get to know, tells me with a great degree of accuracy, over fifty-five million people are currently connected to our conference via a live video pod cast using the reach of the internet."

The audience gasped – not realizing the interest and reach of this event, as Cigdem continued, "some fifty-five million with this interest in our work – are not here to learn the details of the various papers we're researching and presenting, working to move our knowledge ahead based on the scientific method – they have joined full of hope – hope for a new normal – where love and compassion are the mature path, rather than the path of naivety – where ideologies are not boxed into various 'isms' – socialism, communism, capitalism, oligarchism, – divisive – where the act of each ism, is a consequential schism."

Okan noticed his podcast screen filling with floating hearts as Cigdem spoke to the world. Okan realized the world is thirsty for a new direction – an altered perception – chosen by the majority – undivided in their quest to think higher and act kinder.

Nothing to do with money or hierarchical structures of perceived power – all to do with integrity and compassion for all sequential life on the planet.

The consequential end of selfism.

Okan lit up a large screen in the hall showing the hearts and love symbols coming in from around the world. The audience looked on, amazed.

Cigdem continued, as the hall once again broke into a spontaneous applause.

"I am not going to go over the credentials of our two speakers – I think they are well known to all – or at least most. You will find the profiles in your agenda catalogue, if you're not familiar. To those joining us as online participants, you have access to all supporting information through our web site created for this event."

Cigdem turned to stage left, held her right arm out – "Ladies and gentlemen, it's my pleasure and privilege to welcome Dr. Marta Armstrong and Dr. Sarah Thompson."

Caroline started playing as Charlie added the harmonies of two more pianos, like the three piano pieces they played so long ago at the conservatory in Toronto.

The music changed – not lonely and isolated any more – connected and accepted.

The audience applauded and gave a standing ovation – the podcast screen once again filled with floating hearts.

Charlie created the light show – bathing the audience in a soft glow of mixed colors – green, blue, turquois, purple, indigo and white – ebbing and flowing – mixing and morphing – synchronized to the music of the three-piano piece.

Marta and Sarah walked to the center of the stage, each giving Cigdem a hug – then the three of them, joining each other in a group hug of solidarity.

Charlie dimmed the lights as Cigdem left the stage.

"Thank you, Dr. Olpar – also thank you Dr. Mathews-Tranter – our beloved Caroline for the music played, - thank you Adam Mason – for the music created, and to Okan Olpar and Charlie – for the hidden complimenting magic you're providing behind the scenes." Marta started.

"Sarah Thomson came into my life fifteen years ago – her case, referred to me due to the work I was doing, and sill do, with autistic children.

When I first met Sarah, she was non-communicative – a six-year-old child showing advanced development in her earlier years, tested in the top percentile for all physical and psychological metrics – suddenly becoming non-functional, withdrawn and socially isolated. Sarah was an unusual case.

She kept her temporal and sanitary needs in place – using the toilet... wearing fresh clothes - having baths daily, eating her meals on time, sleeping ten hours per day on a consistent rigorous schedule."

Sarah brought some levity to the description by giving the closed fist, raised hand – we are the champions up and down gesture - when her toilet habit was mentioned. Both the local and remote participants appreciated the gesture – laughter in the hall and smiley faces filling the screen.

Marta shook her head and continued. "Sarah became fully functional suddenly one morning. I was shocked as she started

talking with me as if she had never been away. She knew who she was – her speech and comprehension were above her age level – she knew who I was – called me by name."
Marta took a drink of water, then continued. "Over the next few months, a team of neurologists, psychologists and others poked and prodded Sarah – with proper permissions granted – and we found the following differences in Sarah's physiology.
Sarah has a denser and larger brain mass than most of us. Her cerebrum has at least four times as many neurons than most of us, and the cerebral cortex is denser and better connected – including neuron connections between the pineal and pituitary glands, which in most of us is not found. We also found a greater concentration of neurons in the cerebellum, which fire with a much greater frequency than the normal cerebellum. We didn't fully understand the means or ways of these differences, and still don't.
My team and I have written various papers on these differences and have included access to these papers on the conference web site. Please refer to them and other linked resources for further information.
You will also see, the corpus callosum between the left and right lobes, is larger with greater and denser connections.
Sarah is born with a different brain physiology – a further evolved physiology, with some tendencies relating and akin to autistic behavior on some levels – a highly functional, multi-tasking, ethereal connection which goes beyond the functionality, utility and connectedness – not only in the social realms – but also empathic capabilities far beyond the normal scope of our understanding.
I am also privileged to be Sarah's friend – from my firsthand experience – knowing the physiology resulting in the extra sensory psychology Sarah brings to the table. She is the most caring, kindest and smartest person I have ever known, and if she represents the future of human evolution – I am on board to help wherever and however I am able."
The audience again applauded as hearts, wow's, and thumbs up filled the podcast screen.
"Ladies and gentlemen, it is my pleasure to introduce Dr. Sarah Thompson." Marta said happily as she relinquished the speaker spot at the podium.

The room stood up and gave Sarah a standing ovation, as the podcast screen once again filled with hearts.
Caroline also stood by the piano and joined the ovation.
Sarah looked directly at Adam.
Adam understood – climbed the stairs to the stage and walked towards Sarah. Again, the hall and on-line audience offered total approval.
As Adam moved towards Sarah – she opened her arms – they held each other closely – as they both said in sync, "I love us so much – we're ascending upon the transitioning instance."
Charlie did a live broadcast of their words as they were spoken – over fifty million people around the planet, suddenly knew they were part of something magnificent and important.
Marta moved over to the couch sat down, ready to enjoy the proceedings. It was not how they had rehearsed it – and she was happy about that.
Okan sat back and let Charlie do what Charlie did best – interact on a higher level with Adam – positive anticipation - emancipation based, creation.
Adam looked over at Caroline and she started to play – the music inspiring, as Adam spoke, "Close your eyes – resonate - psychology, physiology, neurology, endocrinology, cosmology, musicology, philosophy, religiology, physics, computer science – each 'ist' and every 'ism', in our silos of knowledge."
Sarah moved forward as Adam said, "Ladies and gentlemen – it's my pleasure to stand side by side with my lifetime partner in rhyme – Dr. Sarah Thompson,"
As Sarah moved to center stage – Adam added, "Caroline, will mix our, music as we flow – let your anger, fear, and isolation go, as we move to a higher level. We are the Alters."
After the applause, Sarah smiled and started speaking.
"We're born, alone," she looked directly at Adam, "sometimes together – with different goals and aspirations, where we put our knowledge into silos – becoming experts in a given learning category – as Adam mentioned just now – psychology, endocrinology, mythology, geology, cosmology and hundreds of others including proctology.

In order to make understanding less complicated, we have made silos of specific knowledge and we have become individual experts with many Ph.D. degrees protecting the reverence of the work and the respect of the experts who live it.
This methodology of knowledge makes university life and tenure much easier – the labelling of graduates, easier – everyone fits into their chosen "ology" as an "ist". I became a psychologist – after passing the various requirements in the study of psychology. We break our silo's into sub-silos – clinical psychologists – evolutionary psychologists – forensic psychologists – and one of my favorites – neuropsychologist, and many more as you all know here in the hall. Our silos within our silos ensure those with the knowledge, keep the knowledge.
But, in all of this we can agree, nature sometimes breaks the silo barriers through the manifestation of autistic savants – born with the knowledge of music – as Adam, Caroline, Okan and many others are – born with the knowledge of empathy, as I and Marta, and others are.
Highly functional autism is a rewiring of the brain – an evolution of the human condition – the discovery and intrigue of photo-neurons – beyond the particle paradigms enclosed in three static and one sequential dynamic, dimensions – height, width, length and time - as we live in our prison of blue skies. Autistic characteristics are a communal stretch to a higher purpose.
I am here to say, without equivocation, we are non-sequential 'seeings' of light."
Some in the audience were uncertain of the message – proud of their accomplishments in their chosen field of study – proud of their various degrees – which set them apart and proved their worth and depth of knowledge.
Most thought of themselves as their mother's most brilliant child.
The online viewers were sending hearts and wows to the screen.
Caroline played into the feelings in the room and then to the feelings on the planet.
Sarah continued, "The first part of the piece is heavy – contrived – sluggish – repetitive – hopeless, dark and isolated. A million years of struggle – slaves to the mathematics of it all – to the elements and predatory aggression. The struggle of being strongest first – in some

niche of gene evolution and sense interpretation, based, in some cases on stealth at the microbe level, taking down bigger and stronger bodies belonging to their hosts – or in others based on evolved tools, like the talons of an eagle, designed to kill and carry. Flesh in all cases is sacrificed on the altar of evolving forward.

The human brain – the greatest tool of all, kills for sport and entertainment, as tribal societies enact a continuing hierarchy of horrors against other tribes – the proverbial us and non-inclusive, them – for land or procreation.

All lost by Darwinian logic, and the science of mathematics, as self-evident truths – we're not greater than our confinements.

But then a ray of light seeps in – far away at first – getting closer faster than speed." Sarah paused – as Caroline played on. Charlie added to the impact of Sarah's words – showing supporting images flashing on large screens around the room – Eagles talons, tribes killing tribes – bombs doing their damage and more.

Sarah continued. "There is the possibility for an altering of perception – and direction." Sarah said as she moved closer to the front of the stage. "I can feel it – Adam can feel it – We can feel it."

The podcast screen filled once again with hearts as the audience in the hall, responding to the music, which filled in, with all the instruments of a symphony orchestra, felt a lifting of their individualism, into a greater community.

They ascended then transcended the physical boundaries of time and space – into a place where harmonies flowed into harmonies - towards a resonance of purpose. Finally, reaching past the thickness of the sequential moment – into a place of being, above the physical structures – in pure thought – still creative and will-driven, on a common membrane as a collection of all that exists – every instance and every event, connected by proton wormholes, the gateways from particles to waves then back again in an everchanging flux of energy – building to a final consequence – experienced at one time. The multiverse is small when folded into and observed in the non-sequential thought dimension, where time is an illusion – not reality at all, just the running of a sequence of a consequential instance.

Adam watched the colors of the music fill the room – his music was a gateway – as the energy of others in the hall and on-line, mingled

and conjoined via gamma waves – through the pineal photo-neuron gateways of each – moving towards a final resonance of all.
Caroline and Charlie working it and it was good.
Okan had joined his wife Cigdem and they too were part of the emotional rapture filling not only the space – but also the moment.
They were overwhelmed
"This is not a conference on psychology – or a gathering on-line – it is a rebirth of purpose, in light." Cigdem said, as she held Okan close to her.
The music became less intense – slowly becoming quieter as individual instruments were removed from the flow by Charlie.
Finally – only Caroline played with a purity and clarity no one had ever heard before – it was a piece written to capture the rapture of the moment – the release from physical chains of constraint – the freedom to be free of an instrument perception – yet flowing within the symphony.
"Material is sticky by design," Sarah started. "Yet our value system for individuals, tribes and nations bases our worth on sticky material connections and wealth.
The more we 'own', the more we stick to the lower dimensions – losing the truth where width, length, height, and time - are the lowest part of knowing.
There is a knowledge in non-material secrecies, where we emanate then animate our timeless tome, within harmonic, flawless, frequencies transcending a coded genome.
We reach for and yearn for the 'We're' above, through – resonance, empathy, compassion and love."
Caroline stood up as she played – the feeling of freedom - like a butterfly controlling the wind, fluttering here then fluttered there, filled both the on-line and local space of the conference – as Charlie started adding instruments to the flow - as a wind of change – where the wind controlled the butterfly, as it blew it here, then blew it there.
Marta walked to the pedestal. "Can you feel it?"
Sarah walked over to the on-stage couch, sat down as she smiled at Marta.
Caroline turned and bowed to the crowd as they gave her a standing ovation.

Adam walked then sat beside Sarah, both glowing with positivity as they shared the same space.

Cigdem came from the entrance at stage left, took Caroline's hand as they both walked over towards the couch and sat down with Adam and Sarah.

The room was overwhelmed – emotional – some with tears in their eyes – as they tried to rationalize – try to understand this reaction to the music and the inner joy they had touched together as a common core.

The audience became quiet as Marta spoke. "What we have just experienced - not only here, but also those reached by the live podcast on the internet, millions of people hungry enough to seek, find and resonate, to our common higher meaning.

Thought is the builder – in both directions – a portal to the lower three and a gateway to the upper four. Thought transcends the lowest part of knowing and ascends to the highest part of, 'We'."

Marta walked to the couch as Sarah and Adam stood up, then walked to the stage in front of the podium.

Adam started – "I am an Alter – Sarah is an Alter – we're two of millions, including many of you here. Sarah and I became sequential again at the same time, in response to a root event which has since enabled multiple instances, from her birth in Baton Rouge and my birth in Toronto.

Sarah is an empath savant – I am a quantum savant – Our brains are wired differently than most, but not all.

We're a bridge to non-material energy --- energy which does not exist lower as particles, but rather dimensional waves.

We resolve the hard problem of consciousness."

Adam paused, knowing the audience in the room and many of those on-line would understand the 'hard problem' reference – used by many, in their quest to understand consciousness.

The easy problems are solvable within the mathematics bordered and bounded by the metrics of the lower four dimensions.

Consciousness and communal spirit are more difficult to solve – beyond mathematics – much to the chagrin of many who have spent their lives, making great advances in understanding the lowest part of knowing, as required and intended.

Adam continued, “Bio-photonic neurons are gateway neurons, between the lower four dimensions and the upper dimension of thought.

Einstein discovered the magical formula regarding the relationship between Energy, Mass and the Speed of Light - $E = mc^2$. Mathematics is the study of fixed structures – height, width, length and the continuous vortex of time.

Neuroscience and psychology will never discover a formula regarding empathy, morality and compassion, in an - empathy = morality times compassion squared - relationship.

Feelings are not a four-dimensional construct - Empathy, morality and compassion, are not bounded and bordered by the four dimensions defined, from the middle to the edges, by mathematics. You can’t weigh or measure a feeling of love – it’s not a mathematical construct and goes beyond the boundaries of four dimensions.

Yet, feelings like love motivate actions – actions spawn consequences – consequences spawn sequential events – sequential events are experienced by us, in multiple instances, multiple dimensions and multiverse constructs.”

Adam stepped back as Sarah stepped forward.

“Imagine what is real.” Sarah started – As Caroline walked over to the piano - Charlie set the piano as a background flow of music.

“We’re the gifted, the uplifted – the ones who alter the thought process in sequential instances. Our goal is inter-dimensional resonance – where every event consequence leads to ‘we’ instead of ‘me’.

We’re a collective - a selective collective, within a fractal vortex - in a scalar cascade – turbulent energies - add a sequence to our being - and thus we stick to the lower dimensions - the lowest part of knowing. “

Sarah stopped, realizing one challenge within this instance is overcoming the ineffable depth of understanding required to fully appreciate the simple complexity of us.

She explained further.

“The selective collective is the sequential beings seeking resonance - us.

The fractal vortex is the spiral energy cycling, created on a gravity flux field – adding sequence to our being – The scalar cascade is particle law everywhere, large and small, macro and quantum - following the mathematical constructs of the 'sacred' sequence, over the expanding multiverse.

The turbulent energies are black holes colliding and galaxies forming, staving off the vagaries of entropy.

All these together, provide a sequential instance, of multiple events based on the consequences of decisions made, or not. "

Sarah moved backwards as Marta moved to the front of the stage.

The sequential beings in the hall and on-line watched as the large screen filled with the images of neurons forming images of neurons as galaxies and universes expanded and collapsed in a vortex of decay and creation – and then at one step higher in thought – all was seen as one instance in four dimensions, where every experience possible is inevitable.

Marta started speaking: "My friends and colleagues, as you have seen this morning, we have stretched the envelope of what is familiar in our various professions. I hope you have enjoyed our presentation so far." Applause once again filled the hall and hearts the podcast screen.

"We gain our personal hierarchical relevance in silos and even silos within silos, as we compartmentalize knowledge, building closed tribal values promoting elitism – one class against another - not based on intelligence or empathic capabilities, but rather based on family succession heir associations and tribal inner circle selection.

There is no growth in humanity through cheating, manipulating or violent persuasion.

Innovation moves fastest always when 'we' adds greater benefit to all, than 'me'.

If we don't transcend the Darwinian model - we're doomed to extinction.

The planet will kill us first and start anew, as has happened before in the course of the last 3 plus billion years."

It is time for us to realize, we're not the top of the food chain - prime predator on this planet - Nature is.

We live only as Nature allows us to live.

It is an arguable conclusion, Nature has a conscious sense, in four dimensions with a mathematical definition of itself.
The sequential "we", live within these metrics.
The non-sequential "us" think higher and aspire to a greater purpose."
As Marta talked, the screens filled with images supporting her speech. Caroline added strings of notes to the images, fully complimented by Charlie's synchronization of sight and sound, mixing calmness and chaos as audible particles, matching the calmness and chaos of photonic waves. A masterpiece unfolding as a matrix in a vortex.
"I repeat, we're not the top predator and most prolific creator on our planet - Nature is. Nature has its own level of consciousness, for lack of a better word – consciousness is an ineffable term, and from this natural four-dimensional eco-system – we're, allowed to be.
Nature is a four-dimensional construct – a life driven vortex.
From the flower in the garden producing pollen for the bees and beauty for our eyes, to the amoeba working alone and yet following its purpose – never jumping out of place testing the rules of its existence, to the largest neural networks working together, pushing the envelope of what is possible in these four-dimensions of mathematical and natural rules.
There is nothing mystical about moving higher to a state of pure thought, where all Nature below is animated. Nature too has rules to follow based on mathematics and the laws of physical constructs. The fixed relationship of energy to matter, the fixed relationship between time and sequence, and the unfixed relationship between life and death.
Life and death are exclusive states in exclusive instances – but not mutually exclusive when multiple instances exist.
It is not possible to be alive and dead in exclusive instances, but it's possible to be alive or dead in non-exclusive instances.
In other words, in a multiverse observation of life and death, it's possible to be alive and dead in different instances in different time space constructs - our experience and observations in each instance, are different from the others, based on decisions made and consequences met. We're sequential on concurrent and parallel paths and every decision creates a new path, a new event – where

every consequence is experienced - where everything possible, in four dimensions, is inevitable.

Each of us in different consequences, experience ourselves as tyrants and saints – devils and gods – and through this we observe our hunger to think higher, be kinder - resonate within common thought and higher purpose. Where each of us agree, 'we' includes me."

Marta moved towards the couch – as Adam and Sarah moved forward together.

Sarah spoke first as the music became soothing - the screen images of kindness given where kindness was the least expected consequence. The message being, kindness is the highest part of four-dimensional knowing and a gateway to harmonic thought.

"We each have the capacity and choice to be kind, or not, in any given opportunity to do so, or not.

We transcend the pit of four-dimensions, when all choices lead to the choice to be kind.

I will say 'Choose Kindness First' is our mandate.

We hold the desire to be higher in purpose. The physiology of the brain changes – the psychology of humanity changes as we choose to show kindness first.

Giving the gift of kindness is a gift of continued re-giving.

But it must be our choice to give kindness first."

Adam stepped forward and added to the mix.

"We're music – the energy of particles at the speed of sound and energy of waves at the speed of light, - vibrating strings and membranes – mixed in a multi-instance symphony, bringing us closer to us."

As Adam spoke, Caroline played and Charlie added harmonic vibrations, filling the room with the color of music.

"Close your eyes and see it." Adam said. "Live the wave - be it."

Adam let the music sink in as he watched the tsunami of emotion break over all who were connected.

A sea change was happening in Istanbul and around the globe. A transformation of thought – a higher purpose - a new way forward, where kindness was a key component of every choice. The mantra "Choose Kindness First" was appearing on websites, and all forms of social media. Sarah and Adam were now household names – not because of their individual accomplishments as it was just a week ago, but because they had become coupled and entangled - resonating hope of a better way forward.

In this instance, the world is a tired planet – tired of wars – tired of cruelty – tired of crime – tired of the psychopathic, sociopathic, shallowness of being - tired of being tired.

The decision and consequence tree, over multiple events in multiple instances, eventually curves towards kinder decisions and inclusive consequences, leading to an instance where all sequential beings decide the kinder consequence is the path to take-always.

Kindness is the essence of love – the only path worth taking – the only choice worth making.

In the final instance, we transcend the selfness of four dimensions and resonate together as one consequence – Love.

Chapter 14

Without memories,

Time would be a useless thing.

In Erin, Mr. and Mrs. Cagney moved slowly, as they got dressed. Their hearts were broken, still not believing the cruelty of what had happened.

Jenny was their only child - their entire world – a world now empty - without purpose.

Jenny was following her dream, on her way to Pearson International Airport.

She had a plane to catch – flying to London – full of hopes and dreams.

She was in the airport limousine, on the hill - highway 10, in Caledon, when the out of control gravel truck crossed the centre line, T-boning her limo.

In this instance, Jenny died.

" I GOT TIRED OF BEING ATTRACTIVE "

Made in the
USA
Middletown, DE

74677877R00159